MW00941717

Orion's Light

By

BRUCE BALLISTER

Orion's Light
Copyright © 2015 By Bruce Ballister
All rights reserved.

Cover Credits: NASA Hubble Space Telescope

ISBN: 1-5116-1622-9
ISBN-13: 978-1511616225
LCCN:

DEDICATION

This book is dedicated to my three beautiful daughters.
I love you all, Coral, Sarah, Kristy
Live, Love Life, Grow

Acknowledgements

I would like to thank my wife Christine for her unflagging support of these endeavors, my editor and counselor in things linguistic, Gina Edwards, and my support group and friends at the Tallahassee Writers Association.

AUTHOR'S NOTE

To my readers, thank you for picking up this book. Whether a physical thing with cellulose pages or an etheric entity on your tablet or phone, it's a book, and you are a part of the shrinking number who still reads. My fellow authors and I believe in story-telling as a valid exercise in the examination of the human experience. Whether that experience is past or future history is of little matter.

I have attempted to make this novel work as a stand-alone story. But, as you will become aware, it is a part of a longer experience, one with roots on our lovely gem of a planet, Earth. I am planning, at present, to wrap up this journey in one additional, fourth part. Parts 1 and 2 were included in *Dreamland Diaries*. As a reader, I have always felt that books in series should not end with major business unfinished. A denouement should pretty much wrap things up with a teaser, of course, for that next installment. I've been irked by some writers who leave their volumes in cliff-hanger mode. For that reason, *Dreamland Diaries* included the first two parts. Too much necessarily unfinished business remained at the end of Part 1.

To get the most out of this book and the next, I strongly urge you to take on Parts 1 and 2 in *Dreamland Diaries* first. If you choose not to wait and want to dive on in. I've left enough bread crumbs for you to pick up the trail. Whichever path you choose, enjoy.

Bruce Ballister

PART 3

Chapter 1

Mistakes are the growing pains of wisdom.
William Jordan

Dzuran Space
April 22, 1986, A.D. – Earth Calendar
3,608.27 – Dzuran Revised Calendar

"Oh! Wow!" Connie Chappell's reaction from the rear weapons officer's seat was nearly identical to the pilot's less repeatable reaction. Brad Hitchens took in the view beyond the canopy. The all-encompassing view displayed a vast gas cloud. Bands of orange, red, and violet streaked through with blue-grey spread across the sky, a still-life aurora seemingly frozen in place across the heavens.

Bradley Hitchens, in the forward pilot's seat, emerged from post-jump nausea staring at the overhead display. "Would you look at that?" he mumbled, unable to take his eyes off the glowing gas nebula. He barely noticed the glare of the local sun. The spray of colors overhead was breathtaking. They barely heard Jai's report that the system's planet Dzura was thirteen degrees from their nadir nor his question about whether they wanted to rotate to view it. "We're smack in the middle of a nebular cloud." Within Brad's field of view, bright yellow and white stars in the distance illuminated the dust cloud.

Connie took her eyes off the canopy to review the 3D proximity display on her console. "Brad, I think if we turn over, we can see Dzura, Jai's home."

"Right, I think he just said something about that. Jai? Please orient for the best view of your home world." Slowly, the ship they knew as Jai pivoted forward. The pitch added a nauseating sensation of falling to the temporary nausea that, they had recently learned, came from playing with the ship's jump drive.

"Ugh! Hold it there, Jai." Connie saw the dark backside of the planet with only a bright crescent lit by the much more distant sun. A few degrees to the right, the bright red disk they knew had been called Alal gave the thin atmospheric line a lavender glow. "Brad, look at the atmosphere. It's pink instead of blue."

1

"Yeah, and there are no lights coming from the night side. Remember how visible Earth's cities are at night?"

"Ka-Brad, sensors indicate intelligent species using hailing frequencies." The gender-neutral voice that Jai had adopted for speaker communication was flat, devoid of emotion. Jai, not impressed with the visual field of view, was doing its job scanning for life-sign. Four hundred years ago, Jai's builders had fled this planet while under attack from a warring faction in a system-wide civil war. But Jai was a warship and never off duty.

Hailing frequencies? "Jai, use psi," Brad said. "No electronics."

Yes, Ka-Brad. The response was a thought, transmitted in psi, the subtle, more than thought, and less than speech telepathic voice Jai had taught his human crew to use almost ten years earlier. The tiny ship had dropped into Dzuran space perpendicular to the planetary system's orbital plane, not out of expectation of hitting anything, but due to inherent programming protocols specific to gravity well avoidance.

"Jai, can you tell what is being said. Are they talking to us?"

Communication is to ... unknown craft ... best way to translate ... traffic control want unknown craft to remain on station, not power up.

"Brad, this place is not uninhabited." Urgency in Connie's voice added an octave to her normal register.

"Apparently, Con. Dammit! Damn stupid of us to not consider that there must have been a winner." Brad scanned his instrument console for any clues he could understand in the alien craft's still unfamiliar displays. *Jai, can you tell if traffic control is Dzuran, or the others, your old enemy, the Errans?*

No, Ka-Brad ... traffic control use same frequency old Dzuran Navy ... and Erran.

"Connie, what do you want to do? I think we should jump right now. I was expecting to get a tour of Jai's dead planet. This place ain't dead! We don't know who won the war. What do you want to do?"

"I say jump." Her voice now had a tremulous tint.

Jai, can we jump back to Sol space? Do we need to wait on the jump drive to power again?

Jump drive ready in twenty-four point two six minutes ... Flux drive powering up, available in nine point two two minutes.

"Well, Connie, I think we have about twenty-four more minutes to check out the neighborhood."

"Can we at least back up, use chem jets?" She looked down at her proximity display again. Her voice quavered with increasing anxiety. The view overhead was suddenly a lot less interesting.

Brad tried a calmer tone, hoping for a voice of calm and reason. "Hon, the traffic controller told us to remain on station. If we move it might be considered hostile. Remind me to have Jai run us both through weapons training before we head out again."

"Brad, something just appeared on my screens that wasn't there a second ago. They just appeared out of nowhere."

Jai's circuitry responded, "Ka-Brad, vessels approaching. Thirty right, forty-five down. Translating to bring ships in view." The ship yawed down and to the right. Nothing was immediately visible.

"Jai, shields up." The external view began to shimmer. Light from the distant, red sun broke and danced in soap bubble hues on the deployed shield.

~ ~ ~

When the two-seater spacecraft had popped into Dzuran space, the sensory systems of three huge, orbiting habitats immediately noted its presence. The closest habitat to the drop point was Teeya City. Teeya, like its two sister cities, was the habitat for tens of thousands of Erran citizens: engineers, miners, artisans, cooks, pilots, priests, and whatever else it took to subjugate a conquered planet. The three cities were space equally at thirds around the planet's equator, and by proximity rule, its crew took over navigational responsibility for the newcomer. But the incoming craft's signature was wrong. It transmitted no ID in the approved bandwidth, and once visuals were obtained, a welcoming committee of sorts was scrambled to intercept the foreigner.

The two humans, who had been enjoying their first intra-system drop in their borrowed spacecraft, did not anticipate a

3

welcome of any kind. They had expected a destroyed planet, the home system of their two-seater, a Skeeter class fighter of Dzuran manufacture. The fighter was top of its line at the time of manufacture,

four centuries before. It was capable of linked shielding, atmospheric effect maneuvers, as well as inter-system jumps using a flux drive and intra-system jumps using the gravity-bending grav drive. It was armed with rail gun projectile and high energy weapons. At present, its rail gun ammunition was depleted, but shielding, cloaking, and energy weapons systems were at full power. Its latest generation control system was an AI named Jai.

Jai had waited patiently for aid from sentient beings for those last four centuries. It had found Brad Hitchens, an accidental neighbor in the North Florida woods that sheltered Jai's ancient crash site. Time, vegetation, and occasional use by humans had obscured the crash site. Hitchens had introduced Jai to Connie Chappell. The ship's AI had become dependent on and bonded with the two humans over almost a decade of communication by telepathic link. Their telepathic or psi communication was limited by learned and unlearned languages, but the three were now a partnership as Jai understood it: ship, pilot and crew. Connie as crew occupied the weapons officer's rear seat. They often communicated in thought as easily as on audible systems.

"Brad, those guys are getting awfully close!"

"Just a second." He found the slider control he was looking for and the proximity view zoomed away by a factor of three cubed. He didn't know that; he just knew that the three looming ships that were speeding toward them became tiny icons on his display instead of an imminent collision. He could hear her rapid breathing in his comm.

"Oh, but they're still coming, right?"

"Yes, they are. And probably sooner than later." Despite the shifted scale view, he felt certain that the reception committee would arrive before Jai's jump shift was powered up. "Jai? How long before you can engage jump drive? No psi."

"Two point oh four minutes." Came over the audible circuit.

"Arrival in one minute thirty sec—" was the last message Jai relayed before his audible alarm sounded an atonal blee—eep. And went silent. There were no more psi messages. There was a burst of psi from one of the three ships that physically hurt.

"Jai, engage chem thrusters. Get out of here!" That certainty played out in only a few minutes. Brad and Connie both pushed themselves back into their seat padding in anticipation of the gut-flattening shove. It never came.

Brad pushed at inert controls. Connie almost shouted from her seat behind his. "Jai! Jai! What's going on? Are those Errans?"

No response. One of the three ships came to a stop immediately above the canopy. They saw the other two disappear out of view behind them. The ship above spurted a brilliant white beam at Jai's force field bubble. The image of the alien ship was warped by the force field but the field rapidly diminished. A snapping sound came from the fuselage and the energy field distortion effect dropped out completely.

"Connie, I don't like this at all! I am so sorry!" Brad found himself involuntarily sinking into his seat as a dark, rectangular shape glided closer to the canopy.

"Crap! Are they going to break into the cockpit?"

"I don't know. Get your helmet on. Now! They don't seem to know what we are either." His voice took on a metallic ring as he snapped his head piece onto the suit. He reached out against hope. *Jai, Jai can you hear me? Can you please respond some way?* On his console, the center point of the 3D array glowed green in three short bursts. "Connie, I don't know if this will make you feel any better about this, but I think Jai is playing possum."

"No." Connie's voice was clearly distorted by both the helmet and fear. "That is not making me feel any better." In rapid succession, they felt three distinct thumps on the hull as the Erran intercept force attached physical grapple lines to Jai. The ride down toward the Dzuran orbital city was harrowing. Jai bounced against the three confining cables, jolting as uneven tension tugged toward each of the three ships. Below them, a black and gold monstrosity emerged from the hazy light of atmosphere filtered light to the pure, clear illumination of Dzura's sun. Later, piecing together his first impressions, Brad would remember thinking the gold areas provided additional shielding against gamma radiation and the black was for thermal insulation. He gave thanks, in those memories, that in the midst of a terrible headache, he'd blacked out.

Chapter 2

A step into the dark is a step away from the light,
or a step toward discovery.
Old Elioi Proverb

Asteroid Belt, Sol System
May 13, 1986 – Earth Calendar
3580.220 – Erran Calendar

The stacked-mass thruster pile and its guide ship approached the slowly rotating asteroid carefully. Aside from the slow roll on its long axis, the asteroid's small but dangerous yaw could be hazardous to his approach near either end. The tiny control ship carried on its back five massive system-jump thrusters that it was shepherding above the plane of the constantly shifting field of gravel, boulders, and rounded mountains that were the remains of a failed moon. The pilot's panel had been giving occasional life-sign indications for some time and he had isolated a source further starward, but that investigation could wait a while. This asteroid was compelling. The massive rock in his viewer was the largest of the slowly tumbling monsters in this section of the belt. It was the source of the closest life-sign indicator. He set his auto-wake alarm for a distance that would give him visual scanning. The necessary delay in approaching slowly would permit a sleep cycle. When the life-sign indicator beeped again, he turned it off. He knew the system's only habitable planet had been mapped as off-limits centuries ago due to its primitive life forms and possible micro-bio hazards. He didn't need the constant interruption just now.

Turning back to his video panel, he adjusted the two cameras that provided true-color three-dimensional imagery. The pocked surface of the asteroid sharpened into view. He knew from experience that it had been slowly accreting thousands of small fragments that formed a loose and dangerously unstable surface. Another sensor bleated a warning as a gravel shard evaporated in front of camera three. His ship would deploy its collision avoidance shield automatically if the house-size boulders got too near. The mountain-sized stones in the neighborhood were dangerous to the careless. He scanned side, bottom, and rear viewers to check his surroundings.

Suddenly, his breathing slit flared. He sucked in an involuntary breath at the sight of an unexpectedly regular rectangular shadow. He remembered a lesson from the Riiya Space Academy; "There are no straight lines in space!" A carbon-dark cavity, dimly lit in reflected light from the gravel field was coming into view. When the asteroid rotated, letting in light from the system's primary star, he boosted gain on the multi-spectral viewer. Briefly, and too quickly for him to catch any detail, he thought he saw a construction of some sort obscured by the harsh shadows of planetary space. He let his breathing stabilize and assessed his situation.

Jitep, or more correctly, Nem-Jitep, off-system Erran Miner, First Order, was on solitary "sample and push" duty in a long-neglected asteroid belt with marketable stones rich in heavy metals. His orders had been to follow the G-wave disturbance left by the off-worlder's spacecraft. His mining ship had only minor defensive weapons. Jitep fitted out his ship as an assay vessel with a shield generator for protection from rock splatter in asteroid fields and a small high-energy laser to break up or shape large finds into the appropriate size for jumping back to Erra. He had sophisticated systems for mass measurement, chemical composition, bio-chem, collision avoidance, and life-sign. His systems were always on the alert. In fact, his little ship had no off switch for the vital systems that would alert him in rest cycle or authorize evasive maneuvering if emergencies required.

None of these early warning systems protected him from the surprise of spotting the regular, sharp edges of the dark rectangle that just rotated out of view. He drew the ship closer, matched vectors with the rock, and began a detailed assay with full vid-rec of the encounter—standard assay procedure when detecting an asteroid large enough to have a marketable percentage of heavy metals. Soon enough, the anomaly would rotate back into view and he wanted to illuminate the apparent excavation. At less than five hundred meters, he should be able to train his visual, ultra-blue, and thermal band and gamma scanners into the hole. If he grappled its surface, he could ping its interior with resonant imaging. Now all he could do was wait.

His thoughts ran through the possibilities. One, other miner/assayers had been sent to this system and he had not been notified. This was his best scenario. Two, another Erran miner was at work, deep in the gut of this rock, looking for an exotic ore. Errans were notoriously territorial and despite the territorial filings that protected off-system corporate research, claim jumpers could be testy in one-on-one encounters. This choice would be disappointing because the initial scan of the huge rock was promising. It had shown rich metallic ores with a thin layer of scrabble attracted to one of the larger gravity wells in the belt. Three, since he had jumped to a system mapped by long dead elders and placed on the off-limits list, there was the possibility that this was an ancient excavation from an unknown species. There might be exciting artifacts of an unfamiliar culture down there. Considering this scenario, he reflected on the life-sign indicators and the possibility that an unknown creature from some other arm of the galaxy was in there. But, he thought, why a perfectly square excavation?

His ship interrupted him. *Not probable ... non-Elioi spacing species do not occur in twenty-two thousand five hundred forty-seven astral units.*

"Quiet!" he shot back. *Pay attention to your sensors.*

Not in known space, the ship countered.

At times, he would like to take a torque tool to the psi circuits of his ship's computer, Mug. He always reversed this thought amid protests from Mug and he accepted the fact that he liked the company—usually.

The dark edge of the excavation—if that is what it was—came into view, highlighted against the bright, star-lit surface. Too slowly, the depths became visible as the asteroid rotated.

Mug, detach the thruster array. When we have maximum exposure to the interior of that excavation, maintain position. There was a small jolt through the frame of his little craft as the release springs pushed him away from the stacked array of heavy-push jump thrusters.

The dimensions of the square opening, he estimated, were no more than ten percent of the average diameter of the rock. Taking mental notes, he placed it about a third of the way along the long axis; far enough away from the ends to minimize the effect of the yaw. As the hole deepened before him, he felt a subtle vector shift as

Mug obeyed his order and took over the maneuvering jets. Soon, he was looking into the depths of a nearly square pit much deeper than the measure of its sides. Mug had matched angular momentum and attitude so well that Jitep now felt that he was attached to the asteroid. He waited as starlight from this system's central sun poured bright yellow-tinged light down the smooth side of a very cleanly excavated opening.

Simultaneously, new alarms sounded, and Mug began talking. Jitep jumped back from the sensor screen. Life-sign again! Mug's sensors could detect complex hydrocarbons of any origin and give a sign. But this! The clear heartbeat trumped his previous override command! This signal could only be an intelligent species in this hostile vacuum. But which one? He had thought he was alone in this system.

Mug sorted and displayed the ship's scanning arrays which began to provide high-resolution images in several critical wavelengths. The visual display, augmented with dimensions laid along critical edges, indicated at a glance that the hole was much larger than his ship. He quickly made the decision to explore further. Infrared had piqued his interest because a small crevice in the corner of the pit was shedding heat. This was not right. In this environment, entropy always wins. Any heat sign means a heat supply. That means technology. But, again, whose technology?

Rays of the local star now reached the bottom of the cavity, adding bright, yellow-tinted light and detail to the structure at the bottom. It was Erran. That was evident at a glance. By the eternal Lights! Who's jumping my claim?

Mug sent a calming psi tone, immediately stopping Jitep's conscious thought and opening him to silent pilot-to-ship com. That was not why Mug had sent the tone. In the mental quiet that followed, Jitep could feel distress, fear, frustration, and pain. Someone in there was hurt and endangered. He could feel-hear those emotions now, as clearly as if it was a shipmate. There was an injured Erran down there. Briefly, the band of starlight passing across half of the excavation's bottom revealed machinery long abandoned in place and a ship that he did not recognize. The shadow moved up the wall of the excavation, again obscuring detail. He assented mentally to Mug's query and they slowly advanced into the darkness.

"Mug, forward work lights on," he said aloud.

From the hole came a plea. *Help me, please!*

With forward work floods on, Jitep could now see that the other ship was attached to what had appeared to be solid rock on the lower face of the rectalinear excavation. But its position looked to cover one of the many circular holes that led off into the core of the asteroid. The abandoned machinery arrayed across much of the bottom of the hole appeared to be simple structural supports that had perhaps once anchored mining equipment. "Lord of Darkness!" he swore. "Who would leave behind that much metal?"

Thought images from almost forgotten theology classes flooded his brain from whoever was below. *Precursors! This asteroid may be an artifact from Precursors, the Ancient Travelers.*

He projected his thoughts back. *Where are you? Are you in the ship ... or in a tunnel?* Then the import of the message hit him. Precursors? Ancient travelers. This was astounding news! He looked at the scrap metal pile abandoned in a scrabble of dust and debris blasted from thousands of small collisions with other asteroids.

I am in a tunnel ... look at the ship ... then third tunnel left.

Jitep looked at the ship and then to the third tunnel to the left. Life support cabling led from the ship into the tunnel. Then he scanned the ship again. An involuntary quiver ran down his spine. It was an Erran ship of an ancient design. With few exceptions, most Erran ships with inter-system jump could not pass into an atmosphere. This ship was sleek, like an old Embassy Class ship that could quickly courier messages and dignitaries between the entwined planets Erra and Dzura. But it could clearly jump out of the planetary plane. Looking at the ship closer, he realized it was old Dzuran.

The designs of the old Dzuran system had retractable sensors, grapplers, thrusters, landing gear, and often extendable, atmospheric effect steering built into their hull forms. The ship at the bottom of this pit was a clean Dzuran design. Even now, with its sensors and attitude jets and docking assemblies extended, it was beautiful, sleek as a pylon racer.

The answering comment came out of the tunnel. *Lights be damned. Ask for any or all aid ... and I get an Erran.* The slur was followed by something Jitep interpreted as a curse, but the dialect was old and he did not catch literal sense, only a sensation of disgust, then mitigated with an apology and a request.

Sorry ... I am trapped ... I do need help.

Who are you? Why are you here? What help do you need?

The message came through in bursts as though the sender was in pain. *Called Calantral ... prospecting this belt for ores ... contract work for Erran Pel- council... legs caught in something cannot see.* There was a pause. *Lattice of tunnels interconnect ... can get behind me ... tunnel not safe from your side.*

He considered. The miner below was Dzuran. That in itself was hard to fathom. He had to be from a high-born crèche. But the expressed psi tones indicated he was in trouble. This was an unforgiving environment. Or rather the job was dangerous because there was no environment. Everything needed for life was meticulously planned, backed up with secondary systems and often fail-safe systems for those. In times of extreme stress, psi links to their ships often provided that touch of reason.

He sent Calantral a message that he would suit up and come into the excavation. Pulses of caution, fragile rock structures, and gratitude came in answer. As Jitep and Mug descended carefully into the pit, the two miners exchanged psi introductions. Calantral was on system mapping duty and discovered the excavation by accident while searching for heavy structural metals on this larger than average rock. Nim-Jitep was on similar duty. He did not say that he had discovered the system by analyzing the pre-jump trajectory of an ancient bogey that accidentally popped into local Dzuran space.

Mug anchored to the solid rock of the pit's bottom. Jitep changed into his vacuum capable mining suit and jetted, or climbed as handholds permitted, into the tunnel to the left of the one indicated by Calantral. As he worked and maneuvered, his visor was fed a layout of what tunnel structures looked like within sensor bounce range ahead of him. He detected a large complex void with branching tunnels and carefully advanced toward an inner cavity. Caution, nurtured by years of solitary endeavor, caused him to pause at the lip of the entrance. Dark laser imaging augmented by sub-audible sonar told him the cavern was large and intricate. He had more than one and a half shift's worth of air in his rebreather, but he did not know how desperate Calantral might be. Searching to the right, he saw a tangle of cables leading to an adjacent small tunnel. He pulled hand over hand across a surface covered with intricate detail and pattern. Decoration? Function? He pulled up to the edge of the tunnel and stopped.

He could see immediately that one of the cables or lifelines had snagged on a protuberance of unknown function. He simultaneously tugged at the snagged cables and thought his presence towards Calantral. *I'm here, are you all right? I released the snagged cable.*

He felt then saw movement of the cabling in his gloved hand. Jitep received Calantral's thought, *Coming out of the tunnel ... injured my leg ... out soon.* A moment later, the slack in the cables grew taut and they were drawn further into the opening. He realized that the other miner was heading out toward the surface excavation and the two ships. Was he about to be tricked out of his own ship? Had this been a trap? He almost decided to exit in his tunnel when a helmet emerged, shrouded in dust, into the inner chamber. Jitep looked at the miner, faceplate to faceplate. He heard Mug through his ear set. *Dzuran!* Jitep did not respond. He knew that he could not safely shield his thoughts from Calantral at this close range.

The Dzuran miner touched his cuff pad, firing up illumination panels arrayed around the cavity, then pointed up, actually inward, toward the far side of the chamber. He then pushed off from the tunnel lip and made an expert no-grav jump toward a translucent ball now visible in the light light panel array. Jitep did likewise, being careful with his aim. He did not want to blunder into a foolish heap on the other side of the chamber. Showing off a little, Jitep jackknifed into a reverse toes down approach and braked with his wrist jets.

As he approached the translucent ball, he recognized it as a portable shelter. He understood that its thin membrane was all that kept it inflated so he killed his wrist jets. Instead of showing off his spacer agility, he landed ungracefully near the shelter's tubular double-lock entrance. He felt a suppressed mental grunt of displeasure from the other miner, but he knew he deserved it. He had approached too fast and might have endangered the fragile structure. The shelter was a recent model, portable inflatable with twin force field rings at each end of the entrance tube and the critical spherical shield set at a radius just outside the membrane. It was a simple system in use throughout explored space for survival situations and at high-altitude basecamps, equatorial expeditions, newly explored worlds, or wherever the user wished to be more comfortable than local conditions would permit.

The local conditions inside this asteroid were dark, only a few degrees above absolute zero, and in full vacuum. The little shelter was adequate to the challenges. As he passed through the second lock, he automatically reached for the clip locks on his helmet. He grabbed a corner, stabilized himself, and with the foolishness of a rookie cracked the helmet's seal. For his haste, he felt sudden overpressure in his eyes, pain in several internal organs and a burst of air from his suit chilled the sweat around his neck.

Calantral's voice boomed in his helmet. "Stop! Do not take your helmet off now, wait!"

Quickly, Jitep looked over at Calantral who still had his helmet on. The Dzuran had two hands up and outward in a universal stop gesture. He then turned to adjust comfort levels on the shelter's control panel. As air pressure in the bubble came up, Calantral released the catch on his helmet. "Good air now, it's safe."

Jitep breathed the thinner air mixture that Errans had learned to live on and tasted the slightly metallic ionized smell of manufactured air. Thin and tangy as it was, it was a slight improvement over his rebreather after a work shift. "You said you are hurt."

"Yes."

Jitep noticed now that Calantral was massaging his lower leg and examining a piece of the pressure suit's fabric that looked damaged. "Pressure loss?" Jitep asked.

Calantral looked up. "Yes, but not bad. I had been rigging spare air and power lines from my ship. Something lodged against my leg. I tried to pull myself through and fouled my cables, then my leg became more trapped." A glance at the pressure gauge on his wrist told of a nearly depleted rebreather. His look was both embarrassed and relieved.

Jitep had caught variation in Calantral's accent. He asked, "You are Dzuran?"

Calantral's eyes shifted quickly sideways and then stared directly at Jitep. "Yes, my father is the Ambassador to the Erran Pel-Council." He quickly damped his psi so that no further thoughts could be shared.

Although both Erran and Dzuran cultures were descended from the same Elioi stock on the home world Dzura, Erran features had differentiated over the centuries they had been predominantly off planet. Spacing Errans could not function in full Dzuran gravity and often needed air chair assist even on Erra's lower gravity. But despite their gross differences in physique and proportion, they shared many of the innate emotional characteristics. Their ears still glowed red in embarrassment, their breathing slits still flared with surprise or alarm and their foreheads still wrinkled in pleasure or humor. Jitep wondered what his features had revealed to Calantral.

Jitep said, "I need to look at your leg. It may be injured. I have a med-pack." He reached for one of the numerous pouches attached to his suit. The med-pack was in a lower position, outside on his left leg. He asked, "Is that a two-piece suit? Need to access your leg for blood thickener and patch." Calantral's eyes twitched slightly, exhibiting nervousness. "What's wrong?" Jitep sensed the blocking psi signals. Universally, sharing psi expressed trust. They were quickly losing trust. But honoring one party's request to block psi communication was a mark of civilized upbringing.

The Dzuran miner did not respond verbally but began to remove a tool belt and then to unseal the waist attachment to his two-piece pressure suit. There was a pause and then the wounded miner stood and slid down the lower section to a point below an apparently injured leg. White fur at the ankles shaded to brown above the knees with a few white streaks extending toward Calantral's waist.

Jitep's eyes widened, his lips sealed tight, breathing slit flared, and the rims of his ear ridges reddened. He blurted in amazement, "You are female!"

Ear ridges also reddening, Calantral looked away. Then the telepathic communication resumed as Calantral released the block signal. A confusion of thoughts passed between them in short order. Although the war had separated their races, culture, and distance for hundreds of years, they still shared most aspects of their species' behaviors.

Calantral took several long breaths and hesitantly said, "No, not female. Not male. Parent selected me for crèche mother. Though better for Science and Ambassador training. I wanted to go to spacer school. I got into many arguments at school, at civic hall. Much embarrassment for Calantral, for crèche, and for school. I found a representative on Pel-Council and went to spacer school." The Dzuran paused, trying to choose words that described his abnormal colorations with the minimum of explanation. "I went to spacer academy but too late. Morph change began after admission to school and in classes for two years. Drugs to stop heteromorphic shift to female did not work. Now, not still male, not yet female. Calantral cannot parent or even teach in home crèche and I cannot crew in space." He looked up almost sorrowfully at Jitep. "I am too distracting. So, I now work solitary spacer jobs."

Jitep, doing his best not to send psi signals of pity or disgust, gave the short, bobbing head motion that, on Erra at least, still connoted unequivocal understanding. He said, "Your torso fur did not change to white as well?"

Calantral seemed to shrink two sizes in front of him. "No, that is why Calantral cannot join spacer crews. In cleaning rooms, there's too much trouble with me looking like a freak. Space is too hard for one female on a ship with a crew of males. It is even harder for me; I think, work, and act male because I am still male. It's hard for spacer crews to make that distinction. Some would think I'm a breeder."

Jitep nodded again. He pulled a tube of disinfectant analgesic gel from his pack and began to clean Calantral's wound. He finished up with a cauterizing blade. Calantral stood the pain of the hot blade well. Jitep understood Calantral's problem. Simply handling white fur had stirred unintended emotional responses. He made a busy show of putting his med kit away. "You can dress now." He looked away as the other miner stood and refastened the waist seal.

In the few moments that it took for the Dzuran to readjust his/her suit and reconnect tool belts and auxiliaries, Jitep stared through the environment bubble at the alien cavern around them. The walls were covered with structures or possible attachment points for equipment no longer installed. Surfaces between them appeared to be covered with an intricate pattern that could have been either language or decoration.

Following Jitep's gaze, Calantral said, "I don't know what the markings are. I was moving equipment in to set up a research base."

"Are these from the Precursors?"

"Yes, conclusive. Artifacts found in Gikkan, Telian, and Boeran systems correlate perfectly. This is best-preserved collection of this type of ... decoration, I think."

"You are an archeologist? Not a miner?"

"No, but I studied Precursors in philosophy and religion classes. Studied much, read too much about them."

Jitep nodded side to side again. "How long?"

"How long did I study the Ancient Travelers?"

"How long have you been here?"

Calantral tapped a wrist computer to life and glanced at the readout. "Sixteen shifts. I have a lot of time." The Dzuran's brow wrinkled in a rueful smile. "No one on Dzura is waiting for me to return."

"Have you had a chance to report the find to the Erran Pel-Council?" He immediately realized that the question could be taken as edging on hostile. He added, "Are others coming to help you?" This might have been a mistake too. "I mean if I leave you here, are you all right?" Now he seemed to be condescending. He decided to shut up.

Calantral considered the three messages and the apparent catch of error and embarrassment in the psi overtones. "I want to trust Jitep. Remember, Calantral is fully not female. I don't need your help. I'm not having any young. Calantral attended two years of spacer academy, three years of physics and chemistry, one year advanced stellar navigation, and enough history to know that some Errans are good. Not all bad."

Jitep felt his ears burning red and looked down at his crossed legs. "Sorrow and regret for misspeaking." His psi overtones were easily read and received. Jitep had never had diplomat training and could not mask his emotional overtones.

Calantral continued, "Not yet report to superiors. There would be no additional team to help a heteromorph. Calantral trained for work alone and cannot train Jitep in archeology."

"The Precursors are history for all intelligent species. Dzuran and Erran share history."

"Yes, but a history of war and slavery between Erra and Dzura," Calantral reminded him, "means caution for all encounters with your race." He paused. "The Cho Rebellion was settled over four centuries ago. We get it! You won."

Jitep felt the burst of humiliation and hurt from Calantral. Both stopped talking. Jitep sensed another psi block. Somehow, a moment of aid to a fellow spacer and fellowship, still basic to both Erran and Dzuran cultures, had erupted into a clash over their combined shared history, a history forever marred by xenophobic, theistic administrations in both cultures. Jitep wondered in the silence how Calantral had found this one anomalous rock in a belt of pre-planetary rubble around this out of the way star.

He decided to explore further. "How did Calantral discover Precursor site?"

Calantral, psi blockers removed, spoke candidly. "A Telian prospector made bad star jump; confused coordinates for Gikkan system. The Telian miner rediscovered this star system. No one remembered why it was classified as off limits. Two years later, administrators authorized research effort to explore." With slight overtones of embarrassment, he continued, "Ss-Jarand decided to send an expendable assessor for the first report. Here I am, expendable. Asteroids always best first assay because of zero gravity. Ship's sensors discovered Precursor site."

Jitep felt something missing. "Life-sign sensors?"

"No, visual and thermal select for non-random geometry. It found a rectangle shadow and alerted me." He looked noncommittally back at Jitep, who was not getting closer to his real question.

"Did your ship sensors pick up on background life-sign from this system?"

"Yes, third planet had significant life-sign, radio frequency culture obvious! If you had scanned it and not these rocks, you would have detected it also. Assume you have capable sensors?"

Now it was Jitep's turn to feel scorn. "Yes," he admitted, flushing in response to the jibe. "I have planet scanners. I was searching for ore here first and had turned off the life-sign alarm." Jitep realized it was time for him to leave. He had to make some decisions soon, and he wanted to make them at a distance from Calantral's psi sense. He abruptly stood and nearly lost his traction grip on the surface, which would have been another embarrassment. There had been too many in this brief exchange. "Jitep leave now. Good to talk with a Dzuran, Calantral. Someday, much more talk between Erran and Dzuran will bring even more good." He hoped that sounded right to the son/daughter of an ambassador.

"Thanks for your help. Considered my fates." He stood slowly. "When I finish setting up my scanners, I can study the Precursor artifact in detail." She looked up through the bubble at the swirling lines and could-be characters covering the walls of the chamber. "I have much to do."

After exchanging culturally proper goodbyes, they parted. Jitep tried not to emote sorrow for Calantral's condition. He could not imagine being victim of an incomplete life-sex change. He had heard of it, and he understood why most of those poor wretches were put away as too disturbing for the general population. The thought of encountering another who was neither female tan nor male white, but a splotched half-changed accident, would disgust most of his comrades. Although, while talking to Calantral, he had almost gotten used to the idea that his/her upper torso was still tan while much of the calves and below were cloaked in soft female fur. In full dress, Calantral was male by all measure, even if he was only a Dzuran.

Jitep backed slowly out of the excavation and reattached his ship to the array of engines that he used to jump significant ore-bearing asteroids back to Alal's gravity well. He ran through his mission priorities and decided that, yes, this asteroid was sufficiently rich in heavy ores to make it valuable in its own right. The bonus of the Precursor site might even earn a mention in the council chambers for individual effort.

The decision was made. He had probably made it before he reached the ship and went through the density and mass calculations with Mug. He moved into position on the far surface of the asteroid and attached the first in line of the six jump engines to its surface. He detached the remainder of the pile and backed away. Jitep and Mug made separate trajectory calculations and compared notes. They decided on the average of five runs each and set the jump engine's target.

He felt sorry for what would happen to Calantral. If the Dzuran survived the jump, he would not be treated too badly, but possibly only because of his condition. Besides, he just could not let the important Precursor find stay in Dzuran hands. But sending this stone back would stir up trouble among the philosopher priests. Perhaps this would give the great debate some new grain for grinding.

Backing to a safe distance to avoid the ion wash from the thrusters, he activated the huge motors. He did not want to think of the effect inside the Precursor chamber. Perhaps the bubble shield would protect him from the growing thrust of the drive. In two shifts, the glow of the engines would be reduced to a tiny speck and only the flash of the jump shield would tell him that the asteroid was no longer in this system. He sent a G-wave pulse transmission to Erra, advising them of both the arrival of a large mass with its possible occupation by a live Dzuran and the importance of the archeological site. He had a small tug of conscience as he watched the ion-hot blue light accelerate away. Should I have told Calantral that the two races were again almost at a state of war?

Chapter 3

Follow your Guiding Lights: Darkness will fall.
Cli-Chk Tuk - Erran Philosopher, from the *Cho Chronicles*

Aboard Teeya City – Stationary Orbit above Dzura
3,608.286 – Erran Calendar

Pelma Si-I pulled himself along handholds vaulting through the inner levels of the slowly spinning central core of the city. He took a drift tube down, for there was an "up" here. Located on the central axis, the bridge had no gravity when the grav plates were off. The huge city spun slowly, in counter-force to the more rapidly rotating grav chambers. The growing pods turned slightly faster because they needed to provide at least fifty percent of Dzuran normal gravity for plants to grow "up." Much smaller pods generated incrementally more induced-spin gravity, depending on which one a citizen wanted or needed for exercise. Most did as little as possible because a well-defined set of leg muscles had the distinct look of a grounder. Spacers had not thought much of grounders for generations.

Si-I had always thought of forward, toward the command bridge, as up, and he easily propelled himself up-ship toward his duty station. He settled into the command chair and took a great breath. He cleared his mind and turned his psi off to the crew. The bridge was not a place for intimacy. Here, he was in command of Teeya City, the orbital habitat that housed over ten thousand of his people. As senior Pelma among the three orbiting cities, he was the highest ranking officer off the home world Erra.

He took stock of the status screens as a matter of habit. Status was nominal; good! Although the bridge had a vestigial viewport directly ahead, it almost always displayed a gradually shifting view of the nebular Light. It had never been covered with instrumentation as the habitat grew over the decades from a captured Dzuran cruise ship to a massive agglomeration of manufacturing pods, agricultural greenhouses, dorms, nurseries, and hangars for hundreds of supply ships. That viewport was now recessed in a well created by some of those required additions. But the Light was important. Viewing it was a daily ritual, calming, reassuring, and re-centering. The Light was center to the old Dzuran and Erran theology. In its comforting blanket, within its feathery wisps, the star systems through which the Erran prospectors ventured for ores were tossed as pearls in a web. Their nascent planets—for most of these stars were quite young—held their minerals near the surface, often in molten streams for the taking. Seldom did the long timid reach of the Erran commerce venture out of the comforting shroud of the Light.

Si-I grew up in Teeya City, served as a cadet in this command center, and moved rapidly up the chain of command. He sealed his commission as master of the city, Pelma, Supreme Commandant, and sector commander of this third of the planet's defensive screen. Supreme Commandant Pelma Si-I almost never relaxed, but seeing all screens were nominal and the shift crew not engaged in any urgent matters, he allowed himself a contented whistle. Only a few heads swiveled to the source, most knew better. One of the ensigns caught in the act, caught his eye. "You, Pe-yng isn't it?"

The ensign jumped to attention, nearly losing his tenuous sticky-shoe grip on the floor mats. Low grav pratfalls were slo-mo and often comical, and that would have been horrible here in the Command Center of the city. But he stabilized and straightened to attention. "Yes, sir!"

"Pe-yng, I've heard some good things about you and your training group." His brow wrinkled in a reassuring smile. "I have a mission for you." The young ensign, if anything, grew more rigid. Si-I continued, "I need you to take an escort to Jheln City to retrieve some prisoners. You will need a small contingent. Let's see. At least eight. Select the best from your mess and pick up your orders at the dock."

"Sir, ... sir?"

"Do I have to be clearer?" He looked up from his command chair and the distorted face of the young crewman, wondering if he had been that scared of the Pelma when he had come from cadet school. "Would you rather I selected someone else? Would you like to waste that grav training and spend the next two years at a console?" He glanced at one of the surface monitors. "Looks like good weather down there."

"No, sir. Fine, sir." Pe-yng stammered, "I was surprised and, I am sorry, sir. Nothing."

"Good. How is your surface conditioning for Dzuran duty?"

"Adequate, sir. On the ring, I can run over a hundred revolutions at Erran mass so I should be able to survive the surface of Dzura." Pe-yng felt a tingle of fur along his dorsal ridge running from the base of his skull down to his hips. He could not control the automatic reflex for excitement. At least, he hoped, no one could see it under his jumpsuit.

"Are your mates in similar condition?"

"Sir, yes, sir! They can all keep up or surpass me."

"At ease, Pe. Your ID and orders will be ready at the elevator. You'll take an elevator car down and pick up ground cars there. Any questions?"

"Sir, the off-worlders. Any special treatment or precautions?"

"They'll be in blanker helmets and subdued. You should not have any trouble. Get your detail ready to drop to the surface."

The young officer saluted, performed a perfect about-face, and exited.

Si-I, satisfied that his choice for the mission was actually fit for surface duty, settled in to confirm the day's schedule. He determined to get more squads fit for full Dzuran gravity. It was not a traditional policy, but after all, this was the home planet of his species. He outlined the day's schedule and only as a side thought, briefly wondered if he ought to get surface conditioning himself.

Jheln City Prison – Dzura
May 13, 1986 – Earth Calendar
3608.287 – Erran Calendar

With only a little difficulty, Ensign Pe-yng assembled his crew along the length of the landing craft. This deployment was something new to operations, and he was aware of how important it was to pull off this command. His was the first unit to have had extensive, enhanced grav training and, hence, the first detail to come to the Dzuran surface without a contingent of air cars. They were actually going to walk into the prison compound! He was in low-grade pain simply standing and assumed that his small squad was also uncomfortable in their bones.

He expected that he would have little trouble from the off-worlders even though he had seen them walking with ease in their cells. His squad was armed with come-alongs, and besides, his orders were to bind them neck and neck. They would be able to do little with only a three-hand's length of pialla twine binding between their skulls. If they tried to resist, the fine line would decapitate one of the two. Examining the ready and eager faces of his squad, he looked for signs of strain. He did not see any and hoped they were adequately trained.

He had to perform well. He and his squad were in line to become the future leaders of this planet. They would be the first to rule without the encumbrance of the air cars that confined and restricted all previous generations of Erran overlords. If this operation went well, each new sortie into the planet's harsh gravity would strengthen his and his squad's muscles in ways they could never simulate in orbit and would lead to probable promotion and responsibility. Pe-yng took in deep breaths of the planet's sweet evening air. Especially sweet after the shared airspace of the ten thousand citizens of the orbital city above the thin cloud cover. "I just have to get this mission going," he thought. "The future will illuminate the correct path."

On his command, the small platoon entered the apex entry of one of the few surviving surface prisons on Dzura. The triangular room immediately inside the entry was a sally port, a secured doubling of the gate system accessing the prison. The evening's bright lavender light filtered down through skylights four stories above. An air chair-assisted Erran guard behind a viewing panel opened a sliding door and they entered. First Officer Pe-yng showed his orders at the chest-high counter. The officer of the watch at the rear of the guardroom lifted his chair and floated over to the counter.

To Pe-yng's eyes, the Erran watch officer looked ridiculous. His legs were orbital thin, as if he didn't even try grav training. Fat sacks hung under his arms and his belly fat lay in a roll above the waist cinch of his uniform. His shoulders showed moderate former development that had atrophied since his posting to the planet's surface. After all, he had to lift his arms, and if he couldn't afford Dzuran slave laborers in his homestead, he would have to lift himself from sleeping tube to chair.

The watch officer looked critically at Pe-yng and his companions. He had never had a contingent of Errans physically defy gravity and walk into his prison. His first suspicion—all guards are suspicious by nature—was of brazen grounder imposters. He addressed Pe-yng. "What home are you?" He followed up in psi querie, *and what was your crèche mother's name?* He had half expected the imposter to be a blank.

Pe-yng replied, "Riiya City," and in psi, *Yng-na was my crèche mother.* He tried to control a smirk. *Do you believe I am Dzuran because I can walk on two legs? Ha!* Off psi he thought, You will either learn to walk or these prisoners one day will have you readied for the ritual fire mound.

When Pe-yng placed his cred pack and the capsule containing his orders to transfer the off-worlders to Teeya City on the guard room counter, his day went bad and then worse. The sally port officer took the order capsule from Pe-yng, inserted it into his control console, and pressed decrypt. As he did so, the prison lost power—no flicker and no dimming as was usual when the unreliable wiring in the ancient compound shorted. In the dim light filtering into the reception office through the entrance corridor, the officer of the watch and the young platoon leader looked at each other expectantly. A hard vibration in the floor was the only warning before Pe-yng and most of his squad were thrown against a wall. A terrific explosion followed from inside the prison and, brief moments later, a third blast reverberated elsewhere in an adjacent wing. A blast of dust-laden air billowed out of the inner doorway, obliterating the watch officers from Pe-yng's view. Rising to his haunches, his weapon at the ready, he saw that most of his squad had been knocked down by shock, blast, or surprise. Additional explosions echoing through the structure were unnoticed by stunned ears as the Pe-yng and squad regained their composure.

A piercing wail began as escape horns and whistles blended their high and low warbles in a discordant din. Stunned and filthy Dzuran guards appeared from a back room, startling Pe-yng, who was just regaining his footing. They seemed to be subservient to the two Erran watch officers in their air chairs and waited, expecting orders. Pe-yng relaxed his fingers on the grip of his weapon that, for the moment, was still holstered on his thigh. In private psi, he told his small command, *Loose your side arms, but do not draw.*

He addressed the highest ranking member of the Dzuran guard. "You! Take me to the off-worlders!" He started toward the inner door, shouting at the guard who appeared to be shocked into immobility. "Lead, and have the others follow us. Quick now, move! Run!" He pulled his hand weapon out of its bindings. The Dzuran, armed only with a neural rod, turned and lead the way into the inner compound of the Jheln City prison.

Pe-yng quickly discovered that all electronic devices, including his connection to his uplink to orbit, were as useless as the grounded air cars. His squad's first trip down to the surface had to coincide with a prison break. "Gloom upon you all!" he swore at no one in particular.

The hired Dzuran guards gave chase at first, but as they discovered their energy weaponry and helmet-linked command structure was offline as well, their enthusiasm for a confrontation with the escaping inmates dwindled rapidly. And they had not expected an Erran guard unit that could walk erect on the surface.

Standing beneath blood red clouds underlit by the setting sun, the young platoon leader watched as the last few dozen of the over three hundred escapees disappeared into a line of russet-colored brush. Several would-be escapees lay dead or writhing just short of the brush. The dark red foliage glowed in a sunset tinged with crimson. Two of the jump-suited prisoners stood out among the escaping prisoners. These two were half a head taller than the rest. Their head hair was decidedly not male brown or female white. And they ran easily with the rest as the last of several groups of escapees blended into the tangled vegetation beyond the live-fire zone. Were there secret pathways through the brush? He had no firsthand experience with the vegetation of Dzura.

In a few moments, the majority of his small squad joined him. With an abrupt hand signal, he cut off all psi queries and motioned toward the nearest area where the off-worlder escapees had filtered into the brush line. Extending his pace into a trot, he felt the jolts of the hard ground impacting his joints collectively and individually. This harsh reality of surface gravity was a surprise after the padded surfaces of the running track around Teeya City. The track, designed to imitate soil on the planet had not prepared him for pavement. Real gravity, he realized, was different from the induced gravity of the spin chambers. First, and most disquieting, was the flatness of everything. He'd seen pictures, of course, and driven simulation vehicles under sim-grav conditions, but this was—real!

Pe-yng adjusted his pace, moved his weight forward to the front of his feet and the jarring impacts stopped. The horizon, quickly darkening in the western sky, surrounded him with unexpected vistas. The concept of a full surround horizon was unsettling. He called a halt as they reached the brush line where, through hand signals, he split his team into pairs, instructed them to draw their projectile hand weapons, and motioned them into the brush. The pungent smells of the moist soil and the near total darkness in the underbrush at dusk were discomforting. There was always some minimal light in every nook and hidey-hole of his orbital home, and its smells were familiar. The growing darkness and the uncomfortable closeness of the vegetation caused his deployed troops to pause only a few paces into the brush. Overhead, the orange-red hues of the nebula were beginning to shine through the now shaded atmosphere. That at least was familiar. But, a darker band of the nebula promised scant light to assist his search. With the power grid down, their helmets were useless.

Sir?

Proceed?

Where…

Psi queries flooded in from the pairs of infantrymen to his left and right.

"Forward!" he commanded. "We must find the off-worlder escapees." He sensed the motion left and right and wished he had the same confidence in his leadership as his troops. "All Dzuran escapees are expendable, the off-worlders must be brought back alive."

He holstered his weapon to aid in clearing a path through the thickening brush. He imagined that it had been planted years ago as a barrier that would allow pursuing guards and their predator-hunter crant to catch up to any escapee who had managed to get across the live-fire zone. Even a crant would have difficulty in this thick brush.

He paused and heard only the crashing and thrashing of his troops to either side. "Halt!" he shouted.

Abruptly, noises nearest him quieted. Nothing! No sound penetrated from ahead, at least from where he expected to hear sounds. No sounds at all. No, wait. A faint tinkling of running water. Clicks and cries from night creatures he could not identify.

As he stood in the darkening brush, a tingle passed from neck to waist, the hairs on his back stood at attention, and he wished to the nebular lights above to be out of here. It was dark under the foliage, there was no hope of following a trail, and he felt suddenly unequipped to occupy this alien planet. Training in the workout rooms on Erra was no substitute, he realized, for the reality of its sister world. Dzura was unfamiliar in much more than its increased gravity.

He called a general retreat and tried to retrace his steps out of the thick foliage. To his right, someone cried an alarm. He assumed a stumble on a root or branch had tripped one of his team. Moving out of the brush into the clear zone, he counted off two, four, six, eight ... He waited, with increasing concern. It was now dark enough that he could not see faces. He was aware that his pulse was pounding behind his eyes. He slowed his breathing. A quick poll of his group revealed that Jri-Lian and Jri-Too-ad were not back. Forgetting the command presence he had tried so hard to maintain, he called out. "LIAN! TOO-ad!"

~ ~ ~

Shaand, Kinaan, Brad, and Connie emerged into sharply angled sunlight and collectively paused and blinked, closing circular and slit irises against the brightness outside the prison's wall. The wall's opening still smoked from the recent shape charge that, like the five other perimeter bombs, had breached the prison's perimeter. Their escape offered the first view of the surface of Dzura for the two humans, and they paused to take it in. On Earth, in their many conversations, Brad Hitchens and Connie Chappell received glimpses through Jai's mind's eye or, more probably, a camera lens, but the unexpected coloration and beauty of the scene made them want to stop, if only briefly.

Brad and Connie were in the largest group of escapees who ran for their lives across a cleared area designed to be a kill zone. It was hoped that there would be some safety in numbers, and there was the knowledge that power was shut down in the sector. The chosen zone was covered by three of the six auto-fire positions located on the perimeter of the hexagonal prison complex. The stun pulse and projectile weapons meant to stop any and all movement in the zone stared sightless from their hardened canisters. The power loss to the district was pervasive, rendering all energy weapons and their tracking systems useless.

Shaand beckoned to Connie. His companion, Kinaan, reached for Brad, who nodded, and the four began to move. They ran toward another russet-colored hedge surrounding the clear-fire zone, through it and then slantwise down the slope of a drainage canal. Additional area sirens began to sound in the near distance around them.

Quick ... now, Kinaan psi'd to the two humans.

Following the rough bank at a moderate trot, the four fugitives made time and distance getting away from the prison compound. Other groups took different paths, some parallel on the other side of the stream, some up the opposite bank and into the surrounding fields. At the near approach of a softly buzzing surveillance craft, they all stopped, crouched into the darkening shadows, and waited. With the danger passed, the foursome continued into twilight. The wail of the alarm in the distance stopped, and they settled down onto the rocks and caught their breath.

Shaand led Brad and Connie along the waterline of the small drainage ditch. He showed them how to step lightly into the water so their footsteps made no more sound that the gurgling of the stream itself. Kinaan, Shaand's crèche twin, caught up with them, cleaning a stiletto with a bloody cloth. As they neared a broad, arched culvert, he led the group to the top of the embankment and then showed them how to backtrack in their steps, to return to the water's edge and back into the stream itself. Brad realized immediately that they were leaving a false trail to the top of the embankment and smiled as he recognized the tactic from old westerns and war movies.

The four quietly moved along the stream and into the darkness of the arched tunnel. When his eyes accustomed to the darkness in the tunnel, Brad saw a dim glimmer ahead that indicated the tunnel was possibly a hundred yards long and curved slightly to the left.

Kinaan called to Shaand to halt about halfway through the passageway, aimed a small reddish beam toward the wall of the tunnel, and began to search the stone wall. After scanning the wall for what Brad estimated was about thirty feet of identical stone blocks, Kinaan found one that was slightly darker than the rest. He depressed it then stepped back as a panel appeared in the wall. A dark space, dimly lit by Kinaan's utility glove, was slowly revealed and he led them through the opening. In the darkness of the smaller tunnel, Shaand psi'd that Connie and then Brad should follow.

Stepping into a narrower passage, the two humans stooped to avoid the low ceiling. The walls lining this passage appeared to be much newer, but with less engineering finesse than the moss-covered waterway. Its walls were rough-hewn through native soil and rock, occasionally propped with sheets and piles of organic material that Brad recognized as wood, but which had an entirely different texture. He was reminded of the entwined helical structure of one of the desert succulents he'd seen in Arizona and immediately thought of how far he was from Earth. Kinaan, now in front, led the small group single file through a winding passageway. Their path first rose in elevation then dropped down a short set of stairs and through an opening into a well-lit room with composite pour rock and stone walls.

Shaand, a smile furrowing his brow, said, "All safe here. He," pointing at Kinaan, "is Ss-Kinaan, leader of this sector. He is the Ss who authorized your removal from the prison."

"Removal?" Brad asked. "That was a general prison break."

Kinaan psi'd, *Removal plan keep you from High Pelma Si-I. From Errans.*

Shaand, better at audible communication with humans, said, "Hoomans maybe not survive kestions from Erran priests. Chemical test, maybe bad. Tay bad for Dzuran person, maybe make Hooman dead."

Connie looked at Brad, eyes wide. "Brad, they've just saved our lives!"

Brad asked, "Shaand, how big is this breakout? There does not seem to be any power outside the prison." He looked up at the ceiling that emitted a soft pink glow. "At least above ground. How much plan is this?"

Shaand looked at Kinaan and received a silent go-ahead. "Dzura now in war wit Erra. Before, only some area in revolt. Now," he opened his arms wide, "all Dzuran fight Erran boss." Shaand made a very human gesture of pounding his palm with his other fist then started to lead the way out of the room, but turned back to Brad. "No power on surface. Power in," he paused searching for a simple word, "not surface."

Brad nodded. *You have power supply underground.* He hoped his intent was picked up by Shaand and Kinaan by psi.

Shaand nodded, testing the word, "Unner gond. Underd gond," and finally, "under grond."

In response, Brad nodded assent and tried to psi, *Good!*

"Come, need go." Kinaan motioned to one of the two doors in the room.

The door bore no visible locks or handles. Brad watched as Kinaan placed his hand over a small dot on the frame and the door opened outward into a much larger space. Brad noted that this door was thick, blast-proof thick. Stepping through, they found themselves on a platform resembling any subway or railway station he might expect to visit on Earth. Here, however, there was no sign of advertising. Down in the tramway, there were no visible rails. Overhead, unreadable signage with iconic arrows labeled destinations in each direction. Kinaan drew a small, hand-sized device from his coverall, pointed it at one of the dark tunnels and pressed a sequence of buttons.

While they waited, Connie stepped into an arm-in-arm hug with Brad. Kinaan and Shaand, seeing this, stepped back and away. She felt a wordless psi message of displeasure from Shaand and she became aware of a more distinct sense of distaste from Kinaan. "What's the matter?" she asked Shaand. "Is something wrong?"

"Not wrong," he replied, obviously repressing discomfort. "Hoomans different." His ear ridges darkened. "Dzurans, Errans too, not touch udder sex unless in..." The coloring on his ear ridge darkened further as his discomfort with the subject deepened. "Elioi not touch 'less for making more Elioi."

"EL-io-I?" Connie tried the word as she thought she heard it.

Shaand replied, pronouncing it clearly again. "Elioi are..." He paused, then tapped his chest, pointed to Kinaan, and waved an arm outward as if to encompass all around him. "Elioi are we," he continued, enunciating meticulously slowly for the off-worlder Hoomans. "Dzurans and Errans are Elioi. Ert has Hoomans; man and wo-man Hoomans. Dzura and Erra have Elioi and Elioiti."

Both Connie and Brad expressed nearly silent ahhhs of understanding. They might not be sure of the pronunciations, but clearly, the sexes here did not touch in public. They took a step apart. With further knowledge of the local name for its own species and the implied sexual distinctions, Connie was about to ask a clarifying question when noise to their left and a rush of air into the chamber announced the arrival of transport.

Earth Interlude 1

We must always tell what we see.
Above all, and this is more difficult, we must always see what we see.
Charles Péguy

Ft. Meade, Maryland
May 15, 1986 – Earth Calendar

Colonel "Bud" Henderson glared at the recently retired Master Sergeant Martin Jenks from across his broad, clean desk. Detritus *did not* settle on the Colonel's desk. For decades, Henderson had lead two of Project Bluebook's descendant agencies that tracked possible UFO sightings or contacts. Henderson understood that it was imperative that his agency's hyper-secret activities saw little daylight. His small band not only did the field work of tracking down reports, but also sought to neutralize those reports—one way or another. Jenks had a long but successful record in the unit, before his retirement, a retirement forced by a Senate sub-committee.

"Jenks, uhm, Martin. What are the chances that I can convince you to come back to work for us as a civilian employee? All the bennies, better pay, and no structure to worry about. Just a job and a paycheck."

Martin Jenks settled back in the guest chair and took a sip of the excellent hot Columbian coffee that was always available in the Colonel's enclave. "Colonel H, listen. We've known each other for what, nine, ten years? I started out in your little operation as a skeptic. Understood that there was a certain level of alien hysteria that could be tolerated and that some of the more extreme cases needed intervention. All that has changed. I know what I saw. You saw the corpse. It's as real as my mother and as alien as they come." Jenks had been present when his long-term assignment, Brad and girlfriend, raised a crashed alien ship and its dead pilot from north Florida limestone.

"Sure, sure. It's a game changer to be sure." He'd only seen desiccated skin stretched over bone, but there was no denying the x-rays and the 3D model built from the CAT scan. That thing was not human or anywhere near the terrestrial genetic tree. Oddly, there were a lot of hits of parallelism in the chromosomal analysis—

double helical structure, same four basic nucleotides. "Not much chance of going the denial route on this—"

Jenks interrupted. "And what do we do with the media storm now? I just don't see the point anymore. I've spent almost half my career chasing ghosts, scaring the hell out of good citizens, and wham! One of my pet projects digs up a real live spaceship while I, I just stand there and watch it leave."

"Well, there was a hurricane passing through at the time, if I remember right?"

Jenks sagged back into the chair letting his frustration take shape. "For what? What did we protect and from whom?" The pain of frustration painted lines on his face. "Looking back, I really can't think of any national interest we protected. What the hell have we been doing to people for all those years?"

Henderson eyed his friend and confidant of over ten years. Jenks had been principal investigator on the Hitchens case and had dealt with complex situations with respect and understanding. He had seen and understood the full implications of the alien corpse— that its secret was no longer secret. It had been reported on national television and the media had been hounding Congress for a peek at it for months. He envied Jenks, a witness to the first flight of the freed alien ship. He'd have given up a rank to have been able to see and experience in sound and color what Jenks had put in his report. "Martin, obviously there is a major mission change. We are no longer focusing on containment, but...," he sought the correct phrasing. "Understanding? We've gone from official denial while accumulating a significant database that would prove we are not alone, to going back through that database to figure out what we do know." He shifted back in his chair. "There will be some handwringing and apologies while we do our best at retaining credibility. I see a dangerous release of information about all we know of this particular case and no reason to back into the archives."

He rose and took his ample coffee mug over to the pot and refilled it. Turning to Jenks, he continued. "We're going to go public with the details of the dead pilot and I'm working on getting clearance to go public with your story. People—and by people, I mean the major media—think we've done away with Hitchens and his girlfriend."

"Since when did we worry about what the media asks or says?" Jenks's sarcasm had a hint of bitterness in it.

"Since that little prick's girlfriend went on the God-damned evening news!" Henderson's voice went up a few decibels, as he vented his frustration. He had been drawn before yet another Senate panel on top of the more insipid Congressional panels and had tried to explain why so much of his little department's work had been *sub rosa*. Now that the two principals, Brad Hitchens and Connie Chappell, were missing, fingers were again pointing at Henderson's B-Team as probable culprits in an unofficial snatch. Henderson took a deep breath, a sip of coffee, and sat back at his desk. Henderson also knew that sharing a secret with a sworn-to-secrecy Senate subcommittee was only a little less efficient than calling *The New York Times* news desk.

"Bud, I know this has been tough, but I don't know what to tell you. We saw it go up, it came back down, the kids got in, and it went up again. We left. It was all I could do to keep Fischetti from hauling ass and leaving me with the body. He'd been scared shitless. He babbled all the way from St. Marks to Eglin. Short story? It's gone." He pointed up. "There's a lot of 'out there' out there."

"Too bad we had to neutralize Fischetti's memory. You can't trust a babbling idiot."

Jenks looked down at the floor, letting his head sag into a cradle of his hands. "Yeah, I hated doing that."

Henderson agreed. "Tell me about it." He pulled a file folder from his "active" drawer and opened it for reference. "Other than the enquiries of tower personnel who somehow 'lost power' to their recording equipment on November twenty-first, we've only got the data from the regional towers, except the one at Gainesville. That tower got a case of stupid when this thing began playing around in our airspace." He thumbed through the report from Moody Air Force Base.

"We have an aircraft with no transponder and a thin signature appearing out of nowhere near the coast south of Tallahassee, hovering, then accelerating vertically at unheard of velocities. They thought it was an atmospheric effect from the hurricane, at first. Then it gets higher than the cloud deck and keeps going. Ten minutes later, let's see, yeah, it comes back down to below tree line. Thirty minutes later, it's up and gone off screens."

Jenks chuckled, a smile pulling dimples into his chocolate-colored cheeks. "Yeah, I imagine they were pretty confused. I'm almost not surprised the other towers 'lost power.'" He hooked imaginary quotation marks in the air. "Bud, I really wish I had taken a waterproof camera out there. It could have rocked your world!"

"Yeah, well. Aren't you the lucky man?"

Jenks looked down at his palms and then back up. "No, the lucky man got to go for a ride in a spaceship."

Colonel Henderson leaned back, elbows on the arms of his chair, and slowly put his fingertips together under his chin. "Well, Martin. I want you back on the team. There's going to be a major looky-here exercise up on the Hill, and maybe it's a good thing that you're not on the payroll right now. When it's over, I'd like you back." Looking over his steepled fingertips at the lucky SOB who actually got to watch the launch of an alien ship, he added, "Meanwhile, go up to your mountain cabin and fish!" Jenks started to rise. "Oh, and Martin."

"Yeah, Bud?"

"We know it's been back. Watched it take a few day trips, but it's gone. Hasn't peeped since January!"

Jenks nodded, internalizing that last gambit, gave a perfunctory salute that hovered on the margins of proper form. Then he turned and left. He had a lot to think about if he was going to work for Henderson again.

Chapter 4

The antidote to fifty enemies is one friend
Aristotle

The Dzuran Underground
3,608.296 – Erran Calendar

The car, when it arrived, was less than Connie had expected. She'd thought perhaps, something similar to a subway car or train. A small, apparently engineless, platform car with little more than a windscreen and eight seats appeared, slowed to a stop, and settled onto a guide track. They took their places with Shaand and Kinaan fore, and Brad and Connie aft. With the press of a few buttons on Kinaan's hand controller, the little car lifted on its suspension field and accelerated into the dark tunnel ahead.

In the darkness of the rushing tunnel, Connie reached for and found Brad's hand. He squeezed it reassuringly. At intervals, an overhead dome light illuminated small areas of the tunnel. Brad realized that the infrequent light would be far less than he would be comfortable with if he were alone in the tunnel. He couldn't tell if there were recesses that would permit a pedestrian to avoid a passing vehicle. Maybe the locals had better low light vision. It appeared that his and Connie's best bets were to remain allied with the Dzurans, but he was increasingly aware that they had dropped into the opening moves of a local revolt.

He reached forward and tapped Shaand's shoulder. "Shaand, I know from Jai's memory that Dzura forces were called Coalition. Are revolt forces still called Coalition?"

Shaand considered, wondering how much the Hoomans had learned of his planet and culture from their ship's memory files. He paused, selecting from his limited Hooman vocabulary. "Dzura have two big land, with water." He motioned with his hands to demonstrate the idea of two large land masses separated by water. "Before Erran deceit and war, two Dzuran tribes, groups. Some Dzuran not trust other Dzuran. After start of Erran war, two Dzuran tribes form Coalition." Using liberal gestures, psi, and his limited but growing human speech, he managed to convey that the northern hemisphere was rich in manufacturing capacity, its base metals very abundant in its surface formations and with efficient, planet-based, smelting centers located nearby. The southern hemisphere was or had been rich in research, science, and the arts. It was also the planet's bread basket with vast, richly endowed, agricultural plains. Characteristically different, remnants of the two cultures bonded from necessity after the richest and most powerful abandoned the planet, seeking another home in the stars.

The Cho Rebellion had started in the asteroid mining colonies. In less time than it took for the two planets to dance twice around their center, the various factions chose sides. All of the off-world colonies, primarily Erra and the asteroids, as well as the now dead inner planet Milla, had followed Cho-le Baan in his insurrection against colonial rule by the Dzuran Hegemony. The fighting initially went to the Dzuran military, with the capture of the Erran capital by its superior spacing navy. The inner planet Milla was fiercely contested as Dzura's navy was well matched by ground-to-space rocket installations and ground-to-air artillery hastily deployed by the rebels. In an attempt to break the stalemate, Pelma Gruen-kot made the historic mistake of using nukes designed for splitting asteroids on the ground installations. The horrific results sickened many in Gruen-kot's navy and incensed the rebels.

The retaliation was just as terrible. Erran bombardment of the population centers on Dzura with gigaton asteroids was just as brutally effective. Mass drivers, intended to accelerate much larger stones to the outer system colonies, accelerated asteroids to explosive velocities, taking a greater toll on the Dzuran ecology than the planet could bear. A brief period of volcanism triggered by the impacts added to the atmospheric shroud. As winter settled on the home world, its navy escorted as many of the Dzura's citizens as possible, crammed into cruisers, requisitioned pleasure liners, and even an L5 hotel in the final evacuation. What was to be an emergency escape to one of the several inhabitable systems in near-Alal space turned into a rout as the experienced off-world miners and engineers in technically inferior craft outmaneuvered the escaping Dzurans. The chase did not end until every known fighter, destroyer, cruiser, and city ship was accounted for as destroyed. As there had been no survivors on tortured Milla, no prisoners were taken as trapped and overwhelmed vessels were summarily opened to space.

On Dzura, those who could not buy or swindle passage, those who hadn't the foresight to stowaway, watched as their leadership, their best planners, engineers, and scientists took off for the stars. Years later, those survivors—northern agrarian and southern manufacturing workers—now banded together by necessity. Each huddled from the five years of winter cloud in underground complexes rebuilt on the framework of the old transit system. The atmosphere cleared and Erran forces took control of what was left of Dzuran society. The greatest secret withheld from the conquering Errans was the extent to which the old underground transit system had survived or had been rebuilt.

Jai, after nearly four centuries buried in terrestrial bedrock, knew only that its home world was destroyed and uninhabitable. It also knew from battle records stored in memory that the last stand of its navy was overmatched in numbers and had been losing. Based on the limited knowledge gained from their ship computer, Brad and Connie had believed they would be able to survey a damaged and dead planet. They had not expected to find that not only had it become habitable but that it had been taken over by the race that had defeated Jai's builders. They had been tossed, they thought, into an Erran prison for safekeeping or, thinking about the more unpleasant possibilities, for examination—or worse still, dissection.

Now that he and Connie were in the middle of the revolt against Erran slave rule, Brad had to assume, or at least hope, that their best interests were being looked out for by Shaand and Kinaan. As he thought about this, he realized that he only had the word of his Dzuran protectors that they were being kept safe. But for what reason?

The response came in moments. He knew, he wasn't sure how, that Kinaan was the one who responded. *We need you much ...same you need us.*

The little car was now moving fast, Brad guessed over forty miles an hour, but he realized that this was hard to estimate with only occasional lights whizzing by overhead. The voice returned. *Will talk later in Pel-Council.*

Brad was stunned. In Council? He involuntarily gave Connie a harder squeeze.

39

She leaned over and whispered in his ear, "I heard that too."

"We are going to be introduced to leadership," Brad whispered back.

"Isn't that good?"

"I guess so. We may be important in ways we don't know yet."

Again, their mental space was overheard and interrupted. This time by Shaand. "Plees. Dzuran Elioi want friend wit Hoomans and Ert." After a short pause, "Much good all. Braad talk wit Pelma Sian-Lotan. Talk much good for Hoomans and Elioi. Braad talk wit Dzura Pel-Council."

There was a short pause. Connie had not been mentioned in that exchange. Kinaan took in their involuntary responses. *Ka-Nee not worry, Ka-Nee female Hooman, need go learn from Dzurati.* There was a pause, and then, clarifying, *Elioiti of Dzura..*

Connie gripped Brad's hand to a point just short of inflicting pain and she wished she could block her thoughts.

Shaand turned back to them from his seat in the front and said, "Ka-Nee safe with Dzurati. Learn much. Not good, Ert female go Pel-Council."

Without realizing that he was responding in kind, Brad psi'd back, *Go to see the Council now?*

Not now, not safe. Need more safe. Need Errans not find Braad. Kinaan's response seemed definitive and closed the exchange. They rode on in silence.

In quiet conversation, Brad and Connie balanced elation over being sprung from Jhelen Prison against the unknowns of being delivered to the high command of the resistance.

~ ~ ~

Teeya City: Commandant's Quarters
3,608.296 – Erran Calendar

Stretching his muscles awake, Commandant Si-I rolled out of his netting and pulled on a fresh uniform jumpsuit emblazoned with the three-crested crown of the Erran nobility and the three entwined circles denoting his high admiralty rank. Its vermillion cuffs identified him as a member of the Erran Royal Pel-Council, Representative from Teeya City. He slid into traction shoes and moved into the busy hallway leading to the command bridge. He paused, decided against his usual pre-shift inspection of the bridge, and pulled instead toward the shrine chambers.

By mid-shift, the miner was due to arrive. The so-called Precursor Stone, as the media were calling it, was in a parking orbit above Erra. An interesting find sure, but Precursors? He wanted to have the miner's report before the off-worlder prisoners were brought up. Then there was the matter of the Dzuran geologist, what in God's Illumination was he doing out there, outside the Light. He had not survived the jump back to Alal space and the Dzuran Ambassador was clamoring for severe disciplinary action.

He slid into the recirculating air shaft to avoid as many crewmen as possible. The shaft's current pushed him down-ship along the central core of the city, three-quarters the length of the orbiting megalopolis in a tenth the time it might have taken in crowded pull tubes.

When the color of the shaft turned from command red through gradations of crew tan and green and finally to priest yellow, he braked with his hands and knees, found a port, and slipped back into a much less crowded hallway. This sacred section of the city was appointed in gilt on dark slo wood. Decorative motifs from old Dzuran shared space with new ones from Erra. Many of the decorations were found nowhere else except in the holy shrine in Cresow City on Erra or in similar enclaves on the two other orbiting cities. Slo wood forests once blanketed Dzura's northern latitudes but were now quite rare. Their use as paneling and decoration was a show of wealth and power. Si-I slipped into a side passage, pushed on an otherwise innocuous panel, and entered the antechamber of one of his most troublesome associates, the high priest Eluoi-

Annchda. An acolyte, startled awake, gave a muffled grunt of surprise, quickly composed himself when he saw the rank and markings on Si-I's sleeve, and stood stiffly against the wall.

"Sir, Your Most High Excellency, shall I announce you?"

"Just step aside!" Si-I gave a sharp mental rebuke with the verbal command and the yellow-clad attendant tried to grow smaller, less in the way. He was, in fact, already up against the wall of the chamber and could do little other than disappear, which is what he would really rather have done. The Commandant slid past the relieved priest and approached the ornate vestibule to Eluoi-Annchda's inner sanctum.

"Sir?" the acolyte protested. He suffered another severe mental blow from Si-I as the City's Commandant pushed into the room. The room was dark and, at first, he thought the priest was still in sleep cycle.

After a rustling behind a panel, the priest Annchda emerged, straightening his cloak. "Have you no respect?" asked the indignant priest, composure returning from his surprise. "Do you ever think to see if I am alone?" He glanced at a panel on his desk. "At this hour, I may still have been in my absolutions."

"Shame I didn't interrupt. Maybe you wouldn't waste so much water!"

"Lights of Creation! What—"

"Quiet, priest!"

"I am not just a priest. I am the Eluoi! Senior to the ministry in all—"

"I really do not care about your power structure... your trappings, or," he waved a hand at the ornate decorations in the Eluoi-Annchda's chambers. They were far too gaudy for his command sensibilities. He did not care for the look, the period, or for that matter, the most holy Eluoi-Annchda. The priest was about to gather his mental energies for a new offensive when a psi-blast quieted him. Si-I put a hand out in the universal stop mode and the Annchda took a step back.

"I have news for you that you will find out soon enough." He started to turn on his heel then abandoned his reservations. "You may not like what comes of it, but you will soon know. I do not know why we cannot control the whisper threads in the city, but we can't."

"Is it about the Precursor Stone?" The priest's brow wrinkled in a self-satisfied smile.

"How did you know? I only learned of it this last shift."

"As you said, Pelma, whisper threads, they are insidious." Feeling a little more than proud of the discovery he just this moment confirmed, Annchda continued, "What can you share? Perhaps we can confirm each other's rumors."

"I don't have rumors, priest. I have a report, scans, vids, a dead Dzuran Ambassador's offspring en route, and a prospector ordered back as soon as a grav-jump can get him here." He looked at the display on his wrist panel. "By the end of this shift, the prospector who found the artifact will be aboard." He sighed to regain his composure. "What we will have to determine is whether he will be secluded as a prisoner or hailed as a hero."

He paused, thinking of his course. He had unnecessarily riled the priest. After all, he had to share a modicum of power with the priest. There would be rioting among the workers, mayhem in the crèche schools, and possibly even dissentions among the guard if the priest's flim-flam wasn't given due regard. He drew himself up to attention, gave the formal deferential nod of the head, and apologized. He'd been too angry about the report, too uncertain of all it implied, and what it might mean about the two off-worlders who had been in isolation for almost a third of a revolution already. Yes, they seemed to survive on the food in prison, but he thought, By the Lights! What if they are Precursors, or at minimum, descendants?

The priest nodded in acknowledgement and psi'd in response, *No reason for sacrilege, Pelma.* He said, "What exactly have you discovered?"

"This miner I mentioned was exploring a new system. It's the star system the two off-worlders came from. The asteroid belt is relatively rich in magnetics, conductor metals, and silica, not too unusual. But he found a large one with an intact Precursor sign."

"Are you sure?"

Both calmed. Apologies accepted.

"Sure as vacuum!" He pulled a chip from his waistband, turned to face the priest's com console and placed the chip on the I/O pad. After speaking his executive override to the com unit's start-up sequence he tapped at the screen a few times to find the right scenes. Video began to stream of the interior of the hollow asteroid. The markings were unmistakable. This was a Precursor artifact! Only two others were ever found, one on a habitable world that was populated by carnivorous monsters and one on a minor moon surrounding a volcanic planet. They watched together, silently, the Pelma in awe and the priest in dread. The camera began the same traverse across the highly decorated walls in ultra-blue, displaying altogether different patterns weaving through and complementing the combined sculpture and painting in visible spectra. A third pass in high red blanked out the ultra-blue decoration but also made it clear that there were conduits in the walls.

It began a fourth pass in infrared, when Annchda told the desk computer, "Stop, pan right, return to visual." Something in the heat signature range had caught his attention. The screen reverted to visual and began to pan right. "There, what's that?"

Si-I held his breath for a moment, exhaled, and said, "That is the other, uh, anomaly." He guarded his words. "What you are seeing is a fairly typical shield-enhanced, inflatable shelter." He added, "It's not one of ours."

"Who's is …?" Annchda hesitated.

"It's a Dzuran shield shelter."

"Well, it's remarkably well preserved. That must be a reliable shield energy source. Solar?"

"No. That is, I don't believe the power source is significant. The shelter is new. It belongs to one of the Dzuran Ambassador's crèche brood. At the Choice Ceremonies, he opted for Science against the will of the Ambassador. Something went wrong, either he was too old or just wasn't totally committed. The enzymes didn't take."

"What?"

"The Jann-dk didn't work on him for some reason. His change wasn't complete. He's still mostly male, but the fur change had started, and there were some other issues with organs, but he, it didn't die. Too bad. He or it is an androgyne. He was unfit for either male or female path. Their Pel-Council said it should be sent into space. The Ambassador took them literally and gave the poor thing one of his shuttles, and sent it out to go prospecting. So, there was at least one spacefaring Dzuran on the asteroid and our prospector encountered it." He again emphasized the *it*. "IT is a freak!"

But they are all on ...

Si-I read the thought before it was spoken. "No, they are not all on the home world or Erra." He glanced at his wrist pad. "That asteroid, or thing, and the dead Dzuran freak inside it have been in Erran space since last mid-shift. The prospector will be here toward the end of next shift. But he will have a much shorter de-cel period coming into the system so he will be here when we have our study team assembled, you should watch."

"Where was the...?"

"He found the artifact in a new system, at least from minerals assay records. Star records exist, of course, but only cursory, long-range assessments of planetary assets were on file." He lied. The old asset records from before the Cho Rebellion indicate the system was assessed as having a sentient species at an iron and bronze development stage and a tribal need to be in perpetual war. It had been listed as no potential for trade and refrain from contact and no details were available on microbial hazards.

"What about the Dzurans? Does the Ambassador know we've killed its," the priest paused, "its heteromorph?"

Chapter 5

I got a bad feeling about this.
Han Solo in George Lucas' *Star Wars, Episode IV, A New Hope*

Near Jhelen City, Dzura
3608.297 Erran Calendar

The Jhelen City Prison was rendered useless as a prison by the explosives that preceded the breakout. The power outage rigged from the underground had killed all electric barriers, rendered useless all locks, and shutdown beamed power to guard towers. With no assistance beyond mercenary Dzuran guards, the Erran administration had capitulated its responsibility and called for an evacuation from the surface. The Errans wisely interpreted the well-planned break as a planned stage in a spreading rebellion, in part because their mercenary Dzuran guards disappeared into the mass of escaping prisoners. Those who couldn't were left to explain to the unusually fit new Erran guard unit why they had been unable to restrain any of the escapees except for those in the infirmary.

Ensign Pe-Yng regrouped and set up temporary power from his shuttle to light one cell block and heat rations. He had failed his first mission but felt certain—well, almost certain—that he could redeem his career's future if he persisted. With the two off-worlders gone in the general melee, he would reconnoiter the area in the morning. For the evening, he just needed to secure his perimeter. He laughed to himself. Who would he expect to break into a prison? He glanced up at the night sky and was overcome. The Light spread overhead in all its magnificence. The nebula's display of reds streaked with yellows. Yellow-orange had awed all sentient species in the Dzuran–Erran system since the first creatures became aware of something beyond hunger. From the Dzuran surface, the sister planet hung in crescent beauty, side-lit by Alal and backlit by the nebula.

Ancient generations of planet-bound Elioi had considered Erra to be God's Eye. Its presence moving in stately procession across the nebular gasses filling the night sky offered a different view with each nightfall. The planet, tied forever in a gravity-bound dance with Dzura, had both terrified and inspired earlier generations. The planet had been settled now for over a thousand years, all of its mysteries had been revealed, mineral rich but soil poor. Its thin atmosphere and weaker gravity made for a hard-won existence for the pioneers. The hardy asteroid miners, acclimated to no atmosphere and little gravity, found Erra to be ideal for manufacturing facilities and most of the huge space-built activities had gradually moved to the solid foundations available on the sister planet.

Standing now on the home world, Pe-yng felt its stronger pull on his muscles and bones and smiled. This rebellion would be put down. The odds were for it and by the Lights! He would put his life down for it. These Dzurans were hardy, but it was brute strength conditioned from birth on this heavy planet. They had no organization, no military capability. Maybe some policy concessions would come of it, or maybe things might get tougher for them when it was all over. That was for others to decide.

He inhaled and relished the clean air of the agricultural district. Tomorrow, he would continue his search. He'd found the culvert where the off-worlders had escaped and had only to wait for daylight to follow. He felt good in his bones. Tomorrow would be a good day.

~ ~ ~

Supreme Commandant Pelma Si-I was justifiably upset. The uprising in the southern hemisphere was taking too much of his time. The atmospheric engineering of a recently discovered mineral-rich world had been his most recent passion and the damned Dzurans just would not accept the inevitability of Erran rule. He started in the Service as a space habitat engineer and had risen to Masters Level. Most recently, he had taken on command of Teeya City and its Senior Pel duties in the Erran Pel-Council. Now this damned uprising with the Dzurans was going to complicate things more than he had been prepared for when he took the Pel.

He had been managing the developing Dzuran insurrection when the off-worlders had been captured, entering near space. Separated and sequestered, they were no threat and could be studied at leisure later.

He turned off his favorite hemispherical view screen so as not to be distracted by the swirling clouds, cratered landscapes, and glinting seas sliding below his command headquarters. From his stationary equatorial orbit, he was overseer of activities ranging over a third of the planet's surface, and due to seniority, Supreme Pel for Dzura at the Erran Council.

Si-I was an engineer by training and loved to solve problems—problems of mass, movement, and time. Chemistry was a secondary study, and he was good at it, as good as some of the best female researchers anywhere. He had risen in his crèche and then in engineering school had excelled at weather planning and done his majors study in atmospheric engineering, the lighter vapors, so laden with potential and ruin. Methane rains on a cold planet were almost as erosive as water rains on a warm planet. Load them with sediment and he could move mountains, fill unwanted seas. Learning how to localize the storms was the hard part.

His achievements and attention had come as a new graduate from the academy when he advised the council on how to hasten the thaw on the home world. Its riches, so long deprived by their Dzuran cousins, was now at Erran disposal. As they sought to fill new worlds, they would be unstoppable. There had even been talk of raising Erran crèches on the planet, to force gravity to harden the bones of the next generation, to create the new masters of the future Erran leadership. The Dzuran scum holed up on their miserable asteroid-blasted planet were all that was left of his former masters, and he did not pity them their slavery. He made a note to himself to bring a new policy to the Council to raise all new Dzurans as blanks.

A discreet flash of the light bar above his doorway indicated an interruption waiting in the hallway. "Enter!" he growled. A messenger stood at the threshold as the door opened. "Well? What is it?"

The uniformed guard stepped forward, stiffly extended his hand, and uncurled his three thin fingers to reveal a message cap. Si-I took the small capsule and laid it in a decrypt slot. In the glow of a specific wavelength of ultra-violet light, its thin metallic shell slowly unfurled and revealed its message. As he read, its edges were already oxidizing. A few moments later, the thin shell softened and turned to white dust. He waved off the messenger who gratefully obeyed and left his commander's private quarters.

Si-I looked at the time bar on the console and calculated. "By the Lights!" he muttered. "Someone will pay for this." He thought of the lovely planet five jumps down-quadrant that had just begun to respond to his atmospheric engineering efforts, and his gaze hardened on the thin strip of ash. He tapped at the control on the decrypt slot and the dust disappeared. A thousand years of life off-planet had bread a fanatical fear of dust into the Errans. Dust was the enemy of machinery, and they depended on machinery.

Commandant Si-I closed his eyes and intoned a habitual prayer to the three deities: Light, the carrier of life force; Alal, the Maker of Light whose true name cannot be uttered; and Erra, the dark sister. His mind's eye saw the twin planetary system of Erra and Dzura with the central sun. Alal was surrounded by its planets as their nav computers displayed them in space-truncated projection, the whole image being caressed by a pair of loving hands. He knew it was a silly image, but it had been instilled in crèche when he and his mates were still blanks, unaware of the rich lives ahead of them. If he chose, he could add as a backdrop the visual screen of the nebula that filled eighty percent of the dark void beyond the airlocks. Even knowing that he no longer truly believed, he still went into the long unpracticed trance. He prayed for a solution to the insurrection that could deplete the labor supply they so badly needed.

Now the revolt in the mineral-rich northern hemisphere had spread to the productive agricultural districts in the south. He would have to convene the supreme Pel-Council soon. His joints creaked and popped as he stood. He vowed to spend time in a spin chamber and get some exercise. And he would have to find out where the off-worlders had come from. True, they had stolen an ancient Dzuran warship, but how and from where? The miner said he had followed its graviton trail back to the system where the so-called Precursor artifact had been found. But had that been the origin of the Dzuran warship? Could they be plotting a return or even somehow coordinating this new outbreak? Could there be more Dzuran refugees from the old conflict building their forces? He would need to follow up on the status of the two aliens. He flicked the data port on his thin wrist and said, "Prepare a report on the two off-worlders. Have it on screen at the end of this sleep." The machine bleeped an affirmative and the soft glow of its I/O panel faded.

He had just leaned back in his chair when the panel lighted again. The image of the holy triangle in reds and greys, rotating

49

slowly on the screen, was replaced by a young officer he thought he recognized from the planetary surveillance section. "Commandant?"

"Yes, report!"

"Sir, the off-worlders."

"What is it?"

"They are gone." The unfortunate officer seemed to back away from his display as if the further distance could protect him from the Commandant's rage. "The entire prison in Jhelen City has escaped into the countryside."

Earth Interlude 2

By and large, language is a tool for concealing the truth.
George Carlin

23rd Wing JAG office, Moody AFB, GA
1000 hrs, January 17, 1986

Court of Inquiry, Official transcript relating to incident reporting
Re: November 23, 1985

Col. Harold McIntyre – Presiding
2Lt. Michael Johns – Duty officer
SSgt Miguel Ortiz – Senior Radarman
A1C Delaney Peters – Radarman
A1C Shawnda Jefferson - Radarman
Cpt. Ariel Smithson – JAG
A1C Delores Skinner - Recording

McIntyre: Okay, people. Settle in. It's 1000 hours. Let's get this underway. First, I want to thank you all for being here this morning. Let me state for this record that there is no attempt here to find any fault with the personnel manning tower operations on the evening of November 23, last year. I understand that this is a Saturday and you all have places to be. The events of that evening have, let's say, been elevated to national prominence due to some rather spectacular leaks to the media from other installations, and the records from your equipment appear to provide some correlation. Captain Smithson, please.

Smithson: Thank you, Sir. I submit for the record of this Inquiry, transcripts and backup tapes from the night of November 23, 1985. (Hands documents, cassettes, and floppy discs to bench.) Lieutenant Johns, would you please read for the court the list of staff on duty on the evening in question?

Johns: Yes, ma'am. On that evening, the Moody tower's control staff consisted of myself, as duty officer, Staff Sergeant Ortiz as senior NCO, and Airmen 1st Class Peters and Jefferson, radarmen.

BRUCE BALLISTER

Smithson: Lieutenant Johns, were there any other personnel in the tower during the, uhm, event?

Johns: Yes, ma'am. That evening, a civilian contract operator, Belinda Mason, was working scopes and another civilian equipment specialist, Clayton Potts, who was on hand. He had been called in as a standby mechanic due to the dicey weather.

Smithson: Would you say, Lieutenant, that this was a regular staffing of the tower for the night shift?

Johns: No, ma'am. We were expecting some pretty significant atmospherics due to the approaching hurricane. For a Saturday with no major ops planned, that was a pretty full tower. SRO.

Smithson: SRO?

Johns: Sorry, standing room only.

McIntyre: If you please, this proceeding will probably be turned over to NSA, and the Joint Chiefs, but probably also to Senate and House committees as well. I realize that the SRO is a fairly normative abbreviation in the culture, but as you get into the more technical aspects, could you please do your best to eliminate jargon and acronyms? It will help further down the road.

Smithson / Johns - simultaneously: Yes, sir.

Smithson: Were all of the aforementioned personnel on duty for the duration of the event?

Johns: Yes, umm, yes, ma'am. Once this thing began, we had a crowd around the screens. Afterwards, I am pretty sure everyone was there. Yes, I believe so because we were sitting around later over coffee talking about it.

Smithson: Lieutenant Johns, are you a certified radarman by training?

Johns: No, ma'am. I had squadron watch and drew flight line duty. I normally get HQ but I, well, I drew the short straw that night and ended up with flight line. I had just come up to the tower as the winds picked up. I had already taken a crew out on the line to secure

52

the fixed-wings that wouldn't fit in their hangar, after I supervised the removal of all rotary-wing aircraft to hangers.

Smithson: I see. Who in your opinion is the most qualified to respond to questions on interpretation of screen depictions of what occurred that night?

Johns (uncomfortably): Ma'am, I would suppose that Staff Sergeant Ortiz would fit that bill. But from the conversations afterwards, both of the airman specialists seemed to be on top of their game.

Smithson: One last thing. Have you spoken to anyone off-base about the events of that evening?

Johns: No, ma'am. After Captain Fells had been called to see the tapes run, he called Post HQ and Gen. Harkness came up and swore all to secrecy. I've upheld that oath.

Smithson: Thank you, Lieutenant. Please, it would please this panel if all witnesses will remember that they are still subject to that request and oath until further notified by their commanding officers. (Pauses to consult a list) Staff Sergeant Ortiz. Sergeant, how many years have you been assigned to tower operations?

Ortiz: Ma'am, I've been in the Air Force for sixteen years, and I've been in tower ops for the last twelve. If I may, I worked with the tech crew six years ago when we installed the new equipment. The same equipment in service now.

Smithson: So you might be considered an expert witness for the purposes of understanding what you saw?

Ortiz (coughs):   Well, no, ma'am. What we saw did not meet anyone's understanding of what we would expect to read off the equipment.

Smithson: But you are an expert on that equipment and can help the court understand how it displays what it senses?

Ortiz: Yes, ma'am. Of course.

Smithson: Can you, very simply, for the court and any future persons who may review these proceedings, provide a summary?

Ortiz: Of course. Let's see. Usually, the equipment uses several sensing bands to record the position of an aircraft in the airspace surrounding our airfield and its approaches. We have several settings for looking at the overall region, and we can track in greater detail at a much smaller radius.

Smithson: At the range of the Gulf Coast of Florida, is your equipment usually useful in the interpretation of what is being reported or shown on your screens?

Ortiz: Ma'am, normally, we would have transponder information for any aircraft in the region. We can monitor traffic between Moody to JAX or MacDill, and Rucker and Benning are easy. We also hand off and receive traffic to and from a long list of civilian towers in South Georgia and North Florida. But, normally, we get that transponder information telling us what's out there. That is, say, a 707 comes into TLH, er, Tallahassee from Atlanta. We'd see its transponder ID, with a translation. Say, Delta flight 2202 would show up as a civilian icon or symbol with its ID, D2202, and there'd be an altitude number associated with the signal that reflected both the transponder's info and the geometrical solution from the back-scatter radar.

Smithson: Excuse me, Sergeant Ortiz, could you explain again about the transponder signal and the back-scatter radar?

Ortiz: Well, the transponder is equipment on the aircraft that we use to help sort things out. Each aircraft transmits its unique identifier. It's a who's who for regulated civilian and military traffic. Radar only tells us that there is something out there. Think about your World War II movies when the green screen's sweep bar would highlight a blip, or a signal, reflected back to the radar base from a ping that went out and bounced back. That's the back-scatter signal.

Smithson: Thank you for the clarification. Sergeant, you have not said as much, but on that evening did the object in question have a transponder signal?

Ortiz: No, ma'am. Just a blip.

Smithson: What can you tell from the blip alone?

Ortiz: Using our different equipment and basic geometry built into the system, we can determine the position based on azimuth, or direction, and distance from our tower based on the delay time of the return signal. We can also imply altitude within some limits. It's simple triangulation geometry, but we see it on the radar sets as a white dot with a number and on some of the machines as a red cross with that same number indicating elevation.

Smithson: Red cross? What does that mean?

Ortiz: That's an indication of an aircraft with no transponder. The red cross highlights possible illegal activity or a civie with dead equipment. We get them all the time from aging private civies with a dead panel fuse. They'd get fixed before they'd be rated for air again, but some of the older airframes short out their panels pretty regular like.

Smithson: Really? This is common?

Ortiz: Well, not that common. It happens often enough that usually, we'd think that there was an equipment fault, unless we saw an inbound coming in from the Bahamas or from over the Gulf. Those we'd figure to be illegals. If they get up off the wave tops, we can see them.

Smithson: On the evening of November 23rd, would you please summarize the activity you noticed?

Ortiz: Just as straight as I can remember it, ma'am. Let's see. We heard some tower chatter from MacDill asking for confirmation of a possible bogey just north of the shoreline down in Wakulla County, Florida. It was unusual because it had just appeared, or at least, they just noticed it. We confirmed that what had been a very minor radar signal on our screens was indeed stationary just north of the coast at a few hundred feet.

Smithson: This was unusual?

Ortiz: Yes, very. MacDill thought the bogey was a druggie coming in on the tail of the hurricane. Uhm, for the record, that was Hurricane Kate. It appeared to them that a helo had come in from a boat somewhere offshore. If they are brave enough, they can fly between the feeder bands sweeping onshore on the backside of the storm. The helo was hovering over some obscure LZ, or landing zone, down in the federal lands on the coast. It would have been a lousy weather night for the druggies, but actually very lucky because almost every human for a hundred miles was hunkered down, stayin' out of the weather. And it was unusual to us because of what happened next.

Smithson: Please elaborate.

Ortiz: Well, at first we thought it might be a local search and rescue helo operating in the lowlands, we figured it might be getting ready for an offshore mission or was doing a rooftop rescue or something. The chatter from MacDill seemed to indicate that they were going to deploy Law Enforcement to interdict in case it was a druggie. Then (pause), then it went straight up. (pause)

Smithson: Please continue. Remember, do take your time and try to keep those events clear.

Ortiz: Like I said, based on the geometry readouts from the radar—remember the bogey didn't have a transponder signal—it went straight up. At first, we thought, okay, there is a real helicopter operating out there, but it kept on going. (pause) Its numbers kept on going, above ten thousand feet where it hovered for a while. A few minutes maybe.

Smithson: Excuse me, for the record: Would that altitude have cleared the heavy weather?

Ortiz: No, sir. Those storms can top out at thirty-five or forty-five thousand feet. That's why anyone with any sense stays clear. So, anyhow, it dropped back down below our signal, at least below a coupla hundred feet. From that far out, based on radar alone, we aren't that good at altitude. It did drop below the bottom of our signal. We thought it had gone to the surface but couldn't figure why it would have gone to ten thousand feet in that kind of weather. There were still fifty to sixty mile-an-hour winds coming in according to the Doppler radar. We thought that was that. End of show.

Smithson: Sergeant, who is we?

Ortiz: Everybody! By then everyone in the room was looking over one of the screens or another, trying to explain what we were watching. Damned unusual traffic for a hurricane. Well, then, oh, I'd say twenty-five minutes later, it reappeared. I'm sure we can get the exact chronology off the tapes, ma'am.

Smithson: Exactly, and that has been done, and you're about right. That was (refers to file) twenty-two minutes later.

Ortiz: Yes, ma'am. About twenty minutes later, it's back only it doesn't go up to ten thousand and park. It just keeps on going. Past twenty, thirty. At fifty thousand, we were all pretty much stunned. Although the readouts kept going to sixty, our readouts started indicating error after that.

Smithson: Why is that, Sergeant? Why would your equipment give you an error reading?

Ortiz: Air, ma'am. There ain't no air there. I checked the tech manuals on the screens and found that it will display an error message for slow movers above fifty thousand feet. Above that altitude, all traffic is considered to be ballistic because airfoils don't work except for a very few fast movers, er, jets. And that traffic is classified. I don't believe I can discuss that traffic in this room without checking for clearance.

Smithson: I see. What can you tell us about your conclusions? If you had to discuss this with your mother or a fishing buddy, what would you think you had witnessed, as interpreted by your equipment?

Ortiz: Ma'am, I knew you were going to get around to it eventually, and (pause) I don't really like to say this on the record. That is, I'm uncomfortable putting this in the official record of the US Air Force because I don't know of anything we make, that anybody makes, that can do that. That can do what we saw it do in the timeframes that we recorded.

McIntyre: Please, Sergeant Ortiz. I know this puts you in an awkward position, but this is an inquiry not a court martial. No charges are contemplated, and no repercussions will be levied, and I have this from the Base Commander and above. We are just trying to get to the bottom of what did actually happen. In your opinion. We need to square this with the testimony at some of the other bases that managed to be more, let's say, circumspect about their handling of their recordings.

Ortiz: Yes, sir. Sir, if it pleases the panel. Based on my understanding of my equipment and its capabilities and limitations, an object of unknown make ascended vertically at a few thousand feet per minute through the atmosphere to a region where no known aircraft that I am familiar with can go. It continued to ascend vertically to an elevation where it would have had to either have an onboard source of oxygen or (pause) another means of propulsion.

McIntyre: Plain speak Sergeant, please.

Ortiz: Yes, sir. I think I saw a UFO, a spaceship. It was a flying object and I could not identify it. I'm not a Twilight Zone kind of guy, but I know what's on those tapes, and I've personnaly checked the apparent velocities, and sir, I think the US Air Force flies the finest machines manufactured on God's green earth, and I don't think that thing was (pause)

Smithson: Was what, Sergeant?

Ortiz: Made on Earth, ma'am.

McIntyre: Thank you, Sergeant Ortiz. Captain Smithson, the next witness, please.

Chapter 6

The Light created the sisters Dzura and Erra. Even as the second shone its own light down upon the first. The first looked up at the second for guidance.

Perversion of ancient creation script by Erran clerics after the conclusion of the Cho Rebellion

Dzuran Surface – Near Jhelen City Agricultural Complex
3608.299 Erran Calendar

Land Commissioner Gre-LonnDonn walked steadily toward the rail at the side of his bed chamber. Like most rooms modified for Erran visitors to the planet, all walls not obstructed by furniture had hand rails just above waist height to assist if the air chairs all Errans depended on failed. Centuries in orbit, habituation to low Erran gravity, or zero gravity had bred an inability to survive unassisted on the home world of the Erran Elioi. LonnDonn was disgusted with his own thinly muscled frame. Despite excruciating exercise periods in spin chambers and what seemed like entire days in static machines, he had arrived on planet barely able to stand and only able to move his mass from bed to air chair to desk with difficulty. Twenty-seven days later, a fitting anniversary he thought, he had been able to walk across his room, and now, he was doing rail-assisted squats.

He had heard of the training of special ground troops, physically fit young troopers fresh from the academy who could walk among the Dzurans. He wanted what they were getting, acclimation to full Dzura gravity. Cautiously, he lowered himself to a squat, knees forward, and pushed. This was far worse than walking. This was agony. When those muscles gave out, he tried the easier squat with knees backward. The stronger muscles on the front of his thighs made this an easier exercise. He was no gymnast. Any Dzuran child could do better. But then, they had been raised here, hadn't they? The vertical wrinkles on his forehead expressed his pride and pleasure at having achieved something no one in his clan had done for uncountable generations.

Unsatisfied with this small success, LonnDonn took a step to the left and performed a squat, then another. Then another. He slowly and carefully made his way around the room. Lifting his arms, he stretched them high above his head, smiling at his reach.

Abruptly, he fell backward to the floor bruising backside and elbows. As he returned to his grounded air chair, he swore, laughed, and vowed to become useful without aid of the chair. He also resolved to keep any enhanced mobility to himself. He was determined to be able to walk the planet of his species' birth.

Two motivations guided his actions. First, he thought the triad was a ridiculous excuse for a religion. If he wanted inspiration, all he had to do was step outside any darkside airlock and send his thoughts into the nebula. The giant red arc of gas illuminated in part by their red star and four other giants embedded in its shroud had lit the dark side of the twin planets, probably he thought, since before the two planets' orbits had become entwined. A star and two planets! Psssh! It might subdue the masses, but it was thin on morality, causality, and essence. A made-up crowd control theology short on spiritual depth and long on dogma. At best, it formed the basis for most of his expletives. At root of his philosophical dilemma was the self-realization that he wanted to release himself from dogmatic dictum. Errans had not become superior to the groundlings they had differentiated from almost a millennia ago; they had actually become inferior.

Second. Yes, the Errans had evolved from Dzuran stock long ago. But Errans raised in low-spin space or even those who spent long tours on Erra were now almost incapable of developing the strength of musculature to walk on the home planet. Almost was the key to that phrase. He determined that he, Gre-LonnDonn, would be able to stand without aid and, after that, walk. Maybe even pass for Dzuran. He rose and crossed the room, stretched to full height, and extended his arms, rotating them, feeling the muscles working against gravity. His eyes fell on the little-used air chair in the corner of the room and wondered how useless it would be if the beamed power grid went down. As if his thought had manifest powers, the overhead lighting in his room flickered and died. A thin, emergency, amber-light line energized around doors and cabinets, but these, he knew, might not last until daybreak.

~ ~ ~

Captain's Cabinet – Teeya City
3608.301 Erran Calendar

The Pelma Si-I was furious, but only his closest cabinet officers would have known that. There were no apparent outward displays to warn a young messenger that the Pelma was engrossed in contemplation of the deteriorating conditions on the planet's surface. There had been indications of growing unrest for some time, sabotage efforts that affected little. The usual retribution seemed to quiet those isolated outbreaks. He played back the sequence, looking for pattern or organization. First, there had been simple work slow-downs, especially on the southern continent. These were attributed to simple reluctance of the enslaved groundlings to work under Erran rule.

He had always had his necessarily over-compensated cadre of Dzurans in his employ to assist him in the administrative duties on planet, and also the inappropriately named Home Defense League whose foot soldiers kept their fellow Dzurans in line. All it had taken was for one of his priests to choose a random shift of minors, crop workers, or other minions, and have every third worker taken to the local community commons for execution. For maximum effect, these proceedings were broadcast on all channels. The work slowdowns stopped.

Then there were the breakdowns. Mining equipment seized up in their shafts, freight haulers rolled to inexplicable stops, and then two heavy lifters in a row had exploded on liftoff. This was unheard of. One of them had even crashed on a barracks of Dzuran workers and killed the Erran overseer. Had that been a simple accident or subterfuge? One of the space elevators had been tampered with, causing a lifting car to almost ram a descending empty platform. If it had not been stopped, it could have destroyed the elevator.

The hair behind his ear ridge tingled. He stopped pacing and ran his hands across the back of his head, smoothing out his fur. He slowly spun the small globe projected in front of his desk with the trouble spots highlighted. Glowing blue dots indicated where the most recent sites of revolt or breakdown had occurred. Major manufacturing centers remained intact, but prison outbreaks had been orchestrated to occur at the same time as power outages.

Clearly, some sort of shadow organization had developed. Were his Dzuran lap dogs conspiring?

Communication hubs had been blown up and the power grid shutdowns were becoming more frequent and widespread. These had immobilized the Erran air-chair equipped administrators, and one had been murdered in his quarters. Taken in total, this was a full-blown, orchestrated revolt! Suddenly, seemingly, there were more outbreaks than his ground forces could address. He did not feel ready for the meeting of the Supreme Pelmate scheduled for the end of shift. The Pelma, sensing the presence at the door, said irritably, "Enter!"

The young officer hesitated, seeing that the Pelma was engrossed in study. "Sir?"

"Out with it, Kel." The Pelma whirled around, the globe projection fading into glistening motes as he did. "What news?" May it be good news, he thought.

The Kel seemed to shrink into his uniform. Then, with force of will, he took a deep breath, came to attention, and visibly regained his posture appropriate for a Kel, an officer in the Pelguard, the ship's select guard. "Pe-Yng reports that pursuit led to an underground complex with a portal hidden in a bridge embankment. It had apparently been there for quite a long time. Sir, the escaped off-worlders are gone, along with most of the Jhelen City's prisoners. Pe-yng's report concludes that they have joined the rebellion."

The Pelma considered this, looked up at the stiffened young officer just inside his doorway. He saw a junior model of himself. He wasn't sure if the soldier was from his home crèche. There were some similar bloodlines there for sure. That could have been me years ago, he thought. "At ease, Kel," he said. And then, "What crèche name do you carry?"

"Tean, sir."

The Pelma's brow furrowed slightly in a smile. "Good line. You have the potential of the house of Kel. That is good." He paused, thinking of the ramifications of the news. "Kel-Tean, which sector's prison were the off-worlders in before the break-out?"

"Sector nine-thirteen, the old Jhelen City," Kel-Tean said.

By the time he said it, the Pelma had restored the globe image, rotated it so that sector nine-thirteen faced them, and zoomed in the view until it showed the rebuilt sections of Jhelen City. The area was on the edge of an impact crater wall, the impact that had taken out the original Teeya City. Jhelen was the largest population center nearest to the space elevator that supplied the orbiting New Teeya City. Exploring the visual image of the surface was not informative. He turned to face the young officer.

"What is Ensign Pe-Yng's latest position?"

"He is mapping a series of underground tunnels, the old transit system. His squad discovered that it was powered by energy shunted from the surface grid even when all available power on the surface was disabled."

Si-I sat back in his chair. A tunnel system that had power indicated a high degree of planning. This was no spontaneously spreading insurrection. This was a well-planned revolt. "Kel, what do you know of history before the Cho rebellion?"

Chapter 7

*Some say the "Ones Who Came Before" seeded this system with
their biota, to ensure compatible food crops and creatures if they
should pass this way again. Surely this must be taken as theoretical
foolishness. Clearly, the Elioi have risen to the mastery of the Alal
system through evolutionary progression. Simply consider how old a
culture must be that would plan for habitable worlds thousands of
millennia in advance. Consider too the consistent genetics across the
higher species. The Precursors are no more than a convenient
hypotheses for the non-believer of the primal destiny of the Elioi.*
Sia-Tran, in *Introduction to the Philosophy of Cho-le Baan*

Erran Space – Near Akat City
3608.311 Erran Calendar

The asteroid, known as the "Precursor Stone," dropped into
Erran space two shifts earlier, had been stabilized into a standard
synchronous orbital. It was placed in position immediately behind
the trans-orbital platform above Erra's prime metals reduction and
mass compiler facility. The auto-thruster units were sent, per normal
procedures, to a parking orbit around Erra. The preliminary
assessments of the odd asteroid had been promising. Nem Jitep had
reported that the nearly square excavation and its tunnel network led
to an inner chamber decorated with elaborate carvings and paintings
from an alien culture. His assessment that they were Precursor
glyphs still needed to be verified by a field team.

Nem-Jitep had obtained temporary celebrity status as the
discoverer of the asteroid. He had also barely avoided serious trouble
for having sent the rock on an inner system jump with a living
unshielded Elioi aboard. The creature, neither still male nor yet
female, had perished. The Dzuran Ambassador made appropriate
protests through embassy channels but seemed to be relieved that
one of his progeny would no longer be an embarrassment.

Jitep was selected to serve as a guide for the research team that
would explore the chamber's decorations. A science team had been
assembled from cultural specialists on Erra and one first contact
specialist each from the three orbiting cities above Dzura. Although
there had never been an actual "first contact" with a sentient species
before, they were at least schooled in what were thought to be the

best protocols for initial, friendly contact. They were also fully trained in the hard sciences in hopes of assessing any advanced technologies that might be encountered. Just in case, there were four heavily armed marines. The Supreme Pel-Council on Erra had decreed that the discoveries should be shared and that at the very least, all of the cultural affairs team members would learn something valuable from deciphering the ornate decorations on the inner walls of the hollow asteroid.

Pelma Si-I had invited the Pelmas from the two other orbital enclaves, Riiya City and Aeya City, to watch a live feed of the team's entry into the chamber. The three commanders and their highest senior staff filled a small viewing theatre and observed a series of scenes that alternated between helmet cameras and mounted cameras. The projection space was filled with a three-dimensional image of the interior room and details as seen through the helmet cams. The team first explored the small habitat tent set up by the hideous Dzuran, Calantral. He had not dislodged anything from its original space. This, all agreed, was a good development.

The priest Eluoi-Annchda slipped into the room and stood quietly in back, hoping that nothing would shake his beliefs further. He had filed a protest of the Precursor Stone research on ecclesiastical grounds and had been summarily ignored. Any threat to the worship of the Three, would come from science, and this mission could only bolster the resurgent cult of Precursor worship. Annchda watched as his third in command entered the chamber with the specialists from cultural affairs, the seldom discussed but never before needed alien contact committee. The viewing room was crowded beyond comfort. The room's array of ceiling-mounted monitors were filled with scenes from inside the stone.

A camera was trained on a researcher who was going through the remains of the Dzuran explorer's habitat tent and the small cache of artifacts he had collected. Others followed as members of the team moved over the complicated swirls and contours of the complex chamber. Uniformly grey, the shapes indicated intelligent design but gave almost no clue to function. In Teeya City's viewing room, Pelma Si-I wondered quietly if he should be occupied by something a little more pressing. There was, after all, a major revolt gaining momentum and many of the hot spots in that revolt were in his planetary control zone.

One of the planet-born Erran researchers invited aboard Teeya to help back up the research team pushed off from his perch and yelped as his weightless body flew across the room. The surprised and helpless form flailed as if he had never traveled in low to no gravity. He managed a folded pirouette and hit the ceiling with hands and feet outstretched. He managed to regain his composure and his perch, but the momentary murmur of amusement in the viewing chamber quieted immediately as almost all saw the reason for the bodily eruption.

An indicator light for one of the city ship's external approach sensors flashed to caution blue. The technician in the adjacent workstation flicked a button on the console and one of the exterior cameras swiveled to catch an object still flaring in ion blue and graviton green from a dimensional jump. It had appeared incredibly close to the oddly deformed asteroid and came to an abrupt stop.

The object was a perfect cube. All faces were nearly perfect reflective surfaces, a six-sided mirror. The observers in the control rooms on all three city ships and the major population centers on Erra watched as the cube moved closer to the asteroid. With no visible means of propulsion, the cube aligned to the axis of the square hole in the asteroid. A momentary delay as it oriented to the square opening in the asteroid left some of the watchers holding their breath. As it lowered into the hole, it was apparent that the cube's dimensions were slightly smaller than the opening as rocks, debris, and dust ejected around the perimeter.

The mission commanders watching from their remote position on Teeya began to fear for the research teams aboard the stone. Three shuttlecraft at the bottom of the square excavation were the only means of escape for the team exploring the chamber. Their fears were realized as small pieces of those shuttles joined the ejecta streaming from the narrow space between the cube and the sides of the hole. One life monitor went blank. A marine must have been in or too near the bottom of that hole. Monitors trained on the research team in the chamber showed them scrambling for secure footing or handholds as vibration began to loosen a fine dust into the confined space. In the several linked watch rooms monitoring the event, gasps of horror and cries for some intervention began to build. Frantic calls from the research team blended into a gabble. A marine called for quiet, then muted most of those com lines, rendering an eerie quiet as the watchers observed members of the research team scrambling for a handhold.

A small, brilliant yellow light appeared on a panel near one of the researchers and pulsed, seemingly without pattern. Cameras immediately centered on the yellow spot and zoomed in to provide a better view.

The crowd in the viewing room watched in fascination, as a small, yellow cylinder not previously noted rose from a tangle of sculpted cordage. Without appropriate cultural referents, the cordage had been examined and considered, but since the material did not seem to taper as organic appendages might, it had been written off as a sculptural representation of simple form like so many of the other shapes in the chamber. Some had been simple geometrics, some quite elaborate and exotic. The research team had been debating if they were part of a cultural identification test.

The glowing yellow cylinder rose, slightly elongated to a tube about finger wide and hand long. Abruptly, it emitted a band of high-intensity, yellowish-white light, creating a narrow vertical line along one wall. The thin band of intense light moved, panning across the surface of the interior. As it passed over the walls, dislodged dust rose from the surfaces of the carved shapes. The exposed, once-grey shapes began to take on color as if ancient fossils were slowly regaining vitality. Shapes that had once been only curious design glowed from within. Loose forms fell or rose away from the wall and became low structures. If there had been an atmosphere in the chamber, it would have hummed. The chamber was becoming animated. Two of the research team members closest to one of the exits to the square entrance excavation dove for the opening to squirm through only to find the escape blocked by the silvered cube. The rest of the research team, fascinated by the metamorphosis, watched but tried to avoid being scanned by the slowly rotating slice of brilliant light.

One of the team, backing away, became entangled in lines that had secured Calantral's habitat. First in amazement, and then barely controlled panic, she watched the yellow-white beam scan across boot, then leg, and finally her torso. She was the first to scream. As the beam passed each of the numerous monitoring cameras, the screens in the viewing room went black. Only a few continued to beam horror to the assembled dignitaries and scientists. The team members who could not escape the slowly rotating, yellow light were atomized to the horror of those watching as the cleansing beam removed any trace of foreign matter from the surface of the chamber.

~ ~ ~

Erran High Priest Eluoi-Annchda pulled his aging bones into his chapel in an agitated state. He was unsure of what to ask the Pelma and how to ask it. He had fundamental belief issues of his own, but for the sake of his people, he had to maintain his conviction in the revealed truths as he had been taught and as he had been teaching. He believed—or in his moments of doubt, he hoped he still believed—in the divine forces that balanced his psi, maintained his spiritual health, and purified his soul for transition into Alal. In his moments of doubt, he agonized over the inconsistencies in the Erran interpretation of the Trinity, its imposition over most aspects of Dzuran and Erran physical sciences, architecture, urban design, holy sites, separation of the sexes, and the simple observations of the daily ritual. He had long ago refuted the agnostic views of the Neogene movement that claimed all life in the spiral arm was seeded. By whom? Precursors? But lately, he had begun to doubt his own belief in the divine import of the Trinity and to consider the relationship of the Alal and its twin planets to be a simple accident of planetary physics. If that was the case, what of the Trinity? Would a new order not send its dead into the sun? He decided to meditate.

He carefully lifted the lid from the box and set it aside. The box's contents, the aromatic oils, sacred script coils, and gloves used in the high ceremonies, were neatly arrayed in carved and inlaid recesses. Annchda pulled on the gloves with practiced ceremony, regardless that no one was watching. He draped the necklace over his shoulders and settled the oil container over his chest. He tapped each of the three fingers on his right hand on the tip of the oil jar's wick, staining each a bright red. His wetted fingertips formed a triangle with practiced ease, and he transferred three rose-colored dots of the sacred oil to his forehead. In supplication to all he still thought holy, he bent his head against the mirror-polished surface of the platinum tetrahedron, perfectly aligning his forehead against three, center, raised circles on the face of the cold metal.

The cool platinum against his forehead, the holy oil, and his need for comfort and guidance finally brought some mental relief. He felt the loss of the ever-present vibrations of the city first. So ubiquitous as to be seldom felt or thought of, those essential reflections of the thousands of moving parts of the city always intruded in times when he sought quiet contemplation. Next, he purposefully damped the sounds of the ship and silence filled his mental vessel. His closed eyes, double-lidded, blanked all light. Gradually, as his psi-shield closed, he was alone with his maker. In fervid supplication, he asked for guidance, for understanding, for an interpretation of the morning's revelations.

He opened his eyes when the platinum pyramid emitted a tiny click, audible usually only to the priest conducting the ceremony. Four small flaps peeled back from the apex folding to form a jagged vertical box. A holographic display of Alal and the central planets formed. Soft thrumming, resonant with the chest cavity of Erran and Dzuran alike, filled the chamber. The image shrank and with a deep base throb the twin planets appeared, their dance perfect in display. If one watched the time-shortened display long enough, the slightly larger Dzura would rotate almost twenty-seven times as the pair revolved once around their common center. The smaller, lighter Erra spun only three times. Why would an intelligent species not find base three a logical system? After all, all Elioi had three fingers while most of the dumb beasts had one or two curved hooves or claws. The importance of the Triad MUST be preserved.

He sighed. Sagging now, with most of his enthusiasm fading, he pressed a small indent at the base of the pyramid. The shining metal went dark and silent. The flaps folded slowly closed. He wondered why no answer came. No answers had come for a long time. He had no precedent knowledge to draw on to explain what he had seen in the viewing chamber. The screams of alarm then fear and pain had come first, drawing every soldier, orderly, navigator, officer, acolyte, and other curious passersby close to the entry to the viewing theater. The psychic pain, as the curious light atomized the research team, wailed in a brief spasm felt by all in proximity.

One camera on a dying anthropologist's helmet recorded the glowing bands of light running throughout the serpentine scrollwork previously thought to be hewn from the rock itself. It showed that scrollwork unwinding, recoiling, and reforming into unrecognizable shapes. Early random writhing took on orderly pattern as the tubes and tendrils formed the framework of machinery. Thin film membranes seemed to harden and take on pattern and possibly language.

External remotes beaming signals from the mining control center and from nearby craft showed the sloughing off of any loose objects on the surface of the "asteroid." This allowed the slowly widening fractures on the surface to be documented. Other cameras in the chamber, broken loose from their moorings and relieved of the increasing vibrations of the rock shell, portrayed in lurid detail the last movements of the dying exploration team. One by one, their signals blanked out and remote screens went dark.

"What?" he shuddered, at the memory. "Who, Lord of Light, have we offended? We did not mean harm! Please protect my brothers, our mothers." He almost allowed a cry of prayer to become audible.

He bent over the low altar, sacred to the honor of the Three. Everything he had preached, entreated, spoken, or even thought for his entire life had had the Three at the center. From the oldest memories and oral tradition, there had been Alal and the twin planets at the core of all theology. The complex of seasons and tides, reproduction ritual and later births, and for many, their final descent into the everlasting—all depended on the intricate dance of the sun and the twin planets. Even when he had strayed through doubt and indecision, he had fought his inner weakness and come back to the Light of Alal. But was the "asteroid" a revelation, a denial of everything he had believed in? Certainly it was proof that there was out there, somewhere, an intelligence with curiosity about the other habitable systems in this part of the spiral arm. An intelligence that could afford to leave a sentinel.

He thought its design clever, for sure. Camouflaged and protected by a thick layer of detritus but marked so clearly with the sharply cornered square access pit. Any other inquisitive mind would surely see it as a marker that this particular asteroid was atypical. Why did it wait so long to activate? Was it designed to wait for the curious to play with the interior? To push a button? He paused, reconsidering. Maybe it was less sinister, or at least less devious. Maybe it had been left behind, by necessity, by a far more ancient civilization that passed through, refueled and reconnoitered, and for whatever reason, left this particular craft behind. Maybe it had been left in the Hooman's home system to stand watch over them!

The anthropological team, in its enquiry, had learned how to activate the ancient machinery. Perhaps that was the key! It needed to have been activated by an intelligent, spacefaring species.

Humph! Not the Hoomans! It had been left in their space and for how long? For how much longer would the sentinel have waited for Hooman society to go to space? Well now, he thought, there's another interesting question. How exactly did two Hoomans acquire and learn to operate an ancient Dzuran warship? Why was it in their system and how did they get such an ancient model to work?

These questions, he realized, would have to wait for the interrogations. He stood, used a small cloth to wipe the three dots from his brow, and systematically put the sacraments back in their places in the box. As he handled the objects, sacred to the honor of the Three, he thought again of the explorers in the interior of the sentinel asteroid. They might as well have walked naked out of an airlock.

He somehow was surprised at the screams. Space had always been a quiet place when he had been outside the locks, but the radio channels had carried all the immediacy of the exploring party's terror. There had been a short few moments of quiet on the audio channels before the video panels went out.

The greatest surprise came only moments later. External monitors captured the emergence of a silver ovoid with one-fourth of the clearly defined cube extending from its surface. The ovoid, now free of its accreted layer of debris was beautiful in its simplicity. The surfaces of the ovoid were as reflective as the cube. As the observers watched, the strange shape reoriented, flared, and left. The sudden acceleration out of Dzuran orbit with no visible means of propulsion had stunned the command decks of all three city ships.

Whatever he thought of the asteroid, whatever it might have told them, the only real lesson had been that it was not from here and it was not staying. It was going home, or somewhere. His final, disturbing thought on the subject was obvious. Someone or thing would be able to track the sentinel's path back to Alal, to Erra. Neither Erran nor Dzuran would be preserved from the scrutiny of the sentinel's owners. If the ovoid had been a sentinel, its assigned post had been light years from Alal. Now the owners would be alerted to this system. If they still existed.

Earth Interlude 3

*Look deep into nature, and then you will understand everything
better.*
Albert Einstein

Kitt's Peak Observatory, Arizona
June 9, 1986 – Earth Calendar

"Hey, Chuck! Check this out. I don't know if I'm crazy of if
we have a visitor." Charles, Chuck, the Chuckster, or sometimes
"The Ghost" for his pallid complexion, looked up from his monitor's
screen at Dr. Fatos Jakorian who preferred Jake to the more obvious
corruption of his first name. "Jake" Jakorian and "Chuck" Pender
had been coworkers and researchers at the Peak for over two years.
Pender would get his doctorate in astrophysics and spectroscopy in a
few months. Dr. Jake, two years younger, two inches shorter, and a
hundred pounds heavier had his already and vowed that he was
through with school. He hoped that living frugally, and by
publishing enough to make full faculty status, he could pay off his
student debt by the time he was forty.

"Whatcha got, Jake?" Chuck turned from the screens at his
crowded and cluttered workstation. "Find some Martians?"

"I wish. This is too weird." The rounded face glistened with
sweat beads.

"It better be good. Since the spaceship left, or disappeared or
whatever, there've been *sightings* all over the place—most have
turned out to be embarrassing."

Several months earlier, the now famous Hitchens spaceship
had been reported in numerous, relatively remote locations over a
period of a few weeks but had not been seen recently. Many of those
reports were debunked because of their near simultaneity. It simply
could not have been seen over Ulan Bator five minutes before it was
seen over Alice Rock and ten minutes before a UFO report was sent
by a ship captain near Easter Island. Unless there were more than
one UFO visiting at the same time. Some chalked it up to technology
that we couldn't possibly understand, others to a conspiracy to cover
up secret government negotiations with aliens.

Chuck rolled his chair to Jake's workstation and swiveled to a stop. Jake pointed at the display on screen which, to the uninitiated, would have been recognizable only as static on an old television. "For God's sake, Jake! Zoom out so I can see what the hell you've got."

Slowly at first, and then faster, the image resolved as the side of an asteroid that seemed altogether unremarkable. "There," Jake said, pointing. "That is anomalous." The small dot looked, at first glance, to be nothing more than a small rock undergoing gravitational adhesion to a larger one. With no reference scale, they could have been football-sized or city-sized. "Now watch as I take this view back several nights of successive observation." Pender watched as the larger asteroid was presented in various aspects as it tumbled slowly in the rock field. Jakorian said, "There are two shots per night. That's why the shadow jumps, but here." He stopped the sequence. "Look at that!" Clearly outlined in the view was a black square, caught at the perfect sun angle to throw an apparent excavation into high shadow.

"Whoa!" Chuck leaned in, peering intently at the image. He pointed. "What's that?"

"I haven't the foggiest idea." Jake leaned back in his chair and swiveled ninety degrees to face his friend. "That, my dear Watson, is the mystery at hand," and continuing his metaphoric reference, he added, "I believe the game's afoot."

"Have you called anyone?" Chuck whispered in a conspiratorial tone.

"Only Hawaii, for now. They've been doing some research on tracking the larger bodies for anticipated collisions to see if they can forecast bits being thrown our way. They aren't always looking where I am, but they're going back through their records. They think they've got some stuff in the library." He thought a moment, stroking stubble. "It would have to have been awfully lucky to get the right sun angle and aspect to see that."

Jakorian pointed his chubby finger at the fuzzy but plainly visible square in the face of the otherwise normal peanut-shaped asteroid. "That, what is that?"

"Maybe it's a hole?"

Jake backed the sequence two frames and got one with a less apparent rectangle in a side view. He zoomed in on the frame and made room for his friend to get a good look at the screen.

"But, what the hell is THAT!" Chuck nearly stood with excitement, but his knees buckled on the first attempt and he settled back into his chair.

"What?" Jake prodded.

"There, above the hole, or whatever." What had at first looked like any other collection of space rocks now appeared suspiciously not native to the frame. It was too regularly angular. And it was spotty. No, that wasn't it. There appeared to be shadows thrown by shapes you would not get in the eternal buffeting in the belt.

Jake responded. "That, my friend is not from here." He leaned back in his rolling chair which nearly dumped him astern. He righted himself, a broad grin spreading across his face.

Chuck added, "And it don't look a thing like that bean-shaped thing the kid was driving."

"Good, I didn't want to point it out. Didn't want to push my first guesses on to you." He toggled a control and the view zoomed in on the shape. At higher magnification, it was a very grainy shot of something too geometrical to have occurred naturally in the massive rock tumbler of the asteroid belt. There were many sharp-edged asteroids in the field. Shattered bits broken off from larger pieces took time to get worn into the more typical battered peanut shape. This thing had the appearance of several haphazardly stacked boxes with a cylinder at one end.

"Is that the only shot you've found it in?" Chuck's excitement took on urgency for more.

"Unfortunately, yes." Jake began to advance forward again through the sequence of images. "Now, what do you see?"

"Uhm, not much. What am I supposed to see?" Chuck leaned in toward the screen again, seeing nothing unusual.

"I had to check the tracking software a half dozen times, but this is the same view, the same spot in space." He zoomed out again to the original view of blotchy patches of grey half-lit by the intense light of space. "This is six hours later and all the neighbors are in town, but our friend with the hole is gone!"

The light slowly dawned on Chuck. "So if you report this and everyone takes a look…"

"Right, they won't see a thing except a perfectly normal view of a few asteroids. Except for this one frame you took." Jake waited for the next question.

Charles asked as if from a cue card, "But you got other people looking. What if they report the asteroid with a hole in it, or that stack of hat boxes first?"

Jake closed his eyes and rolled his head back, his heavy frame straining the government-issue chair. "Right," he sighed. "To publish, or not to publish?"

The Chuckster responded in their practiced refrain, "To perish or not to perish."

Chapter 8

Truth never damages a cause that is just.
Mahatma Gandhi

Jhagatt City – Beneath the Verparksransaran Plain
3608.319 Erran Calendar

The small flatcar slowed as it approached a reddish lit section of the tunnel. To Brad's eyes, it might easily have been a subway station in almost any major Earth city. Engineering was engineering. He realized as they came silently to a stop that the red light was probably similar to the high noon illumination of the system's red-tinged light. He guessed that Dzuran vision must be specialized in the red spectrum. As the two Dzurans in the front seats got out, he whispered to Connie, "I think we're here."

"You have any idea where here is?" she said half joking and half serious.

"Well, several miles away from that prison. Someplace safer?" he offered.

They stepped onto a platform that must have been left over from an earlier age. It clearly had the capacity to handle thousands of passengers a day on what must have been much larger trains. The reddish glow was suffused and did not seem to have any particular origin other than up. Up was a long way up. The place was a cavern. Looking across the guideway from their platform, Brad saw at least five sets of platforms leading to similar tunnels. Connecting them overhead, a broad elevated walkway, a connecting concourse he guessed, provided access to ranks of stairs leading up from each platform.

Kinaan drew the cuff of his left sleeve to his mouth and spoke quietly. His three companions looked expectantly and then whirled toward the gaping mouth of the tunnel from which they had just exited. Although the shock wave of the concussion bombs at the other end was surely several miles away, it blew hard. Kinaan's brow wrinkled into a smile.

Shaand psi'd, *Erran no follow!* He nodded at the Hoomans, a silent expression of acknowledgment or understanding that he had picked up in his brief exposure to the off-worlders.

Brad continued his visual inspection of the platform area. Turning around, he saw three more behind him. Nine tracks, he thought. This must be a major terminal.

"Yes, Braad," Shaand said. "Many train in time before."

Brad was about to ask before what, when he realized what had been lost, how advanced the Dzuran culture must have been before their civilization had been stoned from above. If this advanced train mag-lev or whatever system had been below ground, what, he wondered, had been above ground before the war? The war that accidentally sent Ka-Litan to Earth.

Kinaan motioned that Connie should follow, but she had already received a silent impression to do so. She turned in response. When Brad started to go as well, Shaand put a hand on his shoulder to stop him.

When Brad said, "Connie! Wait!" Shaand sent him a calming tone.

Brad was sure he heard a soft "ssssss" and Shaand said aloud, "Friend Ka-Nee go to see Dzuran females. Brad not go."

Kinaan led her toward a down staircase that appeared to be a non-operating escalator. She turned at the top, smiled, and blew him a kiss.

Shaand said, "Come, Braad. Need much talk." They proceeded to an up staircase in line with the set Connie had just descended. He recognized the layout as similar to installations in shopping malls on Earth. Once again, he mused, *engineering is engineering.* However, as they stepped onto the stairs, they silently began to move. At the upper concourse, Shaand and Brad crossed over two tracks and descended on another set of stairs that began to move when they detected weight. He thought, some engineering is better than others, too. From the top of the escalator, the cavern enclosing the terminal was huge, at least as large as a basketball arena, and clean. Dzurans had used this place for quite a while.

"We are conquered above, friend Braad. We Elioi leave surface to Errans. Errans not walk on surface, not discover. We destroy all surface terminals not damaged by war. Errans not come below ground. Tis Jhaatt City. New capital, old storage. " Shaand led on in silence to the edge of the platform and, tapping his cuff, summoned a small car. Brad thought about the long, strange journey he had been on since what, nine years ago?

Always the eavesdropper, Shaand said, "Yes, much to remember, much to tell. Come, Pel-Council need hear Braad story."

~ ~ ~

The Pel-Council's room was well furnished, its polished walls carved from solid bedrock. Trappings and decorations were softly contoured and elegant without being overly plush. One wall was dominated by an animated screen depicting a shoreline lit by the ruddy sunset. With almost no wave action, Brad guessed it was a small lake possibly a live shot to keep the grounders connected to their surface world. The vegetation lining the nearest approach to water was grass-like, and a variety of red-leafed shrubs lined the shore a little higher upslope. He could not tell if the scene was lit from behind. The wall itself appeared to be the screen. Arrayed around a large oval table were eighteen places for Council members with three raised chairs at one end. All Councilmen wore the identical one-piece, grey jumpsuits that Shaand and Kinaan wore. Similar, he could see, to the one he had been given to replace the clothing the Errans had taken from him when he and Connie were first taken prisoner. Unlike his own suit, theirs had differentiating pattern and decoration in the cuffs. The left cuff of some seemed to have the additional heft of communications devices.

Shaand took the only empty chair. Brad realized his "friend" in the prison cell had been planted there. Was he really a member of this Pel-Council? Another Dzuran with greenish, banded cuffs entered and directed him to stand centered on a small, marbled disk. As soon as his weight settled on the disk, a small podium rose. He controlled his surprise and impulse to jump back and instead stepped forward and relaxed his hands on its raised edge. He wanted to appear competent, above all, as he was the only male human in a male-dominated Dzuran society. What he actually felt was something between the fear of a prisoner facing a capital trial and simple stage fright.

The apparent leader, the one in the middle of the three on the raised section, rose and began to speak. Although Brad could tell that it was part speech and part psi, he could not tell what was being said. He thought he heard his and Connie's names a few times. On command, Shaand stood and spoke to the Council and, with appropriate formal gestures and responses, seemed to be answering a series of questions from the leader.

I guess being a visitor from another world is still a big deal, Brad thought. At least these folks are a lot more open about it than the Air Force.

Shaand left his Council chair and continued to talk while joining Brad at the podium. Shaand extended his three-fingered hand as if to shake hands. Shaand paused, hand still extended. Brad hesitantly took it.

Shaand said, quietly. "Not know Hooman hand take hand. Ok. Hand point you to talk now." Shaand's brow furrowed in a grin, then he gave a subtle nod toward the seated leadership.

Brad flushed, and released Shaand's hand. He had mistaken the gesture as a handshake. Where would Shaand have learned that. His friend's perpetual good humor saved the moment but as Brad looked around the room, not all of the Council members shared the smile response.

"Shaand, that smile is for me?" Brad asked. "I cannot make Dzuran smile with my face."

"I tell Council of tis," Shaand responded, "Tey not surprised. Tey want understand how Hooman from Ert come in Dzuran fighter ship. You tell me, I tell Council."

"I did not steal it."

"Yes, you tell me. Tell right. No tell wrong." Brad waited as Shaand paused, looking for the right nuance and psi'd his intention for the words truth and lie. Shaand mumbled a phrase in his native speech, tried it in English, and then looking up at Brad, continued, "I tell Council for Braad."

Brad understood. With studied formality, he turned from Shaand and faced the leadership. With formal Dzuran styled deep nods to others at the table, he told Shaand, "I will tell Council the truth of my story."

For the next several hours, with Shaand patiently translating, testing words for correct meaning, he told the somewhat fantastic story of finding, not only an unfamiliar piece of metal near his home, but also his contact by telepathy or psi with a former pilot, Ka-Litan. How, after many years of contact with the pilot of the ship, he had finally realized how to free the ship from its limestone prison. He explained that he was afraid to tell his home world's military about the friend in the woods because he was afraid of what they might do to a living specimen from another world.

He told them he did not understand how a pilot could survive a crash so violent as to bury it in rock or how he could have lived for four hundred of his years. They stopped him. The assembled council members turned to each other in what Brad understood to be disbelief. Whispers and a few calls toward the head of the table disrupted the flow. He was losing the crowd.

Shaand asked, "You say Ka-Litan live more four hundred years? How long Earth years?"

He backed up. "No, Ka-Litan did not survive the crash. When we first began talking with Ka-Litan, we did not know it was the ship's computer transmitting as if it were the ship's pilot." Heads turned, murmured, and clicked. Heads continued to bob in understanding as the Pelmate at the head of the table called for quiet. Watching them, he realized that maybe none of these living Dzurans had ever developed a three-way pilot-gunner-ship psi connection. They had been living under the surface of their planet, developing resources and rebuilding what could be rebuilt, but none had ever been in space. He explained, "Ka-Litan, or Jai as we later learned to know him, is the ship's computer. Out of caution, fearing a species that would not wish to communicate with a machine, Jai adopted the persona of its pilot. And so, when we finally released the ship from the ground, we found the pilot's body in the cockpit and realized that we had been talking with Jai, the computer."

"You say 'we.' I understand more than one."

Brad took it as a question. "My friend Connie come with me many times. Jai, Brad, and Connie are crew."

Heads turned to talk to their neighbors, but with few social references, he could not make much of their interactions. Surprise, amazement, disgust; Connie was female.

One of the seventeen asked Shaand a question. Shaand asked Brad again, "How long are Ert years? You say nine and half years from you find metal part and later you help ship above ground."

Brad turned and asked Shaand, "Everything I see here is in threes. Even your hands have three fingers. Do you use three as number base? Do you understand me on number base? Ert, uhm, Earth math uses base ten while our computers use base eight." He paused while his translator tried to digest the question.

Shaand's eyes brightened when he remembered the counting and number lessons Brad had taught him when they'd been confined together, teaching each other vocabulary in the other's language. "Ten, yes, we make large numbers base ten. Old priests, Trilogist priests wanted to preserve old counting ways, count in trees. Science say count tens."

Brad turned back to the seated Council, moved his hands two feet apart, and said, "Earth year is three hundred sixty-five Earth days. Jai said that Dzuran or Coalition year is over four hundred Earth days." He widened his hands only slightly.

Shaand translated again for the Councilman who had first asked about the year length. Another question. "Why so much time? You find metal and release ship nine years more."

Brad thought about how to explain concepts that he had no Dzuran words for, how to get around the deficiency. He began slowly. "Nine years ago, Brad," he pointed to himself, "was small, not grown." He indicated himself chin high with a palm lowered from head high. "I find metal and send a small part to chemist. First chemist, then chemist helper, then Brad's father killed by my government." He paused, thinking. "My government not want humans to know about life on other worlds." He shrugged. "Not know why."

Then he continued with pauses for Shaand to consider the story as he had shared it in Jhelen Prison and to translate it for the Council. "Many years metal lost in ocean, hard to get metal returned. Eight Earth years, metal found, send small parts to many chemists. All chemist agree, metal not from Earth. Take metal to, uhm…" He looked at Shaand for help. "Take metal to news?" He pointed at the moving wall screen. "Spread knowledge of metal to all Humans. All Earth knows about long ago visit from other world."

When Shaand finished with this translation, the Pelmate stood, obviously distressed. He spoke rapidly to Shaand who translated the sudden concern to Brad. "Ert knows about Dzura? Ert Hoomans know where is Dzura?"

"No, Humans do not know about Dzura." He tried to remember the time. "Humans learn for first time that Earth is not only planet with life."

The Pelma thought for a moment. "Hoomans know how to find Dzura? Follow your path Ert to Dzura?"

Brad said, "No, Humans only leave planet to visit our moon for three days." He looked to his right at Shaand. Shaand explained that the Ert moon was like a small barren Erra and gave a reassuring psi response. Brad felt the calming effect but began to wonder about how much vulnerability he should express. He had not known what to expect from an appearance before the Pel-Council, but suddenly, he realized he was the de facto ambassador from Earth. Elected or appointed by no one. Here he was, however many light years from his home potentially giving up security secrets. He could see a slight change in the Pelma's stance. Was the Pelma overhearing his thoughts? Can these guys block their own thoughts for privacy?

From his right, Shaand said quietly, "Yes, can block."

The Pelma looked around his Council table, apparently taking a silent poll, prompting Brad to begin talking. With a glance to Shaand, whom he hoped he could trust, he began. "Earth science not travel star to star. Earth and its people are not threat to Dzura. Earth would condemn any race that would damage another race's planet with asteroids. If the Erran Elioi travel to Earth, they can do great damage to Earth with asteroids." He paused hoping to put the right words together in the right order. He needed to sound not only intelligent, but capable of representing humanity. "If you will allow me to speak for Earth and Humans, we all will be willing to fight in our own way, the Erran Elioi if they travel back to my home, to Earth." He paused to let this first diplomatic offer settle.

The Pelma looked at him and seemed to squint with extra concentration. Brad felt a tug at the base of his brain as if he was being probed. It reminded him of the initial contact he'd had with the computer Jai back in the Florida woods. He opened his mind to it and shut his eyes. He was not sure how he felt what seemed to be a series of questions. No, not questions. The sensations were more like an evaluation of his trust. Was it a request for trust? He opened his mind to the probing.

Pelma Ck-Naa like Hooman Braad ... talk alone Braad?

Brad responded in psi. *Shaand talk also. Help talk to honored Pelma Chack Naa.* He hoped he had the sound right as he had 'heard' them in psi. He knew he'd never be able to phonetically reproduce much of Elioi speech.

The Pelma made a short speech to the Council and they stood, bowed in a shallow bow to the raised head table section and, to Brad's surprise, turned and bowed toward him then filed out through two doors on each side of the room. He bowed in return, although he was not sure of the protocol. He sensed a message from the Pelma and Shaand that this was good.

Doors silently closed on either side of the room and the Pelma Chack Naa left the raised dais and approached Brad and Shaand. Brad saw immediately that the Pelma was aged. He was beginning to discern facial differences in the Elioi. To his unaccustomed eye, they had been so similar at first that he thought they might all be clones, but he now recognized the differences in head shape between Shaand and Kinaan, and seeing this collected group of leaders, he noted the differences in skin tone between mature and aged.

Looking at the Pelma, Brad could see the face carried years of worry and strain. This Elioi had been the leader of a beleaguered people. His skin texture had more definition, as an eighty-year-old human might, flesh around his eyes a little more saggy and soft. An intelligent force beamed out of the eyes, however, telling Brad that this was a leader. He found himself bowing out of respect and, out of habit, extended his right hand to the head of Dzuran government. The Pelma took the hand in both of his and holding it, squeezed gently. Still bowed, Brad felt the older Elioi turn his hand over and poke gently at the fourth finger and the meaty lump of thumb flesh. Brad straightened and caught the elder's eyes. They held each other's eye as Brad stood to his full height, looking slightly downward at the Pelma's brow. Brad raised his eyebrows, forcing a row of horizontal wrinkles in his forehead, a Human attempt at forming the Elioi smile response. The Pelma released Brad's hand, and returning the smile, gave a very human nod of the head.

The three sat and, through Shaand's increasingly capable translation talents, Brad explained that there was one world body in the United Nations but that it held no real power over the many different tribes of Humans. That, at best, it was a political body for deliberation to try to settle differences. He tried to explain that the

Pelma of his people had started to develop a system that could attack missiles traveling in near space. He wasn't really aware of the details of President Reagan's Star Wars program. He wasn't really sure if anyone really was. He thought that maybe the Star Wars missiles could be an initial defense force if Errans threatened Earth.

He learned that his translator Shaand was actually a high-ranking official in the Dzuran defense forces and that was why he had been "planted" in the same cell with the "off-worlder." After what seemed like hours, the lights in the room gradually darkened. They explained to Brad that the darkening ambient light approximated surface conditions. Light levels always remained bright enough to allow basic navigation but varied throughout the day to allow for sleep cycles. The Pelma abruptly stood and thanked Brad for his candor. Both Brad and Shaand and stood and bowed as he left.

As the door closed, Brad asked, "Shaand, please let Pelma Chack Naa understand that Brad appreciate talk with high leader of Dzuran Elioi. Very grateful." He thought, Jeez, I think I just had an audience with the President or the Pope or, at the very least, a regional governor.

He hoped that he had gotten across the idea that humanity was technologically very capable and, in many ways, the two cultures shared numerous engineering concepts. He welcomed contact with the Dzurans as trading partners if the current revolt was successful but had emphasized that humans were, however paradoxically, both peace loving and jealously territorial. Later, thinking about the interview, he realized too late that he had shared much about humanity and learned only a little about his hosts.

Chapter 9

You can never learn less; you can only learn more.
Buckminster Fuller

Jhagatt Science Center
3608.319 Erran Calendar

Connie followed Kinaan down a wide concourse that circled almost a quarter turn as it descended to a lower level concourse. She tried to keep abreast, but Kinaan always seemed to speed up or maneuver to have her walk at least a step behind. The same reddish lighting they had seen in the first concourse they had entered suffused this chamber. Somehow she had expected a lower level to be darker. At this lower level, she could see that only a few of the tracks were illuminated. Darkened void space beyond a third track hinted at larger spaces beyond. In the opposite direction, a large pedestrian space faded into darkness.

As amazed as she was at the level of development she found below the surface, she remembered that the planet had been bombed into a wintry oblivion centuries ago and that many of the destinations this station might have linked no longer existed. She was panting slightly as they arrived at a platform, a multicar train passed through with hundreds of jump-suited soldiers in the ubiquitous Dzuran light grey. She had difficulty counting the cars, but she figured there were easily over fifty. These were followed by a dozen flatcars carrying tracked ground vehicles. WAR! It looked the same on any planet, she supposed. But how would the planet-based Dzurans combat the spacer fleet of the Errans? When the huge chamber grew quiet after the troop train's passing, a low whirring announced the arrival of their small two-seater. He offered her the back seat. A clear canopy slid upwards from the side and they were off at much higher speed than the firs trip in the open platform car.

She sensed an appraising probe from Kinaan, but he psi'd nothing. If she had learned anything about the Elioi, they didn't do small talk. She waited as the little car carried them to a single platform station where a small cluster of Dzurans stood. Connie knew very little about native physiology, but she knew these were females. Physically, they were as tall and robust in appearance as other Dzurans she had seen, but their fur showing at collar and cuff was white. At least, she thought they were white. Mentally, her brain had begun to filter out the reddish or pink illumination to register the palest pinks as white, but these locals were definitely not tan or brown as all previous Dzurans had been.

She got out of the car, following the beckoning gestures of the group on the platform. Familiar with Dzuran smiles from Shaand, she felt safe in this group. She barely noticed that Kinaan had stepped away when a track indicator light changed color, and he and the car disappeared into darkness.

One of the females, dressed in a Dzuran jumpsuit, stepped forward and awkwardly said aloud, "Me Clee-Chk." She bowed toward Connie and took one step backward.

Connie, unsure of local formal custom, bowed to Clee-Chk and said, just as awkwardly, "Me Connie." Behind Clee-Chk, a wave of what appeared to be humor passed through the small group of attending females. She wondered if she had committed a social faux pas.

Beyond the platform doorway, the two females, one human and one Elioi, with a small entourage following, passed into a much larger crowd of curious onlookers. None of them came up to her chin. She had never felt especially tall, but of all those heads, only a few came up to her shoulder height. Connie's first impression was that they looked like smiling doll puppets, arrayed in identical uniforms with nearly identical features. Then she started seeing the dissimilarities: variations in height, weight, fullness of face, narrowness of eyes, and even subtle shadings of the fur above the expressive brows. She noted that Clee-Chk had three embroidered, red stripes lining her left sleeve cuff. That must be rank, she thought. Looking at the crowd they were passing in the broad tunnel, she saw that each jumpsuit had slight differences at the cuff. Most were plain though some of the cuffs were white with varied colors of embroidered striping. A few had the added bulk of a com device.

Being led at the front of the group, Connie was conscious of trying to maintain a slight wrinkle in her forehead to broadcast a smile or friendliness. Raising her eyebrows also gave her a surprised look, she thought. Taking in a larger view, she noted the elaborately tiled, barrel-vaulted tunnel they were passing through. The entire upper wall in the curvature of the vault displayed decorative scenes in low relief, intricate patterns she might have described as Moorish or Celtic, and occasionally colored sections depicting daylight scenes in pastoral settings. She remembered, these people have been underground for a long time.

Beside her, she felt an affirming psi agreement from her companion. Clee-Chk spoke hesitantly, "Chk hab lesson on Hooman speak." She was grinning broadly with an expanse of horizontal ridges across her brow, but she was trying hard also to mimic a human smile with her almost perpetually oval mouth. There was a lot missing grammatically, but the psi undertone of the Dzuran's speech revealed her intent. Chk indicated to Connie that Clee was a formal title and that she could be called Chk. Connie grasped her abdomen as a wave of nausea suddenly passed through her and she had the sudden urge to retch. Diplomatically, this could not be happening at a worse time.

A second wave passed and she stopped walking and put her hand to her mouth to prevent an involuntary burp of bile from leaving. Grimacing, she managed to swallow. Her face reddened with the effort. As a chill ran down her spine, she began sweating from forehead and temples. She mimed drinking from a cup then faced her leader/companion and with eye language and psi tried to apologize and convey sickness. Chk took her hand and guided her quickly out of the crowd and into a room that she recognized as a toilet. It was communal, but she had gotten used to the Dzuran lack of modesty. As the lone female in an all-male prison, she had been escorted to a single user facility and left alone. Here, she could see the small, shiny slots that the locals squatted over. There were a few sinks across the small room, and she went to one with a flowing tap and splashed water on her face to cool off and then washed her mouth of the bile.

Was it the growing claustrophobia that had crept up on her, the crowds, and actual reaction to the bland food they'd been fed, or the excitement itself? She wasn't sure, but she was glad that it hadn't been more of a disaster. As it was, the crowd tour was cancelled and she was led to a much smaller room with a low padded bed similar to one she had in the prison above ground. This room had some creature comforts such as a small refrigerated bin, a video screen that she had no idea how to operate, and a small attached room with a toilet slit and sink.

This is a regular underground hotel room, she thought.

She was brought a clean jumpsuit, plain cuffs, and a tray with more of the bland porridge. This time, however, her meal included a small bowl of assorted fruits and semi-hard lumps of something that might have been protein or soap. It was hard to tell from the smell. As the attendant left, Connie thought her fur was a darker grey-brown than those in the reception party and she did not send out any psi thoughts. Like her jumpsuit from the prison, the new one they had given her was also too short.

A tall, slender female entered the chamber and introduced herself as Leeink-Knaa. Unlike the stiffly formal stance of the other Dzurans Connie had encountered so far, this one was completely at ease as she sat cross-legged, mimicking Connie's position. She nodded her head briefly in an informal hello bow and said, "Plees scuse baad Hooman speek." She paused, possibly recalling the set piece intro she had memorized. "Want learn Hooman speek. Try link with you friend Jai."

Connie perked up. "You can talk with Jai? Where is Jai?" The ship's computer had learned human speech as Connie had taught it much of human culture and science while it had been trapped on Earth.

"No, soorry." The smile lines on Leeink-Knaa's forehead refolded from horizontal to a vertical fan. Indicating regret and negative emotion. "Jai, still in Teeya City. Annuder day, want talk Jai." She correctly interpreted Connie's blank stare of incomprehension and pointed up. "Erran city ship. Ka-Nee and Braad come with Jai to Teeya City."

Connie could not help looking up at the concrete-like pour stone ceiling, thinking of the underground bunker these Dzurans had kept secret for so long from their Erran overlords.

~ ~ ~

Leeink-Knaa proved as adept as Shaand at attempting to form the mouth shapes required of human speech. Over the next few weeks, they endured power losses and repetitive rations. As concussion waves from surface battles near and far reverberated throughout the underground complex, the two became better at each other's nuances in communication.

Connie was given an electronic writing pad that amazed and delighted her. When turned off, it was dully transparent. When inserted in its charging slot, its exposed edges glowed in soft blues. When energized, it became an opaque white and could be drawn on with a fingernail or stylus. Pressure points at the corners could project its image to the larger video screen. She found later that it was a child's version of the com pads that some of the leadership had built into their sleeve cuffs.

With gesture and sketches and drawings, they exchanged concepts and cultural information. Connie learned that the flat car they had traveled in was a hrrr, onomatopoetically descriptive of its humming progress as it sped away from a station. Similarly, the longer enclosed trains were harrussh, singular and plural.

The enclave she'd been brought to was a science center. Leeink-Knaa and Connie shared as much as they could exchange about the structure of each other's planetary systems. Connie explained that Earth's sister was called a moon, was lifeless, too small to retain an atmosphere. Humans had explored it but had not stayed. She didn't mention that the exploration was minimal, several-day stays.

She learned that there were two major continents on the planet separated by a wide sea that narrowed to a small treacherous gap with dangerous tides. Jhagatt was about a three-day walk from that coast. Dzura rotated in days that were slightly longer than Earth's twenty-four hours. Erra, its planetary twin, rotated so much slower than the slightly larger but much denser Dzura that it perpetually faced Dzura. Erra had very little volcanism and showed signs of ancient meteoric impacts. It did have an atmosphere and two distinct oceans, but these only covered about a third of the planet. Due to its slow rotation, it experienced temperature extremes and only near-polar regions were easily habitable. Though actively volcanic, Dzura showed the new scars of the civil war with the largest meteor craters near or obliterating the locations of the largest cities of Dzura, its old planetary capital forever erased by the reprehensible attack from above. For nearly a century, the Dzurans who were left behind after the diaspora and the destruction of the surface cities diligently constructed the underground complex based on the remains of its old tramway transit system.

Connie learned from Leeink-Knaa that females selected their sex at the edge of maturity to adulthood. By eating from a cultivated plant stock, selli fruit, a hormonal change was induced and the young Dzuran's body underwent physiological and psychological changes. Females were never blanks. All had psi ability and, according to Leeink-Knaa, the females were better at it than the males. As the females were sequestered by cultural norm, Connie lost her initial impression that they were enslaved by the males as breeders. She sensed the pride of self these female Elioi had since they had self-selected their roles and took an active and culturally important role in managing the nurseries, the physical training, and the education of young Dzurans. At the highest levels, senior science advisors mixed with male leadership in systems and, more recently, war planning.

The young stayed in crèche until their natural abilities began to differentiate individuals into "talent pools." Near the end of childhood, what Connie would have considered late adolescence, a major ceremony was held and new crèches were formed that developed into lifelong relationships as the basis of future working groups. In males, these might become military squadrons or construction teams. In females, they could become research teams in the science labs. She was surprised to learn that most of the science development was in the female crèches. At only the highest levels did male leadership and female leadership coordinate strategies and programs, and these coordinating committees were made up of individuals of both sexes who did not, or could not, participate in the sexing rituals.

~ ~ ~

The following weeks in protective custody, house arrest, or simply in the protection of the Elioi were punctuated by daily bouts of nausea and a tightening in her gut that gave her certain knowledge that she was pregnant. Conflicting emotions of joy and dread fought for supremacy. She was pregnant with Brad's child! Love of her life! She would be the mother of their child! The elation of these brief, happy moments would be followed by questions of where Brad was. Would they ever find a way to return to Earth? Would the Dzurans possibly win their war for independence?

She knew that a war raged on the surface. How had the Dzurans manufactured and stockpiled so many munitions? How was the conflict going? There had been sounds of impacts from above, seemingly from explosives. Or were the Errans once again resorting to asteroidal bombardment? Would she be able to deliver a child on this planet with no more knowledge of childbirth than she had? Would a child develop psi talents on a par with the locals? Would she be able to produce and express milk? Had she been breastfed herself? And most of all, where was Brad? Was he safe?

~ ~ ~

North of Jhelen City Agricultural Center
3608.348 Erran Calendar

Gre-LonnDonn had mixed feelings about the insurrection that had spread into his sector. His beautiful crops spread out to the horizon and, he well knew, beyond that horizon. They were growing with the free energy flowing down from Alal, watered by the nightly rains. The swelling buds promised a record crop. But his Dzuran laborers had vanished and he had no idea where. He was the master of these fields but now had no hope of bringing in the harvest. With surface transports conscripted, and no field labor, he was expected to report to Port Jhagatt on the coast of the Central Sea, by any means available.

He turned suddenly. A high-pitched whisper crescendoed to a shriek. As specks on the horizon approached at high speed, he ran for cover in a grove of selli fruit. From multiple directions, air effect fighters converged over the nearly flat terrain covered in grains, fruit, and leaf plants, and by his own dark lights, this grove. From his cover, he looked up to see which were friend or foe. The aerial acrobatics were confusing as hunter and prey changed by the moment. He finally understood that this was no aerial battle. The air effect and field effect craft were dodging ground-based energy weapons. He involuntarily ducked as one of the combatants exploded above and behind him. Its fiery debris came to ground out of his sight. Briefly, his concern rose for the flammable crops. This distraction was replaced by immediate concern for personal safety as a fighter turned fireball fell in his direction.

His mobility on legs was still slow, but after a painful low sprint, he dove into a nearby drainage ditch. For the first time, LonnDonn began to think that the insurrection might be dangerous to him personally. With his face in mud, he first felt the blast of a nearby explosion and then the heat. A fireball rose above the crash site, baking his back and arms. "By the Lights!" He tried to sink further into the cool mud with no real relief. His exposure to singeing heat was a totally unexpected result of his plan to walk his fields and survey the yield of the approaching harvest. After years of training, he had overcome the inherent weakness of his upbringing in zero to low gravity. He had gotten legs under him for what? Hiding in the mud to avoid sudden scorching death?

A new sound entered his face-down, mud-clinging consciousness. Something between a harsh buzz and shriek approached him from behind. A small ground effect car careened to a stop in the ditch on the opposite side of the road. Smoking from unknown damage, the car nearly capsized then righted and settled. He rose to his knees to see if the craft was friendly. Through the canopy, he could see uniformed Erran figures struggling in their harnesses. Crouching, as if making a small target would increase his chances of not being blasted by one of the circling fighters overhead, he ran to the car. The driver's lifeless body was still smoking. A scar across his chest lined up with a line of damage that cut through most of the materials in the forward cabin. Looking back into the car, he was shocked to see a weapon turning to bear on him. He was only an arm's length from an air-to-ground launcher pointed at his head.

He dropped to the ground shouting, "I am Erran! I am Erran!" to no avail. The air above his head shattered as the projectile burst out of the weapon. Instants later, its drive engaged. LonnDonn felt heat from its thrusters as it trailed acrid smoke in targetless flight. He reached for his ID swipe card, holding it above the line of the car's windows. Confused conversations inside the vehicle ended abruptly at the shout of command.

"We will not shoot. Rise and show yourself."

He stood shakily, more from nervous anticipation of being shot than weakness. A hand reached out and took his swipe card. The apparent leader of the group read then looked up. "How did you get this card? Where is the Gre? We could use a hostage right now."

LonnDonn started to protest that he was, in fact, the Gre-LonnDonn. Agricultural Administrator of the Felldt region when the squad leader stood, obviously accustomed to the atmosphere. LonnDonn stared, speechless with confusion. Were these warrior Dzurans who had procured an Erran ground car and uniforms, or were they Errans who, like him, had mastered gravity? Was he a hostage or was he saved?

A voice, calm amid the chaos, came from behind him. A dark grey uniformed soldier in Erran attack body armor stepped out of tall vegetation. "I am Pe-Yng. I need this car."

Earth Interlude 4

The Elioi explore the dark regions beyond The Light,
shining the light of knowledge upon us all.
Gobad-Tok

Above the Asteroid Belt
July 21, 1986 – Earth Calendar
3608.354 – 1Erran Calendar

Nem-Drit, crèche mate to Nem-Jitep, dropped into the Sol system at the approximate solar radius he'd been given. These were the precise coordinates taken from Jitep's ship. Jitep would have been given the assignment to return to this system, but he had perished with the research crew aboard the Precursor Stone. It had been acknowledged that the artifact was from an advanced, unknown species. Erran leadership was still hotly debating whether the alien species was still alive and capable of traveling, whether they might backtrack to Erra. The artifact was obviously ancient as were all similar indications in other systems, but did that culture still survive? Should they begin to develop new defensive weapons systems to protect against an invasion?

Nem-Drit didn't care about all of that. He'd been given a highly sought-after ten-shift assignment and eagerly watched his near space sensor plot the found gravity nodes in the system and fill in the orbital tracks. Slowly, the lightly hashed indication of a rock and rubble belt appeared between the fourth and fifth planets, floating free of gravity wells, minerals for the taking. But it was a real grab bag. According to Jitep's flight log, many would be pure silica and almost worthless. Many would be nickel-iron and more cheaply acquired in the overturned spoil piles in the craters on Dzura. But some would contain veins of conductor metals, copper, silver, gold. Structural metals titanium, platinum, and specialties such as iridium, selenium, strontium, and lithium. With no real sense of exactly where the Precursor Stone's embedded area was now, he'd begin his assay anew.

He set a course to intercept the approximate center of the band and maintain a Z-axis separation that would keep his ship from impacting most of the outliers. His shields would burn off any smaller outliers. Drit set his sleep clock and went full auto for some rest.

~ ~ ~

Sore bones told him that he had been asleep for at least a short time, but not long enough. A console indicator blinked caution blue. He raised his head slightly to see that it was life-sign. He sighed, yawned for oxygen, and sat up.

Life-sign! Protocol required he check it out. Wasn't that what got Nem-Jitep in trouble with the Precursor Stone? He adjusted three verniers to locate the highest strength on three axes and set a long range camera to see whatever was setting off his sensors.

He blinked at the white and blue bands on the screen. What? A jumble of high-frequency noise filled the cabin.

Drit rapidly flipped radio controls, killing most of the frequencies and the roar dropped to a jumble of still incomprehensible but sortable noise. This was useless. Even if he isolated what must be broadcast signals, he wouldn't recognize the language. Maybe this WAS the home world Ert of the Hoomans. He slowly adjusted a frequency slider and still was met at almost every stop with overlapping and unresolvable noise.

He turned to the video feed and zoomed all the way out. The white and blue bands shrank to a small white dot. He centered that and zoomed in, picking up a planet with obvious weather bands, in three-quarter illumination. That meant that no matter who or what was responsible for all the signal noise, at least he was on the far side of the planet's orbit.

He scanned his system log and this one came up as an ancient entry from before the Cho. It had been listed as non-technical, a highly aggressive though primitive warlike species. The date on the first contact report was over eight centuries old. The most recent was one hundred years before Cho. That would have to be updated! This was a development he should add to the report. This planet's occupants had made a significant jump into broadcast technologies. He made plans to get a good system update logged, get commissions on five heavy loads of metals, and possibly pull down some bonuses.

It only took half a shift to ready a powered drone and set the search parameters into its mapping system. He launched it on a course that would mimic the one he had set for his ship and then set his drone on a plotted course toward the blue-white third planet. If he was patient and did one shallow jump then approached from behind its moon on a chem boost, he might even get in an extra sleep cycle.

Chapter 10

The enemy of my enemy is my friend
Nicolo Machiaveli, *The Prince*

Jhagatt Residential Complex
3608.354 Erran Calendar

A food service orderly hesitated and approached the room with caution. There was an off-world alien in there. Not just "not from Dzura" or not an Erran, but not from known space. And it was ugly. Errans, confined to their city ships smelled bad enough, but this thing? The Lights be dimmed! Nearly hairless, it had a misshapen face, odd skin flaps on the side of its head and its body proportions were all off, long legs, short torso. Hideous! He selected a plate of food for the Dzuran and a bowl of grey-green mush for the alien. He didn't understand how its cell mate could stand the stench of the off-worlder. Tapping the control on the food cart, he quickly moved away down the hall.

~ ~ ~

The room was not uncomfortable. Brad sometimes wondered if instead of this being a dormitory or barracks room that maybe he was on exhibit, but he had come to understand that this was not a zoo and not a prison. It was simply housing for the rebellious Dzurans, and it was thin on creature comfort. He did understand that he was special. He was being given an unbelievable access to the day-to-day life of his hosts, especially understanding how the human species might have treated Ka-Litan if he had lived.

The maxim, "the enemy of my enemy is my friend" seemed to be appropriate to his favored status among the Dzuran resistance compared to his more hostile treatment under Erran control. Bradley fought waking up totally, because waking up meant living in a mental anguish until he could tone down the cacophony of physical and psi noise from the others waking up around him. His roommate was not so bad to live with, but the rest!

By the Lights of Creation! Okay, he realized, I must be awake. I'm cursing like them.

The sounds and senses of fifty conversations bled into his consciousness. He rolled over to see Shaand staring at him. It was disquieting really, but he had to admit, there was really nothing else to look at. Aside from the three grey walls, the flat black portal in the back wall, and the dully glinting energy wall dividing their space from the hallway, the room was absent any decoration. Because of the energy wall they could not see any of the thirty-two other rooms at this end of the dorm's third wing. There were three sleeping pads, one unoccupied. They were set low to the floor and his was no longer doing its job. He pushed, sat up, and looked across at Shaand. Noticing a food tray near the end of Shaand's bed, he saw a bowl of oatmeally mush next to his own. On the wall near the end of his bunk were three groups of five scratches. Fifteen or so days in this place. Shaand called them shifts. But he had forgotten on some days to make the scratch mark.

Shaand's stare brightened as Brad gave him a smile. Early on, Shaand had learned to interpret human facial clues and tried to imitate the mouth-widening twitch that was a friendly greeting. The human had tried to learn how to wrinkle the lower part of his forehead in an answering smile. Shaand's eyes widened in the effort of "smiling" and Brad laughed softly.

"Good try, Shaand."

Brad wondered how he might record this scene for posterity. He catalogued the features of his companion of the past several weeks. Shaand was heavily muscled, humanoid. He had two legs, two arms, head on top of a bilaterally symmetrical body. His proportions were off, longer body, shorter legs. Each hand had three fingers, one of which could rotate to serve as an opposable digit. Shaand's face was not what he would consider cute, or ugly. He supposed he would get used to it in time. Disney cartoonists could make it cute he supposed. Two large and expressive eyes just below the skull's meridian straddled the top of a breathing slit that opened and closed silently, a little slower than his own breathing, he'd noted. The nearly round mouth had soft lip tissue covering what looked like a serrated line of bone, not individual teeth. Did that mean they were or had been vegetarian?

Shaand's nearly black eyes were relatively small and faced outward and forward. The large forehead above the eye ridge was expressive. Brad had noticed it wrinkle in a variety of patterns which seemed to be a part of Shaand's attempts at communication. His speech was possibly imitable, but the clicks and whistle parts would be a challenge. The roommates had learned to communicate mostly because Brad had been taught crude telepathy by his spaceship, Jai. Connie, always better at learning languages, was probably doing better in her quarters.

Shaand's honey brown fur was, Brad learned, the sign of adult males—females had fine, white fur. Juveniles were a darker brown, as were many of the workers he'd seen who seemed to be of a lower class. From comparison with the first creatures he'd seen when he and Connie were taken into custody, he had assumed that Errans and Dzurans shared a common evolution but had become separated. He didn't know the Erran overlords had developed their spindly and gravity-abhorring body types from centuries in space and the development on the low-gravity sister planet Erra. Both races were born with thin light or dark brown covering of short fur protecting all but the faces of the upper classes.

More of the sleepers were awakening and those who had psi ability were reaching out to their immediate and nearby mates. The mental cacophony made Brad wish he had never developed the ability in his long conversations with Jai. The beginnings of the daily constant headache induced by the psi channels began to throb. He told Shaand, loud enough over the overlapping and confusing thoughts from the surrounding rooms, "It wouldn't be so bad if it was in a language I understood." But the Erran tongue was simply too foreign, clicks of all sorts, glottal sounds, and sounds he had never heard used as communication were all in the mix. These, he now knew were augmented by facial nuances in personal discussions that he would never be able to master. The many conversations, both audible and psi, blended into a background babble he often could not tolerate. He could only get rest from the noise in sleep cycle when most of the other inmates were asleep.

In his conversations with Shaand, Brad learned that his wing of the compound was designed to hold two hundred and forty-three warriors, or three to the fifth, a royal number in the old Dzuran base three numerology. Farther along the track, two more identical compounds brought that residence capacity to three to the sixth. The vast underground housing complex was secreted from the orbiting overlords. Above ground, an emergent forest now stretched its ruddy leaves out of the low scrub that had been the first flora to re-inhabit the thawed plain. It had been relatively easy to power up those regions of the planet that had not been obliterated by the bombardment from space and some areas had actually fared well when the planet had gone into an extended winter. The Errans, in an effort to partially restore habitats they'd destroyed in the war, had brought zoo collections and plants back to the home planet.

The snow covering had actually preserved much of the Dzuran infrastructure for decades and as the war between the two old enemies finally resolved itself for the Errans, Dzuran captives were either summarily executed or put to work. A few, smarter and more clever than most, were put to work as bosses, and even fewer of those were given the additional responsibility of translator and work boss for their peers.

Errans had discovered that they did not enjoy planetary gravity. Governing a subject world required that the physical labor necessary to extract resources could be provided by its former inhabitants. Shaand, formally Ss-Shaand, an administrator of public works under this system, was a skilled communicator and facilitator. He had risen to high levels in the Erran/Dzuran administration as well as to regional commander in the Dzuran underground. The orbiting overlords suspected but knew little of the shadow government. As he had been the best translator among the disparate clans of Errans, Shaand had been assigned to Braad in the Jhelen City prison. Shaand now shared a room in the free Dzuran underground compound.

"Shaand?" Brad said, getting control of the headache at the base of his brain. "How long have we been here?" He waited, knowing that it sometimes took a while for his roommate to take in both the spoken word and the intention in psi.

After a moment, he seemed to nod with understanding and replied, *Dirty fie.... light dark.* Light dark was the literal translation for the Dzuran idea of a day or two shifts.

"Days? Thirty-seven days?" Brad offered the new word. "One light and one dark cycle is a day." He said the word, thought the word, and mentally pictured a sunlit wheat field.

"Day, yes. Dirty fie daysss."

"Thirty."

"Dirty."

"TH, th! thirty!"

"Tirty." Shaand got as close as he might ever get to the Hooman's speech.

Brad thought of Connie and wondered how she was getting along with the female side of Dzuran society. He hated that the strict separation of sexes in this society demanded that they were separated.

"Braad leep lon time," Shaand offered, conversationally.

"Yes, sleep. Sleep."

"S-leep lon?"

And so, language, always on the learning curve, made step-wise improvements. Brad stretched and yawned trying to finish the effort of waking up. He did not mention the dreams he'd had of his distant home, driving along the coastal highway with his girlfriend. But that brought back disturbing thoughts. "I did sleep long time." He paused. "Shaand, can you think of any way to communicate with Connie, my friend from Earth? The other human that came with me?"

"Com un i cate?" Shaand's brows widened in the Dzuran expression for wonder/question.

"Speak, talk, send a message, uhm, send words." He ran out of suggestions.

Shaand looked at the floor, head slanted to one side. To Brad, the gesture appeared to be very human-like, as if Shaand was lost in thought.

Did he learn that from me? Brad wondered. Or do we have that in common?

"How do I do that?" he asked Shaand. "How do I get a message to Connie? I want talk Connie."

Shaand closed his eyes and swiveled his head toward the flat black wall panel that filled the room's back waall. His lids closed tight as he scanned the psi patterns of some of the surrounding rooms. His left cheek puckered slightly with an apparent effort to send out a message. Presently, his face relaxed, smiled. "Can do tis. Can find Ka-Nee."

Chapter 11

"Life is a journey that must be traveled no matter how bad the roads and accommodations."
Oliver Goldsmith

Jhagatt Residential Complex
3608.359 Erran Calendar

Brad asked Shaand, "What were the other prisoners in the Erran prison for? What did they do?" There was no response at first. "What did your comrades do to get in prison?"

"Com rads? Pizon?"

"Yes, in Jhelen City, other Dzuran comrades?"

"Com rads?" Shaand said, "Wat is com rads?"

Brad expressed the ideas of *friend, comrade, and mate* and then, said, "Other prisoners."

Shaand's shoulder hair bristled and he reared up to a fully erect sitting position on the edge or his bunk. "Not frens!"

Brad put his hands up in a stop signal. "Right, right, yes. Those other prisoners—what were they in for. You said you were there because you were behind on quotas, what about the others?"

"Udders steal, and not work, not pray." He paused searching for how to express his concepts in the English he was trying to master. "Not know Ngliss for word." He closed his eyes and expressed the thought. *Sabotage* came through psi channels.

Sabotage, he thought, that would certainly be grounds for execution, unless the Errans were short of labor. But there was more to think about in Shaand's last sentence. "English! English!" Brad enunciated very carefully.

"Nglisss, Nglisssss." Shaand could not seem to put the vowel e before the ng or properly make the s-h dash; it always came out as ssses. Brad just laughed. Shaand said, "You do Dzura talk!"

"Okay, okay." Brad thought about the phrase. "Sh-Shaand fezch haa," and laughed.

"No," Shaand interrupted, "Shaand not Fezch-Haa. Shaand is Fezk-Fraa." Still laughing, "We say wit Hooman talk, hand sum."

Good to have a roommate with a sense of humor, I suppose. Brad ran his hands through his hair, stood up, and stretched. Thinking about what Shaand had said earlier. "Not pray? Some of those guys were put in prison for not praying?"

"Yesss, and some for keston." Shaand looked squarely at Brad then, without moving his head, flicked his eyes at the black panel and said, "Keston ... kweston of Erran master some time bring hurt."

Brad looked at the panel with renewed interest. He had always assumed that he was being watched, benevolently possibly, but with academic curiosity if nothing else. If there was malevolent intent, they had never given him reason to think so. One of the things about psi communication as a supplement to vocal speech was its intent value. Thinking about it, he considered whether an adept, born with the ability, could hide intentional thought from another Dzuran.

Yes, is so, was the simple message Shaand sent him.

"Shaand?" Brad looked for the phrasing he needed. "Is this a prison? Am I prisoner of Dzura? Is my friend Connie prisoner of Dzura?"

Shaand looked startled, stood, assumed a position that would have been considered formal in any embassy on Earth and bowed toward Brad. "No, must regret any feel—tink of Braad (undecipherable) prisoner." Still bowed, he continued. "Braad and fren Connie most honored guest of Dzura high Pelma and Pel-Council." He straightened and continued, looking into Brad's eyes and sending a confirming psi signal. *Want Shaand fren Brad.*

Brad stood and took a step and a half forward, closing the narrow space between their bunks. He extended his right hand forward. Maintaining eye contact and trying with his limited psi ability to express intent, he said, "On my planet, on Earth, two friends sign greeting and trust with hands, both hold right hand." He shook his right hand up and down slowly. "And both confirm no weapon and talk in friendship." He did not know many of the Dzuran customs of daily informal or formal protocol, but he wanted to let this custom be known. He thought wryly, if I could only let them understand that human men and women live together.

Shaand looked at his own hand. The opposable finger/thumb could rotate in its socket and center on the middle of the three primary grasping digits, almost birdlike in form. When pressed into the middle of the palm, his hand resembled the three digits of a bird foot or a crant foot, or the three tines of a fork, or the three lobes of a Jann-dk fruit stalk. Yes, the Hooman's hand was odd. He looked at Brad's extended thumbs-up hand, and then with wrinkled, smiling brow rotated the fourth digit to the top of the three digits and awkwardly took Brad's hand. As Brad shook their two hands slowly up and down, Shaand understood the gesture and returned Brad's soft pressure.

"Braad want see Connie?" Shaand asked.

"Yes, Shaand. Human male and female stay together. Can be? Not offend Shaand?" He had learned, in his many language lessons with Shaand, what puzzled looked like, and Shaand looked puzzled. He tried again, ensuring that he left clear psi thoughts as he expressed the sentence. *Can Brad and Connie be together here underground?* He motioned around the small room they had been sharing. "Can Connie come here?"

The expression of puzzlement cleared and Shaand's eyes widened then narrowed. It was hard for a face with an oval mouth to curl a lip in disgust, but Brad could tell that he had suggested something close to disgusting. He thought, I know it's just cultural norms, then asked, "Do Dzuran males and females..." What were the words? "Do Elioi male and female ever stay same room?"

Shaand blushed.

Brad had seen it before so he knew that Shaand was not comfortable with the topic. He tried again. "Are Elioi male and female only together to mate? To make more Elioi?"

Still blushing red at the ear ridges, Shaand nodded. A human response he had learned from Brad. He said, "Brad want to make more humans with Connie. Can she come here?" Almost too abruptly, Shaand stood. He waited there for a moment, composing himself.

After Shaand took several deep breaths, Brad noted that the coloring of his roommate's ear ridges had returned to normal. Shaand looked at his seated companion, smiled, and left the small room. Brad watched him go and wondered if maybe he had finally gotten his message across. Or had he insulted his roommate beyond his dignity?

He leaned back against the wall and thought about an earlier conversation with Shaand that, more than anything, justified his resolve to help the Dzuran revolt in any way humanly possible. He snickered silently to himself at the thought. "Humanly possible indeed!"

He tried to reconstruct the early history of the Cho rebellion from Shaand's description. It would be important for him to be able to retell it with reasonable accuracy if he ever returned to Earth. A simple fist fight in an officer's dining hall over religious differences between off-planet miners and Dzuran Pel-Council staff had been blown by media coverage into system-wide strife. A miner's revolt on Erra followed, resulting in a separate Pel-Council to provide administrative support for that growing colony. The incident was not over as new debates ensued over an ancient religion that championed the belief in a race of superior space travelers who had started life in the outer arms of the galaxy and moved on in their quest to map the expanding universe. A few Dzuran clerics had sought to freeze research, believing that the travelers would be back to deliver revealed wisdom and eternal bliss for their followers.

In generations, political reality trumped clerical skeptics and a resurgence of Dzuran science blossomed. Hard-nosed politics and social inertia had to be overcome, but eventually female-led science teams were allowed in space and the science of dimensional time/space slips became firmly embedded. It was inevitable that the static religion based on untouchable astronomical bodies should wither.

If the technical establishment in the Erran Capital, Cresow City, had never discovered the fifth and sixth dimensional slip space secrets, the Dzura might never have been destroyed. If the resurgent science movement in Dzuran science centers had not developed their effective cloak and shield physics, Errans might never have felt threatened. By the next generation, Erran expansionists urged on by their military arms suppliers and jump-ship manufacturers' guilds argued for suppression of the competition from the newly flourishing Dzurans. They were aided by a clergy who cherished the old triad-based religion of the home world and their new leader, Cho. Pelma Cho-le Baan invoked a new interpretation of old dogma that proclaimed the primacy of Alal and the twin planets as the birthplace of destiny and the basis for expansion under Erran superiority.

The Cho Revolution, as their history called it, forever separated the home world's Dzurans from the expansionist Errans. After all, Errans miners and engineers no longer shared physiology, aspirations, and most importantly, religious doctrine with the home world. After the tragedy of the nuclear death of the Milla colony, the rain of asteroids fell first on Dzura's major population centers and political capitals. The Erran admirals learned far too late that they should have prioritized the space ports. It had taken far too long for the volcanic winter to freeze out the planet and even longer to track down the adept fleet admirals of the Dzuran navy.

Brad figured he had the gist of it. This brief history of the Cho Rebellion's beginnings had taken almost two weeks of gesture, psi'd implication, experimentation with new words for both Brad and Shaand. Their friendship had grown amid trust and the daily trials of mutual confinement. Brad had accompanied Shaand on the occasional foray above ground after dark and taken part in two sabotage expeditions to ensure that harvesting equipment could not be employed. Now, he felt, he had just humiliated Shaand with a request that would be seen as degenerate. Learning the basics of another culture was going to take more than language, but damn, he missed Connie.

~ ~ ~

Verparksransaran Plains
3608.360 Erran Calendar

LonnDonn saw his chance and took it. He was tired from walking. No, he was exhausted. His early pride in walking erect on his species' home world dissolved each evening into muscle spasms and cramps. A ground car lay just off the road, its crew either lifeless or disabled. They had been hit in an apparent ambush by projectile weapons. Except for a few perforations, the car appeared to be useable. He pulled the dead from their seats and laid them between rows of Jaan-dk plants. He found one officer and a weapons specialist still alive and tried carefully to move them. The officer did not revive and was placed with the dead. His wounds looked lethal; the youngster probably would not make it.

The weapons officer's eyes opened as he was being moved and looked with some interest into LonnDonn's eyes as he was being carried out of the car. Something triggered a defense response and the young Erran tumbled from LonnDonn's grasp. As LonnDonn bent to grasp the soldier, his stare resolved itself on the glowing end of an energy weapon. Its menacing, cool blue tip was too close to his face. "Friend, I am trying to make you comfortable."

"Dzuran slave. Remove your hands from me!"

LonnDonn jumped back just as a bright green flash crisped the air beside his head. Instinctively, he kicked out at the weapon. It flew into the field and the soldier winced with pain, dropping onto his back to hold one hand with the other. LonnDonn could see that the trigger finger had been broken backward with the kick. "You would kill your savior?"

"I would kill any Dzuran on sight. Too many of my crèche have been killed today by your friends, perhaps by you."

"But I am Erran!" LonnDonn still believed that to be true. His psi would support that. But his psi also layered in his own doubts. The soldier reached for something in his side leg pockets. LonnDonn again kicked out, breaking a finger on the other hand. "And you, fool, know only how to kill, not how to listen." Perhaps this fool was ckli-mat, programmed only to hunt and kill anyone who could walk upright. The pitiful wreck of a soldier lay back now, both hands ruined in addition to his prior injuries.

LonnDonn stepped into the ground car. Its console appeared to be intact. He placed his palm on the ID pad and toggled the ignition. The car powered up and lifted a few inches off the ground. He now had transportation. Where should he go? To Jhelen City? Ground forces were setting up a command center there. Or north to one of his harvest compounds?

A movement on the ground caught his eye. *By The LIGHTS!* The soldier was crawling toward the weapon. He jumped from the car and reached the hand laser in seconds. He stood and in pure anger, aimed it at the upturned face of the soldier. He paused, seeing loss and resignation in the young face. "If the rebels let you live, then you'll live. You'll not die by my hand today." He pocketed the weapon and returned to the car.

He had moved only a short way toward the coast and the outskirts of Jhelen City before he coasted to a stop. The car settled. He had used his hand print to start a military ground car. The commanders would know this. His Pelma would soon know this. He looked out at his crops, crops that would never be harvested this year. Row on row of Jaan-dk plants were nearing maturity. How would he find the hands to harvest them? *He* couldn't harvest them. He was thinking in the past.

By his actions, by starting this car, he had just compromised his standing. He filled his lungs with sweet air. Air laden with damp soil, fresh rain. He thought about the foul air aboard the city ships. He felt the cathartic moment as a physical and emotional wave passed through his chest as serenely as an acolyte accepts enlightenment. He blew out a last lung-full of Erran air and drew in another as a Dzuran. He energized the car again, and turned it around, slowly at first, and then with confident resolve, he headed north to one of two processing sites, and who knew what kind of future lay ahead.

Earth Interlude 5

"May you live in interesting times."
Attrib, to traditional Chinese saying

Wakulla County, Florida
Hitchens' household – Wakulla Beach Road
July 31, 1986

The Hitchens homestead is one of those generational structures usually found in the rural areas of the south. Its origins as a two-room cabin dated back to before building permits were required in the county. The kitchen and first bathroom were added with the extension of electricity to the coast. Bradley's grandfather had added the large master bedroom and updated the indoor plumbing. His father Whitcomb and grandfather had completed the house with the additional bedrooms and bath when his father had returned from Vietnam and announced his intention to stay in the county. The broad, full-width, front porch built at the first stage gave it the architectural style label of cracker shack.

Whit's widow, Lucy, sat at the kitchen dinette with her sister Susan, trying to enjoy a fresh batch of Sunday morning coffee. Exhaustion and worry lined their faces. They would have probably gotten a little more sleep if the damn military types left them alone. Colonel Henderson had been the last to leave at a little after one a.m.

Brad's mother and aunt were not in the best of moods and the mid-summer heat didn't help. The scene outside was painted in washed out colors as every growing thing seemed greyed or withered. The air itself seemed to suspend and inordinate amount of white dust that rose from Wakulla Beach Road whenever another fisherman gave up for the day and passed by with truck and trailer.

"What a persistent son of a biscuit!" Lucy mumbled as she took another sip of the chicory-enhanced brew.

"Good God, yes," her sister replied. "How many times can you answer 'I don't know' before they get the hint that you don't have any earthly clue as to how their satellites are disappearing?"

"Or unearthly."

"Yeah, or unearthly. Dear Jesus, I'll whip that boy if I find out he's had anything to do with it."

"Sue, those pictures they showed us from the Air Force satellite? That thing didn't look anything at all like Bradley's spaceship."

"No, and that's got me worried." Susan put her coffee down and distractedly mixed the last of the grits in with her scrambled eggs. Her golden retriever puppy, Maggie, sat whining, hoping for another scrap to hit the floor. Susan leaned over, scratched the pup's ears, and added, "Do you suppose that if they went somewhere with that 'star jump' thing and they found other aliens…?" She paused making the next logical step. "And those aliens backtracked to Earth?" She adopted a whining overtone as a supposed alien accent. "Hey, here's a nice hospitable planet, only slightly used."

"Anything is possible, Sue. I might not have believed that for sure fifteen years ago, but now. Hell, girl, I might believe just about any idea you'd come up with." She shut her eyes, picturing the little brush-lined pond in the woods a few miles behind the house where it had all started. The "voices" had come to her out of the blue, speaking grammatically poor English, but convincingly earnest. At first, they had rarely followed her home, but the voice that called itself Ka-Litan had begun to stay with her, giving her visions of another world painted in pink, lavender, and purple.

When she had finally shared with Whit that she was being spoken to by "something" out in the woods, he'd been less than sympathetic. She had learned not to move her lips when responding to the voice.

"You know, Sis?" Lucy said. "Thinking about it now, all these years later, I wonder how different this would have all turned out if Whit had simply gone down in those woods with me and been introduced to Ka-Litan?"

"We'd probably still have Whit here." Susan looked at her sister's pained face and felt her heart break. She casually wiped the beginnings of a tear from her cheek and tried not to crack her voice. "Remember that old saying 'May you live in interesting times'?"

"Hah!" The hoped-for smile spread across Lucy's face. "I just hope they don't get any more interesting." She set down her cup. "Luce, if that S.O.B. Henderson ever comes back, we need to make damned sure we find out if they ever charged the soldier that killed Whit!" All levity, however briefly it had lightened the morning, left the room. Whit had been killed by an agent who had been sent to retrieve Bradley's "artifact." Years earlier, when Lucy had left home, fearing mental incarceration, Whitcomb and Bradley had been living alone. Fourteen-year-old Bradley had found the now famous metal rod embedded in the root mat of a fallen cypress tree. In the early days of investigating why a metal rod lodged in the roots of a three-hundred-year-old tree could be untouched by corrosion, Whit had been shot, accidentally it seemed, by one of the investigating officers.

Lucy raised her mug to her lips, felt in the now cold ceramic a reflection of the hollow gut vacuum she felt on hearing of Whit's death. Even from across three thousand miles the news of his death had been hard. "Sue, between the Sheriff and the Florida Department of Law Enforcement—who I do trust to tell me straight—and that Air Farce cracker jack colonel—who no one in their right mind should trust." She slammed the mug down. "I don't know how in creation the three people who died—who are all attached to the same little piece of metal—were not connected ... at all ... by anyone."

"Come on now, Sis. We've been over it, and over it. It's not going to help to stir that hash again."

Lucy stood, took her cup to the sink, and tossed the cold dregs. Beyond the kitchen window she could follow the beginnings of her trail into the woods. Litan was not there anymore. Or actually, his ship, Jai impersonating the long dead pilot. Jai was the start of the long strange road that led to her insanity, to Nevada, to Brad and Connie going out somewhere, way out somewhere. As much as she missed Whit, she couldn't forgive his lack of compassion when she'd needed it. But she really missed having Brad around.

The mention of Whit's death dampened spirits in the small comfortable kitchen. Both women at different life stages had been either lover or wife to Whit and both had, in turn, mothered Bradley. Both Susan and Lucy grieved not only Whit's death, but worried over Bradley's disappearance. Brad and Connie had been successful in retrieving Ka-Litan's ship from its limestone grave and, after a few modifications for human comfort, took a few joy rides. Their first trip to the back side of the moon had taken only a few days. The second to the Gobi Desert and the Australian Outback had stirred up international tensions as disputes over airspace violations flooded the airwaves. Both the Chinese and Russian governments expressed their outrage at unfounded allegations of shenanigans in the remote desert. Lucy had even come up with ideas on how to order and fit sex appropriate 'relief' apparatus from a private pilot magazine. Those allowed the longer trips to the moon and opened the door to even longer excursions. With the existence of the spaceship a secret to all but a few in the Air Force, Brad and Connie decided that with a few more provisions stored aboard, they could possibly visit Dzura, Jai's home world.

That was the last Lucy and Susan saw of them, and they were very long overdue. The accusations coming from the military that somehow Brad had been involved in the theft of communications and military satellites added to the sisters' worries. A knock on the screen door interrupted the morning quiet.

"Miss Sue? Miss Lucy? Either a ya'll home?" The sisters realized that family friend and occasional caretaker of the family homestead, Sunny Rogers, knew by the presence of both their cars in the drive that they were, in fact, home and that there was probably a fresh pot of coffee on the stove.

Susan called in a controlled yell, "Come on in. You know it's open!"

Before the screen door slammed shut, they could feel his heavy steps on the old floor timbers then heard them backtrack to swing shut the heavy homemade timber plank front door and preserve any coolness against the building summer heat. "Mornin' ladies. I think it's gonna be a hot'en today." He waved his hat at the sweat beads on his forehead. He was more than a generation older than the sisters, but he was of old southern gentlemen stock, even if it was a little rough and unpolished. He kept up his manners. "I see the Feds just left outta here. They give you a hard time about Bradley and Miss Connie?"

Susan answered while Lucy just shook her head. "Good morning to you too, Sonny. No, they asked all the same questions as last night and yesterday and a few days back. I think they want to catch us up in a discrepancy."

"Figures. Any good cop-bad cop stuff goin' on?"

"Have a seat, Sunny. Sit down. Can I get you a cup?" Lucy offered.

"No'm, I'll fetch it." He knew well which cabinet held the good china, but he went for the mugs and grabbed one with a stylized drilling rig logo on it and raised lettering advertising Hitchens Well and Pipe. Filling it at the stove, he said, "I can put a tail on that feller if you'd like." He took a sip of the nearly scalding brew. "At least we can find out where they's a stayin' since they seem to want to know so much about you two." He turned around, leaning on the aluminum-edged Formica countertop. "You know, he's the same one that was here back when young Mr. Bradley was first trying to get outta here."

"Thanks, but no," Lucy said. "I don't see how that would do any good."

"Well, Miss Lucy, if they start disappearing folk again, at least I'd have a thought as to where you mighta gone first if you turn up missing."

Sue responded, "Sunny? That almost makes sense in a twisted way. But since the whole story came out and Brokaw did that interview down here, I think we're too famous, or at least, almost famous enough to have them leave us alone."

"I'm just trying to be helpful, you know. You'd think you'd be safe in your own home. I bet that's what Miss Connie thought when she went to sleep in her apartment and then woke up a day later in a Nevada basement." His deep woods accent rhymed Nevada with Knee Vaa da. The prior year, when the existence of the "artifact" was still a secret, Connie had been snatched from her Tallahassee apartment. Brad had been tricked into the wrong limo on his way to a graduate school interview. Both had woken up in private holding cells in the then secret holding cells in Area 51 north of Las Vegas. That had not ended well for the Air Force and the videos of that installation being bull-dozed flat had also been broadcast on Tom Brokaw's Evening News.

Sue burst out a short laugh. "Ha, I just had a line run through my head: 'They're coming to take you away, ha ha, ho ho, hee hee!'"

Lucy retorted, "Sis, that's just not funny." Then she giggled. Susan repeated it in sing-song and Sonny joined in for the laugh chorus. "Okay, okay, I guess it is funny."

After a pause and shared smiles, Sonny asked, "I guess there's been no peep from the kids?"

He started to count fingertips. "What's it been, three months now?"

"It's been one hundred days today," Lucy said, looking up at the wildlife refuge wall calendar. "Gracious, but those kids have me worried. They had food and water for ten days. Unless they found something to eat, they'd be bones by now."

Sunny spoke their shared thought. "Let's just hope they's alive in those bones." Nods around the table followed. "They're smart and between 'em, I'd place a bet on humans over aliens."

Chapter 12

"Those who make peaceful revolution impossible revolution will make violent inevitable."
John Fitzgerald Kennedy

Jhagatt Residential Complex
3608.360 Erran Calendar

Brad stirred uncomfortably on his bunk. He was tired of being a ward of the state with no responsibilities. He missed Connie's company, her more positive outlook, her dimpled grin. He and Shaand were becoming better communicators. He assumed that if Connie had a constant companion that, by now, she too was a lot more proficient in their language. He and Shaand had made decent progress in their attempts to learn the gestures, primary sounds, and the growing vocabulary needed to understand each other. Occasionally, they made huge leaps when they would gain a new concept of the past tense or spans of time. Shaand's abilities were, of course, augmented by his psi understanding of intent and emotion. Brad was newly proficient with a wrist pad. It had been given to him with some ceremony by one of the elder females. He had no clue as to the technological magic behind its touch pad, but he could draw pictures and display them on a wall to add to the daily game of linguistics and charades.

Shaand was out somewhere doing the Council's business. It seemed everyone else had duties somewhere. There was almost always noise in the hallways outside, but now he was alone. Alone with his thoughts. He began to mull over his first meeting with his Erran captors.

~ ~ ~

He clearly remembered that every moment in the fetid air of the city ship was a moment of near nausea. There was a constant whir and rumble of equipment and a persistent hissing of air vents. An increase in noise levels in the outer hall had brought the two off-world prisoners to high alert. Brad and Connie had been in the low gravity section of the monstrously huge space station for a little over twenty-four hours. Although they thought they were going to see the barren, dead home world of their lost spaceship, they had found that

Dzura was now occupied. The civil war-ravaged planet they had been given glimpses of from their ship's computer memory banks was now the subject colony of the victorious Errans. Dzura was an enslaved world.

The foot traffic in the corridor had been characterized by the sshtic, sshtic, sshtic of low-adhesive magnetic shoes. Foot traffic in the hallway outside their holding cell had been rare enough, but the murmur of unintelligible voices with a military cadence was new. The cell's door de-energized and three guards had stepped into the small space at the end of the two bunks.

One pointed a handheld stun pike at Brad, wordlessly conveying that he was to stay put. The other two directed Connie to get up. When she hesitated, strong arms lifted her by the armpits, and she was soon cuffed and readied for transport. Four more arms held Brad in place when he attempted to get up. A silvered sphere was placed over Connie's head. She loosed a small yelp but tried to retain her composure. "Connie, I'm gonna come for you, somehow" was all he could say to her before a second blanking ball was put over his head. Brad heard her, muttering, "Oh crap, oh crap, oh craa—" But the psi and sound-blanking features of the helmets were turned on and they were essentially blocked off from each other when static noise emitters in the blanking ball filled their ears.

The ball-shaped helmet was silvered opaque from the outside, dully transparent from the inside. It was like the one he'd been in when they were brought to their holding cell. He suspected that its real utility was that psi-waves could not penetrate. Not only could a prisoner not communicate with others, they could not send or receive to their guards who weren't always non-telepathic blanks. Brad did not know all of this for sure yet, but he was beginning to realize that here, as on Earth, there was a hierarchy. When he and Connie had arrived, a few days earlier, they were capable of limited communication with the Erran pilots and guards they'd first met. They had communicated only in the transfer of limited intent and will. It became clear that the good intentions transmitted as "we come in peace" were not a sufficient base for communication.

Their almost immediate transfer into a larger ship, wrist bindings and, shortly thereafter, the psi neutralizing helmets had been a startling and unexpected result of finding their spaceship's home planet. He had stood trapped between two guards as three others escorted Connie away. As he stood watching her go, a pop and crackle indicated that the energy wall that made his cubical a cell was charged. A rumble from some action elsewhere on the ship had rolled through the metal walls of his cell.

A similar rumble brought him back to his present situation, this time from explosions on the surface.

Alone. For the first time since his arrival in the Dzuran system, Brad laid back on his bunk. At least now, there wasn't anyone around to eavesdrop on his thoughts. If he stuck to English, any non-blanks nearby might not be able to understand what he was thinking.

~ ~ ~

Nine years earlier, an adolescent Brad had found a small scrap of metal in the woods near his home in North Florida. He and his father had come to an early conclusion that it might be extra-terrestrial and that's when his world and world view changed forever. Several months before leaving to find Dzura, the nine-year struggle to keep the artifact safe from the Air Force's black hats had ended in his worldwide fame and most of the world's acceptance of extra-terrestrial life. As Tom Brokaw had predicted, the media and philosophical firestorm had been immediate and intense. Book offers, scammers, opportunists of all stripes had bombarded them, and all but Brokaw were given a universal cold shoulder.

He and Connie had a continued purpose in keeping to themselves: only a few people knew of the spaceship Jai. Protecting that secret seemed paramount. They had long and well-deserved distrust of the Air Force and could assume only duplicity and deceit if they volunteered it. They discussed it and determined that Jai's capabilities would be militarized. Jai was a warrior's dream, but humanity didn't need any more lethal tools.

They had been shocked to near speechless wonder to find that the pilot, Ka-Litan, their confidant and window into the lost world of Dzura was dead. He had died centuries ago and the ship's computer, Jai, a cognizant being in its own right had been their "friend" in the woods. They had each learned a lot about each other's cultures as Jai had learned how to communicate with his human contacts on the surface through its psi-neural interface.

Brad closed his eyes and brought up the memories of Jai. Its shields up in an auroral display of brilliant colors, rising from the limestone prison that had covered the Dzuran fighter for so long. He and Connie had laughed with joy in anticipation of meeting the ship's pilot Ka-Litan but then found only a desiccated corpse lying in the cockpit.

Jai had been communicating for years with Brad and Connie in psi-English and readily adapted to the task of teaching the two humans the basic controls of running the recharged Dzuran fighter. After a brief joyride above the atmosphere, they landed in the Hitchens family homestead's backyard and cloaked it against detection. A few provisions were put aboard, and primitive accommodations were made for human biological needs. Brad had introduced ship computer Jai to his mother and aunt and, the next evening, to Connie's thunderstruck parents.

Thinking about the backyard visit and their shared sheer wonder at the existence of a real-to-the-touch spaceship in the backyard, he had to smile to himself. Happy times. The few trips to remote deserts had seemed harmless, but the Australian Abos were none too happy, and a visit to the Gobi had nearly charged an international incident between the Chinese and Russians.

In their earlier discussions, Jai had told them of the destruction of his dead home planet and the trip to Dzura had seemed like a good initial shakedown cruise. They had not counted on what might have happened in the four hundred-plus years since Ka-Litan had fatally crashed the ship into the Florida swamps so close to the seawater that would have saved him.

The ship, Jai, was a Dzuran Skeeter, a tactical fighter designed to attack en masse in sufficient numbers to overwhelm a destroyer's or cruiser's defenses. As individual fighters, fatalities were sometimes as high as twenty or thirty percent. But when the little ships linked in triad formation with their shields combined for protection, their unified energy shield was almost as effective as a Dzuran destroyer's and their combined, neutrino, rail gun and energy wave bombardments were lethal.

Jai was dolphin grey with shields down, a little larger than a school bus and shaped like a slightly melted jellybean. Slightly flatter at the bottom with sloping sides, its smooth lines were broken at the back for thrusters. Most of its sensors, fuel scoops, and airfoils were retractable. Jai could operate in atmospheres under chemical boosters with extendable airfoils. In near-space, it maneuvered with neutron thrusters and in grav-space by slipping outside of five-space, as Jai called it, and moving along a sixth dimensional axis that both Bradley and Connie had great difficulty understanding. The idea that the ship could "jump" or "pop-and-drop" into another star system light years away boggled his mind.

Brad had grown up on Star Trek and its warp speeds. That always implied travel at high speed, speeds at multiples of light speed, but still a journey that required time. The "pop and drop" didn't seem to require travel so much as defiance of physics as any human science understood it. Questioning Jai, he learned that limitations built into the guidance system prevented dropping too near a gravity well, a star, or a large planet, preventing immolation or crashing, and time could not be overridden. A transition always occurred in real time. Safeguards in the ship's design meant that the sixth-dimensional slip could not slide forward or backward along the fourth, or temporal, dimension.

In their early indoctrination to Jai and its control systems, Jai had shown them file vids of the bombed and cratered planet as he had last flown over it near the end of the Erran civil war. He had also shown some older scenes when his two original crew members were taking the new psi-enhanced ship through training drills.

~ ~ ~

Now, lying on his bunk in a Dzuran dormitory, Hitchens realized that he had not actually seen much of the planet since his capture when Jai dropped into a high orbit above Dzura. The alien interception craft instantly immobilized Jai's ability to maneuver by physically harnessing it. He and Connie had watched helplessly as Erran craft surrounded it and pushed it none too gently aboard a fantastically huge orbiting city. Suitless and helmetless, they had been relieved to find the loading dock area pressurized to something close to their Earth normal and it had breathable, if particularly foul-smelling, air. He would later learn that generations of Errans had been born, had lived their lives, and had been recycled, breathing this same air. To the Errans, it smelled like home, to the humans, an urban sewer.

Brad and Connie were shuttled into a holding area and waited in a state of near panic for decontamination teams and biological specialists to examine them. The odor and noise of tens of thousands of alien creatures, however filtered, began to take a toll. Their initial bravery and bravado broke down as their captors pulled and shoved them from chair to chamber, through crowded and noisy hallways, and back. Whether they expected a reception committee or a dissection table wouldn't have mattered at first. They could not know what to expect of the next moment. They realized that some of the same psi skills taught by Jai worked on the alien ship except that the language was absolutely undecipherable. A barrage of clicks, whistles, and spoken alien words, along with unbidden intentions or thoughts, flooded into their partially trained psi centers. It was only after they were seen to react to intentional thought that both he and Connie had been fitted with fish bowl helmets. He realized now how lame his promise to Connie had been. "I'll come after you."

Hah! he thought. How am I going to keep you out of a dissection chamber? What a dumbass!

~ ~ ~

That was the last time he had seen Connie before their chaotic reunion just before the jailbreak. He could still clearly remember her shouts out to him when she saw his blonde head, nearly half a head taller than all the Dzuran prisoners. There were few moments now that he did not think of her. He loved her lopsided smile with one dimpled cheek, her help in solving problems, and above all, her belief in him. Ironic! Find the love of your life, take a surreal dream vacation, lose the love of your life to space aliens.

He and Connie represented two young adult humans, fresh out of college and, potentially, two of the best random samples that these skinny, furry aliens could have wanted to observe. He only hoped that observation was all they intended. He had learned to overcome the odor of what passed for food so he remained nourished. The water was water, clean and purified with only a slight metallic aftertaste. The air aboard the orbiting city had smelled horrible but was breathable. Here on the surface, it had to be, if anything, a little richer in oxygen than Earth standard.

If Connie was being treated in a similar manner, then hopefully, she was still fit as well. He tried not to think about all the sci-fi scenarios he'd seen of probes and needles. She had to be okay. He had been treated, well, decently. From all the conversations with Shaand and his personal audience with the Dzuran high Pelma, he felt he could trust the Dzurans.

Of course, he thought, before we have a shot at going home, the Dzurans will have to survive and win their civil war!

With that, he sat down on the floor, braced himself back on his elbows, and began doing leg lifts. He understood why most prisoners he had seen were thin but fit and although he wasn't exactly a prisoner, he could not go out for a jog. Exercise beat out some of the boredom. He ran through his improvised routine of floor exercises and began to run in place when he heard footsteps coming down his hallway. He waited as the shuffling approached and then stopped nearby. Shaand was back?

An electric snap signaled the release of the door catch. Four Dzuran soldiers stood in close formation at the doorway. They turned and separated slightly, revealing an unmistakable female human form in a Dzuran jumpsuit. "Connie! Good God! You're here!"

"Brad! Oh, my gosh! I've been so worried." She started to move forward toward the door, but the lead guard pulled back on her elbow.

"Easy, Con. It looks like they're bringing you here. Patience!" In short order, she was led into the room, and the guards stood aside. He rushed to her and hugged her close to him. He could feel her shuddering in sobs of relief. He breathed in her smell. Her hair, her neck, he took in a deep breath savoring her. Connie was back at last!

When they broke the embrace, tear tracks ran through the dust on her cheeks. Cupping her shoulders in his arm, he guided her to the edge of his bunk and sat her down. The guards, troubled by the overt emotion and public touching, backed silently out of the room.

He just wanted to look at her, to drink in her face. Presently, she pulled back and with an entirely blank look, said. "Hey, you look good in a beard."

He stroked his hirsute chin. "I haven't actually had the opportunity, but—" He stopped in mid-sentence. Something was wrong. "What is it?"

She broke in on him. "Don't look at it, but there's someone behind that view screen behind me."

He almost did look automatically but checked himself. "You sure?"

"Yes, actually, I think there are at least two of them. I can hear their psi thoughts. One of the administrators is in there with a Dzuran guard or two."

"I figured that's what it was. It bothered me at first, but I figured we've so far been treated very well. I wouldn't trust the Air Force to wait this long before they'd want to dissect a live alien on Earth. "

She nodded in agreement. She almost turned her head toward the view screen in the back of the room and thought better of it. "You haven't heard them before? The psi coming from whatever's back there?"

Brad thought about it. "Not that I could tell that it was coming from there. This whole wing seems to vibrate in the psi and I have all I can sometimes do to hear myself think."

He felt the throbbing headache emanating from the psi center at the back of his skull. "How'd you get so good at it, Con?"

"I don't know, I spent a lot of time last year teaching Jai." She paused, remembering her sessions sitting by the little cypress stained pool reading to Jai when he was still trapped underground. "You know? We know almost nothing about these guys. If they've downloaded Jai's main computer, they have access to a World Book Encyclopedia, a pocket dictionary, an Atlas of the world, some college chemistry and physics and astronomy as Earth understands it." She looked over Brad's shoulder, unfocused toward the energy wall. "And what do we know about Errans vs. Dzurans?"

"A little, I guess. We know there was a civil war and our side lost. I suppose if we sat down with a typewriter, we'd come up with a lot just from our individual experiences."

"Yeah, first contact between Humanity and an alien race and we come down on the side of the losers." She slumped slightly.

"Well, it's the first contact we know about. Except for our long list of buried records in the vaults of the Air Force. We don't really know do we?"

"I know that Jai was sexist?"

"What? How can you say a computer is sexist?"

"Programming, his whole culture was sexist, or at least, the military leadership that programmed him had no use for breeders."

"Breeders? What do you mean?" Brad was puzzled.

"These guys, they're all men, er, males. They think they run the place and they have a word for females which is expressed derogatorily. 'Breeders' is a close as I can get. I think when one of their pre-adults decides to go through the change and the hormones do their thing, their hair turns white and they get written off. They have their litter, raise them and that's it. At least that's the male view of the system. Females can't revert back and I haven't seen many in open society. Just these brown males. I'll tell you about the females later. They have their own world view." She reached over and hugged his head close, nipped an ear and whispered, "I want to get you into a dark room with no viewports! I want to share my female world view!"

Brad felt stirrings that he could not act on. He looked briefly at the view screen, nuzzled into Connie's neck and gave her neck a light nip.

"Ouch!"

"Want a hickey?" He said, grinning.

"Ewww! Not in public!"

He thought about what she'd said about females. Of all the locals he'd seen, he couldn't say that he had ever seen a female. "How did you get to see so much?"

Connie said. "Well, they sent me first to a youth crèche. I guess it was to put me with Dzuran females. Later I figured it was because they seem to have a cultural desire to remain segregated from females except for the breeding rooms. Oh, and I saw how they raise their young, but I could not communicate with the youngest. Almost all except a few adolescent ones were blanks. No psi!"

"Blanks?"

"Yeah, blanks. They're called Cli-mat I think. That's either a crèche name or they are all called that. I don't know. They are specially bred as workers, they have darker brown hair and I guess a little more squat, or sturdy looking. They are still brownish, but with more grey in the brown fur, and it's a more bristly. Like the difference between a donkey's fur and a horse's.

"Worker bees, warriors, breeders. It is almost as if they have ant colony culture. Dang, I wonder what they would think of humanity, we have a lot of stratification that is more related to circumstances of birth. Leaders breed leaders and worker bees breed worker bees. And there's still slavery on Earth, in the third world. But at least on Earth, there's an outside chance an individual can beat the odds and go from worker bee to leadership."

He had been staring at a nondescript spot on the wall, trying not to think about whoever might be behind the screen. "Outside." He looked up at the carved rock ceiling. "What's it like outside?"

"I don't know. Whenever I was moved around, I was in the underground. If I got too near something important it was with a black-out bubble on my head."

"Yeah, Shaand told me those are used whenever they transport a prisoner to keep them from talking to other prisoners in transit."

"Shaand?"

"Yeah, he was one of the guys in the prison break. The tall one who was driving the subway flatcar."

"Oh, right." She said, remembering. "So they're treating us like prisoners?"

"Sort of feels like it. To them it's probably all the hosting they can do and wage a revolution at the same time. What would we do with an alien visitor, put them up in the Lincoln Bedroom?"

"Brad? I'd hate to think what we would do with a Dzuran who accidentally showed up on Earth."

"Right." He continued off subject, remembering that his thoughts were probably being monitored. "Shaand's been my roomie here for, I don't know, about a month. Most of the time I've been down here. He said he was put with me because he had been a translator for the Erran overlords. Because of his language skills they thought he might be able to talk to me. He's pretty good actually. After they separated us, Shaand took me right into a session with this area's super council. I think they call it a Pel Council and their main man is the Pelma."

Connie said very quietly, "Shaand is one of the guys behind that screen. Then asked, "Did you learn any of their speech?"

He nodded, thinking, *Esta verdad! Tal vez no hablan Espanol.* Then aloud. "I can understand a little if they talk slowly and try their best with psi inflection, but I can't make alot of those click and pop sounds. At least I feel stupid when I try."

Connie smiled, pulled her lips into a pucker, and made a rising sucking whistle sound ending with a short tongue click.

"Yeah! Stupid!" Brad laughed. "That's the sound that Shaand used to say a lot at first. He thought I was stupid. Of course, I didn't know it for a while either. Maybe I am stupid."

"Just not as handy with languages; not your best suit I guess."

"Hey, I did learn a little Spanish out in Arizona. But then, I never learned to roll my Rs either." He asked. "So how is Jai a sexist?"

"It's probably just his programming; a cultural thing. When we got in Jai's cockpit. Or rather, when you first got in and you asked him to raise the shield so I could join you."

"Yeah? What?"

"I sensed hesitation. He knew I was a female. He didn't mind me teaching him about human culture, but he didn't seem to want me along."

"That's probably nothing sweetie. I think you're maybe misinterpreting what happened."

"Maybe, but when we were back up above Earth's atmosphere, all packed for adventure. He asked where to go. I said South Pole and you said Dzura. The stars all slid into purple and here we are! We'd be a lot better off now if we'd gone to the South Pole!"

"So you're saying Jai didn't respect you? What if he had some kind of directive to go home?"

"Maybe, but why didn't he just go home at any time after we got him free?"

Brad thought about this a second. "You know, he was programmed to be one of a three part crew. They were already short on crew when his weapons officer was reassigned to pilot his own ship. Since you and I were the two humans he knew best. Maybe he didn't just leave because although he can do all he needs to do to get back home. He needs the orders to do it. I don't think he has will of his own to do anything. Remember, he's a smart robot."

"A very smart robot." Connie rejoined.

"Granted," Brad said, "He's also a superb guidance and control system, armed to the teeth, and dangerous as all hell. I don't think his Dzuran programmers wanted him to have free will."

Connie nodded her head considering. "So, do you think he's missing us? The rest of his crew? As much as we miss him right now?"

"God, I hope so. We're a little thin on friends here."

"What about your old roommate?" She gave the subtlest of eye rolls toward the screen in the back of the cell. "What was he before he was tossed in here to help make sense of you?"

"He said he was a supervisor, jailed by the Errans because the work group assigned to him was not meeting quotas. I think he's a lot higher up than a simple supervisor. The Dzurans got him assigned to me because of his language skills." He thought about the less than coincidental posting. "I suppose maybe the Dzuran elite also wanted to know how to make contact with us."

"What happened?"

"You mean before or after the jailbreak?"

"Today."

"Beats me, he left this morning. I had the cell to myself most of the time which I spent missing you and poof! Here you are. I had actually thought it was him coming back when the guards were bringing you here. But I guess that's him behind the screen, hoping to monitor human sexual behavior."

She closed her eyes, relaxed and turned her head slightly as if thinking or remembering something. "Shsss." Give me a second. She rotated her head slowly side to side then opened her eyes again. "Exactly, the guys behind the wall are wondering if we'll exhibit mating behavior."

He took that in, resisting the urge to glance at the screen or even think about it. "You are one pretty freakin' amazing girl. You know that?"

"What?" She smiled back at him with her characteristic one-sided dimpled grin. "I didn't quite hear you."

"Freaking amazing, and beautiful, smart, a redhead, a telepath or psychic, whichever; and did I say beautiful?"

"And you are a hopeless romantic." She said poking him in the chest.

He sighed, deeply. Holding her close, he wished that there was no view screen at the back of their room and that he had some way of turning the lights down. "Any chance you could forget about that screen for a while?" To their mutual astonishment, and delight, light levels in the room dimmed to the level of a nebular-lit night on the surface. Default lighting for sleep shift.

~ ~ ~

The next 'day', or shift, Shaand joined them and was demonstrating that he could speak English with a little more clarity.

He leaned less heavily on psi and more on gesture and sound. His graphic attempts were hopeless. When he tried to draw, it was too symbolic and they didn't have enough common references. The two humans figured he was trying to teach them to write. Brad used his sketching skills to great advantage in vocabulary building.

Connie and Brad knew that Shaand was one of the few beings on the planet, besides Jai, Kenaan, Leeink-Knaa and Clee-Chk, who could understand them very well or at all. For that matter, they had no idea if Jai was even on the planet. They had been taken out of Jai's cockpit under armed arrest, which they understood with clarity. Brad had shouted out. "Jai! Don't tell them anything about Earth!"

In that next moment aboard the orbital Erran city, they had been separated from Jai and from each other. By Brad's estimation, they had been separated for almost three weeks before she had unexpectedly been brought to his cell in Jhelen City Prison. Then there was the prison break. Only a few hours into that escape, they had been separated again. Now, against their expectations, she had been brought back to the triple bunk room and shared their space. Shaand stayed for day shift but left them for sleep shift. They supposed, to learn more from the off-worlders when they were by themselves.

Brad was staring at the sketch tablet covered with symbols representing the Dzuran alphabet, a basic lesson which Connie seemed to get with ease. "Why do you think your language skills have improved so much more than mine? Unless I'm looking straight at Shaand, I mostly get very limited information and I can't distinguish all that babble in the hall as individual thoughts."

"I don't know, Brad. I think we were both trained by Jai in all those sessions in the woods." She pulled back her wavy red hair and used a makeshift tie to keep it back. Doing so, she screwed her mouth slightly with the effort and Brad had to resist the urge to lean in and kiss her again. They'd been separated since capture and he had no indication until she arrived that she was alive. She continued, "I spent a lot more time with him than you did with all those exercises in math and the sciences. Not only did he get more vocabulary, but I ended up with more training, I guess, in Dzuran telepathy. I think it's something that some humans have the potential for, but most of these guys can do pretty well."

"Not all, sweetie." He said.

"Right, the blanks. The cli-mat."

Shaand appeared at the doorway as the energy screen powered down. "Yess, blanks not psi talk."

Connie expressed why and Shaand replied, "Blanks is Hooman word, Elioi name is ckli-mat. The sound was hard for the two humans who both tried it with varying success until Shaand expressed humor with their efforts. Connie did a little better because she had been told about the ckli-mat. Shaand explained that, ckli-mat are workers. Not stupid, but not planned for more than intelligently competent body work. Lift, push, pull, sort, move, plant, harvest. They can do simple directed tasks and some, older, learn trades. It is a necessity in Dzuran and Erran societies to have a working class that does not hope to be better. He warned also, "Most, not all guards are blanks. Careful not assume guard is ckli-mat."

Brad asked, "Do you know the word slave?" He continued to try to explain it.

Shaand responded, "Ckli-mat not slave; ckli-mat workers. Slave is ckli-tot. Shaand is slave. Erran masters on Dzura make Shaand ckli-tot." He reddened slightly at the ear ridges and added, pointing beyond the doorway shield, "Many farm workers ckli-mat. Most farmer-builder-worker, ckli-mat. Cli-mat not tink ckli-tot, not want more, not need more."

Connie asked in psi, *How many generations, how long have Dzurans been slaves on your own planet?* She then told Brad what she had asked.

Shaand looked away and down, his ear ridges had darkened and what they had learned to interpret as a frown lined his brow. He psi'd back, *Shaand slave birth in crèche. My crèche trained as administrators but also ckli-tot to Erran masters.*

Brad asked, "What about soldiers? Are the soldiers given psi training in crèche too?"

Shaand looked up, interested in the question. "Many Erran soldier crèche ckli-mat. Soldier leader has psi. Erran soldier leader raised in different crèche."

Connie asked, "Ckli-mat not have psi. What name for Elioi with psi?"

Shaand looked surprised. Had not Hoomans been paying attention? "With psi, Elioi!" He pressed both of his hands to his chest. "Elioi." Then he moved cupped hands to his temples, mimicking a dish antenna. "Have psi." He put his hands on his chest again. "Ckli-mat." This time he put his hands on his head and clasped his skull palms inward. "Not psi."

Connie suppressed an OMG impulse but did not suppress the jaw drop reaction in time. The Elioi considered the ckli-mat workers, as a bred sub-species.

Shaand acted at least as if he had not overheard the thought and changed the subject. "Erran Ss-, ah, administrator tink Braad and Ka-Nee stupid, maybe less tan ckli-mat. Not know how you come wit Dzuranti warship from off-world when so stupid." He allowed a smile to furrow his forehead. *Shaand tink Braad not so stupid.e*

Maybe that is a good thing. Connie thought about a possible recapture by the Errans. Maybe they wouldn't ask too much about our home if they think we are too stupid to understand.

"Is good ting." Shaand tried his new human expression, nodding, to show agreement. "Tay more surprise when you gone."

"Gone?" The humans said simultaneously.

"Next sleep, Shaand and more Dzuran take Hoomans gone. Protect you from Erran Pelma."

Brad found himself whispering. "Are we in danger now? Has something changed?" He and Connie shared worried glances and looked back at Shaand.

He psi'd *Erran leader Si-Ano want take you to Erran sky-home.* He pointed up toward the ceiling or orbit and added. "Si-Ano has orders to take you talk to Si-I."

"That is bad?" Brad asked.

"Much bad for Hooman" He made what looked like a chopping motion against his wrist. "Yess, bad for human talk to Si-I." Brad found that he got that last in psi perfectly.

Shaand continued, "Shaand have," he paused thinking of the expression, "Su-pi. Yes su-pi on Teeya City." He again pointed to the rock ceiling.

The two humans looked at each other questioning.

Shaand tried again. "Su-pi?"

This time with the psi undertone, the both got it and said together, "SPY!"

"Yess, have su-pi on Teeya City. Work docks. Talk with other su-pi." Pointing up again, he said. "Pelma Si-I very bad Elioi. Want to talk Hoomans. Not good talk." There was no need to elaborate.

Shaand leaned back against the wall. "Need eat, need su-leep. Next shift all move, more away from Erran soldier. Tey come tomorrow."

The two humans shared another look; this one, full of concern. A wavering in the energy wall announced a presence in the hall. Brad saw two bowls being pushed through an opening in the left corner of the shimmering wall. Soon another bowl slid in on Shaand's side. The holes closed and the wall returned to its neutral static barrier mode. Impenetrable without extreme pain, its bland non-surface hummed softly as it came up to full power and again became part of the background noise. Shaand reached for his bowl, "Eat. Good for you psi talk." He made finger to mouth motions.

This food is good for psi? Connie asked silently.

Brad was surprised that he overheard, but knew that it was not illusory. This had not been a human-Dzuran interaction or human-Dzuran machine, he had heard Connie think talk to Shaand. His psi ability was improving, finally.

Shaand replied, "Food have seed of Jaan-dk. Jaan-dk is plant give to young in crèche to begin psi train."

Understanding flooded into Connie as Shaand transmitted complex feelings and images to her. She got up and reached for the bowls, and handed one to Brad. Taking it, he understood that it was not just a mealy mush; it was an intentional effort by the Dzurans to establish contact; it was the key to better psi abilities. He tasted the grey lumpy stuff as if he had not been served the same mush in two out of three of the meals he'd had each day since he'd awakened in the Jhelen City jail cell. Although its taste was not at all similar to the oatmeal it resembled, and its odor was close to repugnant, it was edible. He caught Connie's eye, smiled and swallowed.

Chapter 13

There is no living thing that is not afraid when it faces danger.
The true courage is in facing danger when you are afraid.
L. FRANK BAUM, *The Wonderful Wizard of Oz*

Jhagatt City
3608.361 Erran Calendar

Concussions reverberated through the barracks. At each blast, fine dust settled from the hewn rock ceiling. Rebel ground-to-air resistance was all but over. All ground-to-air equipment and most of the personnel assigned to it were gone. The best activity most could do was sleep, and if the noise and disturbance wouldn't allow that, talk. Connie asked Shaand about the length of the planning effort. His response, only a little reserved, indicated that the adopted plan had originally been set for the next generation, but physical abuses in the mining areas in the southern hemisphere had precipitated outbreaks. There had been talk of denying all future crèche classes Jann-dk fruit, essentially training nothing but ckli-mat workers. At first, minor clashes, characterized as labor disputes had led to strikes and open hostilities with Erran overseers thrown from their air cars and trampled to death. Simple work stoppages incidents escalated to sabotage when it was learned that the leaders had been taken to Riiya City, tried, and executed by ejection into vacuum. Armed conflict erupted after a long secret arms cache had been found. It had been stripped bare and the weapons distributed among the workers before the news could be transmitted to Riiya City.

Erran reinforcement troops had been shot dead as soon as their ground effect vehicles emerged from transport carrier ships. Their carrier ships were attacked as they tried to leave the spaceport with two of the six crashing back to the surface with the loss of all aboard. News of the successful attack spread quickly around the mining territories and shortly thereafter to the agricultural regions further south. Errans had initially thought to starve out the mining camp insurrections by cutting off food shipments to the less hospitable reaches of the deep southern hemisphere and found that this had no effect.

Another crash sounded overhead. Brad flinched involuntarily as dust settled down from a new crack in the ceiling. He said, "Seems like they know about this place."

Shaand replied. "Yess, we evacuate tis site two shift time. Move all to Old Chookya to make for better defense. His next sentence was broken off by a rolling thunder crash near their hallway. A staccato buzzing which sounded like an alarm system with a wiring short sounded. Shaand was on his feet only a brief moment before Brad and Connie. He went to the door and looked toward the sound's source and ducked back into their room to avoid a cloud of billowing dust that filled the hallway. He went to the door, looked toward the sound's source, and ducked back into their room to avoid a billowing cloud dust that filled the hallway. Dust and debris blew into the room.

Sounds of nearby collapsing walls and tumbling equipment subsided. The power feed to the area went down and the hallway's light cut off with a ziit-snap. A small emergency light panel blinked on providing light levels similar to a dark night under the nebula. The crisp smell of fresh air began to replace the nose-clogging dust cloud that had just filled their space. Cries of pain joined other calls for help. The psi surge immediately after the blast was painful.

"Shaand?" Brad looked at his host for help.

"What should we do?" Connie asked at the same time. "Safe to stay this room?"

"No move now." Shaand cocked an ear toward the door. "Hear for weapons." He cupped an ear bud in demonstration of his intent. "Soon go, Errans come on feet."

Connie and Brad understood the importance. If an air attack was being followed up with ground assault then small arms could be coming. Additional explosions from above and the crashes of collapsing barracks structures continued for too long. Shaand pointed at their bunks and took shelter under his bunk first. Brad helped Connie slide under hers and then followed her in. Having been self-conscious of prurient ever-present eyes, he was conscious of spooning into the curves of Connie's huddled form. As he put his arms around her, she pushed back into his S-curved form. For a moment, they both forgot the immediate peril in the hallways outside and luxuriated in the warmth of each other's body. Any thought of doing more than snuggling was censured by more reverberating thuds from above and more crashing beyond the door. They waited for the air attack to end. If ground forces did come, it would be after the bombing stopped.

A nearly direct overhead ground hit shook the room to its carved rock floor. Shaand was back at the door psi-ing for them to stay put, then he was gone. Green flashes followed him from the far end of the hallway. Dust and debris rained down from the ceiling. The room went dark after a flicker. Connie shuddered and tightened the hug. "Bradley, I think I'm scared."

"Shh, honey. I know, I know." Hitchens pressed his cheek into the back of her head. "You know as long as I'm here, I'll do anything within my power to keep us together and alive. If we never see home again, I still want to grow old with you." He thought of the night, now a distant memory, when her family's shrimp boat had sunk in the Gulf of Mexico and he'd helped comfort her fears. She rolled to face him and he pulled her even closer, found her mouth and gave her a long tension releasing kiss." Breaking off, he rolled to see that Shaand had left a handgun on the floor near him. This clearly had not been an accident. Brad reached for it and fitted his hand to the grip. It was not a natural fit, but he could hold it and depress the thumb trigger. He tested it on a block of pour-rock debris on the floor. It smoked then burst under the green beam of high energy particles.

~ ~ ~

Pe-yng shifted the dust mask on his face. The last explosion had brought down more of the roof than he'd expected. They had surprised and overtaken guards posted at the entrance to the underground warren, but the second tier of defenses had proven formidable. A splatter charge was aimed at the opposite wall and when ignited the wall had disappeared in a spray of gravel.

The first line of Dzuran defense was now dead and partially buried under gravel and stone. Any moving survivors were summarily dispatched. Moving forward through the tunnel system, the next barricade had been similarly blasted. This time the splatter charge weakened the natural stone roof overhead and a massive boulder dropped from the ceiling. Frustrated, he listened through the clatter of loosened gravel still falling from the hole in the ceiling. He could hear shouts and footsteps beyond the huge stone, retreating.

Had this been a trap? He set up a rear guard to ensure that his squad wasn't cut down from the rear. He'd have to call in engineers to safely remove the massive boulder without bringing down more of the ceiling rock above. Walking toward the fallen rubble, he waved at the dust and felt fresh air displacing the dust-laden air. He saw a hole near the former doorway that he could fit through. He signed for his squad to stay back and entered. Skylight filtered into this section of the warren from collapsed floors above.

Footsteps retreated beyond. The Dzuran survivors were clearly in retreat. He began to cautiously proceed further into the rubble filled hall. A nearly collapsed wall to his right showed several doorways. Any of these could mean an ambush. The 3D war gaming techniques he'd learned for taking pirate warships in deep space were of no use here. There are no silent approaches on a gravel strewn floor. He peered into the first and saw only a pile of collapsed wall sections. The next two were similar, but voices, no, not voices. Some strange animal sounds were coming from one of the rooms ahead.

Pe-yng heard the sound of a blaster and then shattering rock. *"Was someone trying to blast a hole out?"* He crept toward the former doorway, stepping carefully over debris and fallen ceiling lights. At the door now, he took a deep breath and beseeched the Light for strength and wisdom. Using his newfound planet-side agility, he stepped into the opening and froze. "By the LIGHTS!" He was only a few arm lengths away from a Hooman.

Brad heard the approaching footsteps and seeing that there was no cover, stood with his gun at the ready. He hoped that he hadn't dissipated its charge on the piece of rock. A helmeted Erran trooper filled the doorway and stopped. Was he alone or a vanguard of a larger force? Light footfalls could be heard, but there was no knowing if they meant help or capture. The trooper lifted his visor and for a moment Brad Hitchens and Lieutenant Pe-yng faced each other. Slowly, Pe-yng's weapon began to lower from vertical to horizontal. Brad put his left hand out in what he hoped would be understood as a universal stop signal.

The weapon wavered and slowed, still pointing at the ruined ceiling above Brad's head.

Pe-yng's orders were to capture the Hoomans alive if possible but to take no extreme measures. This one was pointing a blaster directly at him with that odd extra digit held over the firing button. Another Hooman was huddled under a bunk. Maybe one would do. A sound rattled to his left, he glanced left looking for the source. He looked back into the room. The Hooman now had both hands on the weapon steadying it and it was pointed at his face.

Brad saw indecision on the Erran trooper's face. Was there any way to negotiate? Was the Dzuran cause lost? As he watched, the trooper's face hardened. Slowly the weapon in the trooper's arm began to lower toward horizontal. He did not want to die here, but he couldn't bring himself to face-to-face murder. He pivoted slightly and fired. The trooper's arm burst below the wrist and the weapon clattered to the floor. The trooper's shocked face looked at where his right hand should have been and then at the smoldering cauterized stump. Brad heard more noises in the hall. A flash of green sizzled the dust just over the trooper's head. The Erran turned and ran back to the nearly blocked entrance.

Shaand appeared in the frame of the doorway, appraising the shocked Hooman standing before him. He psi'd a welcome and a let's go message and turned to go. "Come! Now!"

The sizzle and crackle of firing energy weapons could be heard a short distance away. Shaand scooped up the Erran's fallen pistol. The three had just cleared the doorway when fractured rock and debris from floors above tumbled into their room, flattening the three bunks. As the rock fall slowed, it filled their former sanctuary and the ruined passageway. Smoke mingling with dust was highlighted by flashes of burning green rays from behind. A searing pain flashed across Brad's back and he might have faltered if Shaand hadn't pulled him into another room a few doors down. Connie was already inside, wide-eyed with fear. Shaand attempted to shield the two humans with his body.

"Down. Cover you wit blanket." He tossed dust-filled bed covers from the bunks at them. Connie settled into the corner first and Brad sat in front of her.

Wait here! Shaand ordered them silently and stepped into the hallway.

Brad huddled back under the blanket with Connie squeezed tight behind him. Only the muzzle of his handgun stuck out from the blanket. Footsteps and shouts passed by outside. Friend or foe? He had to look. Brad's dun-colored hair blended into the destruction and dust. His eye peering around an edge of the blanket failed to alert the soldier assigned to clear their room. The minor pop of the pistol seemed inadequate to the danger so Brad fired again, and a third time. The surprised Erran trooper fell across the bunk and died, never recognizing that the hand of his fate was, in fact, the object of his search.

No footsteps backtracked to their room. Sounds of close order combat moved steadily further away. Connie shifted to relieve a thigh pinched by Brad's weight. "Did you kill him?"

"I think so."

"How do you know?"

"He's not moving." Brad pulled back the covering blanket.

"No! Shaand said to wait here." She tugged the feeble shelter back over them.

"Okay, for the sake of the only two humans in this part of the galaxy, We'll give it a while longer."

He thought, I have no idea what to do next if Shaand and the rest are in trouble.

"Con, there's no way to know who'll win this skirmish. There's you, me. Do we fight it out?"

"Or what?" She hugged him from behind. "Go back up to that city ship? For testing?" A flash of green slashed the doorway burning a diagonal slash in the metal frame. Her arms tightened around his chest from behind. Footfalls returned in the distance, growing louder. Chirping shouts of command in the Erran dialect grew more distinct. Squeezing him tightly, she continued. "We've just killed one of their soldiers. If you don't see a grey jumpsuit, shoot." She seemed to shrink even further into their corner.

"Yeah, I kinda got that. But in this dust, everything's the color of dirt."

Shouting in the hall ended abruptly in a scream of agony and a helmeted form fell across their threshold. In the dim light falling into the room from gaps in the hallway ceiling, the Erran soldier's face stared into the room, reflecting obvious pain. Brad edged his pistol out of the blanket. He took careful aim at the face and resolved to finish him if there was any sense of understanding that they were hiding in the corner.

More footsteps approached. An Erran, his uniform with officer piping on the cuffs, stopped at the doorway and leaned down to check for life in the fallen soldier. Down the hall, from the Dzuran side, the pop-pop-pop of projectile weapons grew louder. The officer spoke rapidly into his cuff, turned to look over his shoulder, and fled. The wounded Erran raised his head toward the doorway, aware that he was being left behind.

Brad and Connie sighed in unison as the Errans left in the direction of their initial assault. Maybe they'd been beaten back?

More footsteps.

Again Brad's pistol raised, covering a spot chest high in the doorway. The wounded soldier lying on the threshold heard the approaching steps and reached for his laser weapon. Brad fired. The Erran's pistol sizzled and spun out of reach. More footsteps and shots from the hallway, some departing then more approaching.

The running steps slowed to a stop just outside the doorway.

Braad?

Shaand?

Not shoot! Is good. Shaand slowly waved a hand into the frame of the doorway. Brad recognized the cuff insignia and the cracked cover on Shaand's cuff screen.

"Come in, Shaand. Glad to see you." The two humans stood, shaking off dust.

Between short breaths, Shaand said, "We win tis time. Now must go." He looked pained. Brad was almost sorry he had begun to read emotion in Elioi faces. Shaand added, "We will fight again wit bigger guns." Brad and Connie stepped over the dying Erran and followed Shaand toward a pile of rubble the led upward to clear sky.

Chapter 14

*In preparation for battle, I have always found plans are useless, but
planning is indispensable.*
Dwight David Eisenhower

Teeya City Commander's Board Room
3608.362 Erran Calendar

The boardroom directly behind Teeya City's command bridge
was tense with anticipation. The revolt on the ground was becoming
deadly as more of the newly trained surface action crews were
reported missing. Assembled division commanders from Erra, the
asteroid belt factory ships, and the other two orbital cities, Riiya and
Aeya, nervously waited for Pelma Si-I. Elected by the Erran Pel-
Council to supreme Pelma to oversee the suppression of the growing
revolt, he was known to be irritable if not rash in the treatment of
officers who had failed their commands. On-the-spot promotions
were coupled with on-the-spot demotions to maintenance crews or
worse.

The rebellious planet below them was displayed in a slowly
rotating three-dimensional array, trouble spots highlighted in blue.
The three space elevators were highlighted in yellow with a golden
triangle above each with each city's glyph. Red triangles and circles
located the positions of ground teams and other Erran personnel on
the surface.

Breathing literally stopped as the door abruptly swung open.
From behind Si-I's hurried form, a corpsman shouted, "The Pelma
Si-I."

"Sit!" he commanded abruptly, stopping the attempt of the
waiting commanders to get to their feet. "I don't have time for
foolishness."

He went to the head of the table, tapped a few controls, and the
image of the planet went briefly dark. He tapped again and a time
series began.

"Before you, we have a time-lapse of events over the past
months, since the first outbreaks. If you watch carefully, as I have
over the past few hours, you will see a pattern."

Blue lights winked on and slowly faded. At first, most were confined to the equatorial coastline of the southern continent, but then lights occasionally flashed further inland to the south. One area began to glow lightly in blue. As it spread, flashes pinpointed clash locations. Eruptions of light blue shading spread from these locations. Clusters of red dots surrounded some of the trouble spots and then receded.

As the slowly rotating, translucent orb turned, all could see that the southern hemisphere had been the origin of the outbreaks. The orange background display developed dark spots in the northern hemisphere.

"Note the simultaneous power outages on Kranna!" Si-I pointed to growing dark blotches as the power outages spread. "Twenty days ago, all security locations on Kranna simultaneously went down. With few exceptions, we lost most of the inmate population. Many were simple slackers, but we also no longer have in custody many of those we thought were conspiring with the southern fighters." He advanced the time sequence with a few taps on his wrist pad. "Observe."

Blue flashes and ensuing light blue areas spread across vastly separated areas on the northern continent of Kranna. Si-I continued, "Obviously, we are witnessing a concerted, well-planned insurrection. This is no mere labor revolt as we first thought. It is not an outburst against our dominion. This is revolution. It has been planned, apparently, for years. They have vehicles, advanced ground-to-air weapons abilities, and there must be, somewhere, training areas."

He tapped his console and bright orange lines appeared, connecting most of the blue areas on the two continents. "These," Si-I explained, "are the routes of the old ground rail system on Dzura. It has been abandoned for generations. Its records were only recently obtained by one of our ground teams that was not eliminated in the skirmishes. It seems," he said in barely controlled tones, "these lines are still useable and are the key to the spread of the revolt."

He looked toward the door, psi'd a command, and the door reopened. A young officer entered and came to attention before the assemblage of his superiors.

"Meet Ensign Pe-yng." The young officer saluted stiffly with his truncated right arm and resumed his stance of attention. "At ease Pe."

The ensign relaxed only slightly, still wary of the presence of the Erran high command seated around the table. Physically, he was in far superior condition to the rod-thin, ship-bound senior officers and administrators around the room. Except for the somewhat bulkier leaders from Erra, most had the spiderlike limbs of the permanent spacers.

Pe-yng began to feel, for the first time, different, superior almost, to these flaccid, stick-legged, pot-bellied officers. Had they ever seen combat? Had they, in their lifetime of administrative duties and political intrigues, ever had to command crèche mates and friends into uncertain battle and death? He had. And he had lost some of those friends to barbaric deaths on foreign soil. They had never contemplated being personally involved in hostile action, and the physical evidence of its consequences resulted in staring.

His attention drifted from its straight-ahead stare to the rotating image of the Dzuran surface. He immediately grasped its significance. To his embarrassment, he realized he was being addressed.

"Ensign? Are you well? Have you been well taken care of in the infirmary?" The bandaged stump of his right arm had drawn the attention of the assembled senior administrators.

"Yes. Yes, sir."

"Share for us the conclusions you transmitted in your last mission report."

Pe-yng cleared his throat of bile, an eruption caused by the half grav of the ship's outer ring and stirred by the anticipation of his command performance. He recounted his routine patrol after one of the prison breaks and the absence of any prisoners in two of the three prison pods. They had captured a few, killed several, but had been mystified by the lack of escapees after the breakout. On another occasion, he had surveyed the damage of a collapsed agricultural warehouse and found a floor hatch leading down to a tunnel complex. He had fought his way through a small storage area into an apparent barracks area. At first, he thought it was housing for the agricultural workers, but he had found a weapons storage room. Its empty racks for small arms weapons were complete with charging stations for the energy weapons, and all crates of ammunition for projectile arms were empty.

He had lost three good soldiers in the action, but not before he had discovered that the complex had a camouflaged door leading away from the warehouse. It had been too heavily guarded for his small team to enter. Back on the surface, he had oriented himself to the tunnel door and realized that it would have gone west toward an abandoned transit station. He continued to describe his squad's entrance into a large dormitory complex on which he'd ordered an air strike. He had been nearly captured himself but was rescued by the only other fit for service ground team that had been waiting in stand-by. In his unconscious motioning of his ruined limb, he amplified the personal peril that had to be faced to enter and clear the warrens below the surface.

As Pe-yng concluded, the Pelma stood and took over the briefing.

"So, while we have been growing soft, complacent, sure in our domination over the stupid and subservient Dzurans, the vanquished have not suffered that dominion easily and have planned well." He tapped his desk console and the ancient underground tunnel network highlighted again. "Their ancient transit system has been activated, its power sources isolated from surface grid." He drove the point home. "From interrogations, we know that when our ground troops have been trapped in place by disruptions to the power grid, the underground transit system has continued to operate perfectly."

Si-I tapped his desk console and the blue-stained orange globe dissolved.

"Beginning immediately, more ground troops, walking ground troops, are going into surface simulation training. " He scanned the room for any sign of disagreement and found none. "You will each begin D-normal gravity training. You will get at least nine squads each into your D-normal spin chambers for conditioning."

Some bulging eyes of surprise were becoming hard to hide.

"Some of you who have slowed your spin chambers to, ah, more comfortable settings will bring your training modules up to E-normal as soon as you return to your cities. In nine moons, you will all be D-normal capable." His breathing slit flared for emphasis. "In case you missed it, I mean that you personally will begin full Dzuran conditioning immediately. Is there any misunderstanding? We WILL take back our home world and we will do it by the end of this campaign."

He glanced at the senior administrators and officers seated around the cramped board room table. Their glances at each other revealed that few of them were happy to be here before the Pelma Si-I.

"Suggestions for next steps?"

Pelma Juaan-Litan from Aeya City began with ideas of a controlled attack with asteroid drops, this time with less mass, and targeting the nodes of the underground transportation network. This proposal was opposed by an agricultural supervisor from Dzura, who feared they would be out of work perhaps for generations if they triggered another planetary winter. He was joined by the other agriculture supervisors and the Pelmas from the two other orbiting cities who could not redeploy onboard gardening pods for at least a year if the food supply was disrupted by climate change. Si-I agreed as his city was also dependent on foods grown on Dzura. His city's growing population had moved into ship compartments formerly used for growing food crops and protein tanks.

Si-I scanned the faces of the four agricultural managers. "Where is LonnDonn? He had orders to attend as well." Blank faces, a subtle shrug, and a few sidelong glances were the only responses. "Pe-yng? He was last seen in the sector you were patrolling. Any sign?"

"Sir, we encountered LonnDonn in a skirmish. He wanted to commandeer a ground car that had been lightly damaged by ground fire, presumably to get back to safer areas. I needed it more."

"When was this?"

Pe-yng had to think back a few shifts. Or was it more? "At least several shifts, sir. He was on foot, walking. He was at least as comfortable on his feet as my squad." This news was greeted with shocked expressions and more than a few side-bar whispers.

Si-I motioned for quiet. "All right, Gre-LonnDonn is another casualty perhaps." Si-I motioned for Pe-yng to approach. The young ensign did so and stiffened to full attention. Si-I raised his right arm in brigade salute form toward the young officer. Pe-yng responded in kind, raising his shortened salute arm. Si-I reached into his pocket and pulled out a cuff band indicating the rank of a full lieutenant. With full ceremony, he laid the band across Pe-yng's wrist. The newly christened lieutenant gave a half bow, barely controlling the smile ridges on his forehead and backed away, returning to his position against the outer wall.

"Well?" Si-I broadcast to his broader audience, psi-ing to continue the discussion on alternatives.

Pelma Chk-Tkarn, the third Commandant from Riiya City, suggested low yield nukes on the same targets. After some heated discussion, the idea was literally shouted down to prevent contamination of the essential food crops they all depended on.

High Pelma Kaup-Naa, representing military forces from Erra, stood, raising his arms for quiet. "For too long, we have maintained our identity as spacers. I, too, have my roots in the brave forebearers who accepted the extreme risks of vacuum in the deep freeze of space. My bloodline derives from the great Cho, who, led the rebellion almost five hundred years ago that granted the Erran and asteroidal colonists economic and religious freedom. Now, we need to consider going home. Suppression of this uprising offers the perfect reason. Dzuran is the Elioi home world." With a brief sidelong glance at the priest Annchda, he continued. "Old enmities and prejudices have led to some ridiculously circular arguments that would perpetuate the superiority of spacer Elioi over those who were abandoned on Dzura after the diaspora. The best and brightest of the Dzurans left in the diaspora, but they," he smashed a fist into its opposing palm, "they are blasted to space near a score of alien suns never to return. Our fathers ensured the dominance of spacer Elioi four centuries ago. But the Dzuran survivors have proven resourceful." He nodded toward Pelma Si-I at the head of the table. "It is time we took back the land of our heritage. Ourselves. On foot!"

Shouts for and against filled the small room. Two second tier officers from opposite camps nearly came to blows. Si-I hit them with a psi blast that made them cringe. The order, though directed at the two officers, was felt by everyone in the room, even though most had advanced blocking skills. The room gradually came to order again with only Pelma Si-I and High Pelma Kaup-Naa standing. Si-I nodded toward Kaup-Naa for him to continue.

Kaup-Naa outlined his plan for ultimate victory. "I propose that we train our best Erran troops to withstand full Dzuran gravity and go after our enemies in their warrens." A small murmur was the only response this time. "We have already trained a small number of squads for patrol." He paused to noticeably glance at Ensign Pe-yng. "I propose that we train regiment-size units and capture the leadership. This revolt will end when we have put down the leadership." More murmurs, sounding more like assent, followed. Kaup-Naa laid out a plan that would have gravity-conditioned troops on the ground in the next one hundred and twenty days. In the meantime, attacks from air-effect ships would continue on known or suspected underground facilities with conventional explosives. Within the half shift, each of the ministers, in their own way, held a new optimism that the seeming tide of defeats could be countered.

Si-I brought the subject to a close. "Gre-JenDonn, you now have at your disposal any and all grounders that can be captured. You need to prioritize getting as much of the harvest in as you can. Prioritize foodstuffs and Jann-dk. Pialla can wait. The elevator cables are in good condition. You will have at your disposal any of the crant teams for crowd control."

"Crants? Sir, I don't think that will—"

"Yes, by my Lights! We still have some trained crant teams to chase down any grounders who attempt to escape." The Gre sat down hoping that his fear of the fast six-legged carnivores hadn't been too obvious to the rest. "Yes, sir. Just having them in obvious pens near the work crews should let them know that escape would mean horrible death."

Si-I considered that a few horrible deaths by crant would be sufficient incentive for the work crews to stay in line. They should have been taken off hunting duties and used as pursuit animals much earlier.

As the strategy session concluded, Si-I seemed almost relaxed. A major worry was off his mind. His enemy was planet-bound and could be dealt with in time. He was determined to get at least a sustenance level of harvest lifted off the planet to buy time. His small squadrons of ground troops could do essential close-to-ground recon of ancient transit points and destroy their power generators when they were located and, until more were trained, he would avoid conflict with the damned rebel Dzurans.

A quick tap of the console alerted a waiting ensign in the hallway to his place on the agenda. Dzar-yng entered and, seeing the royal green piping on every uniform at the table, swallowed hard.

The Pelma Si-I asked, "Do you have a report on the off-worlders' spacecraft?"

The young maintenance leader stared hard at a minute spec on the opposite wall to avoid making eye contact with any of the seated commanders. "Sir, yes, sir!"

"And?"

"It's not off-worlder, sir? It's one of ours."

A round of inhalations and a few oaths were heard around the table. Si-I prompted the young maintenance hangar tech to continue.

"That is, sir, it's Dzuran manufacture."

"You mean that blob of a ship is Dzuran? They have warships that sophisticated?"

"No, sir. Well, yes, sir. They did, that is. It is definitely of Dzuran make. It's just that it's very old. It dates from between the beginning of the diaspora and the near end of the elimination of the Dzuran fleet. It was probably quite new then, the latest technology they had. It's quite sophisticated for the time."

"Hold on now," one the seated administrators objected. "You say this ancient spacecraft is sophisticated, yet it's over four hundred years old?"

The young officer stumbled over his next thoughts but managed to get them organized. Out of respect, he turned and, with a slight bow from the neck, answered, "We have verified that it is a fighter of the last model they manufactured. We have not been able to get into its operating system. Sirs, we've tried patch cables. We've spent a lot of time in the cockpits working with the controls and it doesn't respond. It may have been damaged by our overrides when it was captured, but—"

"Wait!" Pelma Chk-Tkarn interrupted. "You can't get into its operating systems at all?"

"No, sir. We can't even get it to turn on."

"Please explain that, Lieutenant. It's completely unresponsive?"

"That's correct, sir. It was blasted by a tractor wave when it first appeared. That may be the problem. We've been working on it in the maintenance hangar since we brought it onboard and we haven't even managed to energize the cockpit light panels."

"By the Lights! Move it to one of the docking berths. Continue to work on it, but be prepared to scuttle it if you need more space for fighters. I'd like to know more about its systems and where it's been since the war."

"Yes, sir."

"We will be getting in a number of surface freight lifters from Erra to assist with getting troops to the surface. If it starts getting crowded in the bays and you haven't made any progress, jettison the damned thing."

Earth Interlude 6

"If war comes among us, it will come as a thief in the night."
Eamon de Valera

Asteroid Belt
August 3, 1986 – Earth Calendar
3608.362 Erran Calendar

Ground stations had detected the incoming craft two days out and tracking monitors had determined that its trajectory had been designed to approach in moon shadow as long as possible. Clearly, this was a cautious if not hostile approach. Offensive military satellites had been re-assigned and were closing on the craft. The sensors of at least two world governments watched in horror as the visitor snatched a communications satellite from orbit. Forget that shards of very expensive solar panels would be incinerating over populated areas. The intent was clearly hostile. Though technically redundant, com-sat telephonic capacity had become an important component of global communications. The thought of loss of that capacity initiated the emergency summit of the United Nations which overwhelmingly voted to take action. Only one pass of the armed experimental satellite would be possible every forty-eight hours and the next pass was chosen. It would prove too late.

~ ~ ~

High above the blue-green and tan planet, a small craft maneuvered through an array of smaller but resource-rich satellites. Nem-Drit hadn't noticed them at first, until he had come perilously close to a collision course with one of them. When he told his ship's computer to map orbiting bodies, he was astounded as the list kept growing. By the end of his sleep cycle, it had documented the orbits of hundreds of the tiny satellites. Ordered to this system to finish Nem-Jitep's assignment, he'd found riches beyond his hopes. A thick ring of nickel-iron-silica asteroids offered mining potential for in-system colonial expansion and the third planet had readily breathable air. The third planet's tiny satellites were an even better find.

Nem-Drit was crèche cousin to Nim-Jitep, the discoverer of the so-called Precursor Stone. Same father parent, different crèche class. The discovery of the stone had not ended well for his prospector cousin. Now Nem-Drit was investigating the intelligent activity on the only readily habitable planet in this system. True, it was already occupied by an intelligent species, but two more were ready for engineering crews, and several of this system's moons had potential, but nothing was easier than finding metal-rich asteroids of just the right mass and jumping them to the home world. He had already used his heavy mass pushers to send four nickel-iron asteroids home.

But the riches he'd found near the third planet! He, Nem-Drit, was in uncharted territory and found resources his orders could not have anticipated. Here, mineral riches beyond counting were ready for the taking! Some of the smaller satellites were less than a twentieth of a standard jump mass. These he attached to his own ship's transport pod for the return trip. He wouldn't have to use one of the heavy pushers to get them out of the system. Gold, silver, titanium, aluminum, plutonium, lithium. The list of refined metals from his first find grew on his wrist pad. As he typed in results for the report, dreams of returning to the Erran home as a hero bloomed in his mind. And wealth! At three percent, he'd be rich! He closed on his next target.

He extended grappling arms below his ship while carefully matching orbits with an oblong, gold-wrapped cylinder. He secured it where its mass would not affect his jump geometry, clipped off the energy panels, and jettisoned what looked like a communications dish. He took one last look at the planet below, noting the obvious marks of engineering on the surface and wondered if all its inhabitants looked like the two off-worlders he'd seen on the news feed. Surely, they must be primitive to have left this much hardware in orbit with no weapons platforms to protect them. He slowly added velocity to escape the gravity well that could distort his jump field.

Two sleeps later, the planet was a small blue-white dot on his screen. His transfer pod was full of high-value tech metals, and the gravity fields around his ship showed no prohibitive levels of interference. Nem-Drit called up the jump drive screen, dialed in homing coordinates, and took a deep breath. Depressing the two buttons, his computer began to count down from nine. As it reached one, he tranced for the slide from four-space to six-space. Numb and tingling, he awoke a short time later outside the orbit of Erra,

Dzura's little sister, his home world. Scanning his display, he found the massive orbiting home of over thirty thousand Errans.

The city ship was not graceful, but it was home. The Errans' scant history of designing for ships that maneuvered in atmospheres resulted in deep space habitats that emphasized function and never form. He set a trajectory for an approach and settled in for a short restorative nap while his ship's guidance system plotted the return trip home.

Chapter 15

"New Light, New Life, New Worlds."
Pelma Teeya Adrandonn

Verparksransaran Plain
3608.363 Erran Calendar

The Verparksransaran plain, Dzura's breadbasket, had only occasional tree-lined field boundaries to block the horizon. Lying side to side under the impressive night-time canopy, the only two humans in several light years of space reveled in the overhead vista. Connie shivered and snuggled close to Brad, who stared open-mouthed at the vast red and orange display overhead. He knew, theoretically, what a nebula was but to see one in its glory from within, or at least from very nearby, was fantastic. Why hadn't he noticed this beauty as they were coming in from their jump from Earth? Maybe there were filters in Jai's canopy screen that blocked low light. That didn't make sense. Was Jai's shield up? He didn't remember. The events had become too alarming too quickly. He stroked Connie's arm in an attempt to warm her and to comfort as best he could under the circumstances.

Their situation had certainly diminished. As they were leaving the relative comforts of the Jhagatt City complex, they had come under attack. When the dust had settled after the aerial barrage, dozens had been killed, and hundreds more wounded. Shaand felt certain that if there was to be any follow-up, it would be with air cars and even some of the new ground troops that had been reported. But none had come. At dusk, they had evacuated with several hundred other survivors. All had crept out of the ruins and almost all carried packs of provisions. Some carried or assisted the wounded. Brad had been impressed that the evacuation was so well planned on such short notice, but he remembered that if society had psi connectivity, mass movement could be coordinated. Connie, with her better communication skills, was the difference between being cooperative and helpful and being prodded along as uncertain but willing pets.

In the darkness, he thought he saw white-pelted Dzuran females working their way through the scattered clumps of refugees, providing medical attention. "Interesting," he said aloud.

"What is?" Connie replied, then in a huffing laugh, "What isn't 'interesting'?"

He pointed at two apparently light-furred Dzuran forms attending to a clump of seated figures several yards away. "There, those look like females. They're out mixing with the males and there's no apparent sexual tension." He wondered aloud, "What's that about?"

"Maybe it's due to the stresses of the moment. No, wait. If I remember right, most of the medical teams are females. Only for combat troops are some of the males trained as medics, or that equivalent, emergency medical trauma training and such. The surgeons and general medicine types are all females."

"But I thought, contact was so…forbidden."

"Hmm. Maybe that's a confusion between apparent intimate contact, like we were exhibiting with our hugs and embraces, versus professional contact. These doctors or nurses are providing needed professional contact. And, I don't know," her voice arced in a verbal shrug, "there's a whole lot we don't know about these critters."

"Yeah, I guess. But the sex segregation is so pervasive under normal situations."

"Careful about transferring your cultural norms, Brad." She placed her hand on Brad's, stopping his now unconscious stroking. "There's a whole culture here that works for them. It's adjusted to their biology and psychology. Lord knows how many different social structures humans came up with. We aren't psychic on top of being inquisitive and problem solving, and jealous and vindictive and territorial, and all sorts of other behaviors derived from our recent emergence from tribal existence. Besides, on Earth, there are plenty of cultures that still treat women as chattal."

"So that graduate work in sociology is paying off for you?" He nudged her with an elbow, grinning slightly in the red-tinged light from the overhead canopy.

She nudged back harder, knocking him off his perch on a semi-rigid container of supplies labeled in the still unreadable characters of the Dzuran language.

As darkness had fallen over the ruins, the collected and reorganized rebel forces had divided into nine columns and, in groups of three columns, had radiated away from the destroyed bunker system into the outlying fields. All headed, more or less, to the coast, to Old Chookya. A small guard had been left with a medical team to attend those too injured to travel or keep up. The two "off-worlders," as they had learned they were labeled, were stressed to keep up with the column, finding the Dzurans' endurance enviable. Brad wondered if confinement in the orbiting city, the Dzuran prison, or the rebel barracks had caused him to lose his muscle tone. Any early advantage they might have had when they first came to a planet with a mass lower than Earth's was gone.

As Brad got back onto his portable perch, a reinforced box of food containers, Shaand approached, bent over at the waist and looking anxious. "Come! Move to fields. Hide! Tay down!"

They all scurried into the tall grass-like fields leaving nothing behind on the roadway. Wondering about the change was short-lived as a low-pitched humming from over a hillock grew to a rumble. Over a dozen ground vehicles passed down the road, some on wide tracks and others on flexible metallic wheels. All appeared to be carrying troops in dark Erran battle uniforms. Soon they were too distant to see exactly what was going on, but it was obvious that the new troops were setting up batteries of lights to illuminate the wreckage of the bombed bunker system. Shots were heard, both from projectile weapons of Dzurans and the spitting pulse of Erran energy weapons. Wails of agony and horrible pain drifted whisper quiet across the expanse, telling of the deaths of any survivors at the ruin.

Shaand stood slowly to observe the activity, tufts of grass tied to his headgear. From his position on the ground, Brad saw an expression on Shaand's face that he had not seen before. Although it was new to him, the slump of shoulders, sagging cheeks, and drawn mouth all conveyed grief. A low throbbing came from Shaand's chest although he did not seem to be breathing. Almost a purring. Was that a Dzuran crying?

Connie put her arms around Brad in the darkness. The purring seemed now to be coming from around them, from others hidden in the grass. The throbbing grew and synchronized. The purring became a louder, palpable thrumming that penetrated to the bone. Connie found herself silently weeping, crying as an overwhelming sense of communal loss spread among the band of refugees. She looked at Brad to see on his cheeks two thin bands of liquid reflecting the dim nebular light.

~ ~ ~

LonnDonn was having a very bad day. He needed to get from his ruined offices at Jhagatt to Old Chookya on the coast. From there he might make the Teeya elevator's base complex. The first ground car he'd found had been commandeered by an unsympathetic ensign in charge of a small band of foot soldiers. He'd been chased down by sky cars and barely managed to elude one attacker by diving into a dense grove. At day's end, he had come upon a second abandoned vehicle. Waiting for darkness, he had emerged only to realize his car's tracking mechanism made him easy prey. Any cursory scan of his vehicle found him wearing a worker's jumpsuit. How he had been so stupid as to not disable the tracker? Two fighters had narrowly missed slicing his air car in two, but he'd heard the noise. Looking over his shoulder through the open top of the car, he had run into a low wall and crashed. Crashing had been his salvation as the bright green beams crossed just ahead of him. He leapt from the car and scurried into the grove as the two fighters looped overhead and came in for a final pass that quartered the car. Repeated low altitude passes failed to find his hiding place behind a fallen, charred slo tree. By dusk, they had gone and no ground troops were sent to find him. He was exhausted from three days of immersion in surface gravity with the only respite being the now useless car. He awoke from an unplanned sleep.

As twilight grew in deep violet and orange, the deep reds of the star field above glowed through the darkening atmosphere. For comfort, as he walked, he listed the names of stars he had learned long ago. The gas cloud nebula perpetually illuminating night side provided enough light to move around in but not enough to make out detail. Its concentration of red light gave faint impression of the warmth delivered by Alal, but its pale glow was cold. He was cold and had just tripped into another irrigation canal. If he hadn't been stargazing, he would not be wet as well as cold and tired. A few taps on his wrist pad and he noted that crescent Erra would not rise for hours. He really should sleep again.

LonnDonn pulled down an armload of grain stalks and made a soft mat on the cultivated soil. He gathered several more and laid them over his body to preserve body heat for the night and settled in for another uncomfortable night. He thought back to his encounter with the surviving soldier from the air car and how nearly he'd been shot—of the abandoned warehouse and its mysterious connection to an unmapped underground. And he thought of his crops. HIS crops! The damned air cars were scorching crops to deprive the rebels of foodstuff. The harvest had been intended to feed the orbital cities and even provide export quantities to supplement the more limited agricultural production on his home world. Without a supply of fresh selli fruit nectar, there would be shortages when this year's crèche graduates needed to make the change. By the Guiding Lights! What a stupid way to win a war!

The rebels could harvest for their own needs under cover of darkness and disappear down into their hidey-holes. Was this war winnable? How many rebels were there? For how long had they been planning? Since the insurrection had spread to the Verparksransaran District, all sign of the native population had disappeared, presumably down that hole in the warehouse and others like it. His overworked brain succumbed to exhaustion, and his eyes finally closed to sounds of a distant skirmish.

He awoke to a glow on the horizon. The overhead canopy's rose veil had shifted a quarter turn. He rose to an elbow, disoriented. That was not East? Erra's crescent shone above, but its bow did not point toward the light on the horizon. New Light would not be for hours. The glow was steady and appeared to be an area of lighting around a farm compound. Ahh! The power grid is restored, at least temporarily. His mind was now too busy for sleep. What development would permit such a display of energy? Had the area been secured by Erran forces or were the rebels being reckless in restoration of area lights?

He realized that he would not sleep anymore this night and decided that the best approach to the compound would be in the dark. He rose, stretched sore muscles, felt the firm pull of the planet's iron core, and stretched again. Whoever won, he wanted to stay on Dzura. This was where all the ancients of history, Chupal, Dianon, Teeya Adrandonn, and the rest, had grown and prospered and become aware of their universe. Where they had drawn back the curtain of dogma and revealed the greater mysteries of scientific discovery and, over the millennia, had taken to the stars. Was it right to become two peoples? To be either spacer or grounder? Shouldn't both prosper without the prosperity of one being at the expense of the other? He shook his head to clear it of treasonous thoughts and stepped out onto a rough farm track and headed toward the lights on the horizon.

When a column of armed vehicles passed down the track, he left the roadway since, on foot, he would be mistaken for a rebel. He continued his lone march, but when he heard noises ahead, he moved back into the tall standing crops. Moving slowly, he realized he was entering a field occupied by rebels in hiding. Still at some distance from the lights, LonnDonn felt a drumming in his chest. He recognized the almost forgotten funereal meld experienced when a comrade was memorialized by his peers or when a head of state's funeral was orchestrated for maximum effect with broadcast vids and subliminal thrumming in a soundtrack. This was primal. Then the thrumming started.

Overcome, he fell to his knees, grasping his chest. His senses were overwhelmed. The ache in his chest grew with the rhythmic hum of his grieving enemies.

Enemies? he wondered. These huddled refugees? He lowered himself to his haunches. These refugees are just like me! What separates us? History? A cruel war that's now over twenty-five generations in the past. The need for resources that we should, in truth, all share? He relaxed back on his haunches. Did it take a space-bound Erran with something besides jealousy for the home planet to appreciate the planet for more than its resources? It's our home!

The thrumming in his chest subsided as the huddled refugees nearby shared a psi-bond grief release. Suddenly, he was alone again. Not a part of the thrumming group. And then, much too close, he felt the mental search pattern first, then the gun barrel in his back.

~ ~ ~

In the early glow of daybreak, Shaand gently shook Brad awake. "New Light!"

"Yes, good morning to you too." He sat up, rubbing his eyes in bright daylight. Above, Erra shone as a pink crescent. The red disk of Alal was rising just above the husks of the field crop, not even clear of the distant mountain range. Its rays shone unnaturally golden after passing through smoking remains of formerly prime croplands. Looking past the smoky foreground, Brad thought the ragged peaks in the distance were unusual in their isolation. Scanning the dark horizon to the west, he saw another remote stand of mountains, and he began to wonder. He had spent his college years in Arizona and had the experience of mountains in continuous ranges, not isolated clumps. He pointed to the cluster of mountains nearest the rising sun Alal. "Shaand, what do you call those large lumps of, uhm, soil? Land?" He wished he had Connie's better facility with concepts in Dzuran.

Shaand shaded his eyes against the brightening disk. "Tey, kee-rossh."

Brad tried it out. "Keerosh."

"In war," Shaand said, "Errans drop big rocks on Dzura, make kee-rossh."

Brad was stunned; those were the crater walls left behind by the Erran bombardment. He tried to imagine what it looked like or felt like to have been here in the final weeks of that war when the planet's shell rang like a bell with each strike, seismic waves spreading destruction far beyond the blast of the impact. Those nearest the impact might have been lucky to have died instantly. He put a hand on Shaand's shoulder as they both looked at the distant mountains. He said, "Keerosh, keerosh." And he knew the onomatopoeic root of the word. To anyone removed enough from the destruction it must have been one terrific crash.

Shaand put his own hand on Brad's and softly said, "Teeya City was tere, Old Teeya City. Gone." He turned to look at Brad. "I come wit news." He pointed almost straight up. The reflections off the side of the orbiting city high above could not be mistaken for a natural heavenly body.

Connie walked up to them and followed the pointed finger. "News? Is it good news? Do we need to move again?"

"Yes, Ka-nee. Need move. Then tell of Jai. Jai in New Teeya City." Shaand looked again toward the dark irregular shape, side-lit by the morning sun. "Tat," and the disgust was evident in his delivery, "Errans call Teeya City. It over site old Dzura capital, Teeya. We tink bad joke." He pulled Brad aside and said in low tones, "Jai in new Teeya, not work. Tey tink bad ship. Soon tey trow away."

Connie overheard and rejoined Brad. They both became excited, hoping they'd understood Shaand's English. Brad said, "Jai is going to be discarded? Thrown away?"

"Yes, Jai not turn on, not link wit Erran ship. Not tell Hooman secrets. Not do anytink."

Connie asked, "How do you know this?"

Shaand turned to her, beaming a forehead smile and what passed for a humanoid grin. "Su-pi! I tink Jai talk to Dzuran Su-pi ... Brad, Connie.

A rustling in the fields nearby grew to the sounds of a struggle and a panicked voice was muffled. Shouts, running feet, and more excitement growing at the locus of the original noise caused Shaand, Brad, and Connie to squat back down into the cover of the field crops. The center of the disturbance moved en masse toward the temporary field headquarters of the evacuated troops. They all stood again, tracking the noise.

Shaand said, "Crant. Not worry, crant made go way."

They both asked, "What is crant?"

"Crant is hunter-killer, move low, fast. Can eat not careful Elioi." He looked up over their crop cover toward the noise then aside to Connie. "Not worry, our soldier chase crant way to Erran camp." He was smiling hugely.

Brad glanced over at the snow-capped mountain range. Shielding his eyes from the rising sun, he wondered what damage and loss would occur if an impact like that hit near the San Andreas Fault line or what a deepwater impact in the Gulf of Mexico would do to all of the communities surrounding the gulf. Looking at the Keerosh Mountains, he had a much better understanding of the losses and the enmity between the Errans and Dzurans that would never be resolved. It was much deeper than the inanimate Jai could have explained to them.

~ ~ ~

On the other side of their encampment, LonnDonn awoke with a throbbing headache and the uncomfortable awareness that his arms were bound beneath him. As the figures above came into focus, he saw the lower torsos of four Dzuran jump-suited soldiers. He psi'd a short welcome that he hoped was still universal. It wasn't. One of the soldiers kicked him. LonnDonn hesitated. Then realizing that he had not bothered to concoct a cover, he said. "I am Gre-LonnDonn, High Land Commissioner for this district."

His inquisitor growled at him, gave him a full click of disgust, and kicked his legs. "Do not think I am a fool, Erran. We have seen you walk on your legs like a Dzuran. The only Errans we've seen walking are military elite troops. So, again, Erran. Who are you?"

LonnDonn struggled uselessly against his restraints and sighed. "May I sit up?" Two of the soldiers roughly grabbed at his arms and set him upright. "Light's shine upon you!" He stretched his arms knowing that he could not break his bonds, but just trying to revive circulation. A hand clamped firmly on one shoulder holding him down. The officer instructed his soldiers to stand the prisoner up and they faced off. LonnDonn was struck by the face across from him. They were from the same caste, only separated by many generations. Life in space had begun to morph the limbs of the permanently space-bound, but that, he realized, may have only been a physiological result of low gravity. He was staring at one of the leading class of this planet. A bloodline that had not been able to get off planet. A bloodline that had survived.

"Again, who are you?"

LonnDonn stood at attention. He'd have saluted in what he knew were the old ways—right arm raised in front, palm down, but he was confined. "I am Gre-LonnDonn. I have been working for two years to develop my body, first on Erra, then in the spin chambers on Teeya City, and now..." Abruptly he was slapped, hard. His head rung from his earlier beating, this current assault, and his eyes stung. "May I ask, sir, who are you?"

"I am DjuKlat Saa, Commander of this humble band of soldiers. Why is it that you, who claim to be Erran, stand erect before me?"

"I am High Land Commissioner. I, I felt, to fully see my crops as they grow, I need to see them, feel their buds and leaves, smell the soil. I could not do that in an air car." He couldn't think of what else to say and so repeated, "I have trained for years, first on Erra, then in the spin chambers on Teeya City."

The officer roughly grabbed LonnDonn and turned him to face east. Alal was now half its full height in the sky and the rocky, snow-capped ridge in the distance shone brightly in full morning light. DjuKlat Saa shouted at him in barely controlled contempt. "THAT! Was Teeya City! Over four million died in our Teeya City while your ancestors rained death on them creating that Kee-rosh." Again, a hard slap to the head.

LonnDonn slowly tried again, feeling the animosity brewed by his own ancestors' misguided aggression. "I am LonnDonn, Gre for this district. I wanted to be able to walk the fields, talk to supervisors, to smell the soil after rain, to know these lands. I have argued for years that at least we agricultural managers must learn by walking the fields."

LonnDonn stood rigid, attempting to not react as DjuKlat Saa scoffed "How many of the Gre, like you, walk upon our land, sniff the soil? I have never seen a Gre step out of his car." The commander sent a burst of psi, implying disgust with strong overtones of hatred that flooded LonnDonn's sensory system. The former Gre willed himself not to flinch as the commander held his head in both palms and hissed with hatred. "Which of the killer bands from your Teeya City in the sky are you from?"

"DjuKlat Saa, I understand your hatred." He gave a short courtesy bow. "I have seen better, closer than any Erran, what has happened to this world." He swallowed hard, his forehead tensed to a fine shine, revealing his terror. "I was walking the fields when the battles broke out. My car was destroyed by your forces. I was overtaken by the thrumming last night." He paused anticipating another blow as the commander's muscled arm rose. "I was captured by an Erran ground team who thought I was Dzuran."

"How? How could you be mistaken for a Dzuran? That is a cli-mat work suit. You are clearly not cli-mat."

"This jumpsuit." He glanced down at the grey work overalls that were common to all workers, staff, and administration for non-military personnel. Only colored piping on cuffs and collars distinguished function or rank. "When my car was attacked, cooling oils sprayed my jacket and pants, they began to dissolve and my skin burned. I went to a Jaan-dk processing center. I cleaned off the oils and found clothing in one of the food processing plants."

The DjuKlat asked, "Why are you here? Among us?"

"The lights, last night. After the attack last night, patrols came to the site of the bombing and I thought to get another ground car. I needed to try to get some assistance with the crops. As you see, these are ready for harvest and will spoil soon."

DjuKlat Saa smiled inwardly. The short-sighted Erran warlords in their orbiting cities had miscalculated or not calculated. They had in their haste to destroy and kill, destroyed any chance of provisioning the massive orbiting city ships and, at least in this sector, removed all hope of exports.

LonnDonn felt the psi channels that DjuKlat Saa had purposefully left open. He understood immediately that the Erran cause was lost. DjuKlat Saa was right. The timing of the insurrection may have been spontaneous, driven by events in the southern hemisphere. But the military over-reaction by the Erran masters had assured that the agricultural heartland of the southern hemisphere would be virtually lost to them.

DjuKlat Saa looked at his prisoner, appraising him for visible signs of duplicity and scanned his psi for telltales. *Open your mind to me.* He took the prisoner's head in his hands again and forced him to lean forward. The DjuKlat Saa closed his eyes and focused intently on what had been said, what had been disclosed through psi and looked for a personal connection that individual Elioi so seldom permitted each other, complete servile acceptance of another's probing mind. Soldiers surrounding the two shuffled nervously. This was seldom done and almost never in public. It was a ritual usually confirmed on officers who melded into a command team. This was just short of a reportable offense because it could only be a two-way blending of thoughts, feelings, fears, and most of all, allegiance.

In time, DjuKlat Saa released the prisoner's head. Gre-LonnDonn seemed to be genuine, at least in his most recent account of his being here and in Dzuran worker's garb. "I will back check everything you've told me. Everything!" He turned to an aide. "Remove his bindings. LonnDonn is no longer a Gre in the Erran administration, but he is not yet one of us."

He gave further directions to see that the prisoner got medical attention for his chemical burns and that he be detailed with the off-worlder prisoners. With no further attention to the prisoner, he wheeled, stepped into an air car and left.

~ ~ ~

Near the Keerosh Mountains
3608.365 Erran Calendar

Old Teeya City, the original, had been home to over four million Dzurans, their pets, and beasts. As an agricultural processing city, it had created wealth and abundance for most of its inhabitants. It was a hub for processing the wealth of the surrounding gentle plains. That wealth had produced glittering towers for residents, great machines for harvest processing, centers for training, and crèche halls where the young were conceived and brought to the crest of adulthood. At the crest ceremonies in the grand arena, thousands would gather under a single spun roof to watch the spectacle as the immatures made their way up the aisle toward their moment of decision.

To the right, males ascended toward multiple staircases to various career platforms and, either by choice or cajoling from crèche-mates, chose military, administrative, or other masculine callings. To the left, would-be females took their first sips of the selli fruit nectars that would begin their physiological transformation. It would be at least two years before the transformations were complete, and the continuing education allowed diversification into pure research, applied engineering, birthing, childcare, medicine, the animal arts, and habitat monitoring.

All that changed when a mountain-sized boulder hit three miles offshore in the inland sea. The blast of expanding steam and its following wall of rock and molten crust flattened the towers, spires, monuments, and terminals, erased the ground-level thoroughfares, and scorched any pourstone or metal structures that remained. The dying force of that terrible energy wave left a cooling wall of red hot rock, the Keerosh Mountains. This new barrier between the equatorial sea and the Verparksransaran plain had long ago taken on its mantle of ice. A few centuries of erosion and sedimentation from this mountain-sized crater wall had obscured all other remains of the city. At the center of that crater, a rebound uplift formed a jagged peak that now stood vigil over the four million dead. At the same distance on the east side of the Keerosh range, a seemingly thin filament of woven pialla and carbon fibers rose above the atmosphere. This year, there were very few cargo hoppers moving up to the near-space platform suspended so far above.

At the northern foot of the Keerosh Mountains, seventeen Dzuran soldiers, Shaand, two humans, and an Erran prisoner moved cautiously through the high dry stand of stalk fruit brush. They made slow but steady progress toward Old Chookya Station, one of the last intact portals into the ancient underground network that had fed the ruined city. Subterfuge and cunning several generations prior had led to the construction of a processing plant and warehouse over the site of one of the transit system's old terminals. The overhead patrols had ceased earlier near mid-day so the buzzing drone of air cars at dusk was an unwelcome return to heightened tension. As the buzzing grew nearer, they again spread into small clumps in the tall brush.

Connie Chappell felt that her life had taken one of the oddest turns a life could possibly take. Weird had reached just about the highest level before moving into surreal and she didn't want to consider surreal. She laid back on a soft mat of groundcover that grew between rows of fruit crop. The mat was incomparable to any fungi or grass or combination she could conjure. Its dark brown color would indicate dead vegetation on Earth. Here, it thrived in the red-tinged light of Alal. How strange to lay back on a living, dark brown carpet that had the feel of roughened felt and to stare through blue-veined red leaves at a lavender sky. She knew that when night fell, the lavender would fade to purple, go transparent and thin to allow in the soft glowing bands of the nebula.

The nebula's Dzuran name was more of a concept that seemed to translate into The Light—a proper name, elevated to a religious tone. The Light! She acknowledged that it was incredible, beautiful. Awesome, in fact. If admission could be charged, Earth-bound tourists would spend fortunes to stand on a parapet somewhere and gawk at the red and orange display, then turn to catch splatters of pink on grey, smoky wisps of a super nova's death throes. Many of the stars were brilliant. Were they so close that their disks were visible? Maybe that was an illusion of passing through the millions of miles of dust in the cloud. She wondered if it was visible from Earth, if from that direction, it had a name. She thought of a few: the Crab, the Horseshoe, the Cat's Eye. Noise in the undergrowth brought her back from her reverie.

The refugees from the bombed-out bunker complex had broken up into smaller groups of thirty or so to make less worthy targets of aerial attack. Each group made its independent trek through the long rows of planted fruit grasses. It would have been an easy trip if their goal had been parallel with the rows, but it was not. Their locals, as she and Brad were calling the Dzurans, took turns hacking a narrow trail through the tufted grasses for a single-file passage. When the sun had hit zenith, a large circle had been cut in the vegetation to allow all to sit and rest. Although she never had any military experience, she thought this was not good practice because the circle in the long expanse of tufted grasses would be easy to spot from the air. She thought they would have tried harder for stealth as her group was escorting two 'off-worlders' and a high-ranking enemy captured the night before.

The prisoner, Shaand said, was an Erran. Odd, he did not look discernibly different from the Dzurans guarding him. He regarded Brad and Connie with unbridled curiosity.

Something crawling in the groundcover moved against Connie's back and she shot up. She turned on her knees to see what it was but found nothing. Looking around, there were smiles on the foreheads of the guards that had noticed. Whatever the creepy crawly had been, it must not be dangerous. Sitting now and glancing around, she saw the prisoner looking at her. She felt a tug at the back of her brain. He was trying to have a psi conversation with her!

She stood and found Shaand talking with the commander, DjuKlat Saa. Waiting for their conversation to end, she asked, "Shaand, do you think Erran prisoner knows where Jai is?"

Shaand eyed the prisoner thoughtfully. "Gre-LonnDonn." He corrected himself, "LonnDonn, stand!" The prisoner tried to flex cramped legs to get vertical and his two watch guards helped him to his feet. One of the guards plucked fruit from a nearby stalk and casually took a bite. Held elbow and elbow between the guards, the former Land Commissioner for Verpaksransaran District was hobbled closer to the small band with the red haired off-worlder. Brad, waking from a short noon-time catnap stood as well and moved to join them.

Shaand said, "LonnDonn, did you have any knowledge of these off-worlders? Is it common knowledge in the Erran cities that off-worlders are here in the Alal system?"

LonnDonn considered. What do these groundlings know?

He said, eyeing Shaand carefully, "I have been an administrator in the Erran rule of your planet. I understand that I am under your guard. Who are you, with all respects and all regard for your Lights?" He bowed his head slightly, in deference. "I ask only to know." This was as courteous and formal as he knew how to express his question.

Shaand was startled. "You ask who am I?" He took a breath, tamping down his anger with difficulty. "I am Ss-Shaand, Senior Dzuran Administrator under YOUR rule of MY planet, your district, in fact. You say you are the land administrator for Verparksransaran. Then you should know me, I am—was—under your chain of command. One of my sections at Port Jreya was late in deliveries, and you had ME jailed." Shaand's voice had been rising and anyone still enjoying the noon break was on their feet and closing a circle to listen.

"I, I am sorry," LonnDonn started. "There are protocols handed down by the imbeciles in Tee—" He almost said Teeya City. He stole a nervous glance at DjuKlat Saa and continued, "The leadership demands protocols for dealing with the growing insurrection. Delays are seen as sabotage. It frustrates me to carry out orders that only increase dysfunction; I had nothing to do with

166

your arrest." He bowed his head and held both hands out, behind him since they were bound, palms open in supplication. "You already have my surrender. I offer you my service." He amplified this with a psi message of supplication.

Connie whispered her interpretation of what was happening into Brad's ear. "I think the Erran is switching sides."

He whispered back, "Ask Shaand if LonnDonn knows anything about Jai."

Whispering back to Brad, she said, "I did, just a sec." She turned to Shaand. *Shaand!* Connie started with a psi-blink, an attention-getting exclamation point that she had recently learned. "This prisoner is not hostile. Does he know about our spacecraft?"

Shaand's composure was returning to normal. With a side glance at his two off-world companions, he asked the former Gre, "Prisoner? Did you have any knowledge of these off-worlders? Is it common knowledge?"

Without pause this time, LonnDonn replied, "Yes, most of the higher ranking officers know of the off-worlders and their useless antique spacecraft." Shaand translated this for the Hoomans.

Brad asked, "Why does he say useless? Have they destroyed it?" Concern for the only possible ride home wavered in his voice.

"Why do you say 'useless'? Has the ship been destroyed?"

LonnDonn answered with a smooth forehead and straight stare back into Shaand's eyes, a show of trust and respect. "I have not been in formal briefings; I am agricultural administrator. This was a military matter." He waited a breath. "I have heard from others, the off-worlders' ship is old Dzuran manufacture. I don't know how off-worlders found or even could fly an old Dzuran ship. Erran technology has moved centuries beyond that. Still, our engineers cannot start or breach the ship. It is soon to be jettisoned to make room for new fighters in the ship bays. That is all I know."

Again, Shaand translated the commentary as simply as he could. Brad asked, "Does he have any idea of when it might be jettisoned?"

The answer that came back stunned everyone. LonnDonn spoke freely to a captive audience. The antique two-seater was not a priority. It was, at most, a distraction for the maintenance crews in the hangar that were already overburdened, repairing damage from ground actions. More importantly, a Precursor object had been found in the star system where the spacecraft had come from. It had caused an uproar among the priesthood and old philosophical arguments had risen about the dawn of creation and the start of life on Dzura. But the Precursor Stone had departed and the Pelmas and priests were arguing about what it meant.

The off-worlders, too, had been more important than the little spaceship. They were the first apparently intelligent life from another star. Hastily removed into quarantine among Dzuran prisoners, they had been scheduled to be returned to the orbital Teeya City just as the prison break took place. Specially trained Erran ground teams were now searching for the off-worlders.

Brad squeezed Connie's hand in reassurance as the news kept getting worse. Shaand, DjuKlat Saa, and LonnDonn left the group to talk privately. The two humans sat back down, cross-legged, kneecap to kneecap.

"So they can't get Jai to start?" Brad always found himself a little behind on communications.

"Yeah, they haven't been able to get him to do anything."

"If they fried his circuits when we had hailing frequencies open, they might have somehow overloaded his circuits. It's been a long time. Imagine an encounter between an iron-age artillery battalion and a Sherman tank. No contest!"

"I don't know, they might be able to jump faster, farther, but if they haven't been in conflict, why would they have better weapons? Except for their personal weaponry for keeping down the locals, the Errans haven't had to advance military technology."

Brad mulled this over. "You could be right, but Jai is still old, battered, and as far as we know, he's about to be dumped overboard."

"That's our ride home, Brad." She grabbed at her gut as a panic wave doubled her over.

Despite the nearness of too many locals, Brad leaned over and put his arms around her. "Sweetie, no promises can make this better. Just," he searched for anything that might comfort her. "Just know we're in this together. We'll be okay, somehow. I just know it. Remember that feeling I had that he might be playing possum?"

"How can you possibly know it?" Her voice quavered, full of emotion.

He held her quietly for a moment then heard sniffles in the dark. "When I first left home, I tried to paddle from the Wakulla River bridge to Apalachicola." He remembered the terrible night, almost nine years earlier. "I worked all night, blistered my hands, nearly ruined them. By morning, I hadn't gotten any further than Wakulla Beach. When I got near the beach, a head wind was picking up. I thought I'd be blown clear back to the lighthouse. But Sunny was out crabbing and picked me up. He took me in, got me coffee, comfort, and counsel. I'll never, ever be able to repay him for the help that night or later. The thing is, I trusted my friends and your family, and I got through the worst experience of my life."

"Worse than this?"

The sniffling stopped. "Well, at the time it was pretty damned awful, but you all helped me, and look what we accomplished. We proved to the whole world that there were others out there!" He waited for a response. "You mean you're not having fun? Not taking notes for that first novel?"

Despite herself, she chuckled and picked nervously at a shred of the ubiquitous ground carpet. "Bradley, I don't know what to think! Our little joy ride was probably the stupidest thing I've ever done." Tears began to well up. "We've been gone for who knows how long and who knows where. If Jai wasn't right about no time losses during the jump, everyone we know might be dead and gone by now." She sniffed. "Mom, Dad, and your Moms! They might all be history. Who knows if we'd ever even get a chance to go home if Jai is destroyed?"

Brad sighed, in sympathy and confusion. "Con? I'm sorry I got you into this. We've been a team, together on so much of the last eight, nine years... I figured you should join me."

"I'd have been pissed if you left me behind." She tossed the tiny brown shred into the air where it was snatched by one of the few things that flew in Dzuran air, a small thing that looked like a cross between a butterfly and a hummingbird. It buzzed off, spitting the shred out.

They both followed its erratic flight to the fruiting bud of one of the nearby selli trees. Brad continued, "And, damn! I'm as uncertain about our immediate future as you are. I didn't know for a long time if I should totally trust Shaand. I think we can now, but it's pretty much been day-by-day for me too." He cupped her clasped hands in his. "This might not help, but if I have to spend the rest of my life on an alien world, I'd be happiest if I could spend it with you. And that's the worst-case scenario."

"If we aren't blown to bits tomorrow morning."

"Well, yeah, short of that. That's kind of the worst-case scenario." He smiled at her resilience. "Look, I hate to get too simple but these guys seem to be taking care of us. Those guys?" He pointed up at the lavender sky. "We have no idea. They're on the verge of a Pyrrhic victory. If they win this war using their steamroller methods, they're going to be in a serious hurt when the onboard food storage is depleted. They'll be desperate to get down here. They can't walk, or just barely, and the local workforce is in revolt. As I understand it, if these crops don't get processed, they rot on the stalk and that's it till next year. I think our best chances, either way, are to keep on with the locals and do anything we can to help frustrate the spacers."

"Not sure that we have any choice in the matter," Connie responded glumly.

"I really don't think they have the option of asteroid bombs again. If they induce another long winter on this planet, they won't be able to support the population that's grown under the current system. What would they do, cut off one of the orbiting cities and say good luck, Charlie? They're going to need hand-to-hand methods to clean out the warrens under the surface, and I can do hand-to-hand." He grabbed one of the ripe pods off a stalk and peeled it like he'd seen the guards do. Split open, the yellowish fruit seemed to have the texture of peaches, but the aroma of dung. He wrinkled his nose and tossed it on the ground.

Connie said, under her breath, "Well, they know where Earth is."

"Right."

"And, Brad, what's a Precursor Stone?"

~ ~ ~

3608.367 Erran Calendar

Three day's travel in the brushy crop known as, or at least translated as, stalk fruit had tired everyone. There was little shelter and their progress was slow unless all movement was along the rows. Lateral shifts were made very carefully to avoid leaving a trail of broken stalks visible from the air. Shaand had called a food and water break to wait for dusk. Brad pulled Connie close as they huddled at the base of the stalks. Even here, several million miles from home, hiding from death delivered by indiscriminate killers, he thought she was beautiful. Her red hair took on a living glow in the rosy light from Alal. Her figure was terrific, even in Dzuran field hand dungarees. He felt an odd mixture of pride in being her man and guilt for bringing her here, but he never felt as bad as he had when they'd been separated.

As they passed recent battle scenes, he had seen enough destruction to know that the Errans gave no quarter to their Dzuran slave class. Despite breeding, training, or ability, all were considered less than blanks by the orbiting overlords. If he and Connie were accidentally blown to bits in the effort to put down the rebellion, the Errans probably would not care.

There had been recent near passes by aerial patrols. Most had pursued false trails purposely set in the stalk grasses. Danger had been ever-present that day. Still, holding her face in her hands, he blew her a kiss.

"You, sir, are hopeless."

"I know, I think it's the dimples. I can't help it."

"Shh, I think they're getting closer."

Brad raised to an elbow, aiming an ear toward the sound. A new sound, reminding him of someone crumbling dry leaves, joined the buzzing from the air cars. That's familiar. What the—? Suddenly he knew. He lifted quickly to a low crouch and then, pulling some stalks together for full cover, he stood to see just over the tops of the tufted stalk fruit tops. Smoke, and below it the orange glow of fire. Standing, he could clearly hear the rumbling distant roar of a blazing fire.

"Fire!" he hissed at Connie. "Get up, but stay low. Be ready to run." He stepped through a few rows of thick brush and found Shaand, still distinguishable to Brad only by the black cuffs on his grey overalls. Shaand was standing in a crouch looking toward the rising column of smoke. "Shaand! Fire!"

"Yes, Braad, all leave now." He materialized a small signal fife from a side-leg pocket and blew it softly. The fife's rising, hesitant tones imitated some of the night animal noises heard in the trees lining the neatly arranged crops. An immediate rustling in the brush nearby indicated that it had been heard. He made a few quick hand signs and pointed toward a line of taller brush. In small groups, again in single file, the band made for a tree line opposite the approaching brushfire. Running at a crouch, the individual groups made visible disturbances in the planted rows. Over the noise of the group's crashing through the brush, Brad could hear the ominous buzz of an Erran air car. The cars themselves weren't armed but they could be opened to atmosphere and troops onboard could fire hand and shoulder weapons over the gunnels.

A green flash and a yell of pain indicated one of their party had been hit. More green flashes went unanswered. One of the buzzing air cars approached the head of their column, took several hits from ground fire, and began smoking. Abruptly, its buzzing drive motor stopped and it fell, capsizing just before it hit the ground. Two more closed in and were hit as soldiers rose from the cover of the brush and sent projectile ammunition and high energy beams into their drive ports.

Lying on the ground, Connie listened to the sound of battle around her and the increasing treble crackling of the approaching flames. Looking beyond Brad's head, which she held in tight embrace, she focused on some movement near the roots of the next row of stalk fruit. Two small animals, covered in grey-to-white scales were apparently dancing in complete disregard of the mayhem going on at a larger scale. They were not arm-in-arm, but certainly there seemed to be some ritual to the bob and weave. Eventually, one got the upper hand and forced the other to its back. She thought, what a surreal time and place to get a lesson in local biology. She briefly wondered if she'd get a clue as to how the sexually secretive local population did it. That thought line was brief as the one on top took the head of the other in its mouth and wrestled it off. The loser twitched a little and lay still. The winner, still laying on top, extended its jaws to pass a head the size of its own down its throat. The winner then mounted the loser, belly to belly, and exacted the last offering its mate had. While it's lower half contorted in its effort to extract the needed genetic material, the upper half continued to consume its partner.

The surrealism of the miniature tableau was short-lived. Fire from two more air cars began to target troopers on the ground, squeals and shouts of pain joined the pop-pop-pop of projectile weapons, and the zzz-zzzt of energy guns surrounded them. Brad held Connie close as sounds of battle and motion around them stopped, making the sounds of the approaching fire more ominous.

"I'm certain," he said quietly, "they can't have all been killed." The quiet was broken by the ominous buzzing of an approaching air car's drive. They were soon shadowed by one hovering almost immediately over their position. Connie gripped Brad so tightly he had trouble breathing. Sheltering her head in his arms, he looked up at the craft. Wheel wells with retracted flex metal wheels, intake ports, and an exhaust at what would be near ground level if it was in surface mode. The layout seemed very familiar somehow, not as exotic as he might have expected. Once again, he reasoned, engineering is engineering, and some answers to universal problems should look familiar, or at least understandable.

From behind, the crackle and pop of burning crops grew ever closer. Roiling grey-black clouds, curled and flecked in yellow, rose to darken the setting sun. Even with a light evening breeze deflecting the fastest spread of flames away from them, the popping of stalks in the nearing heat became an irresistible force for motion.

Brad loosened Connie's grip and rose to a crouch. Small arms fire continued to come from the open-topped vehicle targeting his companions. Neither he nor Connie had been trusted with a weapon, but he had an idea. He broke the stem of a stalk fruit plant off at the base. In a few steps, he was under the car's air intake. With a simple jump and thrust, he shoved the fluffy fronds into the intake. As expected, the intake fan pulled the rest of the stalk into the opening. A grinding whine rose from the innards of the craft and white smoke began to pour from the exhaust. Grinning, he stooped to grab a few more stalks. In a moment, the second batch of stalks joined the first with the desired effect.

White exhaust smoke turned to black, and the whining complaint of the air car's drive deepened to a rumble. The car began to waiver. Firing from the car had stopped, replaced by excited, unintelligible yells from its crew. Taking Connie's hand, Brad moved them toward the rear of the car and ran. The car slid and tilted. It landed on its side, spilling crew and its armed troops to the ground. Unable to stand against the pull of the planet and outside the artificial field of their air car, the Errans were easy targets. When the field effect generator died, so did any hope that they could lift, let alone aim their shoulder weapons. The surviving Dzuran troopers closed in and quickly dispatched all but the ranking ensign. Three more air cars began to move in on the group, but kept their distance and, as the sun angle sharpened, moved off to the safety of their temporary surface enclave.

Shaand's remaining healthy troops helped up the wounded, gathered in the two humans and LonnDonn, and moved on toward the shelter of a bomb-damaged agricultural processing building. LonnDonn recognized it as an agricultural packing center near the approaches to Old Chookya. It had other significance for their team too, as it was a portal into the underground. The spreading fires behind gave them all the urging they needed to reach the safety of the underground.

Chapter 16

"Speak the language of high intelligence, and thus you speak the language of God."
Mehmt Murat ildan

Teeya City, Maintenance Hangar
3608.365 Erran Calendar

Jai waited with the innate patience of a machine. He had waited four centuries to be released from a prison of limestone on an alien planet. The latest internment in the hangar bay on Teeya City was a brief stopover by comparison. He had not wasted either stay. On Earth, he had learned a new language, a different, though incomplete interpretation of physics, and how to analyze his own operational needs as a thirst for materials rather than simply as lower levels on his scalar readouts. He was the first machine to understand the concept of need and grasp how to satisfy it. In the past, his pilot or second officer might have read those scalar reports to know that hydrogen, for example, was low and fly to a refueling bay or the thin reaches of a hydrogen gas planet.

As a fully self-cognizant A-I command and control system he was designed to learn how to learn. He'd learned from his first pilot Ka-Litan that he could replenish hydrogen deficiencies in the outer fringes of most gas planets or in the liquid bath of a water ocean. He had synthesized hydrogen from groundwater to maintain his fuel cells on Earth. He'd learned from his second pilot Braad that he could find salts for his nuclear power plant's cooling system in any salty ocean. He was a most versatile machine, built in the final days of the flowering Dzuran civilization.

His Dzuran builders had created beautiful liners to take tourists to exotic corners of the nebula. Pilgrims to The Light paid half a year's wage to experience the nebular display from the vantage of frozen moons, or to find new sights beyond the gas cloud where entire fields of galaxies opened up to view. Those liners had required sophisticated jump drives to clear interstellar space by cheating the fourth and fifth dimensions and looping the sixth. With his own jump drive, very much smaller and not quite as elaborate, his passengers did feel slight disorientation and minor nausea, a huge improvement over the earlier Erran-designed equipment. Its installation on board allowed for his kind, Skeeter class fighters, to jump independently of the carriers, destroyers, and city ships built for the diaspora—a tactical advantage for a fleet on the go.

He had high-efficiency shields that, when coupled with two more of his kind in triple-fighter formation, could deflect most non-explosive projectile arms. His most effective stealth system was cloaking, stolen from the Errans in the early days of the war. Cloaking was also his newest system, but it was out of date by current standards. His crown jewel of design, though, was the malleable poly-crystalline hull metal. Flexible on command, it could form cockpit access steps, extend airfoils, and unless fried by high energy laser fire, even self-heal minor wounds. The teal-grey metal antennae lost in his crash landing on Earth had led to his ultimate discovery and rescue by Brad Hitchens.

Self-preservation loops had been built into his programming. With the unanticipated adversity of confinement, this attribute developed in his self-awareness a first for machines in this part of the galaxy: curiosity and guile. He had waited, circuits nulled on purpose, while clumsy Erran mechanics swarmed over his skin, played with his data ports, and tried to connect power and data cables. They had somehow managed to make a patch cable to match his I/O ports, but he had simply shut down the connections to that port.

He did use them to his advantage. When he sensed no psi-capable mechanics nearby, he used the patch to download petabytes of information about this new Teeya City. These were Errans, sworn enemy of his creators and his pilot. He had killed many of them in the multi-system chase across the galactic fourth arm and might have been destroyed centuries ago if Ka-Litan had not missed a key input sequence and jumped to the wrong planet.

Jai had sbsorbed psi communication around the hangar bay and occasionally, when there was an emotional outburst elsewhere in the city ship, he got glimpses of life aboard the vast orbiting city they called Teeya. Confused by this at first, he verified that there had been a huge metropolis of that name on the old maps of Dzura. It had no longer existed when he was launched; more reason not to trust the coaxing and pleading of the Erran mechanics. He listened to scuttlebutt in the city's hangar bay as workers discussed the off-worlders who came in "this old can." Being a non-emotional sentient entity, he could not take offense. He was actually uncertain about the line of discussion until the maintenance crew had mentioned "some place called Ert."

Jai had remapped his original psi crew bond from his original crew, pilot Ka-Litan and weapons specialist Jen-Mitran, to the Hoomans, Braad and Ka-nee. His loyalties to his new crew insisted that he carefully monitor any discussion of off-worlders. He was eventually rewarded with information that they had been imprisoned west of Old Teeya City. Later, when the hangar bay boss was discussing space for new Erran ground effect vehicles, Jai had learned that the off-worlders might not be coming back to Teeya City because of a prison break. Only a few references in storage from the World Book Encyclopedia file saved this from being a meaningless comment. So much of what biologicals said was meaningless.

Still, he waited for reunion with his bond crew while his enemy's mechanics tried new strategies to make contact. He waited as the hangar bay filled with new fighters brought in to fill Teeya's transient bays almost to capacity. Ultimately, parking bay hull clamps were loosed and an ungainly ship hoist moved him toward a launch door. Good that this took a while because he barely had time to boot flight ops circuitry before he was given a retrograde push. Being let loose with planetary back spin had been designed to lower his orbital velocity so he would slowly drop into the atmosphere and burn. The fall was gentle at first, but every planetary physicist, even artificially intelligent ones, know that gravity is cruel and persistent. Jai had already lost ninety percent of his original orbital altitude when he deployed airfoils and hydrogen scoops. The small canal crossing that would have been his target narrowly avoided destruction by the blast of braking jets as he flared and assumed a horizontal vector.

A small cadre of soldiers walking along the canal at the time flattened upon hearing the atmosphere tearing into a white-hot streak above them. None knew that they had narrowly missed a tragic encounter with the oldest spaceship in the spiral arm.

~ ~ ~

Old Chookya Terminal
3608.367 Erran Calendar

A twenty-seven car train roared through the switching station, pulling with it wind tainted with the odor of mixed grades of damp ores and machine oils. Sh-Shaand smiled as he counted the cars. Over the blast of rumble and screech, he leaned to hoarsely shout into Connie's ear. He had gotten over his initial reluctance to talk to a female in public—after all, she was an off-worlder. "Tese not ores destined for great freight elevator. Tese are proof of our final plans for victory."

She turned, psi'd a question for further explanation and received her answer in kind.

This one is good, he thought. She understands nuance. The Braad is good for action when the opportunity avails, but this Ka-nee is better at language. She knows how to properly pronounce Teeya City with the tongue click rather than the simple T sound they both used in the beginning. Braad cannot. And she is more adept at understanding the intentionality of psi when used in conjunction with speech. Braad has a much harder time with his language, but better understands the mechanics and necessities of war planning.

The last of the cars passed, trailing two flat cars with mounted laser cannons. The spoil from the excavation would be distributed in the dark of night near the mining pits to avoid notice.

He extended his hands to lead both of them up the stairway to cross over to their required platform. "Tat train," he explained, "is almost last of train taking rock away from Teeya ground gun. Two others ready soon."

Brad asked, "You said that the ground guns were to be powered by atomics. Did Errans not have atomics during the Cho War? Before the diaspora?"

Shaand paused. He asked, "Do Hoomans have," he struggled for the word. Ethos? He said, "Atom weapon?" He explained that early atom research a thousand years before had killed many Dzurans. "Poison water in ocean. For twelve hundred year, Dzuran use atomic for power, for light, for propulsion, but Pel-Council forbid creation of atom weapon. Atom weapon kill many fast but kill many more for long time."

Brad thought about the hundreds of nuclear bomb tests done in the Pacific and Siberia and underground all over the world. "Yes, Shaand. Humans have atomic weapons." They climbed the steps in silence for a while and, at the platform, he stopped. "Humans used atom weapons two times. They were used to end a long war." He wondered how he could explain the global horror of World War II. "In the time of my father's father, there was a great war on Earth." He began walking with Shaand and Connie again. "The war killed many for over eight years in some places," he continued. Knowing that, when they had attempted to teach each other the numbering system from each of their worlds, Shaand had understood the concept of "thousands," but likely would not grasp millions, he spread his fingers wide. "Sixty-thousand-thousand humans were killed with guns and bombs and rockets. Two atom weapons ended the war." He had used various gestures and his limited psi to try to get across his message but he came to a stop near the middle of a track overwalk. "Two atomics killed two human cities. Very bad and, yes, the atom bomb poisoned water and land. But the war ended."

The three walked on in silence. Nearing the end of the overwalk, Connie said, "Humans have many atomic weapons. So many that humans are afraid to use even one. If one is used, all afraid that many will be used and too many humans will die. Maybe, all humans."

Shaand paused, taking in the further implication. "Hoomans have many atomics. Hoomans have atomics in space? Around Ert?" He gestured a small circle then a larger circle.

Brad wondered about Reagan's star wars weapon's platform. Had it actually been built? He'd heard a lot of complaints and debates on TV news, so maybe it had. He guessed, "That's not my area, but I think yes. My country on Earth is building a space weapon, but it is not atomic. It is high energy gun, like the Erran's green light gun."

Shaand nodded at this. "We talk about more. First, let me take you to surprise I talk you about."

~ ~ ~

After a short ride in one of the platform cars, Sh-Shaand and his two humans debarked onto a noticeably dingier platform. This site was clearly not one of the cerametal-clad mass people-mover stations. It had the musty sweat odor of the access they had taken near a ruined agricultural building. Bolstering that fact, just inside a hall doorway, several racks of shelving held disposable trays of stalk fruit and Jaan-dk.

At least, thought Brad, this crop isn't going to total waste. They took a steep set of stairs up to a landing that led into the working bay of another processing building. This one seemed to be intact. Heavy curtains along a back wall blocked their view of something beyond them. Connie and Brad felt it immediately upon clearing the floor level of the processing area, and when facing the building-wide curtain, they knew. Almost simultaneously, "Jai!"

Hello friends ... B-rad ... Ka-nee

They broke into a trot toward a slit in the curtain near its mid-point. *Jai, how did you get free?* Connie sent the sub-vocal message. They reached the opening and stepped through. Their transport from Earth sat on its pads, apparently undamaged by the Erran mechanics. The silver-grey ship was about fifty-five feet long and twenty wide. Its round nose and jelly bean oval squared off at the rear to house main thrusters and the peculiar hexagonal array near the center of the stern plates that they now knew to be the G-space driver. Below the darkened panel of the cockpit, a thin line appeared and the cockpit opened.

Good feel friends again, Jai psi'd in English, but Shaand could sense the emotional content. He nodded in appreciation. This had been a good idea.

Two workers with unfamiliar orange-colored cuffs on their jumpsuits approached. They balked, seeing that two of the three grey jump-suited figures who had just entered their workspace were not Dzuran. News of the off-worlders had reached most quarters of the planet, but no one expected to actually see them. The lead tech addressed Shaand with a polite bow, "Administrator, we did not know to expect your presence. We were sent to keep out the curious."

"You have done well. Have you had any success in getting the ship to communicate?"

Jai talk no one, the ship answered.

"I see." Shaand said. "Braad?"

Brad walked forward to the side of the cockpit. As he neared, a set of steps depressed into the smooth side of the hull. *Welcome, Braad ... Jai worry Erran find Ert ... not talk Errans.*

"Well done, Jai." He stroked the side of the ship and put his hand up to one of the steps. Connie approached with eyebrows raised in question.

"Brad?" Her eyes were welling with emotion. "We have a ride home!" Her tears began to cut tracks in the accumulated dust from their travels. She waved toward the open barn door to the pink sky and fields beyond. "I thought this was it, that we'd never see home again."

He turned and embraced her, feeling the shaking in her chest as she allowed full sobs that had been building for weeks to release their stored emotional energy, to let loose fears she had kept to herself that she would have to bear a child under a red sun with no sort of neo-natal care and no experienced hands in human childbirth. The two guards turned in something a little less controlled than disgust mingled with pity. Shaand simply stood and waited. These Hoomans were prone, he'd learned, to uncontrolled emotional fits.

Brad stroked the back of her head, whispering calming thoughts. When the sobbing slowed to heavy breathing interspersed with heaving sighs, he said as calmly as he could muster, "Yes, we have a ship. We just don't know if we can leave. This is a very old spaceship and there's a very new navy up there. We might not last long enough to break the atmosphere."

Another long sigh registered that this had been absorbed. "Hhh, Hhh, I know. I was just so relieved to see Jai again. We have a lifeboat!" She let a few more shudders pass. "Hhh, Hhh, hhh. Bradley, I do want to go home!"

"I know, hon!" he whispered. "I do too. It'll have to wait. We have to see what plays out here. I think, from what we've been told and what I can interpret in overheard Dzuran, that things are coming to a head." He turned to Shaand who had gone to talk with the two sentries.

"Shaand?" He walked over, hesitantly. "May I ask, by your Lights? What are our, er, your chances? I mean, is there a final confrontation coming with your underground forces somehow taking over in a way that the city ships cannot damage Dzura? Is there an end coming to this war?"

"Friend Braad is what ship Jai call you. I tink you friend, but we, I, cannot tell military secret to off-worlder. You know tis?"

"Yes, certainly." Brad did understand. Who was he to be let into sophisticated military planning that had obviously been going on for generations? "Shaand, can I help? I have maybe the only spaceship in the Dzuran navy, and I might be the only pilot it will let control it."

Shaand looked at the ship and attempted a psi link. There was no response.

Connie tried, in sub-vocal psi. *Jai, can you help us? Are your shields and systems able to fight Errans?*

Jai responded in audible circuits, *Jai can help ... much danger from Erran ships ... need to fight city ships first ... fight Erran navy.* They had never heard his audio channels from outside the cockpit and were surprised at the soft, almost feminine tone he projected. Brad's first impression was that he sounded like his mother, Lucy Hitchens.

"Great, Jai. Thanks. All we have to do is kill the Erran city ships, then it will be easy?"

Jai responded in English audible and Dzuran psi so Shaand could understand. Both Brad and Shaand were instructed to enter the cockpit. Out of habit, Brad took the forward position and then realized that Shaand was the native, the local who might need precedence. "No, Brad. Tis ship know you as pilot. Shaand not know how. You pilot."

They settled into their respective fore and aft seating. Jai said over the internal audio circuits, *Jai not waste time on Teeya City ... watch.* His command center display, which usually provided three-dimensional scaled views of the major objects near the ship and labeled them as friend or foe, instead displayed the interior of the hangar deck of the city ship. The view slowly panned until a full view of the city ship's multi-tiered docking hanger was fully displayed. The hangar appeared to be nearly full of small craft, with a small armada of transports tethered below the hangar. The panned down view showed that the opening of the hangar port was still well away from the upper platform of the space elevator anchored in the far distance below. Shaand gasped, astonished. The view of the space elevator platform and its anchor of woven pialla and carbon fibers was the first time Shaand had ever seen one of the platforms from above. The view changed, becoming clear that it was from the nose camera as Jai had been jettisoned from Teeya City's hangar. The view rotated upward as the craft rolled, providing a detailed shot of the underside of the city ship.

From the front seat, Brad hoped that the information would be useful to Shaand. The view went dark and then began to flash through view after view of the interior of the ship. Brad saw glimpses in fast rotation of corridors, dormitories, mechanics bays, kitchens, gardens, armories, meeting halls. He had not really considered how many of the space-bound Errans occupied the ship above. Sure, it was visible in the night sky as a dark shadow drifting above, outlined in fine detail by the glowing nebula. But the numbers he saw absorbed in the mundane activities of their daily routine struck him. There were a lot of them and they wanted his friends dead!

He heard Shaand communicate with Jai from the back seat and the views changed. Shaand let out a gurgling chirp that Brad had learned was joyous laughter in an Elioi. Detailed drawings began to flow past the viewer, details of construction, deck layouts, circuits, cooling systems, and shapes and details of machinery Brad had never seen.

Brad was distracted from the stream of images when he saw Connie's head rise over the edge of the cockpit. "What in the world are you two doing in here? I've been twidlin' my thumbs for at least half an hour.

"Connie, Jai was absolutely tremendous!"

"What? How?" Her look was both comic and quizzical.

Shaand said, "Jai Su-pi!" He was beaming with ineffable Elioi good humor.

"He is the ultimate spy!" Brad turned in his seat to give a thumbs up. "He downloaded hundreds, maybe thousands of schematics of the Erran city ship. I certainly can't read them." He turned the thumb toward the back seat. "But Shaand is having a blast with them."

Connie stepped up another rung and leaned into the cockpit to see the view screen. "Holy cow!" The images kept flooding past the viewer, barely resolving before fading to the next.

"Jai, stop reveal." The last image took form and slowly faded. "Jai, set data transfer to open."

Open data port dangerous, Braad. The ship computer, still in mental bond with its pilot, was protective of information it had stolen from the known enemy Errans. *Erran data ... some useless ... some good ... some dangerous.*

"Jai, Ss-Shaand is friend. Make Ss-Shaand bond link."

In the weapons officer's seat behind Brad, Shaand placed his three-fingered palm against the com panel. The palm pattern was read into Jai's memory and Jai opened its memory area to Shaand's mental probing. Shaand placed a data cube onto Jai's I/O plate and watched as the antique cube glowed blue, indicating it was receiving the upload.

Chapter 17

"Political power grows out of the barrel of a gun."
Mao Zedong

Old Chookya
3608.368 Erran Calendar

Connie was missed. For four days, as best he could determine from the changes in underground lighting, she had been "training" at one of the research enclaves. They had had precious little time together and a lot of that on the run. As mundane and boring as life underground had become, he missed her face, her smell, and her touch. They had taken to making mental lists of things they missed about Earth. This ranged from ultramarine blue skies and green vegetation to family and the familiar surroundings of their North Florida coastal communities. They talked at length about their adventures on her father's shrimp boat, especially the sinking of the shrimp trawler *Lou Anne*, and the later recovery of the artifact that had catapulted them to global fame.

Finding the artifact, a simple teal blue rod of advanced metallurgical origin, and losing it aboard the lost *Lou Anne* had brought a much younger Brad and Connie closer as friends. Their later estrangement at separate colleges had been frustrating but, in the end, had cemented their relationship. Unmarried but bonded, they were now loose in the universe. Or, as Brad sometimes thought, Lost in Space.

Was war universal? Having finally met a species from another planet, he found them in the middle of a centuries-long conflict. Wasn't there a hundred years' war in Europe? Or a four hundred years' war? As he considered his scant knowledge of European history, he reasoned that Homo sapiens had been efficiently killing themselves since they'd wiped out the Neanderthals.

He thought about the Elioi civil war between the spacer variety Errans and the planetary Dzurans. He knew they were all products of evolution on Dzura, and Erra was the more recent colony. Had they always been a warring species like humanity? Would they see Earth as expansion room? Did they live on other planets? Had they found other intelligent life?

Brad was in the middle of trying to figure out how to present these questions when Shaand entered, smiling. "Come, friend. Need show Brad view of soon victory."

"What?" Brad got up, brushing dirt from his dungarees. "Victory? How?"

Shaand beamed with knowledge that he had just been permitted to share with the off-worlder. "Come, war room ready. When talk in Pel-Council of ship Jai and Teeya City su-pi, Pelma say good Hooman come. Pelma want see Hooman."

Brad followed as Shaand turned and left in an uncharacteristic hurry, wondering if he was a good human, or if it was good for the human to come. See what? He'd have to get a lot better at nuance in a language with few modifiers. He remembered his high school Latin and how so much depended on context and idiom.

The drab entrance to Dzuran high command led down a steep, stone-carved staircase, left into a much better-appointed hallway, and right into a crisply decorated foyer. He recognized the trappings of the offices of a Pelma. These, he thought, might have been brought from their last underground refuge as those quarters were being evacuated, or this might be a different regional Pelma's office.

Shaand placed his left arm up to a sensor at the door's center, rotating his wrist so the sensor could read something in the cuff of Shaand's uniform. An indicator light turned red and a latch clicked. Shaand opened the door for Brad to enter. Inside, four guards flanked a shimmering energy wall that seemed superfluous given the heavy armor and weaponry on the guards. Now this, thought Brad, is an inner sanctum sanctorum. Then he wondered if he remembered his Latin correctly. That was religious, this was a keep, a fortress. What was the Latin word for fort? Arix? Arx? Shaand offered his cuff again to one of the guards who waved it with a ringed hand. The ring briefly glowed red and the guards stepped back from the energy wall.

The wall's quiet humming diminished, and the glowing energy thinned to transparency then dissipated completely. Brad looked through a broad portal into a darker chamber down a narrow hall. Finally, the armed escort ushered them into a darkened executive media room. Its curved walls were parallel to the slightly ovoid table that was the prominent feature in the room. High on the walls, scenes from all over the planet were displaying on panel screens. Shaand took a seat opposite the standing Pelma, as his leader nodded assent, telling Brad to sit as well. The Pelma began to talk in what passed for stirring tones among the Dzuran leadership. To Brad, it had the same sing-song clickety musicality that could use a good base beat, but was usually unintelligible unless considerably slowed and accompanied with psi intention and mimed hand motions.

Shaand had the floor and spoke too rapidly for Brad to understand. He was being praised for his action on the Verparksransaran plain when he assisted, unarmed, in bringing down an air car that had pinned down his group. A general murmur of good will and smiling ridged brows made him feel at least he was a good alien. Shaand continued with a description, for the Council's benefit, of the intelligence gathered by the Hooman's space craft.

The agenda moved on and lights went down in the room. The center of the large table rose and retracted into the ceiling, revealing a glowing map of part of the Dzuran surface. The opening in the table, Brad guessed about twenty feet across, shimmered in golds and reds. Shadows indicated a low sun angle. Time must have been accelerating in the time sequence because the shadows began to flip back and forth between dark and light periods. The days lapsed by while the Pelma narrated. An indication of an underground train showed cars full of excavated materials being hurried away from a large circular pad in the center of the display. Rising from the center of the circular pad, a thin glowing streamer rose out of view toward the ceiling. Brad realized this must be one of the three space elevators located immediately beneath the geostationary city ships.

Shaand reached over and placed his hand on Brad's to get his attention. "Now it good!" Brad looked over at a smiling and reassuring face. He liked this guy. He no longer thought of the face as a lipless primate. He'd learned to read facial expressions in a limited way and could identify several of the individuals he'd been introduced to. He thought he could probably pick Shaand out of a crowd.

The detail in the modeling was incredible. The real-time simulation depicted an elevator partway up the strand descending with an empty cargo bin. On the ground, service crews were loading the next bin to be sent up to the upper freight platform. *This amazing!* he psi'd to Shaand.

Amaze, yes. Wait! They both turned back to the developing display. Highlights in ghostly white indicated a growing excavation beneath the foundation, or anchor, of the space elevator. The massive pour-rock base was not to hold up the elevator. Its mass held down the long pialla fiber filament that made up the track of the elevator. Centrifugal force pulling on the loading platform assembly at the top of the fiber kept the track taught and the platform in place. Convenient to the loading bays of the city ships above them, the elevators were the crowning achievement of the Erran mastery over the old home world. Errans built the first space elevators over the industrial complex near Akat City on Erra, a second more efficient elevator at the capital Cresow City, and now there were the three built on sister planet Dzura, one beneath each of the city ships. By freighter, they supplied the less hospitable Erra with the bounty of the home world. Brad had the idea that this was about to change. He could not have guessed how much he underestimated the subterranean engineering he was seeing modeled before him.

In accelerated time-lapse, the excavations grew under the foundation. By comparing it to the size of the train cars hauling out soil and rock, he estimated the foundation to be a few hundred yards across. The excavation grew slowly and, along with its increasing size, six boreholes were developed deep into bedrock. Suddenly, it seemed that all excavation stopped. Liquid, probably water diverted from somewhere, began to flow into the excavation through the train tunnel. The time scale of the display slowed and the view panned out to show the entire length of the elevator and its upper platform.

The Pelma's narration stopped and he nodded for one of his staff to take over. Several different configurations of bright lines that Brad did not completely understand played across the pour-rock disc. Shaand leaned over to explain fracture or break lines. Abruptly, small explosions placed under the disk split the foundation into six wedges. From the bottom of the six deep wells, brilliant explosions detonated in unison. Their combined fireball steam-flashed the water-filled excavation. The media room was filled with intense light. A combined plasma-steam column leapt from the surface of the planet, blasting the six pie-shaped chunks of the foundation through the atmosphere.

Two of the six slabs became entangled in the elevator filament and began to drift off to the negative side of planet spin. Two of them made it as far as the upper platform itself, destroying it utterly with bits of the platform bursting in all directions as chemical energy fuels onboard the platform exploded. A fifth flew past the city ship and arced away to fall back to the planet. The ship was deflected slightly off its orbit as the diminishing blast wave swept past it, but the burst of superheated plasma lacked sufficient heat and mass by the time it reached the ship. The city ship's outer skin flared red and withered on one side, but the interior structure held.

Only one of the pie-shaped foundation pieces made it to the city ship and its impact was spectacular. It severed major structural supports. An entire life support appendage sheared away. Propelled by its outgassing atmosphere, it accelerated away and began a long descent into the atmosphere. The city ship lost considerable air, but automatic locks in the structure closed and the stream of detritus expelled into cold vacuum stopped. No one had really watched the descending debris. All eyes were on the ship. The undamaged hangar bay loosed squadrons of fighters escorted by high altitude destroyers. These fanned out to demolish any ground installations housing remaining Dzuran workers.

Breath seemed to have stopped because, suddenly, a more or less simultaneous inhale was heard around the table. A few who had risen to their feet stopped and gaped. A few turned to each other in quiet conversation. Some arguments broke out until the Pelma turned off the display and all eyes turned on him. Brad turned to Shaand. Shaand was no longer smiling. Room lights came up and the Pelma began to talk quietly to his staff.

Brad thought of a mortar, or shotguns, the biggest damn gun ever built. They used a massive hunk of concrete as a load of shot for a directed charge. Learning from the effects of the near-shore meteor attack of four centuries earlier, the flash of water to steam added significantly to the generated blast wave but not enough to significantly disrupt the city.

Across the table, an excited exchange between three of the techs erupted into argument until the Pelma squashed it, apparently in favor of one of the lower ranked individuals. A female with high-rank insignia on her cuffs entered from a sliding door and sat at the controls. The loser of the preceding argument stood, in limited control of his furious objection, against the wall, eyes darting between the Pelma, the lower ranked tech, and the female at the controls. His controls. She dialed the display back to an earlier point where the excavation for water was nearing completion. The room grew silent as she made some adjustments. The six wells were drilled as before, and to Brad's eyes, only a small distance further out from the center than the previous points. He could see though that the balance point for these holes was a little further out from the apparent centroid of the pie-shaped fragments that would be hurled into near space.

Maybe this would help confine the blast? Perhaps she had taken into account the mass of the outer ring and these well points. The sites of the six nuclear explosions more nearly fit the center of mass of the pie slices when that outer ring was taken into account. She sat back in her chair and pushed a slider control forward. The scene advanced again, more quickly this time, through the remaining excavation, filling with seawater, and the explosion sequence. Again, the foundation disc was fractured with sub-atomics along six radiating lines and the synced nukes blew all into the fractured heavens above the elevator site.

On this run-through, only one of the pie shapes tangled in the elevator. Two others slid off the side of the mushrooming fireball and one smashed point first into an edge of the loading platform at the top of the elevator. Two of the anchor remnants slammed into the model of the orbiting city. Again, severe damage was inflicted. This time none of the appendage structures was severed, although serious damage had occurred to the areas impacted. Obviously, the chunks of pour-rock had penetrated several deck levels and done serious internal damage, but after the automated pressure doors closed, the damage was limited. At the end of the sequence, a fleet of ships exited the hangar deck and began a descent to the surface before the tech shut down the display. As the lights came back up, few spoke above a whisper.

~ ~ ~

Old Chookya Science Compound
3608.369 Erran Calendar

Connie found herself once again among a cluster of white-furred females. Her confidant and companion, Clee-Chk, came forward as she stepped out of the personal rail car. The same long formal bow with a step back and a subtle smile. Connie tried it with much better luck this time, or possibly, the entourage had been warned not to laugh. She was guided into a polished metal room that looked like a modern surgical room finished out in polished stainless steel rather than American-style green or white tile. Her first thought was something like, "Oh crap, here come the probes!" but Clee-Chk reassured her by lying down on the inclined plane of the examination table. The table tilted to horizontal and a robotic arm, one of several at rest in recesses in the ceiling, descended and made a pass over Chk's abdomen. As it did, a holo table beside her built a three-dimensional model of Chk's torso and its organs. On her signal, one of the room's operators, nurses? doctors? made an audible command to the table and it cycled back so the patient's feet again rested just above the floor.

Chk motioned for Connie to rest on the table. What the heck, Connie thought. She just proved it's safe.

One of the operators carefully removed the three-dimensional Elioi torso off the model table. The imaging arm made a slow double pass over Connie's lower abdomen and, in turn, created a model of Connie's torso from below the hips to above the diaphragm. When the table cycled back down again, she got off and turned to look at the body of a pregnant human. When it was placed on a viewing table beside Chk's form, the two sat down in front of their respective models. A tray was placed beside them with identical sets of surgical tools.

Chk had learned that Connie was not only quick to understand language, but very quick to understand by doing. She nodded at Connie and picked up one of the knives. She cut away the modeled outer garment and waited for Connie to follow suit.

When Connie finished cutting away her model's dungarees, she gasped at the half-sized model of herself. She looked over at the lightly furred form in front of her teacher and gave an expectant "I'm ready" nod. She watched as Chk cut away layers of dermis and muscle tissue, exposed in natural colors. Connie held back her urge to vomit or run and began to do the same on the model in front of her. It helped that there was no odor beyond a slight aroma of what reminded Connie of warm plastic tinged with ammonia. To her relief, the machine had colored everything on her model a uniform reddish grey. It had no prior knowledge of human anatomy and had simply filled in with an assumption of the average color of body tissue.

Chk resumed, with slow deliberation, exfoliating layers of tissue protecting an elongated organ the size of a small spaghetti squash. When it was clear of connecting tissues and supply vessels, she laid it on the table. Connie was unsure what to take out of her own model and psi'd a question, *What organ?*

Chk answered, "Not know name or purpose." She put up a hand, signaling Connie to wait. Chk slit the squash-shaped object down an apparent seam and peeled it open. Along a central cord, ten small lumps were attached to supply arteries and protected by a matrix of thin supporting structures. She made a point of counting out the ten positions where ten young were budding.

Connie felt her jaw slacken as she saw and heard the count. Ten tiny bodies were going to develop along that double row of buds. Ten! She turned to face Chk who, not surprised by what she'd uncovered, was taken aback by Connie's shock. Chk nodded toward the human torso.

Connie drew a breath, held it, and slowly exhaled through pursed lips. With scalpel in hand, she made a vertical cut down the center of the stomach from rib cage to pubis. Two horizontal cuts near the top and bottom of the vertical allowed her to pull back the skin and muscle layers. She took several tries to get deep enough to cleanly pass through "her" abdominal wall. She was not sure what to do next. She had seen the colored illustrations of the reproductive organs in her doctor's office, but she didn't have enough confidence on how much deeper to cut. She peeled back the slightly sticky layers of tissue exposed by her first efforts and found that she could make out the inverted gourd shape of her uterus, just beneath the next layer of muscular tissue. Well, biscuits and grits! she thought, slipping back into her Floridian colloquialisms. This was me, real time just a few minutes ago.

Connie lost her inhibitions and took the knife blade to the wall of tissue. She pulled down, cutting through the uterine wall. Tenderly, lovingly, she rolled back the thick musculature with about the effort it would have taken her to cut and split a good sized grapefruit. She gasped as her senses took in the reality of the thumb-sized embryo and its thin placental mass gripping the uterine wall. Carefully, she allowed the small form to fall into her palm. Crying with unleashed emotion, she turned to show the tiny human shape to Chk.

Her Dzuran friend and guide did not understand completely the emotional response of tears, but could very easily interpret the psi messages Connie was unconsciously emitting. She smiled her wrinkled-brow smile back at Connie and attempted to form the human mouth smile as well. "Utra Sond?" Chk was puzzled. "Wat is Utra Sond?"

Connie, controlling her thoughts and rampant emotional state, enunciated what she had last thought. "This beats the hell out of an ultrasound."

Chapter 18

"Another such victory over the Romans and we are undone."
Phyrrus

Teeya City Commander's Board Room
3608.377 Erran Calendar

"*!*" Si-I seldom swore, but *By the Lights! These inbreeds seem not to comprehend the simplest concepts. How do they ever stay in power?* "Ss-Giromk, I understand that there are difficulties in supply! That is precisely the problem. As long as this insurrection strangles our supply lines from the surface, all of us will experience supply shortages." He had to turn away; the wrath on his face was not politic in any situation. He had let his frustration and anger go. Pelma Si-I did not like addressing the Supreme Pelma from Erra in these tones, and he made a note to apologize personally after the meeting, but he was frustrated by the Supreme Pelma's idiotic notion that his favorite foodstuffs and other luxuries available only from Dzura could no longer be obtained, much less be jumped to Erra. The meeting had taken half a shift already and there was a growing list of real things that had to be done. He was High Pelma of the three orbital cities, but technically subservient to the Erran Supreme Pelma. He turned to again face Ss-Giromk and continued in a firm but respectful tone with psi overtones of firm finality. "I also refuse to send down any more troops in unshielded troop vehicles."

Pelma Si-I had called the meeting against the advice of his closest advisors. Coming only fourteen days after that last major conference, the Supreme Pelma from Erra demanded to know why the slave revolt could not be crushed. The other members of the Pel-Council had increasingly stressful schedules due to the swelling demands of the insurrection below. Besides supply issues, security on the ground had melted away as most of the Dzuran home guard had gone over to the rebels.

Senior Engineer for engineered systems, Ss-Taidik, felt the anger in the room and regretted that her agenda item was next. Si-I continued with his agenda. "Ss-Taidik, what if any is the status of installing first order shield generators on our troop carriers. I can't lose any more soldiers to simple handguns."

Ss-Taidik stood, unaccustomed to doing much more in these meetings than reading a prepared report. "Sir, your worship."

"Damn your Lights!" Si-I retorted. "I am not a damned priest."

The hanger manager continued, with a little more control. "Sir, the generators are being fitted with appropriate brackets and control circuits are being wired into the first squadron of nine cars. I expect the next batch of field generators will be delivered in two lights. When those come in, we will be able to fit out two more squadrons."

He swallowed the bile that was trying to disgorge at the back of his throat. "And when will that be?"

"Conservatively, another four lights."

"So conservatively," he growled in disgust, "in six lights we will have only one flight of three per sector?"

"Yes, Pelma. Three flights in six lights." She glanced nervously at the small display pad shining just above her sleeve computer. "In another ten lights…"

"No, Ss-Taidik, as soon as the first squadron of nine is completed, you will release three each to the base of the elevators. They will stand guard over those launch sites and not go on reckless search and destroy missions. As each set of three units is completed you will equally reinforce each of those elevator launch sites until ground commanders can deploy a full squadron in force from any base. Understood?"

Ss-Taidik sat, shielding even her private psi channels in precaution against any uncomplimentary thoughts being overheard.

Si-I turned his attention to the priest. "I will assume you have dropped any objections on religious grounds to the destruction of any historical sites on Dzura?"

The High Priest Eluoi-Annchda blanked, his normally wizened scowl going expressionless. He had not seen the Pelma Si-I in this temper since three of his crèche mates died in a training accident. Privately, he hoped, he wondered if any of the Pelma's anger had to do with the rumblings of discontent spreading through the cities, since the arrival and sudden departure of the "so-called" Precursor asteroid or the impending loss of this year's crops. He said, "Pelma, may the Light forever illuminate your path." He gave a full head bow, down and to the side, as a sign of humility and deference.

The Pelma acknowledged this with a quick nod. Annchda again addressed the table. "The Dzurans, we now believe, have been breeding like ground worms—increasing their numbers far beyond our understanding. They have been planning this insurrection for at least one, if not two, generations. And no," he looked back at Si-I, "I don't believe the timing has anything to do with the arrival of the two off-worlders." He scanned the faces around the table and settled on the Supreme Pel from Erra. "That was unfortunate perhaps, but you will remember the insurrection in the southern hemisphere started long before this trouble spread to the northern hemisphere."

"Pelma," the priest adopted a mode of servile humility, "I believe it was your decision to imprison those off-worlders at Jhelen Prison."

Si-I couldn't believe it. This anachronistic excrement was trying to deflect and somehow attach blame on him. "Those off-worlders were in quarantine, you fatuous fool. Why would I entrust the population of my city to who knows what kind of germplasm those creatures might have carried?"

"Did not the rebellion in the south start after the releases at Jhelen and the other city jails?"

"I—. Yes." Si-I took a few deep breaths, convincing himself not to strike down the robed priest. There were still some who followed the old ways. "The fact that they happened to be in that facility has nothing to do with why that breakout occurred or why it coincided with outbreaks in the north. It happens that one of their cursed underground warrens had a connection within a quick sprint from the prison's perimeter." He stopped, deciding not to waste more time defending himself against these baseless charges. He turned back to the gathered leaders around the table.

"It's unfortunate that this conflict has spread from our mining installations in the far south, to our breadbasket, but we Errans are strong. With rationing, to be enforced immediately, we will get through this temporary lapse in supplies." With an appraising glance around the table, he added, "We have grown weak and fat. Our limbs have withered while we relish the comforts of our homes in the stars. We must recognize that our cities in the stars are our prisons."

Angry murmurs rose from some of the others, but he pressed on. "Our most effective troops have been those trained in full Dzuran gravity. But there were not enough and we have lost a majority of our first independent ground command. Hundreds more are training, and soon we will have ground-capable troops with shielded ground cars, and we will squash this rebellion."

He paused. I'm becoming too preachy, he thought. These were not recruits or even graduates. He was addressing the assembled leaders of his Erran nobility.

He took a second look around the table and, picking up the ceremonial bowl, signaled for each seated member to do likewise. "To Erra, may our Sister shine forever bright in our skies. To Alal! May her warmth bring comfort in the eternal frigid Dark. And to Dzura, home of all homes, may we once again walk in her fields and wade in her cool waters as owners and masters of the realm." He took a long draught from the bowl and set it down. He allowed the priest a small nod. He no longer had any belief of the holiness of the triad, but it couldn't hurt to honor the old ways for ceremony's sake. "I think we have at least settled the issue of sending down more ground troops. This will happen only when we are more secure in their victory. Colleagues? Do we have further business?"

At this prompting, one of the aides standing behind the Deputy for Cultural Affairs tapped his senior on the shoulder and whispered a private note. The Deputy, typical of the group, was fat from success and spindle-limbed from lack of exercise and a lifetime in low gravity. He stood, addressing first the Supreme Pelma and then Si-I. "Our teams have been going over records of the so-called Precursor Stone. After the unfortunate incident, our full attention has been focused on study of those vids and transcripts from the voice recorders. We have concluded," he stopped as all attention on him made him queasy. "We have concluded that we had awakened an abandoned spaceship from an ancient alien race. We believe, due to the decorations in the ship's main hall, that a race of spacefarers may have had direct intervention or contact with the ones known as Precursors." He stopped again, realizing he had confused his own conclusion. "Excuse me, let me correct that." He sighed, pausing to collect his resolve. "We believe that the ship that emerged from the Precursor Stone has a high probability of being of Precursor manufacture.

The priest released an audible "*-*" The double click had slipped out, but no one doubted that he opposed the fantastic belief in an ancient Precursor race that seeded potential planets. Wishing he had kept the oath silent, he nodded in deference to the table and the Deputy continued. His wasn't the only response. Pelma Si-I had to call for quiet.

"The markings in the chamber, before it became activated, are consistent with sites found in other systems. Each of those systems has a breathable oxygen atmosphere and developing plant and animal ecologies. We believe our team somehow activated the ship's controls and its automated defense mechanisms killed our research team. Perhaps it considered them to be an enemy or," he paused, "merely an infestation. From the scale of structures and what we think were control surfaces, we believe that race to have been at least twice our dimensions if not a little larger."

The Supreme Pelma interrupted. "Do you have any idea where that ship's destination is?"

The Deputy seemed to draw in, remembering details. "Sir, at first, we believed it was headed for the system of the off-worlders, but that was only its initial vector. A mining surveyor in that system reported that the stone or ship, dropped into that system, took on fuel in the atmosphere of a gas planet, oriented its exit parallel with the axis of the arm, and jumped again." Hoping he was through, he sat. He wasn't.

"Why?" asked Pelma Si-I, "Why do you think it went back to the off-worlders' system?"

Flustered and thinking on the spot about a question he had truthfully not considered other than as a report entry, the Deputy took a shot. "Sir, we can't know, but that is the system where we found it. Our speculation is that it needed to get its bearings to go back to its origins. We can't know for sure."

The Pelma gave him one last question he could not answer. "Have we definitively concluded that the off-worlders are not themselves Precursors?"

"Yes, sir."

"So they are expendable," he said more to himself than to the group or the Deputy.

Ss-Taidik stood. "Pelma Si-I?"

"Yes, does the Science Officer have something to add?"

"If they can be located, they would be interesting subjects: comparative biology and physiology. It would be relevant to our discussion on planet seeding." After a short pause, she added, "We've been curious about the coincidence of their bipedal erect locomotion, speech, grasping digits. It seems too coincidental to be an accident of evolution."

"You could perform these analyses on corpses, could you not?"

Sagging, she replied, "Yes, sir. If they aren't too spoiled."

"That is all." Si-I set his water tube on the table and turned to leave.

"With respect for your Lights, sir. We will learn a lot more from live subjects."

Si-I was already across the room, heading for the door. "I said, THAT IS ALL!"

Earth Interlude 7

Though it be honest, it is never good to bring bad news.
William Shakespeare, *Antony and Cleopatra*

The Pentagon, Washington, DC
August 24, 1986 – Earth Calendar

The seated generals and senior staff were called to the meeting for what was billed as a SITREP on a serious matter of national security. The return addresses was The White House, and it was cc'd to all five military branches, and to the FBI, the CIA, the NSA and NASA. A full bird colonel in Navy dress blues entered and announced, "Madam and gentlemen, the President of the United States." In unison, all rose.

POTUS entered with the smooth easy grace of a professional politician made president and said, with palms out, "Please, keep your seats, I need to get off my dogs myself." A few chuckles arose from those on casual terms with the Commander in Chief. Others seemed to simply sit back into their poses of seated attention. "Gentlemen and lady." POTUS nodded toward the single high-ranking female in the room. "We have a situation you all know I have been preaching on for some time. I don't seem to have gotten a lot of support for it on the Hill, but I'm sure some of you may have an interest in what our guest today has to share." He let his gaze sweep the room, ensuring that each one present felt, if only for a moment, that electric contact. "We need to get that weapons platform in space, tested, and operational."

He again nodded toward the lone female.

"You all know each other well and I'm sure that beyond the Army-Navy game squabbles back in December," he paused for another chuckle to circle the room, "that we can come up with a solution to our problem. Our guest, Commander Lorene Platte, has joined us from NASA, and as soon as we go live on the phone, we'll have with us the representatives of the seated bodies of the Canadian Armed Forces Council, the UK's Chiefs of Staff Committee, the Israeli Defense Force, and the General Staff of the Armed Forces of the Russian Federation." He picked up a small notecard and read. "On the civilian side, we will also be sharing with the Chairmen of the European Space Agency, the UK Space Agency, the China

National Space Administration, and," he put the card down, "a host of others with a dog in the hunt." He motioned to an aide standing in the darkened perimeter of the room and with hisses, pops, and introductions by representatives, most of the other international connections were confirmed.

After welcoming the newcomers in appropriate style, the President continued. "You will all recall the uproar last fall when that boy from Florida and his girlfriend showed us apparently conclusive proof that we are not alone. Or rather, that we have not been alone. It has been attested that the piece of scrap metal he found was buried for at least four hundred years." Growing a little horse, he took a sip of water, coughed and reddening, coughed again. "Some of you," he let his eyes wander across the hardened faces of the CIA and NSA chiefs, "will disagree with my opening this report to the heads of state of anybody with a satellite in space. I've given it a lot of thought and, with equipment being stolen at random, we don't know whose surveillance birds are going to be taken. I don't want anybody getting an itchy trigger finger." Adopting his well-practiced 'ya with me yet?' smile, he panned the table looking for agreement. He motioned to an aide who turned on the video equipment and set the com patches for the overseas participants. "Please, Mrs. Platte, would you provide us with the salient backstory?"

"Yes, sir, Mr. President. Of course." She stood, collecting a small set of cards of her own and grabbed the clicker remote for the impressive array of video panels lining the side wall of the room. "Gentlemen, you will certainly remember the media storm when Bradley Hitchens and Connie Chappell shocked us all with their discovery, or I should say final disclosure of a piece of exotic metal that has since been proven to have extra-terrestrial origin." Murmurs, nods, and a few chuckles circled the table. "It's been quite a while since that disclosure, and I believe that most of us accept the implications with some excitement, or possibly dread." She'd been smiling and, looking at the frowns around the room, realized that she might be alone or at least not in the majority on the excitement, dread, or even belief level.

"The young couple went to ground, we believe, to avoid the media's incessant coverage of their diets, love life, and daily minutia." She shifted to her second card. "When things quieted down, a curious set of radar sightings triangulated from several military and commercial air traffic towers conclusively demonstrated that, not far from Mr. Hitchens's homestead, a craft—not an aircraft as we might hope to know it, but a craft or object of some kind— rose vertically in the air, hovered in the tailwinds of Hurricane Kate, and then settled below the radar horizon." A cough from the Navy Admiral interrupted her. Seeing the smirk on his face, she directed her gaze to the Air Force General seated across the table. "Sir, can I count on you to corroborate that evidence if requested by other branches or agencies?"

The Air Force general's eyes bored into his Navy opposite and in a guttural grunt that hinted of too many cigars and a love for hard liquor, he said, "You have my utmost support of that line of evidence Ms. Platte, and I might add, we appreciate your tracking of the object after it left the vertical maximum of our radar coverage." He wanted to add that much better equipment is available now, but he settled back into his armchair smiling not quite malevolently at the Admiral.

The President interjected. "Gentlemen, I would not have called you all into this meeting if I thought anything about it would, in the least way, give rise to humor or levity of any kind. Mrs. Platte?"

Platte continued, "On November twenty-first, nineteen eighty-five, four Air Force towers and two civilian towers noted this object's rise into hurricane force winds to an altitude at which only the most insane Coast Guard rescue pilots would attempt maneuvers, and held station perfectly. As we calculated the tracks, the only displacement was vertical. It might as well have been a calm July afternoon. There were, in that area, fifty mile-per-hour winds at tree top and eighty mile-per-hour sustained winds at three to five thousand feet which had no discernable displacement effect on this craft. Roughly half an hour after its descent below the radar coverage, it again ascended and never deviated from that vertical azimuth." She paused for effect. "That is to say, sirs, it kept going. We have to assume that the object that left our atmosphere on the night of November twenty-first, nineteen eighty-five, did not originate on this planet."

The com panel began to light up across the board. The President intervened on what could easily become bedlam. Picking up his handset, he spoke to the international attendees. "Please, my light board is full. I know you all have questions and I know this is pretty stupendous news, but if you will please wait for the end of the presentation from NASA." He paused. "Okay, Mrs. Platte, if you will?"

She sipped a water glass, composed herself, and continued. "As I just said, all evidence indicates that a significantly large object left the Earth in a vertical trajectory and blew past the coverage limits of our satellite tracking equipment in less than fifteen minutes. Later examination of some lucky ground-based telescopes doing routine measurements seems to have located an object maintaining a geosynchronous position at about thirty-two hundred kilometers." She looked at her cards and then back at the highest ranking officers of the US military. "There is a lot of technical information that I do not need to share here that I will include in a full report later. But, put simply, a geosynchronous orbit is usually higher at just under thirty-six hundred clicks and are almost always located at the equator. This object was not only matching the rotational period of the Earth, but maintaining its position over the ground. In short, it was being flown, or guided to avoid the inherent elliptical shape of most orbits."

One of the Generals in tan dress camo—she guessed Army or Marine—asked, "Mrs. Platte, if I understand your brief, this object went straight up to an altitude that would not normally provide a geosynchronous orbit, and then somehow managed to maintain its original latitude as well?"

"Yes, General. That is what we've concluded."

For the next half hour, Lorene Platte dug deep for the resolve to convince both the seated and the linked audience of the facts of the events of November 21, 1985, including the craft object's eventual rapid descent to near the location of the original launch. She did not share with them the desiccated alien corpse that had been transported to an obscure Nevada testing ground for study and storage. She continued to document sightings over Australia and the Gobi Desert as probably being associated with this same craft. When the steam of the disbelievers had dissipated and the concerns from overseas had been somewhat mollified, the President asked her to please have a seat. There was no extra seat in the room so she stepped back into one of the darker corners of the softly lit chamber.

The President took up the agenda again. "I see that we haven't reached one hundred percent acceptance of what NASA and I believe. I assure you, I do believe this interpretation of the observed facts. And to reinforce my beliefs, these trajectories are based on the mutual and simultaneous records from Air Force, Army, and Coast Guard tracking stations, as well as two civilian airports whose personnel have been extensively questioned.

"So! We have established, I hope, some kind of spacecraft associated with those two kids in Florida may have left this planet, and after making several forays to remote regions, may have left for good." Several silent sidelong conversations struck up locally and the question board again lit up with enquiries. "Now, and let me emphasize, that was then, November of last year. This is now, and we move on to the second and a more serious issue on the agenda. Someone seems to be knocking out our communications and military surveillance satellites."

Chapter 19

"It is said that the present is pregnant with the future."
Voltaire

Old Chookya Terminal
3608.381 Erran Calendar

Connie felt the breeze in the tunnel pulling at the roots of her hair. It had begun to grow out from the bob cut she had adopted shortly before leaving Florida for the test cruise. That had been months ago. At least five, if the developments in her abdomen were any measure. She had tried to hide the condition for a long time, hoping against instinct, for a miscarriage. She never thought she would have considered it, but the idea of birthing a human in an underground chamber beneath the surface of an alien planet? Suppose we get back home, she wondered. What would the birth certificate say?

She smiled as she felt a motion in her gut. Was that a roll? Is it too soon for a kick? God, I wish I could talk to Mom! Gently, she smoothed her hand across her swelling belly. Apart from the bizarre circumstances, she shared the hopes, anxieties, and fears of any first-time mother. The breeze felt good—the tram must be moving at upwards of forty miles an hour. She would be meeting up with Bradley at the next stop. She had come to trust her friend and teacher Clee-Chk, but oh, how she missed Bradley. She smiled again. When they were apart, she always thought of him as Bradley. When he was with her, it was Brad, or Sweetie, or Hon. Their intimacy had been long in building, satisfying in its completeness, and all too rare recently.

All personnel not directly connected to the destruction of the elevators, and hopefully the disabling of the city ships, were being evacuated. The ground blasts were anticipated to have seismic repercussions. The outer shell of the planet would ring like a bell and, with three nearly simultaneous sets of explosions, harmonic waves magnifying at various points might get super critical for some of the underground chambers. The modeling indicated they could not stay put. They were going deep, below the water table into mantle bedrock.

Swaying in the dark tunnel, the car rounded a corner and light appeared ahead. Unlike every subway, train, or car tunnel she had ever been in or heard of on Earth, these tunnels were dark unless lit for a purpose. Merely passing through did not constitute a need for preciously guarded electrical power. The light ahead meant a stop. Connie craned her neck to see over the passengers ahead but could not make out the platform. She'd been put on the car with a simple comment: "Hooman friend ahead. Not worry." The car slowed further, indicating a stop and, with heart leaping, she could see, among two groups of evacuees on the platform, one male tow-headed human.

The car came to a stop just a moment after Connie leapt from her seat. She ran toward Brad. He met her motion halfway, lifting her and twirling. Foreheads in both groups blanked in amazement at the uninhibited display. Oblivious to the stares, they felt the psi shock around them. Brad slowed his twirl and set Connie down.

With her fingers linked behind his neck, she leaned back, grinning. She pushed her swollen belly into him. "Hon, I have news!"

His smile froze, a tiny kick from within objected to his pressure from without. He raised his eyes from the outer evidence of the miracle inside.

"Wow! Is that?"

"Yes, there are now three humans on Dzura!"

He pulled back and saw that the standard issue light grey jumpsuit had modified pleats added. He said, appraising the half watermelon bulge straining against her altered jumpsuit, "You are really becoming quite the mama-san."

She had done the stitching herself. She had seen in the crèche that their maternity suits had extra fabric in the back between the shoulders. She needed that extra space in front. She placed his hands on either side of the swelling. With good timing, he was rewarded with a fetal elbow punch that made her wince.

~ ~ ~

Old Chookya Residential Complex

Old Chookya was one of the cities near enough to the Teeya City Keerosh to have been erased above ground but far enough away to retain most of the underground facilities deeply dug into bedrock. The attack force deployed to make final arrangements for the attack on Teeya City's space elevator included Shaand's personal detachment, Dju-klat saa's remaining forces, and a detachment of mining engineers. For the convenience of security, the recent convert LonnDonn and the two humans were billeted together. LonnDonn's conversion, treasonous from the perspective of his former allies and just above despicable to his new allies, had been kept near as his understanding of Erran psychology was helpful in war planning. The two humans were protected as possible friendly agents in any outcome that included an end of the Erran tyranny over the home world.

LonnDonn looked at the tall Hooman across the small room. He was peculiarly shaped but still oddly Elioid in overall form. Bilaterally symmetrical, his sensory systems were concentrated in an obvious head. It had two eyes for depth perception, although they weren't nearly wide enough to give adequate peripheral vision. He had protruding ears, similar to some of the more primitive herbivores here on the home world. Hooman speech was a fast-moving mishmash of soft sounds he could not make. The coloration of its long head hair reminded him of river's mud. Two legs and hips adapted for a vertical stride although the knees could only bend backward. That must be limiting in tight quarters. Two arms arranged much like his own, but too many digits! Why do they need so many fingers?

But his eyes! It was easy to see this was not only a sentient species, but a highly intelligent one. As they looked each other over, he could tell he was being assessed as well, which made him a little uncomfortable. Did he look like prey?

The message came unbidden but perfectly understood. *Not worry, not bite, not eat Errans.* LonnDonn literally jumped back in surprise. Shaand was standing in the corner watching the two, amused by the shocked surprise of the Erran Gre.

Brad said again, this time nodding to let LonnDonn know the origin and vocalizing it in English in addition to a repeated psi note. *Not worry. Hello.* He had only a few hundred words in his vocabulary. While Connie was quite a bit better, he had learned how to color or flavor speech with psi intent, an important component of Elioi speech.

From Shaand's corner of the small room, he took a new appreciation for his Hooman. His student was doing well.

Brad asked the Erran, *LonnDonn come Dzura for walk?* He mimed two fingers walking.

LonnDonn was again stunned. *The Hooman Braad had been told of my interrogation. He is trusted by the Dzuran command.* LonnDonn had no measure to gauge the level of language sophistication, but these humans could psi! He answered. *Yes, Dzura is way to future, not Erra leadership. Erra only know consume and use. Make more crèche—make more Erran soldiers—make Dzurans do more work.* He wasn't sure how much these Hoomans could understand. But he suspected the Hoomans were present as a double-blind interrogation. They were to find out about him and his Errans as much as might be useful to the Dzuran cause.

Sensing that the communication was going well, Shaand stepped forward and, with a bow to Brad but not to LonnDonn, left the room. Brad took this as being left in charge. LonnDonn reassessed the Hooman's possible level of importance to the rebels. What aid could he possibly provide?

Brad started with an attempt at speech that, based on LonnDonn's blank stare, failed miserably. He asked again in psi, *LonnDonn want help Dzura?* He waited for the look of understanding on the Erran's face. *Dzuran Pel-Council need know most vulnerable weakness Teeya City, Riiya City, Aeya City.* A frown lined the Erran's forehead in an spray of vertical wrinkles.

Brad added, psi-ing slowly for understanding, *Humans want help Dzura.* And with a short pause to make sure he was understood, he added the question, *LonnDonn want help Dzura?* He repeated the same question hoping for understanding. He wished that Connie was here to help with the conversation.

LonnDonn considered. He had seen the newsvid of the Hooman's capture, coming into Dzuran space without even bothering to put up a defense. He had followed their escort right into the hangar at Teeya City's elevator and transfer to Teeya City in bubble head suits. The newscaster had said their little two-seater ship was pretty but primitive. The ship had been immobilized in the capture, but all knew that it had been taken into the gaping Teeya hangar for study. He also knew that it had been determined to be inert. Possibly, it had not put up shields as its energy piles had been depleted. What else did he know about these strange creatures other than that they had possession of an antique Dzuran craft? He tried a simple question in psi. *How will two Hoomans help Dzura fight Errans?*

The answer was immediate as Brad replied, *Any path, all path, any time. How can LonnDonn help Dzura?*

LonnDonn smiled and was astounded to see a smile wrinkling the forehead of the Hooman. *I can help Dzura.*

Standing in an adjoining room with a few other ranking council members arranged around a pinhole camera's monitor, Shaand forced a grim smile. "We shall have to test this one, but perhaps he's genuine. The Hoomans we can be sure of. They have been tested under fire. This Erran?" He shrugged to several others' nods.

~ ~ ~

Brad handed the tablet over to Shaand with some humility. He knew that some very advanced thinkers had been working on the problem for years, but having watched the test explosions go through several series of tests, he'd thought of two serious flaws. Had the Dzuran's been victims of tunnel vision, seeing only one way to take down the orbiting cities? The engineers seemed bent on blasting the ships with massive chunks of concrete. In all of the simulation runs he'd seen, even with two and three impacts, the ship's defensive systems kicked in, shutting down all airlocks, minimizing loss of essential atmospheres, and accepting the losses to systems that had redundant backups. And the bulk of the "bullets" themselves deflected the blast force from the blast pit. Those ships needed a crippling blow or the destruction of the planet as a revenge strike would be catastrophic.

Shaand took the tablet and saw the first of several panels drawn crudely with a stylus, but understandable as the space elevator's anchor disc. The first frame was labeled with a simple /, the second // and so on. One through six, //////. Brad had not yet mastered writing Dzuran letters or numbers. The second frame indicated a small explosion and the severing of the elevator filament. The third showed the filament drifting away. The fourth showed seven hexagons being cut out of the disc, leaving the heavy rim intact. The fifth indicated the boreholes dug with one explosive placed under each of the outer six hexagons. The sixth showed the blast extending upward with the seven hexagons being blown into a city ship. The city ship, though crudely represented, was shown being impacted by five of the seven pieces. The force of the blast, which had never before reached as high as the ship, was shown blasting through and past it.

Shaand studied the six frames, scanning back and forth through the series. He pointed at the fifth frame, nodded, pulled a stylus from the pad's frame, and made a few marks on the drawing. He then backed up and made a few notations on frames two and three and then changed all the frame numbers to Dzuran characters. He scribbled a note or two on the margin, tapped a corner of the pad and the image vanished. Watching Shaand's facility with the stylus and pad, Brad had to wonder what kinds of technology the Elioi were capable of and how far ahead of humanity they were. If they were capable of hyper jumps, or pop and drops, or whatever they used to get through space, how much more was there to their culture that he was unaware of?

Lost in these thoughts, he didn't notice Shaand smiling. He looked up to see Shaand checking the data band on his cuff. Shaand tapped it for the time and looked up at Brad. "Soon! Soon we see!"

Brad was pleased that the idea seemed acceptable, constructive. "Think they try this idea on the model?"

"Yes, good is idea!" Shaand was still working on verb placement but had improved tremendously.

"Shaand"

"Yes, friend."

Brad paused, he didn't want to sound overly intrusive, but he had seen so many things that bordered on magic that he had to ask. "Shaand, how does that tablet thing work? I mean not so much the drawing part. But didn't you send those pictures to someone?" He mimed throughout, he hoped he implied picking the pictures off the surface of the tablet and sending them away.

Shaand appeared thoughtful; Brad wasn't sure if their language skills were up to the question. Shaand placed the pad on his wrist and made simulated strokes on its face. He then pulled Brad's left wrist and set the little tablet on it and then set his own left cuff with its embedded com unit beside Brad's wrist. With his right hand, he motioned back and forth, and Brad got the impression the tablet could communicate the same way that the cuffs did. He had seen them used as voice communicators, limited text communicators, and signaling devices that controlled anything from the arrival of personal train cars to electronically locked doors. Okay, so there was a very complex little radio in there.

Shaand left him in contemplation of the disparity between their cultures. He wondered how many hundreds of years ahead of human technology the Elioi were. After all, his old piece of Dzuran scrap metal, the bit broken off Jai's hull, was advanced compared to human science and it had been developed four hundred years ago!

The following morning, in the simulation room, Brad, Connie, four techs, and a few of the male administrators watched the simulation. As Brad hoped, the first small explosion severed the filament. Centripetal force that had been keeping the cable taught now began to pull it up and to the west. While the rest of the shape charges were cutting the interior of the anchor disc into pieces, the tail cleared the boundary of the anchor. The six atomic charges blew a clear hole in the foundation, leaving the heavy foundation perimeter ring behind. The remaining foundation ring, instead of adding to the mass that needed to be lifted, acted as a choke on a shotgun, focusing the charge. A chant developed as the cloud grew, dangerous, ugly, beautiful, and with a focused upward component that the roiling balls of the earlier unfocused explosions did not have. He was not sure if he heard it correctly, but Brad thought the chant was, "jha, jha, jha, Jha, Jha, Jha, Jha, JHA, JHA, JHA!" or translated, go, Go, GO! At full voice, the small group watched as pieces of the anchor plate and the white hot blast of plasma boiled past the elevator platform and burst through the skin of the city ship.

The ship in the model, Riiya City, rolled with the blast, venting as it did. Automatic doors still closed, sealing off the venting gasses, but it was apparent that its gyro stabilizers and automatic positioning jets could not keep the huge structure from rolling. Cheers broke out in the room. The heat of the blast had sheared off a significant portion of the city. The spinning grav chambers collapsed in a tangled mass of structural spokes and venting chambers. Thousands would die if the scenario worked. The ship could eventually be stabilized, but the city would have to expend a huge amount of energy to regain a circular orbit. By that time, it might already be an elliptical orbit that would ultimately bring it down.

In the discussions that followed, the design was tweaked, timing of the events and the shape of the liquid chamber remodeled to maximize the height of the blast column. In two days, the final model was selected in which a strong ring was maintained around the outside of the foundation disc and the liquid chamber was developed as an inverted cone. The last few meters of liquid were replaced with a volatile petrochemical soup of fuels scavenged from a variety of sources. Each of the three sites would have a different final mix since there would be different sources.

The model was run twenty-seven times. Three cubed was a sacred number in Dzuran numerology. The model resulted in the destruction of the city above twenty-five of the runs.

Chapter 20

"If a man be gracious and courteous to strangers, it shows he is a citizen of the world."
Francis Bacon

Old Chookya Residential Complex
3608.395 Erran Calendar

In their second 'interview' with LonnDonn, the Hoomans were led into a room with only general instruction given to the former Gre. Brad, Connie, and LonnDonn had frequently been guarded together and kept together for convenience, so the Erran didn't find it unusual. The reunion came as a surprise to Connie who wondered that the normal take-no-prisoners warfare she'd witnessed had spared this individual.

LonnDonn actually welcomed the company; isolation in the damp and dusty underground quarters made him long for conversation. Very little news was shared with him by passing guards. He had felt the concussions from above as rolling seismic waves passing through the bedrock. The only upper class Erran on the planet shut his eyes in the habit of praying, but he realized he no longer knew to whom or what he should pray. He stood in the corner as they entered, determined to let them share anything. LonnDonn had not opened up to others in questioning like he had with the two strange Hoomans.

Brad noticed LonnDonn rubbing dust out of his eye with his peculiar nail-less fingertip. It seemed a very human gesture. He asked the Erran, *What make your change of mind? Change to Dzura?*

It took him off guard. It was not an easy question to answer. The answer was the only thing that made it possible to get over the loss of so many lives. LonnDonn understood that whichever side lost would suffer catastrophic loss of life. This was Elioi warfare at its worst. He still considered that aerial superiority would eventually win a war of attrition.

He answered slowly, remembering. *When I am small, new in academy, I study war history. Military archive has vid of destruction of Dzura. Watch terrible death from above. Much same as feeling death from below.*

Connie prodded. *How much did you watch?*

LonnDonn watch too many. Not know number. See first Teeya City. Then Jaakra, Clubidik. Asteroids fall in water near city, much destruction. Big wave, fire, steam, more fire then water. Death fast for most, horrible for rest. After all stop, just smoke, water, wreck. All dead. He thought back to the tapes, to images he'd suppressed. *Riiya City, old Riiya, asteroid land on old temple buildings in city center. The city ... disappeared in dust.* He stopped, noticing that the Hooman was writing on a piece of cloth with a strange object. The Hooman did not have a data band on his wrist! He considered the technology that brought the Hooman to the Alal system was in fact, old Dzuran technology. How much intelligence had been inferred simply because they had gotten here? How much because they had the ability to communicate with psi? He decided to change the subject. After all, the Hooman was interrogating him.

LonnDonn asked, *Hoomans only pilots for Dzuran fighter name Jai? Is so?*

Brad responded. *Yes, Jai allows Human pilot Brad.* He pointed a thumb at his chest. *Only pilot, and Connie or Shaand as only crew.*

You friend Shaand tell me of plan to kill my city. Teeya still much danger. LonnDonn unconsciously looked up at the ceiling then over toward Shaand. *Destroyers from Erra come soon. Mine ships come too. Maybe bring back planet death to Dzura.*

Brad stared at the ceiling as this was being explained. He asked, *How is this important to who flies Skeeter Jai?*

The answer was immediate and its psi overtone convincing. *One place, to kill city.* He said, "Pa-Kaa le meek la."

Brad asked, *Please translate, not understand.*

Kill shot in the eye of the beast, Shaand translated.

Brad practiced the sounds. "Pa-Kaa la mick la."

LonnDonn nodded, then corrected, "Pa-Kaa le meek la."

~ ~ ~

Teeya City – Surveillance Section 3
3608.396 Erran Calendar

Remote sensing specialist Mre-Cle scanned his sensors, looking for heat signatures, voids, or anything else that might solve the current riddle. It had been established by numerous survivor accounts that the Dzuran fighters could appear, almost without notice, inflict heavy damage on manufacturing or transport facilities, and seemingly disappear. Often, there were no survivors, but when a few had been rescued from their disabled float vehicles or air cars, the Dzurans had fled, leaving little sign.

Mre-Cle had been enlisted from the mining corps and was an expert at remote sensing systems designed for assay analysis of subsurface materials. As he played with band sensitivity settings and deepwave channels, an anomaly briefly flared and vanished. He had found a combination that seemed to create straight linear patterns, but he'd lost it. Starting over with sensitivity too low to pick up hard rock, he began to slowly increase it. No results. Nothing, nothing. Wait!?

Faint lines and anomalous rectangles appeared near one of the most recent attack sites. "By the Lights! I've found it." Excitedly, he pulled up file images of the latest mineral assay sweeps. Dzura had been surveyed, studied, and meticulously assayed a century ago, but in an attempt to track the elusive rebels, a survey drone had been commissioned to re-fly the entire land mass, starting with areas recently attacked. He pulled up a new set of remote sensing layers covering another attack site and reset the displays to the settings that had been successful. He pushed off the console with such effort that he lifted free of the tacky chair bonds and flew into the back wall of the room.

~ ~ ~

Hangar bay technician Dzar-yng watched as the huge blast doors opened. He always loved to see the surface open up below him. It was one of the few times that he actually felt that there was an 'up' and a 'down' in his normally weightless world. Because fighters, fuelers, munitions drones, and shuttles entered from space, there were no grav plates in the hangar. There was usually fore, aft, and an array of directions typically denoted by bay number rank and file. When those doors opened, there was most definitely a down. Above him, the loading machinery tracked a new set of g-field ships over the opening. He saw the static claws pull back. The smaller ship bobbled slightly, in the city but no longer of it. As this flight's leader gave the command, the nine ships dropped toward the surface. On a powered dive, they became tiny very quickly and disappeared. In the past, as they veered out toward a ground target, atmospheric trails would appear to let him know where the last flight had gone. Now, he knew they were being stationed near the elevator bases to provide additional security at those critical supply points.

Usually though, he was assigned to watch for glitches in the machinery, any loose items that had been released to very low grav that could interfere with a launch sequence. The next flight slid into position above the bay doors. As the grapple claws released, the tiny craft fired a small burst of chemical jets required to clear the Teeya's minor gravity influence and then sped away. Before the shift was over, nine flights had dropped to provide security at the elevator bases. New orders! As hangar tech, he did not know their mission this day, only that it was unusual. These were shielded craft and although they could rain starfire on any ground positions, they could not possibly hope to secure those positions. To land, they'd have to drop shields, extend clunky 'feet,' and settle at ungainly horizontal rest, susceptible to even ballistic weapons. Must be important, he thought, but those considerations were above his grade.

~ ~ ~

Pelma Si-I mulled over the various options. He could continue trying to hamper the Dzuran resistance with aerials or wait for the full complement of ground troops to go into the recently discovered warrens and root them out. Now that they had found a good number of the entrances, it was only a matter of time before the rebels would need come up for air, water, food. How many could there be after all? His display showed the tracks of the nine flights as they spread out over one of his districts on the north coastline of the southern continent. "I almost forgot, it had a name." He tried to remember. Jhianna, or was it Chianna?

One of the flights, the one traveling along the coast, slowed and sprayed a suspected tunnel entrance with enough explosives to destroy any tunnels leading away from the area. Those temporary bright spots flared silently on his screen.

He wondered, how many of you are down there? Why persist? We will eventually win this war because you cannot come out of those warrens without facing our superior air forces. When we can get ground troops down into your tunnels, there will be no escape.

As he sat, watching the display, the smell of the air circulations system's disinfectant briefly flooded the room. It had to be done periodically, but By the Lights, he hoped the new formulation was not dangerous. He briefly considered getting the schedule and ensuring that he was in another part of the city when command and control was being treated. That train of thought brought up a visit to Erra he had taken as a cadet nearing graduation. He had seen a structure that was being treated for sucking lice. A field generator had been set up in the house with a three-shift timer. Noxious gas reactions were set off inside and, he was told, all the lice would be guaranteed to be dead, even the young in their eggs. An idea grew, almost against his own will. The thought that took form made him a little sick at first. The more it developed and the logistics began to take form, he realized that a sudden end to the war would be possible—preferable to a protracted effort that depleted his city's resources, Erra's resources, and wasted the remainder of this year's crops. Eventually, his troopers would have to go in and mop up any remainders, clear the tunnels of the dead, but perhaps this was the course to be taken. Gas!

~ ~ ~

Mre-Cle pushed back his visor and rubbed his eyes. He'd been scanning his instruments for too long. He was confirming strike targets for so long that he was beginning to see things. He thought he had detected a circular void underneath the space elevator pad directly below him. That was ridiculous, without a foundation, the whole elevator would be unstable, unusable in fact. A weather system had just moved into his work area, blocking most good signals from the surface. He gave up. Hunger reminded him of how long he had been at it. He swiveled out of his work station, grabbed at a hand bar overhead and vaulted down a hallway toward the growing bays. He needed to suck the core out of a stim fruit.

~ ~ ~

Chookya Ag Processing Facility
3608.396 Erran Calendar

Shaand had been introduced to his trust circle but had not been given flight release status. He wouldn't know how to pilot the craft anyway as Jai's controls were half psi-control and half manual and, without a release from Jai's semi-sentient programming, no pilot could hope to take command. Brad and Connie had convinced Jai that Shaand and his delegated data techs could have access to those parts of their journey after the drop into Dzuran space. Brad had asked Shaand that, until the survival of the Dzuran revolt was assured and until Brad could ask to diplomatically represent Earth, Jai's extensive knowledge of human culture be kept in confidence.

The information Jai downloaded *was* significant. Jai's logs provided detailed information about the arrangement of Teeya City's hangar bays and armaments. Any captured grounders taken up to be interrogated had always been required to wear blank-out bubble helmets. If any were returned to service on the surface, none was able to report on the layout of the city ship above. Jai's download of systems aboard the ship had been indiscriminate, as his inquisitive mind added whole libraries of information about the Erran super city to its encyclopedic knowledge of Earth and its prior storehouse of Dzuran geography.

If the Dzuran revolt did not succeed, Jai's perfect memory might be the only historical record of the planet's first culture. It is the curse of history that it is always edited by successive generations to satisfy the sensibilities of the survivors.

Jai's sensors went to alert status. No one had been in his makeshift hangar-abandoned agricultural warehouse for days, but activity nearby trembled its sensors; rhythmic motion –footsteps. They were not outside; they were approaching in a tunnel, climbing stairs. A door opened and, his psi channel activated in response to a greeting.

Hello, friend B-rad…friend Ka-nee.

"Good to see you, Jai! Have you been taken care of? Resupplied?" Connie asked.

Yes, Ka-nee...as say at NASA, all systems go.

Where in the world did you learn that? Brad wondered.

On Ert...Ka-nee show Jai books...learn about solar system...learn about NASA.

Connie shot back, "I never told you about NASA."

No...Ka-nee not talk it...Jai learn read from picture books...NASA always big letters.

Well I'll be damned! she thought.

What dammed?

"Nothing. Well, it means all your parts turn to rust." Brad said. "Never mind. It's a human thing. You said all systems go. Do you mean all energy weapons are fully charged and you have full chem fuel tanks?"

Yes...full charge ... grav-nav antennae repaired ... full load heavy arms.

"Heavy arms?" Brad realized that as Jai's pilot of choice, he'd learned only basic techniques of maneuver, and how to deploy and drop the energy shielding. He had no idea of Jai's complement of weapons. "What kind of heavy arms?"

Jai, latest Skeeter model.

The statement seemed to have pride expressed in it. Could a sentient machine express pride? It certainly was protective of the two humans who had rescued it. "Okay, fine. You're the latest model. What kind of heavy weapons does Jai have? I may need to know."

Ballistic weapons include light machine cannon and heavy railgun ... cannon good in short range ... railgun most excellent against unshielded target if Skeeters combine fire ... can break down energy shields.

"We're not likely to be able to have you combine fire with another Skeeter."

Shaand came up behind them. He had ordered his complement of troopers to spread out to cover the perimeter of the building, disappearing into the dried and wilting stalk fruit brush. Since they had not been harvested, the rows of stalks still stood almost head high and would provide good cover if his troops could withstand the stench of the unharvested fruit that had lain too long in the sun.

Shaand said, "Tese Skeeters design to fly in trees." He held up his three fingers to clarify. Then with his fist, he poked the air twice with his hairless knuckles up and once just above it to indicate the third ship flew inverted. He and Brad had become adept at gesture as an aid to communicating when Shaand's growing vocabulary remained insufficient. "Tree Skeeters share shields, make hard to hurt." He smiled. "But tree rail gun aim one spot? Bad for Erran destroyer shield wall."

Brad wondered to himself how he could use that information and how many rounds were on board. The number appeared in his thoughts. *19,683.* He asked aloud, "Is that how many rail gun rounds."

Yes.

A runner entered the ruined east wall of the building, the pink morning light backlighting him in silhouette. He spoke rapidly to Shaand who quickly barked commands to the young trooper. As he ran back to his squad outside, Shaand ordered the remaining guards inside to reinforce those outside and then said to Brad and Connie, "Need Hoomans get in Skeeter. Raise shield. More safer. Now!" He turned and ran to follow the last of the departing soldiers, reaching for his sidearm as he ran.

To their surprise, Jai cracked its canopy which opened with a light whirr. Steps formed in the wall of the fighter. As the handholds took shape, Brad climbed to the canopy wall and got in. Connie followed behind him and settled into the weapons officer's seat.

The design was a two-seater with pilot in front and weapons officer positioned behind. On the ship's last missions for the Dzuran Navy, its crew had been down to one, pilot and weapons officer's duties combined. On the last mission, only the command squad leader Ka-Litan piloted the ship, with Jai's learned skills replacing the crew member who had been inducted into pilot duty on the last push to escape Erran forces. Brad and Connie had used any spare room for groceries on their early shakedown flights and to store water bottles for drinking and waste.

Settling in, Brad found himself reorienting to the control panel. He did find that he could now read the number displays on some of the readouts. He just didn't know the meaning of what was being reported. Although he couldn't read the panel's many labels, he had learned how to operate the three-dimensional navigation screen and could perform basic maneuvers. It helped that with the grav-drive engaged, the ship didn't actually have to 'fly.' It could hover just fine; it was just more maneuverable in an atmosphere with fins extended.

Gunfire, or rather laser fire, erupted at the open end of the hangar. "Hang on, Connie! Here we go!"

Thin green lines extended from the row of withered crops beyond the building's perimeter. His companions were taking fire. Brad followed the lines of fire back to three ground cars concealed just below the level of the crop's wilted fruiting heads. The intensity of the barrage indicated that his friends were soon going to be overrun by superior forces. "Jai, shields up. Full cloaking. Hover and orient to open building."

The ship lifted a few feet off the floor and whirled to the right pointing toward the open end of the makeshift hangar. "Jai, move to the open end of building." The ship moved into an exposed position, facing the row of crops where concealed Erran ground cars were pinning down rebels and slowly chewing away at their shelters with sustained laser and explosive tipped projectiles. Brad sent out a psi signal to Shaand to have all rebels lay flat. In a moment, all return fire back at the Errans stopped. The Errans never saw anything but a faintly shining bubble before Jai's guns opened up. Jai's rail gun laid down sustained fire that swept the withered stalks chest high. When the stalks finally stopped falling, cries of pain and dying erupted from the wreckage of the three smoldering ground cars beyond the ruined field.

With a yell, rebel soldiers, far more mobile than the recently trained Erran ground forces, leapt from their cover and systematically swept the killing field for survivors. From his viewpoint in Jai's cockpit, Brad turned off the forward camera. There was no need to share the scene with Connie as any crawling, groveling, or otherwise moving Erran on the ground was finished off. He had an unguarded thought that he immediately regretted, that this finish was unnecessary. That total elimination of the enemy invited similar tactics from the other side. He wondered what the implications might be if humans and Elioi ever became other than allies.

Earth Interlude 8

"Always listen to experts. They'll tell you what can't be done and why. Then do it."
Robert A. Heinlein

NSA Headquarters
September 14, 1986 – Earth Calendar
3608.396 Erran Calendar

"So you're telling me that this thing has been actively collecting our satellites and stealing them?" The young Brigadier General in charge of the reconnaissance satellite section was at the limit of his willingness to comprehend. Was the even younger Lieutenant Colonel, fresh from NASA's Houston HQ, really saying that the reason for so many failed orbital platforms was that they were, in fact, being stolen?

Colonel Rennie hesitated. He had only been assigned to the recon for a few months but felt he had a handle on it. He knew McDonnell-Douglas and Northrop Grumman specifications from his liaison work and understood the capability of all deployed and planned systems. He had been chosen specifically because of his work in the still secret laser fitted systems. Although not fully operational, and still untested in space, the system was state of the art. "Sir, with all respect, our own tracking systems are backed up by ground observation from Australia, Hawaii, Arizona, you name it. When we got the word out to take a look, we received video of something no one has ever seen before, packing satellites almost at random into a bundle and moving on to its next target."

General Aldenberg blew softly through pursed lips. "Have a seat, Colonel." He looked at the too grainy photograph in the file, knew that a lupe would not help. The photo had already been blown to the maximum pixel density of the image. Further enlargement would just look like grey boxes. "Have you tried image enhancement on this? See if we can figure out if it's the damned Russians?"

Colonel Rennie sat on the front five inches of one of the two spare visitors' chairs facing General Aldenberg's desk. "I almost wish I could conclusively tell you that the thing was Russian. Then, at least, we'd know what we are up against." Aldenberg just puffed his cheeks, waiting. "We are pretty sure that the pirate is not from here because it's taken at least two of the Russian satellites as well."

"You know that for sure? It's taking more than just ours? Any chance that it's that Florida kid and the spaceship everybody was saying he had? He hasn't been heard of for a while. Maybe he's figured out how to make a living stealing satellites for the Chinese. I think I remember that he was verified as the bogey over the Gobi." Aldenberg chortled at his own poor rhyme then caught himself.

"Don't believe it myself, sir." Rennie quickly assessed how much he could say about the little he knew. "That bird has flown. A lot of the commentators and even some of the NASA insiders say he may have gone out of the system and been compromised."

"Compromised?"

Rennie coughed into his hand and looked furtively left and right to signify that he was telling the General more than he should. "Sir, they've been gone, disappeared for far too long for anything that could have been stowed aboard. Conventional wisdom says they're toast."

General Aldenberg looked thoughtful, weighing alternatives. "So, not the Russians, who?"

"Huge guess, my own guess. Someone else, something else, off-planet. Something may have retraced the course of wherever the two Florida kids went. Assuming they went somewhere and didn't crash on the moon or crack a vacuum."

"Those kids are still MIA?"

"Yes, sir. They haven't been sighted or suspected in anyone's airspace that we can confirm in months." He shrugged honestly. "From the chatter we're getting backchannel, the bandit's taken a Brazilian Telefónica satellite and a French TV relay as well. It's apparently an equal opportunity thief."

"The Brazilians have telecom satellites?" Aldenberg was genuinely surprised.

"Yes, sir," Rennie offered, appreciating the reduced tension. "It's an ATT model. With only a few decades down since Sputnik, space is already getting a little crowded."

Aldenberg sat back, puffing again. "So, what exactly can we do about it? What options can I take to the Secretary?" He looked up at the wall clock. "He'll be asking me that exact question in about half an hour, and I hope like hell he doesn't want to take me to the meeting with the Joint Chiefs. That crap is way above my pay grade."

"General, we have one bird up there that is a little more capable than she seems."

This seemed hopeful. Maybe he could do more than sit back and get reports on his diminished orbital inventory.

"One of our latest orbital birds has laser capabilities. It was originally designed to take out satellites whose orbits were degrading into the paths of other designated orbits, to slow them down or if possible, get them to fall out sooner and burn up. We have it figured out that if something has to fall down then it will do so over empty ocean."

"You can do that?"

"It hasn't been tested yet. There're a few candidates that have lost transmission capability, dead fuel cells, micrometeorite damage, or some other malfunction. We were going to experiment on those."

"And find out if you could do it to the Russians in the future?"

"Well, that would be an obvious plus."

"But this isn't the 'Star Wars' stuff the President has been hot about is it?" Aldenberg looked up expectantly, hopefully.

"No, sir. That's still years away, if we ever get there. Those are much more powerful and designed to track and kill multiple ICBMs coming over the pole at us." Rennie gave a short whistle as he gestured with his hands. "Those birds will aim and fire anti-missile warheads. It would be nice to have them up there now. We could blast that little pirate into scrap."

"But we don't have it now?" Aldenberg knew he was asking questions a step above his clearance, but he didn't care at this point. His next request to his superiors, probably during his immediate interview with the Secretary of the Air Force was to get that additional clearance or be taken off this assignment. He didn't really

225

want to be reassigned. He actually wanted the clearance. It was a prerequisite to the next promotion anyway.

Rennie answered carefully, "Sir, I can tell you that at this time, we are still years away from the initial orbital testing of the Star Wars birds."

"So what does this thing do that you already have up there?"

"It's target practice, sir."

"Say again, Colonel."

"Targets and guns are moving around up there awfully fast. An orbital gun firing at a bird in a temperate zone orbit is moving at…Well, imagine you're on the interstate, standing on top of a moving semi, and you want to hit a driver in a car that will be crossing over that interstate in five minutes. You've got to take aim, hold that aim for all of those five minutes and keep up a targeted rate of fire the entire time to be effective."

"Sounds tough," the General grudgingly admitted.

"Yes. Now speed up everything from sixty-five miles an hour to two miles a second."

"Oh!"

"And that's for the high geo-synchronous orbits. The LEOs are much faster."

"LEOs?"

"Yessir, the low Earth orbital satellites are moving at about twelve miles a second. But the delta-V between our bird and the bandit is…"

Although Aldenberg grunted and nodded appreciatively for the rest of the description, he was certain that he only understood about two percent of what he'd been told.

Rennie finished and waited expectantly. He wasn't sure if Aldenberg had full understanding of the magic involved, but he'd hit the basics often and emphasized the test nature of the project. No need to pin too much expectation on the first couple of tries. Heck, the bandit might shoot back with a lot more firepower.

Aldenberg didn't break the silence immediately, but pulled the top secret dossier toward him. He flipped through the first several pages of text until he got to the diagrams. These he studied for perhaps half a minute. He then went back to the cover page and scrawled his ornate signature across the 'approved' line at the bottom. The General looked up at the Colonel who was statue-still, barely breathing. "Son, do this right and you're going to be a hero. Screw this up and you might as well come back in here and ask for Greenland. Understood?"

"Yes, sir. I've been weighing that."

"Don't screw it up." He handed the dossier with its bright red TOP SECRET band secured and watched the young officer execute a parade ground perfect about face and depart. He muttered softly, "God help you, son."

Chapter 21

Cry havoc, and let slip the dogs of war.
Marc Antony in William Shakespeare's *Julius Ceasar*

Teeya City – Surveillance Section 3
3609.000 Erran Calendar

Mre-Cle took his position at the beginning of his shift with a new sense of purpose and, he thought, a bit of well-deserved pride. He'd been called into the Pel-Council's New Year's celebration, praised and called out as a model of resourcefulness and dedication. The pinning ceremony was carried throughout the city's media channels and resulted in a new braid of rank on his cuff. He was temporarily famous. Better still, after the insurrection, he would be given leave on Erra, or one of the pleasure ships on the Charn system's garden planet. That newly discovered system offered growth potential for empire building. As he stood at rigid attention in the ceremony, he'd listened with special interest as the Pelma had insisted on new crèche groups being raised in higher gravity conditions so planetary expansion could be accomplished without depending on the black-souled Dzurans.

The previous surface monitor had shifted field of view to an unfamiliar point, forcing Mre-Cle to re-center the view. From directly beneath the ship, the leading edge of the elevator platform rimmed the bottom of the screen. Pointing toward its center, the dark elevator filament thinned to almost nothing as it reached downward to the small disc of the anchor. Of course, he knew the disc was as large as one of the revolving grav-rings that slowly spun around the axis of the ship's central corridors. Absently, he zoomed in toward the elevator disc itself. Sometimes he could tell what supplies were going to be sent up if he could get a good look at the loading vehicles.

He focused his reticule on the scene. Wisps of the cloud cover that had obscured earlier observations were clearing. A lift unit had just been loaded and was leaving the surface. Odd? A small group of workers was running at speed toward a ground vehicle. The car sped off, raising a small dust trail before it converted to hover mode and its speed increased even further. That was strange! he thought. It looks almost like they were running *from* something. He panned his view back toward the base of the elevator's thin pialla-reinforced filament. The fiber's incredible tensile strength made possible a lightweight physical connection between the massive ground anchor and the near-space docking and loading platform. The platform, attached to its tether well above the altitude of any significant atmosphere, made possible the transfer of material and personnel between ground and city with significant savings in chem fuels.

Motion caught his eye. A bright flash was followed by a billowing cloud of smoke near the base. "What?" The recently loaded car disappeared in a flash! A ripple traveled up the length of the filament. A light surface wind blew the tiny puff of smoke away. He again zoomed into maximum magnification to the base of the filament. "Something dark and lumpy seemed to be laying in a heap just off center. His hand reached for an all-ship alarm, just as one came on with an ear-searing whoo-O whoo-O whoo-O from another source. Someone else had seen this too! Maybe the operators on the elevator platform had sounded the alarm. The filament had been severed. Sabotage!

As the newly promoted shift supervisor, Mre-Cle could not simply hand off the alarm to his supervisor and go back to his view screen. He badly wanted to keep watching as events unfolded below him, but others could do that. He set his screen to auto-record, transferred the signal to the command bridge feed, and bolted straight up for handholds. He pivoted into an express tube and made rapid hand-over-hand progress to the bridge. He was too late. The entire assembly was watching a wall-sized screen. Someone had switched on a view from one of the down-looking cameras on the elevator platform. No one could mistake that the center of view was shifting off center. Without the anchor and much of its cable, the elevator platform would be closing on Teeya City. Untethered, its vector would intersect the orbit of the city. Its crew would have to be rescued and its long out of service drive motors fueled.

For the immediate future, the biggest concern being hotly debated was whether it would impact any fragile structures on Teeya City itself. Most of the heavy movers in the hangar bay had been moved to Erra to make room for the assembled fleet of air cars that were being retrofitted with shield generators. Si-I wasn't on deck yet. The first officer on the con called up the loadmaster on the platform. Over sounds of bedlam and panic, the first officer managed to get across to the loadmaster that there were long disused positioning jets on the platform. He was to impose a northern vector immediately. All attempts would be made to rescue the shift crew on the platform.

The Pelma Si-I dropped from his personnel tube into his command chair. He was already in a terrible mood. More of the screens lining the room began to display a downward angled view of the nadir point directly below the ship. Normally, many of these views would have been blocked by the elevator platform, but oddly, it was no longer there. Abruptly, the surface of the anchor disc fractured as several lines of small explosives began to chew up the surface of the disc. It was being destroyed as they watched.

"How could this be?" Si-I's mind reeled with the implications. This was not an attack on the city itself; it simply removed any possibility of efficient resupply from the ground. "Heart of Darkness!" He jabbed at a com channel switch and shouted, "Hangar doors open, deploy ground crews, NOW!" This was not an unreasonable command given the information he had. But it wasn't to be. All screens flashed white then black. The cameras' sensitive optics had been fried by the intense heat of the nuclear explosions below. Onboard Teeya City, crews scrambled into action only to reach the location where they would meet their ultimate Light. The blindingly bright fireball rising through the atmosphere reached the city only a few moments later.

~ ~ ~

From the ground, behind the protection of a hardened pour-rock ridge, the demolition team sheltered from the rising ball of flame. It rose hot and angry, a roiling white-hot burst of energy. The final design of the attack had called for the complete destruction of the anchor disc into as many large pieces of rubble as possible. The explosives design had simply called for severing the reinforcing beams in as many places as possible. The model design showed that, once the anchor disc was fractured, the intense heat of the nuclear fireballs would melt any reinforcing rods. The masses of fractured pour-rock anchor disc would separate into hot shrapnel. The additional thrust of the water flashing to steam, focused by the perimeter foundation ring, and the shaped basin below was more than enough to send fractured pieces of pour-rock into the vulnerable bottom of the city ships. They were all the more deadly as the boiling column of expanding nuclear fire blasted through those breaches.

Teeya City took the blast slightly off-center. Its main structural members melted but did not sever. The forward hangar bays and their fuel storage pods flashed into a hell storm. The rear hangar bays were wrenched by the violent punch to the city's gut; most of its craft were bashed into each other or the launch equipment. Chemical and munitions explosions ripped through the rear hangars. The two destroyers attached for permanent protection duty died in the fires. The stern hangar bay, recipient of many of the new shielded ground cars, had no power source. Several dozen fighter craft hung uselessly in their powerless unmoving rack storage. There would be no answering wave of vengeful fighters from Teeya City.

The attack was nearly simultaneous at the three city ship locations. Horrified observers on the nearby and adrift elevator platforms watched as the focused blast burst into the base of the three cities. All were crippled immediately. As the events of the next few minutes matured, the three city ships were subjected to radioactive fireballs and perforated by incandescent masses of pour-rock that collapsed walls, struts, pressurized vessels, and hangar bays. Teeya City resolved into an elliptical orbit with severe rotation and no useable connections between what had been forward and aft sections of the city. Riiya and Aeya Cities were severed along their axes. Their major portions tumbled initially into elliptical orbits that quickly degenerated as their perigees scraped atmosphere. Hasty evacuation procedures managed to remove a few thousand desperate space-born Errans to a cruel introduction to Erran gravity.

Riiya's remains crashed, trailing incandescent trails into the central ocean two days later. A day later, Aeya followed, breaking up into a thousand fireballs on the shores of the northern continent. Teeya alone remained in orbit, despite its horrific damage. Teeya's new elliptical orbit did not find atmosphere, but its remaining crew members were unable to stop its rolling. The age of rule from above was coming to an end. In time, intense efforts by two destroyer class ships managed to slow the rolling and damped the more sickening yaw. Its life support pods were essentially wrecked, as were the huge wheels of the half-grav hydroponics sections. Over ninety percent of the orbiting warren had lost pressure. Thousands of dead were found, extracted, and given a hero's funeral in descent through atmosphere. Their myriad smoke trails could be seen from the surface when the rising or setting sun caught them. The remaining crew was left to re-pressurize portions of the formerly grand city and see if its former stable equatorial orbit could be re-established. Eventually, when the Pelma Si-I realized that there was no way to communicate with portions of the structure aft of the burn hole, he called for the two destroyers to begin evacuating those survivors to Erra.

~ ~ ~

Old Chookya
3609.002 Erran Calendar

LonnDonn had felt the rolling seismic waves passing through the bedrock. He shut his eyes in the habit of praying, but he realized he no longer knew to whom or what he should pray. Any lingering reason to hang on to the old trilogy had just died. His crèche, too, had died or would soon. The lucky ones perished in the initial blast. Unlucky survivors of that first boiling wave of plasma would find their home hopelessly crippled, powered down, and most likely losing its air pressure through a thousand minute fractures. That was a death reserved for the most heinous criminals whose offenses were punishable in the airlock. Innocents of all ages, young and aged, were perishing along with pilots, troopers, and crewmen of all ages. It was a city. It was complex and it too would die. He had given the Dzurans and their Hooman helper the secret to the city's final death blow.

He muttered to himself softly, "Pa-Kaa le meek la. This first strike will just tweak the crant's tail. Before it can turn on them, they will have to shoot the beast in the eye." From so far away and so far underground, he could not feel the psi-waves of panic, dying, and death. He knew that he was a traitor of the worst kind. He had betrayed his crèche oath, his city, and his "side." Why had he been put in the position of having to take sides against his city for the love of this planet? He pulled at the brass clasp of his overalls, tugging ever harder until the stitching tore. It was the only piece of metal he'd been allowed, overlooked because of its ubiquitous presence on every uniform issued. It was tiny, but it would do.

He recited the birth name of every crèche mate he still knew to be living before the grounder's attack. In the slow cadence of a reverent prayer, he spoke them aloud. With each invoked name, he rubbed the metal edge against the stone floor, sharpening a corner. Softly, slowly, their nearly rhyming personal names representing the great names of his family's past and the birth mother of the crèche. With a final appeal to the Maker of Lights, he pulled the sharpened edge of the clasp across the small vein above his double-jointed knee, the vein used for transfusions and tests because of its ease of access. It was also the favorite vein for those seeking the relief LonnDonn now sought. He could no easier live now among the eventual victors than he could permit their systematic destruction. He had chosen a path on the planet of his ancestors and it had led to this.

He repeated the names again, a soft muttering personal poem, and watched the small circle of blood grow at his feet. Most of it pooled beneath his feet so it wasn't detected by the guard assigned to look over the not-quite-trusted Erran until it was too late.

~ ~ ~

Near Teeya City's orbit
3609.002 Erran Calendar

Jai had been convinced that he must allow a new weapons officer. Connie had insisted and she thought only her intervention had convinced Jai to accept new programming. He would not allow a replacement pilot. Brad was the Hooman who had released him from his stone prison on Earth, and their bond was so complete that he would have had to go under a complete reboot and training to bond with a new pilot. Brad had been chosen by the Pel-Council's tactical planning committee because there was not time and there were no trained pilots anyway. Shaand was selected as weapons officer because he could most easily communicate with Brad and had already been given trust status. Now, as they approached the slowly tumbling monstrosity, the hasty plan seemed to be overreaching. The smallest warship in the old Dzuran Navy was now the only warship in the new Dzuran Navy. Ahead lay one of the largest armed satellites ever built by sentient beings in known space.

The biggest unknowable factor in the plan known as Pa-Kaa le meek la was whether the city had enough crew to serve its defensive batteries. The second biggest factor was whether the batteries could be powered up and fired. Visible ahead of the main body of the mangled structure, several components that had been blasted loose spun on new centers of gravity in completely independent gyres. A few large pieces had already fallen over a large area on the planet below. Some would be lost to exaggerated elliptical orbits that would, like the sister cities, drag through the atmosphere too often and eventually fall to the surface. Smaller pieces of hull components, damaged and tenuously connected components, hung on to the main body of the remains of Teeya City by cables, or bent and tortured structural members.

The Dzuran ground guns, super mortars, or whatever the future would name the shaped ground charges, had been extremely effective. Two of the three cities were destroyed, with the third badly, but not quite totally, rendered useless. If its orbit could be re-established and its attitude stabilized, it could be a base for the ultimate destruction of the Dzurans below. Cloaked, shielded, and in night shadow of the planet, the little Dzuran Skeeter slowly closed the distance toward the command bridge. Scatterwave cloaking gave it near invisibility, but no one knew the extent of the functional status of Teeya's defenses or if newer technologies could detect the cloaking. Against the darkside view of the planet below, only the sharpest eye would detect the tiny dot of nothing that Jai's reflection offered.

~ ~ ~

On the command bridge of the wrecked city, an ensign flew into the bridge and nearly overshot the end of the tube. At the last moment possible, he grabbed the perimeter ring, folded his legs, and pivoted. The ensign misjudged his target and splayed against the back of the seat he'd intended to sit in. A slow roll to starboard added to the disorientation of the yaw at either terminus of the city structure. Most of the city's midsection had been blasted away, and weakened trusses merely held the former forward and rear sections together in space. Flexing and groaning structural members sent metallic shrieks through areas that still held atmosphere. It was a rough ride for the few thousand lucky enough to have survived the ground blast. The Pelma Si-I was exhausted from five straight shifts of repair and replacement of damaged control systems. He still clung to the hope that, with reinforcements coming soon from Erra, his command could be stabilized and restored.

He had come to understand that with no elevator connection to the surface, raw materials could not be lifted. Of course, he was no longer located over his former nadir position, and that position was now a water-filled crater with a heavy radioactive signature. He and his ship were now totally at the mercy of the aid expected to arrive before the end of this shift.

Si-I knew that leaders of the two planets had been beaming diplomatic messages since immediately before the attack. Dzura had initiated the exchange with a demand that Erra cease its attack on ground positions, remove all administrators from Dzura, and disband any remaining mercenary militia for trial. The summary refusal was expected. However, news of the three terrible blasts aimed at the orbital cities was unexpected. Diplomacy rather than stubborn hubris began to take hold on Erra.

The Erran Pel-Council absorbed the enormity of their losses. Si-I hoped the talks could go on long enough for him to get power back to the hangar bays. If he could launch his contingent of newly shielded ground cars, he would make Dzura pay a heavy price. A final price. Mining ships could be brought in to begin shunting asteroids to high orbits around Dzura. There were plenty of asteroids available without mineral worth and more than enough mass to finish off Dzuran civilization forever. It would not matter to him that his generation or the next would not be able to colonize the old home world. Eventually, Erran culture of the home world would be capable and they would not make the same mistake. They would not be absentee landlords.

He turned his attention to the map of the ship. A twirling projection of Teeya City, with missing parts displayed as transparent. There were too many pieces missing. The remains of the damaged low gee wheel section had already been cut away. The high gee cylinder had been blown apart and most of the inhabitants had been fried by hot gasses before they had been carried away to vacuum. At least, he hoped so. So many others had been involuntarily sucked into space, their last moments of existence filled with terror as they tried to suck nothing into their lungs. He was considering where to dock the expected destroyers from Erra so their thrust would provide the best result in reducing first the rotation and then the sickening yaw that was most pronounced here at the forward prow of the city.

He was startled out of his exhaustion-induced reverie when the ensign dropped into the command bridge. "Sir!" The ensign hastily recovered his composure and a respectful posture. "We have been trying to contact the bridge for a while. The circuit we rebuilt this morning seems to have broken again."

"What is it? What's so important at this hour?"

"There is an unidentified craft closing in on our position from behind. It has to be the Dzuran craft that was jettisoned as junk. It's cloaked, but it has a heat signature."

"Can you get a positive fix on it with any of the impact avoidance systems?"

"We've been trying, sir. The automatic tracking modules are unreliable."

"As soon as you can get a line on it, blast it from orbit." He continued in thought but did not say, *There will soon be no more Dzurans to worry about. While the light still shines on my heart, I will kill them all for what they have done!*

An officer from the com console said loud enough to be heard over the other conversations on the bridge, "It's hailing in code!" Then after a beat, "Whatever that is, it has our hangar codes. It wants to dock." After another beat, "It's dropped its cloaking."

"Get a camera on that thing!" a tech officer called.

"Can't! Our visual controls are out. I can only see it when the ship's yaw passes the camera's range across it."

Si-I ordered, "Get what you can, take a still from that and magnify."

The com officer said, "It's coming on your screen ... now." A shot of a squat grey triangle appeared on screen. By its general shape, rounded corners, and the black canopy, it was recognizable. "Sir, it's the Dzuran Skeeter class fighter, either the same one the off-worlders commandeered, or one just like it."

"Ss-Shaand of the Dzuran Pel-Council hailing the ship known as Teeya City." The signal came in over the command intercom. Si-I's first thought was how do they know our internal com frequencies. They are supposed to be secure. Again the transmission filled the bridge, "Ss-Shaand of the Dzuran Pel-Council hailing the ship known as Teeya City. Are you able to communicate?"

A rumble ran through the ship's beams, followed by a wrenching screech of metal. Abruptly, the sound stopped and the yaw lessened a little. A mechanical voice came over one of the ship's channels. "Aft personnel, bay twenty-two, cut away, sir? Orders to scavenge or jettison?"

Si-I hated to lose city space that would become necessary in times to come, but these were extreme times now. "Permission to scavenge affirmed. Negative on jettison. Place in orbit fifteen degrees behind Teeya." He addressed the com officer again. "Switch weapons systems to automatic. If it's hostile, it's dead."

"Sh-Shaand, this is Pelma Si-I, of the City Ship Teeya, I'm in command here and I'm busy. Why shouldn't I blow you to dust?"

"Pelma, diplomatic channels with Cresow City are not going well. Those furthest from danger do not realize your peril. Do you surrender your ship?" This had been at Brad's insistence. When they overheard the conversations on the bridge that they were detected, he dropped shields to Shaand's complete amazement.

"Surrender?" Si-I had leapt to his feet to stare at the monitor that displayed the tiny craft. "Surrender to what? To whom?"

Shaand improvised, knowing now that they were probably visible on one or more of Teeya's monitors and uncertain of the city ship's defensive capabilities. "Pelma, I have onboard a representative of the planet Ert. Your aggressive actions against the peaceful representative of Ert include your capture of his ship, captain, and his crew and their quarantine in Jhelen City. Under his authority and the Dzuran-Hooman coalition, we demand your surrender or suffer your final fate. We will not make this offer twice."

The ship suddenly winked out. The two ships, one immense, the other a mere speck by comparison, had passed into shadow. Si-I considered. The blasts that damaged his city and destroyed the other two were ground blasts; he had seen the glowing craters. What else could unsupported Erran ground forces do to retaliate? What could this puny ship do to him?

The insistent voice on the com interrupted his thoughts. "Pelma, we require an answer or we will take aggressive action."

To the room in general, "Where's that ship?" Si-I's urgent tone was unnecessary, everyone was scanning their instruments in multiple wavelengths to no result.

"Gone, sir." One tech spoke for the group. The tiny speck of a ship could not be seen.

"Gone?" He whirled on two of the techs monitoring the spinning images on their screens. They had almost always shown static views of the planet below and could be switched to hundreds of points around the exterior and interior of the city. Many of those cameras no longer existed.

"Sorry, sir. If it's anywhere, it's not where it was."

~ ~ ~

Jai had pulsed forward when one of the trailing, damaged dorm wings blocked any view of the larger mass ahead. It had apparently taken a direct hit from one of the foundation pieces and had degassed even as it was being torn from its connections to the main hull. As they drew closer, a frozen corpse dangled from its last handhold. Looking at its position, Brad guessed that the poor soul had been trying to keep from being blown free of the ship and been frozen in place. He shuddered. "Jai, move closer to the ship and stay as close as possible without being wrapped up in it." He thought about it in more detail and psi'd. *Jai, if you can, match spin with the wreckage and be ready to put up shields.*

The little ship began a series of slow maneuvers and soon Brad and Shaand were looking up at hull metal with very little slip apparent. *Great job, Jai. I'm turning manual control over to your automatic guidance systems. Move forward to the command bridge. Stay as close to the hull as you can. If you see a camera, fry it.*

Shaand appraised the Hooman's skills as a pilot from the weapons officer's seat. He could never appreciate the eye-to-hand coordination that Brad had picked up in his dorm, playing numerous video games. He was just pleased that the ship-to-pilot coordination seemed to be thought-melded as well. They were on a delicate approach to the nose of the ship, the eye of the beast.

A practiced eye might have been able to see the lines of the captured Dzuran cruise ship that lay beneath layers of added compartments, pods, bays, and even other larger ships, including one Erran carrier that had become the city's forward hangar. According to LonnDonn, the command bridge was not a prominent structure. It had been once, in the early deployment of the city. It still faced forward or east, but had limited visibility through its clear screens. As generations had passed and additional structures had been appended, it was actually in a shallow depression with very little actual view that wasn't provided by cameras and other remotes. Its secret weaknesses were that it was connected by personnel tubes to most sections of the old cruise ship and there was not a redundant command position located elsewhere. Those tubes no longer had functioning airlocks. The loss of the bridge would mean the loss of the city.

~ ~ ~

"Sir, we're being hailed."

"Have you got them on visual yet?" Si-I was more than annoyed. The tiny craft was interfering with the important work of rebuilding his city. How dare it demand surrender?

"Sir, it's the *Plaut*. It's one of ours."

The communications officer cringed as Si-I exploded. "I KNOW the *Plaut* is one of ours! Where's that little ship? ANYONE!"

No one answered. No one knew, but everyone on the bridge was scanning all remaining inputs for any sign of the ship. They received notice from two Erran destroyers that they were in final approach and had them on visual. That seemed a stupid perfunctory comment. Teeya, though damaged, was still enormous and could be easily seen in the night sky from the planet's surface and, with a decent set of hand scopes, from Erra as well. What he might have said is that they were now close enough to be seen from Teeya. Si-I asked, "Have you found them on any screen yet?"

"I think I saw them on approach from back orbit. That's the safest line of approach, sir."

"Get an auto-cam to lock on to them if you can. I need to set up a secure link."

He knew it would be a while and went back to his study of the ship. His simulation was now smaller by about thirty percent of its mass before the attack. Great sections of ruined structure had been cut away. He muttered, "Fall where you may and bring havoc with you!" Most had fallen harmlessly on croplands or seas. With almost no forward velocity, the fall to the planet when they began to accelerate rarely lasted long enough for incandescence of the leading edges. They fell without visual warning at random across the surface below.

He decided where the larger of the two destroyer vessels could dock and how to rig a stable gantry system. It would be a tripod made of scrap ship metal and it might take several shifts to get the connecting structures up, stabilized, and the destroyers docked before he could correct the yaw and then stop the roll to starboard. Maybe, I've got it backwards, he thought. I may want to stop this cursed roll. Then we might be able to reduce the yaw with more subtle controls. He remembered back to cadet school and the steps required to stabilize the erratic course of a ship that had been blasted into an erratic fall toward a simulated planet with a poisonous atmosphere.

~ ~ ~

Shaand psi'd to Brad, not wanting to use Jai's communications equipment. *Erran destroyer class ships approach behind.* Jai immediately cut its drive and went silent. Compared to the size of

Teeya, the destroyers were minuscule. But compared with the Skeeter Jai, they were formidable. Gun mounts formed a belt around their center of mass. Three large batteries faced forward and three smaller batteries faced the rear. Brad took manual and began to drive Jai aft, hugging the shadows and maintaining the cloaking shield. As they maneuvered around a protruding light reflection structure, they saw one of the destroyers attaching grapples forward of the ruined spin structure. Brad asked, *Has Jai seen this design before?*

Not see before... long time before... different design.

Brad considered LonnDonn's strategy of approach. "Shaand, can destroyer see Jai? LonnDonn's codes were to make Jai look like Erran shuttle to Teeya. Will be same for destroyer?"

"Must keep Jai drive engines off—must turn off unnecessary electronics."

"Understand." *Jai, where is the second destroyer? Teeya's bridge said there were two.*

Yes, two. One ahead now ... taking forward static position ... over support structure for weapon platform now gone.

"Where's the other one?"

Back orbit ... may wait orders ... may provide cover fire.

"Great!" Brad wondered, what next. Then the brilliant light of Alal turned off as both the remains of Teeya City and its tiny hunter-predator passed into planet shadow.

Chapter 22

"Pa-Kaa le meek la" a kill shot to the eye.
Old Dzuran hunting technique

Teeya City
3609.003 Erran Calendar

The blurred pink line of the sunset below drifted west. The reddish glow on the horizon gradually gave way to the pink and orange display of the Light. At night, Dzura sent very little light back out into space. Brad remembered his views of the eastern seaboard at night, Atlanta, Charlotte, and distant Chattanooga. Looking north, a bright yellow band ran north almost continuously from what he guessed was the Richmond-Petersburg area and fell away beyond his horizon. He noted how different this view was when Alal's rays sank below the western horizon. Black below, freakish nebular light above. Somewhere below, in that black expanse, Connie was waiting, and he had no way to communicate with modern Erran/Dzuran electronics.

~ ~ ~

Old Chookya Terminal, Surface
3609.003 Erran Calendar

Another group was looking upward. Moments before, silhouetted in the nebular glow, a dark shape side-lit in Alal's greater Light had been the center of attention of an elite group of science advisors. The group was primarily white-furred females, one red-haired human, with two aged male administrators. Connie could not help wanting to look at the telescope's display screens, but all she could see was a slowly tumbling black mass of shapes she could not recognize. When the view pulled back, it made no sense at all. Large pieces of the city could be seen in a short train to the right. One of these, the last, was not tumbling out of control.

She caught enough of the discussion to understand that it was probably an Erran warship. Another one had been seen moving into a position near the great city's leading edge and had seemed to attach itself. No one had seen any indication of the little Skeeter. Was it attacked by the destroyers? Was it hanging back waiting for an opportunity? She only knew that it had been gone for a day and a half and had been scheduled to give its death blow to the city hours ago.

"Look!" someone shouted.

The screen zoomed in to display a tiny grey blob moving slowly along the ruined forward hangar bays of the city toward its nose. Although the image was too small to see its positioning jets firing, it seemed to be angling in a diagonal around the ship a little faster than the inherent spin, and keeping the huge bulk of the city between it and the forward warship which now seemed to be stationary.

~ ~ ~

Teeya City
3609.003 Erran Calendar

Jai, good work avoiding the destroyer. Brad had seen the vessel as it moved into docking position and all progress had stopped before they realized that a second destroyer was back orbit and even more dangerous. *Jai, maintain a general course forward but impose right yaw and roll.* The little warship, began an awkward tumble forward and to starboard, mimicking the erratic motion of a piece of flotsam. They were now nearing the leading edge of Teeya. "Shaand, what about second destroyer? How fast do you think it will respond?"

Shaand removed an earpiece; he'd been listening to a ship-to-ship channel. He considered for a moment. "Fast, but it will need to understand what happened. Only first destroyer can talk with Teeya command and it not know what happen. May think more structural failure." After finding the right phrase, he continued, "Need time to … not attach to Teeya."

Brad was impressed with Shaand's increased language skills; they were not using gesture in their fore and aft seats. Brad agreed with the assessment. He asked, "Can they follow us to the surface?" but he thought, *if we can get out of here?*

"Not know. Do not tink destroyer ship go into atmosphere."

"Can they target us as we escape?"

"Yes."

Slow as a bug climbing a skyscraper, Jai made progress toward the leading nose of Teeya. Downloaded plans of the city fortress indicated that its command bridge was at the forward terminus of the huge structure. Jai would have to cross the locations of probably hundreds of external cameras. Hopefully, those had been fried by the plasma wave that blew past and through Teeya City. Any report of their presence could easily be transmitted to the trailing destroyer holding station behind the debris field.

"If that destroyer comes forward, it will find the surprise we just left."

~ ~ ~

Destroyer *Shin* was no longer trailing back orbit. Through secure channels, it had been requested to move forward, to search for the Skeeter.

Jai and crew took shelter in a recess formerly used to store foodstuffs. In the deep shadow, ship and crew hoped to remain invisible. They had seen the small red dot to the rear grow, and ominously, take on the shape of the first docked destroyer. This was not to be an easy ambush. Amid the wreckage of a former housing pod, a static nuke had been left behind. It would go off on command, but they had to survive to set it off. Their position was forward, so … "Jai, ease out so I can see where that destroyer is."

Slowly, imitating floating debris, Jai slid out of cover.

"There, it's athwart the docked destroyer."

Shaand said from the back. "What atwart?"

"Uhm, alongside, next to." Then, *Near.*

"Need destroyer to move forward."

Jai, orient Teeya forward, fire chem jets so they can see us, then put up shields.

Neither Brad nor Shaand had been prepared for the sudden acceleration forward, but the blast of hydrogen gasses had its desired effect. They immediately began taking fire from the destroyer. Jai's shield glowed every color imaginable as it absorbed the laser fire from Shin. Green blades of hot light flashed around them. No fire erupted from Teeya.

Too close to Teeya for its weapons systems to maintain a sight line, Brad thought.

They ducked into a hollow in the city's complex folds and waited for *Shin* to get underway. Carefully, on manual control, he backed Jai away from Teeya so only the black canopy extended into any view *Shin* might have.

Shaand waited patiently with his remote firing apparatus at ready. Carefully monitoring Jai's rear cameras, he judged the approach of the accelerating destroyer. It wasn't moving very fast. Perhaps it didn't think it would take too much energy to take out the little Skeeter. It was taking the most direct route, very near the remaining intact hull structures forward of the blasted areas.

Brad began to count down. "Shaand, on chee. Gri, gra, gru, kit, ka, tak, chip, chu, CHEE!" Shaand depressed the remote's single button. A final nuclear blast shook Teeya's tortured. The fuel cell it had been mounted under added minimally to the blast. Pieces of the big ship hurled toward *Shin*.

The burst of high energy plasma so close to the unshielded destroyer was too much for its static gamma defenses. Anyone aboard not fried outright would soon be dead from massive radiation doses. The wave of debris washed into the destroyer, pushing it down toward the dark planet. Teeya began to fold on its axis. The blast had severed enough of the key longitudinal members. Its inherent yawing motion began to force a slow flexing of the remaining main beams. Jai backed away to avoid being swatted by the city's new gyrations. From their short remove, the massive city appeared to be writhing in agony.

Brad was no longer concerned with being overheard. The leviathan just needed to be finished off. "Jai, forward. Begin final approach on the bridge tunnel." Jai resumed a slow spiraling approach forward. Teeya's normal dependence on cameras for remote observation was not total. It was a city built on the bones of a pleasure cruiser. Passing over a ridge in the city ship's hull, they came into view of a lighted array of view ports. Workers could be seen moving chaotically through the area that had once been a promenade deck on the original cruise ship. It had become officer country on Teeya City. Below them, *Shin* began to light the night sky as it reached the lower atmosphere. Its explosion on impact would one day make a recreational lake. This night, *Shin* dug its own grave.

None of the overworked crew visible in officer country took notice of the small craft moving steadily forward, and in moments, any chance of detection passed.

"Shaand, I don't remember seeing that observation deck on the model we studied."

"Me not see too. Maybe Jai not get all info."

"No problem, we'll be there soon."

Abruptly, a suited figure in a jet suit appeared in front of Jai's forward canopy. The figure appeared to be a worker making a surveillance report of damage in that sector. At Jai's relatively slow rate of travel, a collision would not be fatal but it would be soon. Even though Jai's cloaking rendered it nearly invisible at distance, in proximity, it would be seen, and then, if the worker was slow to react, felt.

From the back seat, "Braad, need kill worker."

As they watched, the jet-suited worker pivoted to face them. Before the worker's right hand could reach its left hand's control and communications array, Brad's thought translated into Jai's action and the worker disintegrated in a spray of munitions meant for much more substantial targets.

~ ~ ~

Si-I was relieved. The explosion had rocked the command bridge, but the city still seemed to be whole, repairable, and the Skeeter would soon be of no concern. He turned to the watch officer. "What do you have?"

"I have an unusual heat signature near fuel storage, unit six six," the officer replied.

"You're bothering me with an unusual heat signature?" Si-I was trying to control his outburst. He knew he was worn and tired. So were his crew. He had yelled too often at his stressed and overworked bridge officers who were pulling their third straight shift. The explosion aimed at the destroyer *Shin* threw everyone on the bridge into a heap against the nominal ceiling. Power auxiliaries took over on battery alone. He thought it admirable how quickly they made it back to their duty stations. Fewer monitors were functioning.

"Do we know where that came from?"

The watch officer spoke up. "I no longer have any signal from the fuel storage pile. It may have gone off."

Another tech spoke up. "Sir, we are losing contact. Wait, I can't pick up anything behind bulkhead six two." The ships lurched again. It seemed that a new motion had been induced after the second blast.

Si-I wasn't satisfied. "That was more of a blast than I would have expected from a fuel pile." To the com officer, "Any word from *Shin* on the Dzuran?"

"I can't raise the *Shin*, sir. No channels are open."

"Keep trying."

Another station reported. "*Plaut* is disengaging, sir. It's broken transfer seals and is releasing its tether." He turned to face his captain. "Sir, they report that the *Shin* has been destroyed. It was in the line of debris from the fuel cell blast."

"Destroyed?"

"They say it's falling out of orbit."

"Have the *Plaut* come forward and take out that Dzuran ship."

One of the external monitors caught an unusual view of something with a string of bright yellow lights too close to the ship. "That's the elevator platform. It managed to get out of our path," one of the techs scanning the feeds from the remaining external cameras reported. The tech captured a frame still and zoomed. He had never seen the space platform from the side before. There it was, framed against the blackness of space with the remains of its elevator tail hanging below it. Without its anchor, it was now on a long elliptical orbit that would eventually return. He quickly considered how much mass would need to be attached to the elevator's tail to anchor it again. His calculation concluded that it would have to be written off.

Si-I thought about the platform crew's chances of surviving the heat of the plasma blast. Could they survive the radiation? A grey blob resembling a liquid storage bladder momentarily blocked the view of a monitor. He pulled the monitor up to his main screen and backed up the image. His heart nearly stopped when he clearly made out a cockpit on a rounded ship. That was no fuel bladder. "There you are!"

Si-I moved over to see the monitor. "That! That is the Hooman's ship. What is the location of that camera?"

A few control clicks later and the watch officer said excitedly, "Sir, it's," he raised his left arm and pointed to port, "it's just outside the bridge. That means it's moving forward slightly faster than ship's motion. It should soon be directly ahead."

Si-I could not believe it. What could they possibly do? Were they actually looking for and picking off survivors? Why hadn't the *Plaut* seen it?

He floated to the remaining transparent view screen that looked directly forward. With the motion of the ship, stars shining through a thin section of the gas cloud described an oval path. "Teeya to *Plaut!*"

"Yes, Pelma Si-I." Static hissed on the line. "We are moving forward. Should be on your bridge in..." An excited argument broke out between two of the camera technicians.

"Damn your Lights! Quiet! *Plaut*, the fighter is immediately on our station, now!" Si-I and the assembled crew on the bridge watched through the only view forward, the remaining viewport not blocked by add-ons. A dark shape blocked the few stars he could see. What?

The last thing they saw was a bright flash from Jai's forward rail guns and the forward view portal shattering. He and most of the occupants of the bridge were riddled with heavy metal munitions that pulverized the compartment, its rear bulkhead, and the Pelma's personal quarters. With the complete demolition of those compartment walls, the rain of heavy metals began to chew through bulkheads and finally reached their target. The hydrogen tanks that would have fueled long dismantled positioning jets were still used for other energy needs. Its explosion blew the head off the structure formerly known as Teeya City. The blue white wave of exploding hydrogen removed the remains of the bridge but also shattered internal compartments to its rear. Blast door circuits no longer told isolation doors to shut. Si-I's favorite shortcut through the city's circulation system now thundered as gasses from the few remaining airtight sections began to vent forward.

Jai backed away from the huge ship. Originally propelled away by the impulse of the rail gun, it was now being blown further away by exhausting gasses. The little ship was pelted with debris being blown out of the ruined bridge and adjacent forward compartments. What began as a strong blast of exploding hydrogen gasses slowed as the remaining compartments vented through the ruined bridge. Jai backed further, turned tail, and accelerated as fast as possible toward the dark surface of the planet. The commands between pilot and ship had been spoken, understood, and executed only a little slower than thought.

The darkside view of the planet at night was sliced by waving beams of high energy guns. The *Plaut* was on them. Jai's shields energized slightly sooner than Brad expressed the command. "Down, now, fast!" Jai's shield glowed white then bright pink as it absorbed energy from the destroyer's weapons. Some spot on the planet, either burning, or otherwise illuminated was the only thing visible forward. Erra must be on the other side of the planet. Now. There. Reflection of the Light on the doughnut-shaped lake in the center of the Teeya Keerosh. "There, Jai, head for the east wall of the Keerosh. Shaand, we might be chased. What do you think?"

"I tink we go to ground, wait. Not good fight destroyer."

That seemed like good advice. There were no pursuing flashes of green death. Jai settled onto a narrow rock shelf overlooking the waters that erased the pain of Old Teeya. As Jai powered down and rigged for silent, Brad realized that he could hear the blood in his temples. His mouth was dry, palms wet. That had been too close.

~ ~ ~

Before the ground gun attack, the new Teeya City had been massive. That is, its mass would have equaled any similar city on the planet if only its superstructure were included, pavement not being necessary. At its glory, Teeya City housed a hundred thousand Errans. Survivors forward of the ground blast area had just died in one of the two last killing explosions. Aft of the original blast area only a few thousand remained. These were now rushing to find pressurized compartments or pressure suits. Most did not succeed. The effect of the atmospheric blast venting directly forward began to have a miniscule but inexorable effect. Forward momentum began to drop. The most important function of forward momentum is orbital velocity. The crippled city no longer had the velocity needed to remain in orbit. It drifted slowly west and inexorably downward. It would take some time, but with loss of altitude, the acceleration would only continue. The city was following its two sisters, falling to the surface.

~ ~ ~

Old Chookya Terminal, Surface
3609.003 Erran Calendar
By Brad's watch, as Connie now held it, the atmospheric gasses seemed to run out pretty quickly. After a little over twelve Timex minutes, they could no longer see the white mist blowing out of Teeya City's leading edge. By everybody's estimate, the outgassing alone should have been sufficient to degrade the orbit of Teeya City. A sudden eruption of emotion swept the assembled watchers. No one else on the planet knew it yet, but that small group of watchers did. The reign of Erran supremacy was over.

The elevators were gone. The orbiting cities were finally gone. There was no longer a base of operations for a class of rulers ill-equipped to walk on the surface of Dzura.

Chapter 23

The right decision will be illuminated tomorrow.
Cho-le Baan

Port Jhagatt
3609.016 Erran Calendar

Brad woke up to an empty bed well after midnight. He understood. Connie was dealing with emotional weight he could not help her lift. Unlike hers, his hormones were not preparing him for motherhood. He rolled out of his sleeping pad and tightened the belt on his jumpsuit. He found Connie sitting cross-legged near the end of their row of shelters in the new tent city at the foot of the Teeya Keerosh Mountains. She was leaning back, staring moist-eyed up at the swash of nebular pinks and tans. He spoke softly, not wanting to startle her.

"Con, couldn't sleep either, huh? Big day tomorrow."

She didn't respond immediately. She seemed to need a moment to come back from wherever her reverie had taken her. She wiped at her eyes with her sleeve and rolled onto her side propping her head up with her left arm. He sat cross-legged in front of her. They had finally learned that to ensure privacy, they could get nearly face to face, remain in near whisper mode and focus directly on each other. Now at least, almost everyone except the posted guards was asleep.

"Hey, good lookin'."

"Watcha got cookin'?" she answered the refrain.

"What's on your mind? I mean other than having survived a civil war, gotten ourselves on the winning side, gotten our ride back home, and basically being proclaimed wonderful people by the locals. Besides that, what's got you up?"

She smiled at him. Her eyes, shining with moisture from her recent tears, took in his boyish innocence. He had changed in so many ways since he first showed up at the docks back in Apalachicola. He'd been alone, trying hard not to sound scared, and in need of a safe haven. He'd been a surrogate brother, then a lover.

251

Together, they'd done some amazing things and so many times they seemed to be linked at the frontal lobe – thinking and acting in unison. How could he miss this? She rolled her right hand around the tightening skin over her belly. "This little guy is what's on my mind." She sighed. "I'm really concerned about taking him through jump space tomorrow."

"Him?" His grin was visible in the dim light of the night sky. "Do you know something I don't know about?"

"Well, yes. Remember the imaging thing I told you about? It's a little version of you."

Brad looked down to the ground, embarrassed. He'd become so excited about the imminent return home that he'd forgotten her disquiet about traveling pregnant. The excitement about tomorrow's jump was why *he* couldn't sleep. Anxiety about it was why she couldn't sleep. "Hon, I'm not sure what to say. Do you want to wait and we'll go home after it, … when he, is born?"

"Well, that's what I've been up trying to put my mind around. In answer to that, yes, I'd like to stay. No Erran or Dzuran can tell me it's safe, because their females don't go to space pregnant."

He swallowed. What would that mean, another three or four months approximately, then maybe six more to be able to travel with an infant. It would certainly be easier to have her get her pre-natal and birth and all that on Earth and to have Lucy and Susan and her mother to help out, and coo, and burp him, and whatever grandmothers did. But this was *his* child too. He certainly didn't want a monster if the jump proved unsafe for the fetus. He looked up. "Con. Honey, we'll do whatever you want. These folks are good to us, thankful for what we've contributed." He looked up at the brilliant canopy overhead. "I'm sure we can count on their hospitality for a while longer. Heck, we might even get better at teaching Shaand to speak English."

"And we might both get better at psi and Elioi speech." She let out a soft sigh. "Folks? You called them 'folks?'" She shook her head in amusement. "No, I don't think that's what we should do." She reached out to cup his head in her hand. "I think you should go back home; take Shaand. I'll stay here with the muffin. They say an ambassador-level ship is going to be made available. I can go back later with the baby and maybe Clee-Chk and Leeink-Knaa; see if I can get those ladies up in space."

"Connie, no! It's all right. We'll come home together after it's safe for you in one of the ambassador ships. We can tell Jai to play nice with the Dzurans and we can use him to teach the first class of Dzuran Navy pilots in four hundred years."

Connie smiled with absolute joy that Brad would offer to put off the homecoming he was so excited about. "Brad, you need to go home tomorrow. You need to take Shaand as an Ambassador from Dzura. If you go back alone, with only stories about aliens, the media will go nuts with fabrication, hearsay, and outright lies about an impending invasion of space aliens. You know how xenophobic humans are." She poked him in the chest. "And what if the Errans are the first ones to make contact? What if they spin their side of the story and paint the Dzurans as bad guys? We need to make sure that our side, and I mean us—we need to tell the story. If we don't, there'll be hell to pay by the time we can actually get Humans and Elioi together."

"Con? That's crazy! I'm not going to leave you here alone. It's—"

She cut him off. "Not alone. I have friends here, girlfriends mostly. It's not like I haven't been wishing I was home. Two weeks ago, we were getting bombed every other day, and earlier when we were being hunted down like prey. Yeah, heck yeah! I really want to go home, to be home. But that's—" He started to interrupt and she shushed him. "I think we've been gone for at least five months. Susan and Lucy, and even Sonny, will think we've killed ourselves out in the great beyond. They probably think we're dead already."

"But, damn! I can't leave you here, Con. Not going to happen. There's no telling what could happen. What if the idiots in the Air Force quarantine me and dissect Shaand?"

His voice was beginning to rise. She put out two fingers to his lips. "Shush now. I've made up my mind to stay through the pregnancy." Brad started to open his mouth in protest and she tapped his lips again. "Shss!" She smiled so hard her trademark lopsided dimpled grin was visible in the Light. "Think about what Shaand said about the Erran miner that's been stealing our satellites. They probably think we're to blame. You're smart!" She tapped his forehead with her forefinger. "Use that and you'll both be just fine."

He looked up at her, considering the more immediate issue. Earth might need whatever meager defenses Jai might be able to provide. Jai could certainly police a mining ship. He crab-walked behind her and sat, leaning against her back. They sat back to back until their breathing synced. She began humming softly. He could feel the vibrations being passed from rib cage to rib cage. Finally he caught the tune. Swing low sweet chariot, indeed.

He realized the resolve in her voice matched her mother's and knew the argument was over. Her mother, Lou Anne Chappell, was one of those soft-spoken southern women who could let you know in no uncertain terms you were not going to win any given argument. The next decision was whether he would be going. They sat in silence for a few moments. He idly picked at the ground moss that carpeted the area. A small cry of one of the smaller predator animals in the distance broke the quiet. A few noises from the camp now and then would normally be ignored as background. Now they seemed uncomfortably loud. A sea breeze full of unfamiliar scents displaced the ground smells he'd become accustomed to. The central sea was just a few hour's walk north. He looked up, studying the bright crescent of Erra, shining against the banded colors of the Light. A few hours to daylight and local high tide. Fifteen trips around Dzura was a year here. Twelve to thirteen back home. The local precision was almost exact, the extra day a holiday on the calendar. Here versus there. Getting there from here was the problem.

"Gotta hand it to you, Con. You're right as usual. All points." He tossed a nit of ground moss he'd pulled loose. "I just hate it. I hate leaving you here. I hate leaving both of you here."

"We'll be fine, Chk can do everything for me with their medicine except breast feed for me."

"What about—"

"Stop it! You're just making this harder than it needs to be."

"When did you decide this?" He tried very hard not to sound hurt, or petulant, which is what he felt.

"I guess I started thinking about it when Leeink-Knaa mentioned that, except for the diaspora, no pregnant females had ever gone through the jump that anyone knows about. And no one knows if there are any survivors of the diaspora."

Overhead, a brilliant streak to the west flared and died to a red ember as another of the hundreds of stray pieces of the demolished Teeya City fell to ground, a burning cerametal cinder. He turned and leaned over, hugged her, felt her slip into his embrace. He pulled her close and onto him. In a fluid motion, he continued a roll ending up on top of her and then off the other side of the growing mound in her belly. In the roseate light of the nebula, he found her mouth and feeling her respond, he cupped her head in his hands, dusted her brow, nose and cheeks in flurry of kisses, and took in her special scent.

"Brad?"

"Yes, my sweet? Mother of my child?"

"I think we need to take this inside the tent."

~ ~ ~

The departure ceremony was a grander production than Brad expected. He made a note to notch up his "war hero" status and take justifiable pride in being named Ambassador for Earth. He had to admit to himself that his departure for Earth was only a small part of the ongoing celebration for the end of the war—the end of over four hundred years of slavery. The scene he thought he would always remember was one of the musical ensembles. He had heard wisps of something in the underground that he would classify as music, but he never expected the excellence in musicality that was on display at the ceremony.

A lone musician came onto the stage, piping a mournful melody, in the Elioi version of a minor key. It evoked sorrow and loss in building complexity that wrapped intricate variations on the original theme. A deep, thrumming percussive bass built from somewhere behind the stage and reminded him of the heart thrumming he had witnessed out on the plains when their comrades had been massacred. A string ensemble slid onto a separate platform, sawing multi-stringed instruments with bows. The stringed instruments seemed organic, as if the sound boxes had been grown from a gourd-like plant. As additional instruments joined in, each picked up the original melody expressed by the piper. When the new instruments became fully engaged, a deep, resounding bass drum began a slow dirge. The simple arrangement was a slowed down pattern based on the Elioi's three-chambered heart. The volume and tempo slowly, slowly grew, drawing gasps from some of the crowd as others beside them fell into a trance.

He and Connie had been transfixed, struck by the emotional content of the music. They became aware that the thrumming had begun in the seated crowd around them. Connie wept quietly as the low mummer of the crowd throbbed with more intensity. Electrified sounds from instruments he could not describe joined the melodic line, first picking up the base theme as previous instruments had done, and then adding their own complexities. Brad found himself grinning, enjoying the show immensely. He looked over at Connie and saw tear tracks running down her smiling face.

With a shout, three dancers leapt onto the center stage and began to slip into contortions impossible for humans. Their double-jointed elbows and knees must have been stretched from an early age to permit those gyrations. Around them, the Dzuran locals swayed back and forth in time with the dancers as they recreated in dance the long story of subjugation, endurance, rebellion and finally, victorious success. When the action stilled, the music had reached a crescendo. All went silent except for the base drum's slowly beating heart.

After the performance, the stage and seating area went dark for several minutes, allowing those in the crowd who had been overcome to regain their composure. Many had fallen into the aisles, transported by the emotional performance. When the lights came back up, a simple podium was in place and members of the Pel-Council filed onto the stage. Brad's action in finishing off the last of the city ships took a minor place in the long list of heroic actions resulting in the final victory.

The ceremonies continued well into the night with one surprise left for those following the story of the two Hoomans who had become so important in the final stages of the revolt. The announcement of Connie's wishes to remain until her child was half an Earth year old was welcomed and Clee-Chk had been summoned to accompany Connie to the new female encampment being set up a day's walk south along the Keerosh range. Ss-Shaand agreed to accompany Brad to Earth as the new Ambassador from Dzura and temporarily for the Elioi.

Terms of surrender between the two warring Elioi parties required the delivery of five six-passenger shuttles from the Erran Navy for Dzuran use. One of these would be put at the service of Ss-Shaand after his return from Earth. The first trip would be made in the armed Skeeter, Jai. Final goodbyes and hugs and farewell kisses made most of the locals extremely uncomfortable. Shaand was given a small box of slo wood with decorative inlays of an iridescent material Brad had never seen before. He had the momentary concern that there was so much about this culture that he had not seen. Maybe he was premature in going back, leaving Connie behind.

Before that thought could linger, one of the seniors from the Pel-Council approached Brad and presented a small tetrahedron, also of slo wood with similar iridescent inlays. It's four sided shape reminded him of the tetra-pack milk cartons he'd had in school, but it looked like a national treasure. With some attempts at Elioi speech, he attempted to give thanks. Shaand interrupted and indicated that Brad was to present it to his Earth leaders as a sign of trust. Ranks of guards had formed up, creating a clear path through the onlookers to Jai's cordoned area.

Brad scanned across the assembled forms and quickly picked out a bright redhead among the brown-furred Dzurans. She held up a V-fingered peace sign, or victory sign. Whatever she meant, both were applicable. He blew a kiss and turned for a ceremonial climb into Jai's cockpit. Shaand turned to salute the dignitary stage and followed.

~ ~ ~

Above Dzura
3609.017 Erran Calendar
October 8, 1986 – Earth Calendar

The ascent away from the circle of dignitaries was slow and solemn, nowhere near Jai's actual lifting capability of either grav lift or chem boost systems, but Brad wanted to save chemical jets for near Earth maneuvering. Much too soon, he thought, the crowd was a multi-colored splotch on the ground. The century's long use of the grey jumpsuit had given way to yellows and whites and reds, orange, and probably colors he knew his eyes might not even see.

As the curve of the planet began to dip away from them, he looked out across the horizon. In front of them, the central crater mount of the Teeya Keerosh sparkled in mid-morning pinks as Alal's dawn highlighted it against the dark stone crater walls. Lifting above the atmosphere, the thinning violet faded to an outer band of pink and then darkness.

The nebula's bands were no closer, or maybe only a little closer, but with no horizon or atmosphere, they seemed touchable. They were insubstantial gasses, lit by a few dozen stars, but he knew he'd love to fly into that cloud someday. He knew that Erran mineral explorers and, earlier, Dzuran pleasure liners had flown through the cloud, revealing a spectacular supernova on the other side. He wondered again if it was visible from Earth.

"Jai, energize the starfield nav display." On the recessed 'dashboard' in the pilot and navigator positions, the system display appeared with the twin planets of Erra and Dzura in the foreground with Alal shining behind. The nominal start for the display always presented the equilateral triangle of the two planets as base and their central sun, Alal, at the upper apex. He called to the back seat, "Shaand, can you control this to expand out to see the entire system?"

Before Shaand could say yes, the view zoomed out to display Alal as a bright dot with a glyph labeling it. Thin, light blue lines formed the elliptical display of the orbits of the several planets in the system, more planets than Brad had known about. The scale of the nebula was barely diminished by the zoomed out view. Shaand had never seen this display before and allowed an inhale to betray his surprise. There was much his Dzuran peers would need to learn about near-space to take a peaceful and rightful role alongside the more experienced Erran spacers. Shaand realized that no living Dzuran was a competent navigator, although most finished schooling with an understanding of geography and a little geology. And they were excellent excavators, but there was so much lost knowledge to relearn as they rebuilt their civilization on the surface. Some would continue to prefer the catacombs and tunnels that had been their lives for so long.

Brad asked about the planetary system. As their canopy view of the planet shrank from the half-lit region below them with a broad terminator to a crescent in blues offset by the light-swallowing darkside, Shaand described Alal and its dependent children, for that is how they had always thought of the planets from the earliest days of their astrology-based religion, starting with the nearest, little sun-fried Allon with molten metals swimming across its inward fixed face and ice mountains on its backside. Immediately Brad thought, half-baked!

Next was Milla, just far enough away from Alal's stream of radiation to permit colonies; those had not been rebuilt after the Dzuran nuclear attacks. Then the war-entangled twins: hospitable and life-giving Dzura and its little sister, Erra, forever embraced by Dzura's stronger gravity and lost in a fixed stare at its big sister.

Beyond these two, a hydrogen-methane bubble known as Daja shone, decorated with its ring of stones stolen from the asteroid belt. These stones were the wreckage of some proto planet that had succumbed to the tides of massive Paja, a gas giant so immense that Elioid science still did not know what lay beneath its roiling cloud deck. An eternity's worth of hydrogen fuel forever out of reach. The planet's magnetic storms swatted any approaching craft with lethal lightning blasts. Icy Kreona lay outside them all on an elliptical orbit that some thought would someday cause it to be sucked into Paja's grip.

As Shaand finished his description, Brad looked down again at Dzura's shrinking crescent and appreciated the cabin's grav-field neutralizing system. The system isolated the crew from otherwise deadly G-forces as Jai accelerated away from Dzura's gravity well. They needed separation before the grav-drive could be used for the jump to Sol. The planet was now a small half disc he could encircle with thumb and forefinger. He remembered the view of Earth taken by one of the Apollo astronauts and how similar the two looked. Even in the pink light of Alal, it looked like it could be an Earth with a different shoreline. He considered the mysteries still to be discovered about Dzura, Erra, and the Elioi. He'd heard about a garden planet on another system used for vacationing tourists before the Cho rebellion. He thought about Connie. Was she still standing with Clee-Chk somewhere, looking up? He thought about the tens of thousands of Elioi he had helped kill. Should he feel remorse for participating in the Elioi's final, crushing blow? Was it analogous to the final crippling bomb on Nagasaki? He shook his head to clear the morbid thoughts. Scanning the rear cameras, he could easily pick out sister planet Erra in slightly narrower crescent, tiny but distinguishable.

War. What was it about his species and the Elioi? The Milky Way spread across the void in a brilliant spray of stars more brilliant that he could ever see them from his Florida beach. How many others are out there? How many might be dominated by a single dominant species? Do all creatures who have become masters of their planet or their star system get there tooth and claw and never lose the need to climb to the top of the power ladder? Is warfare the price for planetary supremacy? Surely, there must be a brake on the upward spiral that brings a society to its senses? It certainly isn't a sense of history! The Balkan races had never forgiven transgressions against their ancestors. The Japanese and Koreans were not likely to become more than statutory allies. The tribes of Africa were ill-equipped to master nationhood because of tribalism. Could the Elioi and the Human races ever forge a partnership, an alliance? And these guys, as soon as they had the technology to do it, the Elioi almost killed their own home planet!

"Shaand?"

"Yes, Brad."

"You spoke before about the Precursors. You said there had been a Precursor ship in my star's asteroid belt and that it is known to have gone away?"

"Tat is true. We know from peace talks on Erra. News of Precursor big news. Many scientist tink old civizashun. Gone now."

"Gone as, gone from Erra, or gone from Earth?"

Go from Erra to Ert, ten go from Ert. Not know civizashun system in tat direkchun."

"I think you mean civ-i-lie-zae-shun." He sounded out each syllable carefully.

"Tanks, civilachun."

Brad sighed and hoped that he could protect Shaand from the authorities. Could those xenophobic twits understand that Shaand was not a specimen? "So you think the Precursors no longer visit or come to our part of the galaxy?"

"Not know, friend Brad. Tanks to idiot miner, if tey still can travel, tey now know about Ert and Dzura and Erra. Maybe always know."

Brad had grown up on stories of spaceships and not all of the descriptions jived. Maybe Earth had been commonly called upon by Precursors and maybe many others. Maybe they were just being used as a fuel stop, or a handy source of liquid water. Maybe in this part of the Milky Way, Earth was considered a primitive backwater. So primitive, we had to be shown how to build pyramids.

Well, he thought, I have a spaceship and time on my hands. If I can figure out how to store food and water and how to get rid of it later, Connie and I could—

Shaand broke his reverie. "Ka-Braad?" He gave his Hooman friend the honorific of squadron leader. "My instruments speak ready make jump soon."

"Jai?" Brad asked, "When can we make the jump to Earth? How long before we can go home?"

"Five point three two six Earth minutes," the ship's voice called out.

Still looking down at Dzuran, Brad asked, "Jai? Set the nav display to show the region of Alal space as seen from Earth. Can we even see this system from Earth?"

The soft voice responded, "Calculating, solution in two, one..." Click.

The speck of light that had been Alal disappeared as the Nebula rotated almost ninety degrees and began to shrink. Stars and their labels rushed toward the center of the display and continued to fill the spherical holographical space with only the largest retaining their glyphs. It stopped when the nebula itself was little more than a speck. Behind it, or around it, a thin wash of far more distant stars washed across the background.

From the navigator's seat, Shaand gasped. His forays above ground had always been dominated by the Light, feint veins in daylight and awesome displays at night. The brilliance of the Milky Way stole his breath. In a moment, he said, "See many stars from your Ert. Not so many from Dzura."

Brad was struck by something familiar. He tried to imagine this view from his north Florida coastline. He could imagine standing on the grassy flats at Wakulla Beach with no city lights fogging the atmosphere with scattered light. Stars began to line up in familiar ways. He turned his head sideways to look at the view in a normalized 'up' and gasped. "I'll be dipped in gravy!"

"Is okay with you?" Shaand asked.

Recovering from his astonishment, Brad finally responded, "Yes Shaand! I know where we are. I know how to find you in my night sky! We are in Orion's Sword. We have a name for the Lights, the Lights of Creation as you call them. We call them the Orion Nebula!"

Jai interrupted, "Ka-Brad, all systems ready for jump Dzura to Earth."

"Shaand!" Brad tried to control his growing excitement. "I know this place! Or at least of this place." Brad couldn't help grinning. He knew where he was! A wave of unexpected joy filled his chest. He knew he had no idea how to approach the United Nations or the President or even his family back home, but he knew he missed being under a yellow sun. But standing under his yellow sun, he could tell with certainty, where Alal was, where Connie was, and where he would have to return.

"Tat good, friend Braad." Then, "O Rie-onn, O Rie-onn, is good name!"

Brad thought of the years that he had spoken to this ship, when he believed it was no more than the disembodied essence of a crashed alien. That strange essence had called him friend Braad. He had spent many hours in the night-shrouded desert looking up at the Orion constellation and could pick out the nebula as the bright spot in the hunter's scabbard. What a trip! He thought he had definitively proved extra-terrestrial aliens had been to Earth last year with the broadcast on the evening news. Wait till they get a load of Jai and Shaand! He was at the edge of closing the circle.

He settled into the pilot's seat and began the jump bond with Shaand and Jai. Before he let the jump trance take over he said aloud, "Jai? Shaand?"

"Yes, Ka-Brad," they responded in unison.

"Let's go home!"

The End

Part 4

What is past is prologue.
William Shakespeare

Sol System
3609.017 Erran Calendar
October 8, 1986 – Earth Calendar

High above the planetary plane of the system known locally as the Sol system, an insubstantial flash of light preceded the unbending of gravity waves that allowed for interstellar travel as developed by the Elioi dating back to 2937, Erran Calendar. As the flash dimmed to black, the small two-seater known as Jai re-entered the physical world to the real discomfort of its two passengers.

"Jai, systems report please, where are we?" Pilot Brad Hitchens was still nauseous from the jump, an unavoidable side effect of the small ship's gravity jump drive. He was also concerned because on his departure from Sol system over five months ago the swirling blue and white bands of earth had been visible clearly a little larger than his fist held at arm's length. The sun, if that's what it was, seemed right at thumbnail sized by the same measure. Brad couldn't read the glyph's on Jai's readout because in the five months immersed in the Elioi culture, he'd never learned to read more than the counting digits of their language.

He called to the back seat, "Shaand, are you all right?"

He received a psi message in reply. *Not feeling good, maybe need be sick.*

"Don't worry. It will be over soon."

Jai's 3D positioning array began to build a model of the gravity wells in the system, locating each of the major bodies in their orbits as delineated in thin blue ellipses. Brad counted out to the third blue ellipse and did not see a planetary symbol.

For the return to Sol Space the conclusion of the

Dreamland Diaries series,

please check for the Author,

Bruce Ballister,

at Amazon Books©

Due out, 2017

Connie said, under her breath, "Well, they know where Earth is."

"Right."

"And, Brad, what's a Precursor Stone?"

41193105R00155

Made in the USA
Charleston, SC
21 April 2015